TIME
AND THE
CONSEQUENCES

IAN MEACHEAM

APS Books,
4 Oakleigh Road,
Stourbridge,
West Midlands,
DY8 2JX

APS Books is a subsidiary of
the APS Publications imprint

www.andrewsparke.com

First published worldwide by APS Books in 2020

ISBN9781789961478

For Ann

...past, present and future

PART 1
Broken Barricades

CHAPTER 1

"Cheers!" said Peter Burlington, Head Teacher of Whatmore School.

"Cheers!" came the chorus from the rest of the senior leadership team.

The five members of the Senior Leadership Team, the SLT, sat around the circular table in a private room of the Palace Hotel. It was 9:35 pm on Friday night. Peter's team should have been with their loved ones but felt morally obliged to celebrate with their head teacher. They toasted their success with cheap champagne in cheap champagne flutes. On close inspection it would have been obvious that only two of the five glasses were filled with bubbly. Charlie hated champagne and had filled his glass with cheap lager instead while Neil didn't feel like drinking at the moment and Sobia had been advised not to drink alcohol and so they'd opted for soft drinks. Conversely, Julie and Peter were magnanimously happy to down more than their fair share of the bubbles.

"Well team, thank you and well done," said Peter feeling the need to make a speech. "I know you all heard what I said to the staff but I want you to hear the unabridged version with a few things I couldn't say at the meeting last night. It's great you could all come tonight for a celebratory meal and I'm really pleased that you can all stay overnight. I realise The Palace isn't the most palatial hotel in the area but they did accommodate us at short notice. The food and drink may require some improvement but the company is definitely good. Now, talking of good...well, we did it. Good. An Ofsted judgement of *Good*. We managed to pull it off. I should say that I never had any doubts, but I did. We all knew Whatmore was a good school but we had to fight hard to show the inspectors we were right. After the first day of the inspection I was almost sure we were going to be given *Requires Improvement* but we managed to persuade the inspectors...or should I say bluff them, that we were better than that."

"Let's raise our glasses to our Head Bullshitter, Mr Peter Bluffington...cheers," said Charlie.

"Mr Peter Bluffington!" repeated the other three members of the team, laughing and taking mouthfuls of drink.

"Thank you, Charlie. Your loyalty, support and respect, as always, is noted and will be reported to the Chair of Governors," replied Peter smiling at his loyal and supportive deputy. "We're a great team and we've worked hard to get this result. I know we were a good school before this inspection but Ofsted has raised the bar over the last few years so we can legitimately claim we've made progress. We can also be fairly certain our jobs are safe for a few more years. With a bit of luck, we won't be inspected for another four or five years."

"Does that mean we all have to stay working at Whatmore for that long?" asked Julie looking down the barrel of her empty champagne flute. She looked up, realising that no-one had reacted to her question and was relieved to discover that she hadn't moved her mouth in posing her barbed question. The question had remained in her squiffy mind although she had moved her hands to replenish her empty glass.

"Well, I plan to have retired well before another inspection comes along." Charlie Briggs, the Deputy Head in charge of all things pastoral, had been saying this to anyone who would listen since...since he started teaching. The trouble was, no-one took him that seriously on his planned retirement or, to be honest, on few other matters. In dealing with pastoral issues Charlie was a serious professional but when it came to marking pupils' books or analysing progress he was out of his depth and relied on wit and cynicism. He was the longest serving member of the team at Whatmore having been promoted internally years ago from Head of PE. He loved his job and could not contemplate life without Whatmore. Most other members of staff respected him, loved his devil-may-care attitude to life and his sense of humour, particularly the younger men on the staff and pretty much all of the women he came into contact with.

"You've been saying you're going to retire ever since I came to this school. I don't think you'll ever hang up your boots," said Peter.

"It would, however, help in balancing the books if we could get rid of the highly paid senior citizens and get some young cheap teachers instead," said Sobia Didially, Whatmore's Business Manager. Her remark was met with an uncomfortable pause followed by a chorus of laughter commenced loudly by Peter and Charlie and followed without quite the same enthusiasm by Neil and Julie and then finally by Sobia, merely going through the motions of laughing.

"Perhaps we should both give up now Charlie..."

Julie was just about to suggest an immediate SLT vote on this when Peter continued, "......but I have a mortgage to finish paying, a daughter and her family which needs funding and a wife who wants me out of the house most of the week."

Julie examined her half empty glass. She wanted to fill it with tears of regret, sadness and disappointment but had to settle for champagne.

Peter continued, "I want to thank you for all of your efforts recently to prepare the school for this inspection. We're a relatively new team and we're clearly moving in the right direction but we know that as the senior leaders we have to keep moving forward. If we stay still and become complacent then we won't do as well at the next Ofsted inspection because our masters will keep moving the goal posts further and further away."

"Peter, I know that we have to keep moving and improving and I know we have our inspection targets to meet but can't we put Ofsted to one side and lead the school in the direction that we think is right?" said Sobia sharply. "Are we not allowed to think for ourselves? As you said yourself, we are a developing senior leadership team that has been judged as Good, so why can't we make our own decisions about the future. Surely, Ofsted will leave us alone now that we have their stamp of approval."

Peter held up his hands as if surrendering. "Sobia, you'd like to think we would be left alone as we're deemed Good ol' professionals but I'm afraid that counts for nothing if our GCSE pass rates go down. One dip in the year 11 pupils' performance and someone down in London will be asking questions. And if things really start going downhill then the Man from the Academy will be insisting on changing the lock on the front door. With that in mind, I'm afraid we can never be sure about our future."

Sobia, rather like Ofsted, would not let go. "So, our jobs are no safer today than they were at the beginning of the week. We are still under the microscope from Ofsted...well, a sort of long distance telescope any way. So Big Brother continues to watch us all of the time." Her celebratory mood was slowly diminishing.

"Well...yes...you could say that..." said Peter trying his best to sound as positive, "but we ought to be thankful that we weren't judged *Requires Improvement* or worse *Inadequate*. If we had been, then we'd be over-run with HMI inspectors turning over every stone in every nook and cranny in the school."

"It seems to me," said Neil, putting down his iPad and using his hands to enhance the point he wanted to make, "that only *Outstanding* schools have it easy...they're the only ones who're pest free."

"I suppose you're right, but the head teachers I meet from outstanding schools say they're under tremendous pressure because they have to keep their schools at the top and have to help other schools who're struggling."

"Are we supposed to feel sorry for head teachers of outstanding schools?" asked Charlie sarcastically , his tongue loosening due to the alcoholic lubricant being applied liberally to his mouth. He was sitting opposite Peter across the round table, lager than life, so to speak.

"No Charlie, I think we should feel sorry for all schools and everyone who works in them. Every teacher, teaching assistant and pupil. You and I know what it used to be like. And we know that the job is awful nowadays. Everybody's all over-worked and under-valued. It seems to me that the lives and careers of teachers are defined by the Ofsted cycle and pupils' lives revolve around tests. We're all slaves to statistics. And over the years we have gone round in circles time and time again in a downward spiral. I just hope someone someday soon sees the way it's all going and tries to stop all this. Unfortunately, successive Secretaries of State for Education feel the need to keep the cycle of change spinning."

Peter took another mouthful of champagne and a breath before delivering his vent's final throw-away sentence. "I suppose we're the ones to blame...we voted for these idiots."

"Did we?" questioned Charlie. "I don't remember having a choice about Ofsted. It was just brought in one night when we were all sleeping peacefully in our beds and we woke up to the sound of school alarms sounding, Inspectors setting foot inside our schools and targets for everything."

"Can we stop talking about bloody Ofsted for just a few minutes at least!" pleaded Julie. "We're supposed to be celebrating our success. We've been living in a constant state of doom and gloom for the last six months but now we have a *Good* judgement from Ofsted, we can look more confidently to the future, so let's all enjoy the moment. The staff and kids did us proud. The teachers all turned up for the two-day inspection, taught good ten minute lessons when the inspectors were in the classrooms and kept the pupils' books marked up-to-date. The pupils all pretended to work hard and talked positively about the school when the inspectors grilled them. I think they all deserve our thanks. I think we should raise our glasses and toast them."

This was a great excuse for Julie to reach for the bottle of bubbly and replenish her half-full flute. She also topped up Peter's glass, hoping to get him drunk so he'd fall asleep before he could make any further speeches. Julie then raised her glass again. "The Whatmore staff and pupils...cheers!"

There was a chorus of cheers followed by sipping or gulping of drinks.

To avoid the awkward silence that was bound to follow, Charlie piped up mischievously, "OK Julie, you start us off. Change the subject from Ofsted and schools to something else. Why don't you tell us about the real Julie Osborne, the Julie Osborne that lives and breathes when she's not at school?"

"Me...me? No...I didn't mean...you don't want to hear about me surely?"

Unfortunately for Julie, the rest of the team were all eagerly awaiting the audio version of her autobiography and uttered such encouragements as "Come on Julie" and "You can do it" while cheering and applauding her.

Julie slowly and reluctantly tried to stand up, defying the forces of gravity and alcohol. "Thank you, thank you, my adoring fans. I'll keep this brief as my life isn't that interesting...I was born...some time ago in London and after university and training to be a Maths teacher, I was employed in a secondary school in Solihull becoming Head of Maths before applying for the post at Whatmore..."

Julie was interrupted. "Boring! You 're talking about school...tell us about the juicy stuff," said Charlie smiling and winking.

The rest of the baying mob joined in with whoops and whistles.

Julie's cheeks went from alcohol pink to fire engine red.

"Erm...I suppose you all want to know about my love life. Well, that won't take long. After a procession of boyfriends that didn't stay the course, I eventually found a guy I could trust, we shared a flat and were planning a life together. Then for a variety of reasons, we grew apart and he moved out. I've been on my own a while now. I'd love to tell you my weekends and evenings are jam-packed with parties and fit men are queuing at my door to take me on dates. But that would be a lie. See, I told you it wouldn't take long."

Julie lowered herself back into her seat and examined the bubbles bursting on the surface of her champagne. Her audience sat trying not to look at her, feeling uncomfortable and embarrassed. Even Charlie could not readily find an appropriate quip to fix the moment.

It was left to Peter to change direction and the mood before everyone became maudlin. He started talking about the possibility of a party for the staff at the end of half-term to thank everyone for their efforts. Charlie and Neil enthusiastically picked up the baton and started discussing an event that would probably never happen but it did lead them away from a difficult situation.

Sobia, sitting next to Julie, was not interested in helping plan a party. She just felt sorry for Julie who had inadvertently upset and humiliated herself within the blink of an eye. Sobia surreptitiously placed her hand on Julie's wrist for a second while the men were behaving like boys and then re-adjusted her position in her own chair. Sobia was feeling awkward and sad anyway– not just for Julie. Unlike Julie, Sobia had a husband and two young children, twin boys but all three men in her immediate life outside school failed in any real sense to appreciate her. Her husband was a difficult man to please and was often controlling when it came to both his wife and his children. All three of them were often scared by his actions and reactions so, when he arrived home from work, they'd all tip-toe around him physically and metaphorically. Consequently, when Daddy wasn't home, the twins would be terrible for Sobia. They would fight, they would shout and they wouldn't listen to her. Sobia recognised very early on that they were growing into Daddy and it wouldn't be long before she'd be a punch bag for all of the men in her lonely life. So, Sobia sat there next to Julie feeling sorry for her but also envious that at least Julie could go home in the evening and relax and enjoy the comfort of being alone.

After a few more uncomfortable minutes, Julie announced she was popping to the loo and asked if anyone wanted another or a different drink from the bar. Neil promptly offered to take orders and then meet her in the bar to assist so Julie thanked him and hurried off to the toilet in order to let the tears flow in the privacy of the Ladies.

"Blimey, that was awkward!" said Charlie showing little emotional intelligence or indeed basic intelligence of any sort.

"How do you think Julie feels?" said Sobia sternly. "Forget about yourself just for a minute, Charlie. You know she's finding it hard coping since her boyfriend left her. She's still really upset about the break up and you made her talk about her love life in front of her colleagues. I know you'll say that you were just joking about but sometimes you need to think about things before you say them."

"She was the one who told us to stop talking about school and Ofsted and I just thought it would lighten the mood," said Charlie defensively.

"Well it didn't, did it?"

"OK guys. What's done is done," said Neil, grasping at a platitude to stop a row breaking out. "I'll go and help Julie at the bar. She's already a bit worse for wear and it may be better if I have a chat with her outside."

"Thanks Neil," said Peter.

And so, after a mere twenty-four hours, the *strong and stable* senior leadership team at Whatmore School experienced the first signs of weakness and instability since its Ofsted inspection.

CHAPTER 2

Neil found Julie at the far end of the bar. He had walked along a shabby corridor from their private room and into the public lounge. The corridor had similarities to the grubby walkways at Whatmore and the lounge had echoes of the staff room; people sitting around in twos and threes, trying to talk over other groups of twos and threes; everyone drinking, some laughing, most attempting to put the world to rights. The only difference between the Palace lounge and Whatmore's staff room was that the patrons here were drinking alcohol openly and legitimately and the conversation was more sensible.

Neil perched on a stool next to Julie feeling self-conscious. Anyone watching him might have misconstrued his motives as making a move on the poor unsuspecting woman.

"I've got the drinks order," said Neil cheerfully and loudly in case anyone else was listening.

"Great," said Julie in a softly resigned tone.

"What do you want Julie?" asked Neil.

Julie lifted her whisky tumbler up.

"Oh...you've already got one."

"No, yes; I'll have the same again, whisky no ice."

"OK," and with that Neil waved at the barman and ordered the round of drinks for the SLT.

The drinks arrived and Julie reached for her handbag.

"It's OK, I'll pay." Neil fished into his jeans pocket and hooked out four or five twenty-pound notes.

"Grief! Real money. I thought you'd be cashless?"

"Oh...God...no...I like to keep some cash on me just in case. It's just a bit of spending money."

"Lucky you," said Julie wistfully with a whisky mouth wash.

"I'm not that lucky. Just a flat for one and a fridge full of TV dinners."

"That sounds like my life. But at least you have time on your side to change things. My clock is starting to run low on batteries," said Julie looking at the bottom of her tumbler. "You've got plenty of time to share your bed with the man of your dreams."

"Pardon me?" Neil stared at Julie with wide eyes and then checked round the bar for ear-wiggers.

"You know...Mr Right or even Mr Better than Average."

"No...no...you said man of your dreams and Mr Right... Do you think I'm gay?"

"Well, yeah, we all do," said Julie examining her glass from a different angle.

"What do you mean all?" asked Neil frantically.

"The senior leadership team, the teachers, the TAs, possibly the governors. How the hell do I know? You're not worried that people know, are you? For God's sake, it doesn't matter, does it?" said Julie getting louder by the mouthful.

"It bloody does to me! I'm not gay...I'm just single. What led you to think I was gay? Who the hell told you I was gay?"

"Fuck knows, it was some time ago...I think it was Charlie..."

"Charlie! Why does he think I'm gay? It's not as if I've been hitting on him."

"Good old Charlie...you know what he's like...always drawing the wrong conclusions if it creates a punch line."

"So did you think I was gay?" asked Neil staring deeply into Julie's blood-shot eyes.

"To be honest Neil, I didn't give it too much thought. I've been a little pre-occupied trying to find a bloke for myself."

"Bloody hell. So everyone at Whatmore thinks I'm gay?"

"Well I haven't conducted a poll on the subject but I think that's what the women in the staff room think. Sorry Neil."

"Bloody hell! Bloody Charlie!"

"Yes, here's to good ol' Charlie, good ol' discreet Charlie." Julie raised her glass and emptied the contents in one journey from counter top to mouth and back again. "So he spreads the word that you're gay and embarrasses me in front of the rest of SLT about my lack of a love life."

They sat there in silence for a short while, reflecting on the lack of lustre in their lives before ordering another drink. Neil decided on a manly pint of the black stuff and Julie had yet another whisky. Neil peeled off another note and paid the barman.

Out of nowhere Charlie crept up behind and in between the two oblivious drinkers and made them jump announcing his arrival. "Hey up you two, we thought we'd lost you. I was sent out as a search party."

"Well, well. We've just been talking about you Charlie," slurred Julie.

"Nothing good I hope?"

"No, nothing good or even satisfactory," said Neil.

"Excellent. It's all true."

"The fact is we were discussing your lack of discretion and judgement," said Julie.

"Look, I'm sorry about back in the room just now... asking you about your love life. I was just trying to lighten the mood," said Charlie sheepishly.

"Well my mood was certainly lightened by you asking me to bare my soul in public. Luckily Neil had the decency to come to my rescue and comfort me. We went outside for a bit of bare body ballet.,"

Charlie looked confused, looking first at Neil, then Julie, then Neil and back to Julie.

"Sorry Charlie, maybe we should have told you that from time to time Julie and I have a bit of face time, if you know what I mean. Nothing too serious but we like to keep it to ourselves. It's been our little secret. It's been easy to hide because everyone seems to think I'm gay. God knows why! Do you, Charlie?"

Charlie had no answer. His lower jaw had dropped below the collar of his shirt.

"And I performed my little charade in front of SLT so you'd all feel sorry for me and Neil and I could maintain our play-time pleasures well away from teachers who are quick to judge...and it seemed to work. Don't you think Charlie?" Julie glared at the deputy head.

"Well blow me," said Charlie.

"No thanks," said Julie and Neil in unison, smirking at each other.

"Am I missing something?" asked Charlie.

"Yeah," said Julie, "how about sensitivity, self-awareness and a brain?"

"You're drunk," said Charlie trying to go on the offensive.

"Yeah, but I can sober up by the morning," replied Julie. "What's your excuse?"

"Hey, why are you both giving me a hard time here?"

"Because you told everyone that I'm gay!" said Neil rather too loudly which interested a few people in ear-shot.

"There's nothing wrong with being gay, Neil," responded Charlie trying to climb towards the moral high ground.

"No, of course there isn't, but I'm not...I'm just bloody single! That's all...and yet you've been telling everyone I'm gay."

"Well I just thought you were..."

"So you thought...well done...you have got a brain then. But you didn't use it when you asked me to talk about my personal life in front of the team an hour ago did you?" Julie said, squaring up to Charlie.

"Look, I've apologised already, OK. Now can we keep it down," said Charlie looking around a bar trying to give the impression that no one was remotely interested in their heated conversation. "Let's move on and go back to Sobia and Peter. They'll be wondering where their drinks have got to."

"OK," said Neil, "but I would appreciate it if you could spread the word around the women on the staff that I'm not gay."

"Are you really sure?" said Charlie trying to be funny, and as Neil's eyes narrowed, tried to rescue the situation comedy, "Just joking...just joking!"

"You see Charlie, that's the issue. You're always just joking...the sad ageing comedian who never grew up, the staff clown..."

Charlie glared at Julie, no humorous come-back to hand, grabbed the tray of drinks and walked back in the direction of the head teacher and the business manager of Whatmore School.

Julie and Neil followed a few paces behind. Julie winked at Neil and he smirked. They looked to all the world like a young couple making silent fun at the older generation.

Charlie backed into the swing doors at one end of their private room, protecting the loaded tray. He was a past master at carrying and consuming drinks having belonged to various fraternities associated with various golf, tennis, football and squash teams and clubs as well as ancient society of PE teachers throughout the local authority who took over the back room of a pub in the middle of the city on a Friday night, come term time or school holidays. Non-attendance or lack of commitment by staying less than an hour at some point on a Friday night would lead to *fines* and *penalties* usually involving paying for other PE teachers' drinks the following week. The group of teachers were not exclusively full-time PE teachers but each paid-up member had to either teach a class or take a team after school. Over the years the society's membership had become exclusively macho. Very few right-thinking female PE teachers would even entertain the thought of an evening with well-oiled sweaty male members. Charlie, on the other hand, felt as if he was missing out tonight. He was pissed off, firstly for having to be with the rest of SLT tonight -they were hardly his favourite people - and secondly because he was missing the PE gathering and that would hit him in the pocket next week.

Charlie tried to smile as he made his way towards where Peter and Sobia were sitting away from the dining table on a leather settee. They appeared to be in deep discussion and as Charlie approached, they lowered the volume control of their conversation and then muted it. Charlie started to feel paranoid. Behind him were the two young lovers who hated him and in front of him sat the old guard who didn't want to include him in their conversation.

Charlie put the tray down on the low coffee table and passed the glasses around. Neil and Julie slumped on the other sofa leaving Charlie to sit alone on an armchair feeling as if he was the host of a game show or about to answer questions himself on a specialist subject. He raised his lager and invited the others to join him in "Cheers." The response was neither loud nor heartfelt but the other four team members went through the motions.

"So boss, what do we do now? We're a *Good* school; we've fooled Ofsted for a while. Do we just wait for another set of idiots to change the rules on inspections or do we all retire while we're on top?"

"Well Charles," said Peter in a mock posh voice, "we are hardly on top of our game just yet, my boy. We are not quite Eton or Harrow. Maybe in another year or two and we can become a fee-paying private academy and we'll be able to wear our gowns and the kids can wear boaters."

This was supposed to raise a chuckle but the response was low key for the following reasons:

1.Neil was not quite sure what a boater was.2.Sobia and Charlie did not possess gowns. Sobia left school at 16 to work for her father while Charlie went to a Teachers' Training College and left to start teaching PE with a Certificate of Education qualification - it wasn't necessary to have a degree in those days.
3.Julie was sure she did have a piece of paper somewhere that said she had a PGCE in Education after gaining her Maths Degree but at the moment she was unable to focus on anything or remember very much about tonight let alone some years ago.

Peter moved on, "Well I guess we have to keep improving our results and aim for *Outstanding.*" The word *Outstanding* triggered a negative response from the SLT that Peter wasn't expecting.

It was Julie who was first to launch a missile attack having been fuelled by enough alcohol to reach Cuba. "So we can't have a break from all of this *must do better bullshit.* We can't tell the staff to relax and just enjoy the moment. We can't just enjoy teaching for a few months without the fear of being inspected, judged or graded like farm animals. So *Good* isn't good enough?" she said, provocatively.

"The trouble is Julie, if we take our feet off the gas for a while it will be difficult to regain the momentum. We have to expect more from the staff and the pupils...that's the only way to improve."

"Is it?" said Julie with slurred scepticism. "I mean, how do you do that without making everyone feel as if they're failing or not good enough? Our teachers are dead on their feet and fed up to their back teeth with the marking and preparation. The part of the day that our teachers enjoy are the lessons, but they hate the other crap. Unfortunately, that's the stuff Ofsted are now interested in - he paperwork and data not the students. If we expect more and more from our staff and students then we'll have some very unhappy children and adults. If we go in on Monday and chant *longer and harder* then it'll sound as if we're running a slave ship."

Normally Charlie would have jumped at the chance to say something after Julie said *longer and harder* but his quick wit and repartee were out of gear after her earlier quip about him being the staff clown.

"No Julie, absolutely not!" said Peter raising his voice to a new level that showed his annoyance at his assistant head criticising his proposed tactics for school improvement. "We can't give the staff the impression that we're content with *Good*, we must strive for *Outstanding.*"

"Why?" asked Neil, backing up Julie.

"Yes! Why?" chimed in Julie and the two of them glanced at each other on their cosy settee.

Charlie wondered just what was going on between these two youngsters. Up until today the two of them had hardly spoken to one another. Now they seemed to be as thick as thieves.

"Because...if we stand still for a second, we'll have other schools overtake us..."

"So, it's about our position in the local league table?" said Julie.

"No...well...yes...but it's about being Ofsted-ready for the next inspection. They will, undoubtedly, make our next inspection harder so we have to keep moving forward in order to just stand still in the eyes of the Department of Education. So if we aim for *Outstanding* we might just get another *Good* in a few years' time." Peter was both pleased and saddened by his argument. It sounded logical and tactically correct knowing how Ofsted worked but it disappointed him to think this was how the game had to be played with his staff.

Charlie tried to change the mood of the conversation by bringing more positivity to bear without changing the subject. The last time he had tried that it had left Julie bitter and twisted and that was the last thing he wanted even though she probably wouldn't believe him just now. "And what's your thinking about getting the school to *Outstanding*, boss?"

"Well, Charlie, I suppose we'll have to wait for the full Ofsted report to be published but, as you know from the other night, the feedback from inspectors indicated areas where we will have to improve. Your areas of responsibility namely the well-being of students and staff, behaviour and attendance came out of the inspection very well. But it's no surprise that the key area for further improvement is Quality of Education. Developing teaching, learning and assessment is a priority in order to raise standards and results. We need to think seriously about some of our curriculum areas in the school and a handful of our staff. We can't afford some of our teachers and subjects to let us down as we move forward. I suppose the bottom line with Ofsted is that they want all pupils' GCSE grades in every school to be above average so they can then move the average higher!"

Neil's natural inhibitions were now drowned out by the alcohol he had consumed and the anger he was feeling towards Charlie and his mouth which he felt had lost him potential girlfriends among the staff. He couldn't stop himself breathing fumes and fire onto the already heated discussion. Even though he knew that Peter's last sentence wasn't meant literally or indeed seriously, he still needed to protest at the numbers game. "This is madness! Every school has now got to be better than average and every school has got to be number one in the national league table. Someone somewhere has got their numbers all wrong. As a data cruncher I always thought numbers were supposed to be helpful and a positive force for improvement. It seems the DoE, along with all the other departments in London, just want to use data to prove that inequality exists in an unequal world. How can schools compete with each other fairly when not every school is in the same position and contains the same mix of children? It's neither scientific nor credible as a way of trying to gain accurate and believable evidence. It's easy and convenient for governments to just look at outcomes of pupils in tests and blame some schools for failing kids by drawing arbitrary lines in a list or a league table. They should be looking at the reasons why children don't all have the same life chances before they even start primary school and not blame certain schools for being unable to overturn and cure all of the ills that face our sick society. I know we can only do so much at little old Whatmore but what we can do is improve the chances of our pupils turning out to be outstanding citizens who're kind and considerate and tolerant and...and don't jump to any quick or bigoted opinions on someone else. What do think? Isn't that a better way to behave than judging people on snap shots or partial evidence? What do you think Charlie?" It was a very pointed question.

"Er, yes, I agree Neil, but we do have to play their game, don't we?" said Charlie feeling embarrassed and angry that both Julie and Neil, two young upstarts, were having a go at him. Over the last year or so he had supported both of them over school issues and now they were more established, they were ready to conveniently bury the past in his back with a dagger apiece. "There's no point whinging or crying like a little girl. We have to face up to what we are and compete in the big boys' league!"

As Charlie finished his latest awkward sporting analogy both Neil and Julie sat more upright on the settee and Peter and Sobia finally began to realise that this dialogue wasn't necessarily about education. Nor was it sporting.

"OK, OK," said Peter raising his hands slightly to suggest a break in proceedings. He would have suggested a drinks break to relieve the tension but more drinks might have made things worse. "Would anyone like a coffee or a tea perhaps? I can see if they can bring a tray in here and maybe a few biscuits? Anybody?"

It was agreed that most of the team would appreciate a hot drink. This appeared to be the only thing that SLT were agreed upon.

Peter steered the small talk as far away from education as he could, leading superficial conversations about drinking coffee at night, different types of coffees served in coffee shops, favourite biscuits and the teams' choices for a final death row meal.

Somehow, some forty-two minutes later the topic headed back into troubled waters when a reference was made to school meals. This was led onto the issue of the rising number of pupils on free school meals and the lowering of the standard of school meals and before anyone could shout "Iceberg ahead!" the ship was back on collision course followed by the school stodgy pudding course. Various observations were made about how disgusting the school canteen was...disgusting food, disgusting manners and disgusting prices. There then followed comments about the quality of canteen supervision and the lack of duty staff at break times and lunchtimes.

It was at this very moment that someone lit another blue touch paper with a general comment about how employing more staff would make life more civilised which would in turn improve both the performance of pupils in lessons and their behaviour outside the classroom. Neil, Julie and Charlie, possibly for the first time all night, were all agreeing and nodding their heads.

Peter and Sobia turned and stared at each other for a second or two before both lowered their eyes slightly to hide a tell-tale sign that a ticking time bomb had been exposed.

"What?" said Julie who had used her three black coffees to sober up enough to just about read the covert body language on display.

Sobia had kept out of the discussions on teaching and learning and merely observed the playground antics of some of the rest of the team. She had joined in with the safer topics of tea and biscuits and the extortionate price of high street hot drinks but now felt it was time to give the rest of the team the news she'd given to Peter while the others were ordering the drinks at the bar outside and clearly falling out with each other.

"While you were out at the bar, I gave Peter some difficult news. I didn't really want to spoil the night by bringing this up but in the light of...anyway I might as well tell you all now. Is that OK, Peter?"

Peter nodded and lowered his eyes.

Julie, Neil and Charlie all braced themselves, seeming to sober up immediately. In the 3.7 seconds of thinking time they each had before Sobia spoke again, all of them had concluded independently that Sobia was going to mention a serious health issue and each of them had readied themselves for the news with faces of concern and sympathy but when Sobia spoke again their responses were far from sympathetic. Instead their reactions ranged from shock, disbelief and anger to disbelief, anger and shock.

"Over the last few weeks I have been closely monitoring the school's expenditure as I usually do half way through the financial year. To cut a long story short our costs on staffing are way above the recommended 85% of total budget. We can't make any other cuts to our spending with the increasing costs of services and supplies so we will need to make some redundancies for the next year to balance the books..." Sobia stuttered. As the only genuinely sober one amongst them she was trying vainly to explain the facts to a group of drunken dim wits.

"Pardon me?" said Neil, who had heard every word and did not need the announcement repeated. He just wanted the statement retracted.

"You've got to be kidding me!" said Julie loudly, knowing full well that Sobia wasn't the kidding type.

"Surely you're jumping to conclusions. All sorts of things might happen before next year. There could be opportunities to reduce the staffing bill. How about natural wastage? If we lose a few higher paid members of staff then we can replace them with younger, cheaper models," said Charlie, too caught up in this news to even contemplate making a lewd joke about his last suggestion.

"Charlie, I know what you mean but even if, let's say, three heads of department left and we replaced them with NQTs, we would not be saving enough money to have a neutral budget...not by a distance," reported Sobia. "Clearly it is too soon to tell you how many staff will have to go but my estimate at this stage is...well over five!"

There was a well-timed chorus of one word replies to this statement. Different words at different volumes that sounded something like "FSHUCITHINEKLL!"

Peter jumped in and tried to appease the angry mob. "Look folks, let's not get too wound up about this. This is only a forecast at the moment, right Sobia?" He was looking to Sobia for some reassurance that everything would be OK but there was no hint of that from her lips or her eyes. "If we have to make some people redundant then we can take our time and hope that some staff will leave of their own accord."

"Yeah," said the deputy, "probably our best teachers who'll be able to find a better school to go to. We'll be left with the rubbish. How does that help our results in the future?"

"Hold on a minute, Sobia," said Julie. "It doesn't have to be teachers does it? We could get rid of other staff first, yes?"

"You mean the non-teaching staff?" replied Sobia expecting this line of attack from teachers.

"Well, yes," Julie replied.

"OK, let's take the admin staff first. We have twelve admin staff at Whatmore. They handle the front desk, the typing, managing and collating learning resources, the finances of departments and they are paid roughly a third of most teachers. We could get rid of all of them which would be equivalent to 4 teachers' salaries. Is that what you want? It would mean that teachers would have to do all of their admin work themselves and there would be no-one at the reception desk interfacing with the parents?"

"No of course not…OK, OK, what about TAs? We could get rid of some of our TAs." Julie looked around the gathering for support.

"Well if we had enough TAs to make it worthwhile, we could do that. But TAs are paid even less than admin staff so we still couldn't balance the books even if we sacked all of them. And how would the rest of the teachers feel if they were on their own in class with some of our pupils?"

"There must be another solution?" said Neil.

"Well I would love to hear some suggestions?" Sobia stared at Neil in a way that burned into his eyes, the sensation travelling down his body and stopping at his heart and the wallet hiding in the inside pocket of his jacket.

Neil looked back at Sobia and his eyes pierced her skull, his x-ray vision taking him out of the Palace Hotel and into a different reality in an alternate universe. In this world he was confident, self-assured and desirable. In this virtual world he didn't need to survive by teaching grown-up idiots how to use IT equipment. In this game world he collected coins by slaying dragons and rescuing maidens. There were no financial worries in Neil's alter-ego life. Unfortunately, Neil's real world was a little different.

In the safety of his own flat he had discreetly started to talk to women online and one fling led to another before he settled on a chosen maiden who needed rescuing. She lived many miles away in a land of inequality and unfairness. Neil could not slay her masters but he could provide her with some funds for her to live a better life. So he used his savings to pay for safe passage for his loved one so that they'd be able to live blissfully in his world of happily ever after. Unfortunately, it didn't turn out like that. There was no happy ending and nothing left in his bank account.

Neil needed his two-bit job in a two-bit school earning a few bit-coins a year. He couldn't afford to be made redundant. He would need to become indispensable and keep his job while others about him were losing theirs. He would keep quiet and play a new game. A game of survival.

"Neil, any suggestions?" repeated Sobia.

"No, not at this time," replied the cowardly lion to the wicked witch.

"Charlie, anything to suggest?" Sobia was clearly enjoying her moment in the spotlight armed with a sniper's rifle.

Charlie stared down the barrels of his life and career. The two barrels were in effect one, his life being his career and vice-versa. Just an hour ago he was happily jogging down the road to retirement. A day somewhere in the future, a day of his choosing, a day when the politics of education stopped him from doing the real job. That day was fast approaching anyway but now the economics of education was also a major road block in his path. He was not enjoying the role of continually trying to make savings to an already bankrupt system. It was not what he signed up for many years ago as a PE teacher who liked to kick a ball around with a bunch of enthusiastic kids. But even in his role as deputy head in charge of pupil welfare, dealing with naughty children and biased parents, he still got a kick out of the job. He had a laugh most days, he was appreciated most days and the sun kept rising and shining...most days.

And what about his wife? She appeared to be content, even happy with him working and then going to the club afterwards for a game or two and a beer or two. However, she wouldn't be happy if she discovered that some of Charlie's extra-curricular activities involved exercise of a different sort with the Head of Year 11. These sessions were regular and often and from time to time spilled over into weekends or school holidays. As yet these trysts were easy to keep under cover and they remained undetected. Both were married, both felt guilty but neither of them was able to call a halt to their secret fun and games.

So, while Charlie was in the clear, he kept jogging along improving on his personal bests in his professional and unprofessional worlds – a job he enjoyed, with staff that rated him highly and a personal life where two women believed they were his number one fan. But now the coast was not so clear and he felt the axe beginning to position itself above his head rather than his head teacher. His salary, or lack of it, would save the school a good deal of money. The governing board could well move Julie into his position on a reduced salary and then not appoint a replacement to her post. Perhaps, if Charlie talked to Peter discreetly, he could do a deal that would give Julie the deputy head post, the school a reduction in wages and a small golden goodbye to give him a leg up on to the plane heading for Spain and retirement. *That'd work out quite well for Julie and me*, he thought. It was a noble thing to do. It reminded him of the guy in *A Tale of Two Titties* who took the punishment for some other bloke. Charlie was not quite sure about the names of the main characters, the plot and the author of the book, but *What the dickens, did it really matter in the big scheme of things?* Can't remember, couldn't really care! Or did he? Charlie wasn't that certain that he wanted to go just yet. *Why the hell should I?* Whatmore was a good crack. He could stay for another three years or so and then quit before Ofsted visited the school again. *I'll go then*. That seemed like a plan...

"Charlie?"

"Sorry Sobia...no suggestions at the moment," said Charlie tamely.

Julie was watching the inquisition by Sobia closely, or as closely as she could through beer goggles. She knew it was her turn next and she was ready for Sobia's parlour game.

"I suppose you want me to suggest something else…a magical plan, formula or solution to reduce wages and keep the school *Good*. Well, I can't, not right now, I've drunk too much, I'm tired and fed up and I need to have some sobering up and thinking time. I'm not sure I'll be able to come up with an answer to the budget problem but I'm going to damn well try."

"I admire your commitment, Julie, but I doubt if you will be able to find a palatable solution to this problem. We have been spending beyond our means for some time now." As Sobia made her point she glanced sideways at her boss and Peter was clear that the spotlight was inevitably moving back towards him.

Julie took this opportunity to shut down. Her eyes remained open but invisible shutters behind her lids had closed for the day and night. Her shop was closed but would it ever be open for business again? She scrolled through her mental autobiography and wondered when, rather than if, her life had lost its way.

There was no exact bookmark but up until university everything had seemed to be fine - a supportive family, good grades at school, popular in class and a steady line of steady-ish boyfriends. She moved away from her home town to go to university where she became fairly serious with a few guys but one after another they disappeared off the scene. A year or so after starting teaching Maths at a local secondary school she had met a serious contender to be her perfect mate. She loved him unconditionally, but her other love - teaching – began to consume her life and their plans of marriage, kids, mortgage and happy-ever-after faded into the background. Two years into their rented life together, her boyfriend, prospective fiancé and future husband had had enough of the neglect, rowing, making up, neglect and more rowing and walked out of the door, taking their hopes and dreams with him in the back of his car.

Julie was on her own again. A single Maths teacher. No plus one. She was broken in half. The lowest prime number. To compensate, she threw herself even further into her work. It distracted her mind from the mounting number of her sad yesterdays. And with every day she tried to move on as most of her friends moved on and away from her. In reality she had stalled and life's busy traffic seemed to veer past her in order to avoid a collision.

Her other compensated lay in acquiring the taste and company of wine and spirit in any colour and strength. It helped her through the nights and often through the days. She took to internet dating but had little luck in finding a normal, baggage-free bloke. Her first dates ranged from guys who were fixated on her large chest and didn't seem at all interested in the somewhat smaller grey matter resting above her shoulders, to those men, who were interested only in themselves. She would sit there across a table for two in a restaurant listening to each man's life story, their adventures and daring -dos, their amusing anecdotes, their successes and their connections with influential people. She would smile from time to time and metaphorically smell the lie detector overheating under each man's seat. If she was truthful, she preferred the cleavage watchers in some ways, because at least those creeps were more honest and easier to delete from her internet site. There were a couple of guys who made it to the second or third date but in time their issues surfaced and the mental scars became easy to spot. Their hang-ups often revolved around past relationships, children, debt, jealousy or lack of emotional intelligence and no amount of hide and heal on their faces could prevent Julie from seeing through to the blemishes and scars.

So her sheets and duvet saw no action for month after lonely month, her alarm clock kept ticking and she stopped looking too closely in her bathroom mirror and weighing herself on the scales as she put on a few pounds by spending more than a few pounds on booze and takeaways.

The one part of her life that was a permanent, reliable fixture was work. She moved to Whatmore to escape and start afresh and became an assistant head. A good assistant head teacher. Her colleagues rated her highly, she was competent and relatively popular, even as the member of SLT who created the annual timetable and produced the day-to-day cover list. Mind you, it wasn't difficult to appear to be competent compared to her two immediate bosses. She didn't have a great deal of time for Peter or Charlie. In Julie's mind they were both nice men who were easy to work with but lacked leadership qualities such as vision, drive and backbone. In different ways they both just wanted to please the staff. Peter was a democrat who wanted to talk through everything endlessly before not making a decision and Charlie just wanted to cruise through life entertaining staff and the older pupils with quick-witted quips. She found both men ineffective and ineffectual. She thought these two words might mean exactly the same thing, but she wasn't sure, particularly as she was quite drunk. Consequently, Julie was happy to use both words to describe them. In her present state of mindlessness, she couldn't pick out too many differences between the head and deputy. She pictured Peter as a harmless, bald telly-tubby who couldn't make up his mind, whereas she believed Charlie would be better suited to being a stand-up comedian or an aging internet porn star rather than deputy head of a secondary school. There was no doubt that both of Julie's bosses drove her to distraction in different ways.

Julie believed that Peter, the Wobbling Womble, could not even stick to his own policies. Peter would moan at the kids in assembly for dropping litter around the school, claiming it was the pupils' individual responsibility to keep Whatmore tidy and then would spend over ten minutes each day picking up litter in corridors and across the playground. Julie felt that this gave the wrong message to the litter-droppers as well as the nit-pickers. When looking at him once, bending down to pick up a discarded item from a food fight in the Science corridor, she wondered why all this bending hadn't strengthened his spine and back bone.

Julie was irritated by Charlie not so much in a professional way but on a personal level. She felt that his automatic mouth lacked gears, a clutch or a brake. His job was to entertain the masses, not take anything too seriously and use any opportunity to make his audience laugh. Unfortunately, Julie didn't always feel like smiling. She knew deep down that most of the time Charlie was teasing and it was harmless banter but deep down below his tanned skin and muscular fit body Julie wondered if there was a serious brain ready to pop out. In some of her sleepless moments under her duvet she would think about Charlie's bulging brain quite a bit.

Julie should have left Whatmore by now and re-invented herself somewhere else but at the present time in her life had neither the strength nor inclination to explore new worlds or opportunities. She was no Columbus! Some mornings she found it hard enough to cross her bedroom floor in her slippers let alone the Atlantic Ocean in a sailing ship. Julie knew deep down that she was becoming alcohol and work dependent in order to get through the days and terms of her life. She couldn't quit, though. She needed her job and her booze. She needed to work to pay for the drink and the drink helped her survive the job to pay for more drink.

So, Julie thought, if Sobia wanted some suggestions about how to save money at the school, she would provide them in time but her plans would not include her own erasure. She was going nowhere unless she chose to go. She summoned up what was left of her sober brain and decided to keep quiet and not say anything else on the subject.

There was only one person sitting around the heat of the cosy camp fire who had not commented on the financial problems facing Whatmore - Peter Burlington, arguably the person most responsible for the deficit in the first place, along with the governing board. Peter had known about the problem for some months now. He had had several meetings with Sobia that gradually should have led to him realising that he couldn't bury his head or the accounts in the sand anymore. During this time Sobia had ratcheted up her dismay and anger that Peter was keeping all of this to himself as if it would all go away if he didn't deal with it but Peter wanted to tell his team at the right time; once Ofsted had been and gone;

once the school was settled; once world peace had broken out. But manyana was no longer an option or an excuse -Peter and Sobia's big little secret was to be outed. When Charlie went to help Julie and Neil at the bar, Sobia had given Peter an ultimatum – either the rest of the SLT was told tonight or she would ring the Chair of Governors on Monday morning and explain the situation. Peter had had to accept that the day had arrived when the fan had been switched on and the brown stuff was about to hit it.

Peter's response resembled a performance imitating an imaginary cross-breed of Mr Bumble and Mr Mumble. There was considerable *umming* and *ahhing*, coughing and spluttering, and general nonsense spouted in amongst a lengthy soliloquy delivered by an actor about to die slowly on stage.

"I asked Sobia to delay this news for a few weeks while we checked out the facts and figures and considered some possible solutions. Um, it does seem that we have no alternative but to reduce the workforce and the resources at Whatmore School. We...we...may be able to ease the situation through natural wastage. It could be that if a teacher or a TA leaves during the year we will not replace him or her. And ah...we will also have to conduct a root and branch analysis of every job within the school to see if there are any areas where we can...merge responsibilities or eliminate them. Remember folks...we are looking at roles, responsibilities and structures...not people. But er...we will have to make Whatmore a leaner and meaner teaching machine."

It was difficult to tell when the first pair of eyes in his audience started rolling but at the words *structures* and *leaner* those eyes stopped rolling, stared at the portly figure of the fat controller and started to think of easy ways to make Whatmore a slimmed down organisation.

Sensing tension and potential riot Peter changed tack. "Come on folks. This is a night for celebrating our success. We are officially a *Good* school. Ofsted have said so! We'll be able to recruit new people to the school to inject adrenalin into our veins!"

"Do you mean young staff, boss? Young staff who're cheap and don't cost as much as the experienced teachers who got Whatmore to *Good*? Do you mean young teachers who need their hands held for two years before they're half-decent in the classroom?" said Charlie beginning to see the possible problems that lay ahead for him and the school.

"Well, Charlie, we were all young teachers once. I know what you mean but we'll have to ensure that we keep the best teachers here, if we can," said Peter.

"So how do we keep our brightest and best at Whatmore when we can't offer them any more money?" asked Julie.

"We definitely can't offer any promotions at the moment and we will have to freeze incremental rises!" asserted Sobia.

Peter interjected again to try to take some of the heat out of the discussion. "Look folks, behind all of this is naturally that we are all thinking about our own positions and careers. We're the highest paid people in the school and we know that when the rest of the staff learn about our...predicament...then all eyes will be on us. They will bound to be asking for our heads or some of our heads first. You can hear the talk in the staffroom now *Just get rid of the five members of the SLT and the school will be free from debt and will run much more smoothly.* This could get very uncomfortable and unpleasant so it's important that we introduce this issue to the staff carefully and sensitively for all our sakes. We will need to keep this quiet for a bit longer while I have a discreet word with the Chair of Governors and we, as a team, discuss this calmly and sensibly without the aid of alcohol. I want....no, I expect you all to keep this hush hush until I'm in a position to announce our situation to the staff. Is everyone OK with that? I suggest we don't even discuss this with our partners or close friends or family at present. OK?"

There was a general nod of agreement. There was also a general nod of approval that Peter was slowly growing a pair of cahoonas.

"Now let's talk about something different," pleaded Peter.

"I know," Charlie said quickly, "let's talk about ourselves..."

At this suggestion there was an adamant chorus of "NO" followed by the first signs of a break in the dark clouds hovering above the heads of the SLT.

Thankfully, the conversation moved on to politics and while the four members argued the toss over Brexit, Peter took a back seat and reflected on the redundancy situation at Whatmore and what he should do both professionally and personally.

Since moving to headship several years ago, Peter had always felt uncomfortable. Each day as head teacher he had self-doubts. He questioned his own ability to lead an organisation and what everyone else thought of him and his performance. At times the job felt too big for him. He worried constantly that he would never be able to fill the boots of his predecessor. No matter what measures were in place to assess his effectiveness and how positive the outcomes were, it never felt good enough. Each year since becoming head at Whatmore he had met his targets from his performance management review. The Chair of Governors, two other governors and a head teacher from a school some distance away had picked through the evidence that Peter had presented to the panel and they had accepted that his targets were met for this year, given him a couple of extra quid in his pocket each week and promptly set him more targets for the next year. His SLT seemed relatively satisfied with his leadership. No-one on the team had any real issues with him – well no-one voiced them anyway. The staff, generally, were fine with him. There were, as with all schools and organisations, those who were for the boss and more than half of the workforce who would prefer someone else to captain the ship - that captain might be no better but some of the crew always seemed to harbour dreams of mutiny on the high seas. The pupils and parents also seemed to be fine with him. There were, of course, a few difficult children in each year that he would gladly, if allowed, send to Siberia. There were some obnoxious parents who were never satisfied with the staff, who, in their eyes, always seemed to have a personal grudge against their angelic little angels. But all in all, the governors, his leadership team, the staff, pupils and parents were OK.

There were some elements that required improvement but overall, he would say that the big and little human beings who were connected to Whatmore were good people. Unfortunately, the good people of Whatmore were sparing with their praise of Peter, so he received very few pats on the back. Like one of the young insecure pupils in his school, Peter craved appreciation, praise and affirmation. So Peter just kept trying to do better, driving the school onwards, avoiding as many twists and turns in the bumpy road of education as he could. Of course, one day, a day unknown to him, he would pass the wheel on to a new head teacher to steer the school even further away from danger.

Peter was really pleased that the school had remained *Good* in the eyes of Ofsted but now the budget cutting was going to have major repercussions on the journey to *Outstanding*. It would cause unease with the staff and some of his key practitioners would look elsewhere for a more secure place of work. Resources would be spread more thinly, that was for sure, and again some members of staff could vote with their feet and walk towards the glittering prizes of a big fat academy or private school. Having just avoided one car crash of a poor inspection, he was now heading for possible union action and a revolting set of teachers – a multiple pile-up in the making.

He was, however, determined to ride this out. He wasn't done yet. He had fuel left in the tank. He was only fifty-three years old and still going strong. He didn't want to quit yet. Also, he was not sure that his wife, Rachel, would be over the moon having him at home all day. She was happy to see him in the evenings, weekends and school holidays but all day, every day, might prove too much for her without a lengthy period of adjustment. Rachel liked her maternal time with her daughter and grandchild and Peter was not sure that she wanted another dependent to look after. Their only child lived some distance from them, a point of constant reminder from Rachel to Peter. When he was appointed as head teacher of Whatmore, it meant that Mommy and Daddy Burlington had had to buy a house further away from their daughter, son-in-law and grandchild. From day one this had been a problem for Rachel in particular – a problem that still remained a dark undercurrent even today. At Rachel's unhappiest moments her anger and frustration surfaced and she would make it crystal clear to Peter that she would have preferred that he had remained a deputy head on a slightly lower salary if it meant that she could visit her daughter and her granddaughter more often. She quietly resented the fact that Peter was pre-occupied by his Whatmore family while Rachel was separated from their real family because of his selfish need to prove himself a capable head teacher. Peter was living in a world of doubt. Was he a good head teacher, a good husband and a good father? He was trying to provide comfort and support for both the Whatmore and Burlington families and appeared to be failing on both counts.

Peter let himself drift back in the room and tuned into the bickering and banter of his senior leadership team. Various political leaders were being pulled apart and mocked while they drank tea, coffee or, in Julie's case, the remains of a second bottle of wine. Peter looked at his team, wondering if this was the start of a new chapter at Whatmore or the end of an old one.

Within a few minutes of Peter re-joining the discussion, a phone rang and the debate paused. Sobia grabbed her handbag from beside the settee and walked towards the door to answer her mobile. She took the call in a whisper but between the four remaining members of the team and their eight prying ears, they could pick out various parts of the one-sided conversation.

"Are you OK?...are the boys asleep?...no, just soft drinks...no, I'm going to bed soon...yes, yes, I'll be home after breakfast...I have to...I can't...I'm sorry...it's just the once...tell the boys I will be home by eleven at the latest...I will take them out for lunch...you can have some time for yourself...it's OK...I'll tell you about it over the weekend...are your parents coming over on Sunday?...Yes that's fine...I will need to get some extra food...I will take the boys to the supermarket when I take them out for lunch...OK...OK...I'm sorry...yes...I'll see you in the morning...bye...bye...I..."

Sobia stared abjectly at her phone as she pressed the red button and placed the mobile back in her handbag. She walked back to the group and quietly sat back down, placing her handbag on her lap.

"Everything OK Sobia?" asked Charlie as innocently as he could.

"Yes fine thanks. Just my husband seeing if I was alright."

Charlie persisted. "You mean he wanted to know if we were behaving ourselves and acting responsibly."

"I told him you were acting normally...no more, no less!"

"Oh heavens," responded Neil. "In that case he won't let you come out with us again."

"Probably not," said Sobia and looked down at the handbag concealing her phone.

"Well Zebedees, it's time for bed," said Peter looking at his wrist watch. Only Charlie understood the reference to *The Magic Roundabout* but everyone realised that this was the cue to leave the party and make their way to their rooms at the Palace Hotel.

"What time is breakfast , Peter?" asked Neil.

"I've booked it in here for nine o'clock."

"Nine o'clock!" exclaimed Julie. "That's not morning, that's still the middle of the night..."

One by one, they stood up, said good night to each other and slowly made the trek to their rooms. Up three flights of stairs, single file keeping to the left as if in school. They each found their own room, used the hotel's key cards and let themselves in.

The senior leadership team from Whatmore School allowed their hotel room doors to slam closed behind them. Almost at the same time, each of them leaned back against the inside of his or her door and breathed a sigh of relief - the evening of celebration was over.

CHAPTER 3

Peter

Peter surveyed his hotel room.

He had not had much time to consider his bedroom for the night when he arrived at the Palace Hotel. He was late getting away from school so he'd quickly signed in at Reception, half-listened to the directions to the private room reserved for the team's celebratory meal and then headed upstairs. He'd dumped his overnight bag on the bed, changed his shirt, brushed his teeth in the pokey ensuite and left the room. He wanted to be the first to arrive in the dining room so he could welcome his team as host. He just about made it before Neil who had, as always, arrived on time.

Now, some hours later, Peter looked around the rather dark and shabby room and drew the curtains. He abluted, undressed and put on his rather tight pyjama top and bottoms before sitting on the edge of his bed and considered phoning or texting Rachel. It was late, too late to ring her...she'd be asleep, but he'd send her a text to wish her goodnight, even if she didn't receive it until the morning. He dutifully sent it and turned his phone off knowing that he would get no response tonight and may be not in the morning either. He was almost ready to turn the bed side light off. He just needed a glass of water so he could take his tablets. The nearest thing was a mug next to the kettle.

Tablets taken, Peter switched off the bed side lamp and drifted away from the Palace Hotel to a world where he was young, slim, athletic and a babe magnet.

Neil

Neil's first task in his room was to punch in the free Wi-Fi code for his phone and tablet. Once connected, he made himself a coffee, closed the curtains, stripped down to his boxer shorts and sat on his bed to begin the second part of his evening.

He had tolerated the meal, the discussions on life and everything but he hadn't enjoyed two points in the evening. He was furious to have learned that Charlie, and for that matter, the rest of his colleagues assumed he was gay, Julie included. It pacified him slightly that at the bar, he and Julie had managed to get their own back on Charlie. Even if that was only a very small victory.

Neil was also very anxious about the news that Whatmore was in financial trouble. It made him excessively nervous. It was not the first time Neil had come close to losing everything. Mostly he had managed to rescue his fortunes but his steady wage was something he relied and banked on. It was the only certainty in Neil's uncertain world of thrills and spills. To take his mind off financial worries and uncertainties, he chose his favourite gambling site on his tablet and spent the next two hours watching his world spinning in front of him until he passed out through exhaustion.

Sobia

Sobia closed the door to her room, sighed and started crying. She walked past the door to her ensuite and sat on the edge of the bed. Her gentle tears soon became frantic sobbing. She was too depressed and unhappy to analyse the whys and wherefores at this moment in time. All she knew was that she needed to cry. She also needed to shout and scream but she worried that she'd be heard by a neighbouring guest in the hotel, particularly any of the Whatmore staff along the corridor. What would they do or say if they heard her screaming through the paper thin walls? What would she say to them? Did she have to remain suffering in silence, playing the dumb role of happy wife and mother, while she wanted to explode and expose her anxieties and depression, her fears and tears to the watching world. But protocol meant that she had to remain calm and carry on, in control of herself while it seemed everybody else was controlling her. Deny everything. If she could, she would lose control, lose herself and run away.

So, Sobia wiped her eyes with a tissue from a pack that she always kept in her handbag. She composed herself and composed a text to her husband explaining that she was now in her room and going to sleep soon, she would be home as quickly as she could in the morning and that she loved him very much. She decided not to apologise again. She pressed send and knew that he would not reply even if he saw the text. His response would come tomorrow.

Sobia went into the ensuite and slowly started removing her make up revealing a sad, ageing actor who was finding performing harder and harder as the years went by.

Charlie

Charlie's exit from his stage was less dramatic. He headed for the mini bar and the remote control to see what was available. There were a couple of cans of lager in the fridge that no-one would miss and he went up and down the channels looking for sport and free porn. No such luck. Just a few terrestrial channels that held little interest for Charlie – the international news, a chat show with some over-bloated film star pushing his next movie, the middle section of the re-run of a re-run of *Die Hard 2* and an American sit-com that seemed to be lacking in comedy and over-flowing with sit! He turned off the TV, swigged his can and would have analysed the evening he had just escaped from but he couldn't be bothered. All he knew was that he gave up a night with the lads to talk school and education.

The worst take-away from the evening was that his career was perhaps coming to an end and his life would have to change. This annoyed him. He was happy to keep doing what he did. His golf, his tennis, his five-a-side footie, his lads' nights out, his job, his pastoral team, his head of year 11 and of course his home and his lovely wife. His third lovely wife.

That reminded him, he ought to open his phone to look at his messages. He rarely used his phone, particularly at home, as he didn't want his wife seeing what he was up to. He wasn't into social media but he did receive texts from his mates inviting him to various activities or sharing jokes. He knew from his role as Pastoral Leader at Whatmore, the dangers of Twitter, Facebook, Instagram and the like. So, he kept his exchanges on a one-to-one basis. The first text he noted was from the Head of Year 11. It wasn't school business. It was a short text but in less than 100 characters it left Charlie in no doubt that she was looking forward to their next one-to-one at the end of school on Monday. He smiled and turned off his phone completely forgetting to send a text to his lovely third wife.

Charlie finished the second can of lager and stripped down to his M&S briefs. He had travelled light tonight. No change of clothes, no toothpaste or brush, no just-in-case case – just his phone and wallet – and his wallet contained everything he would need in a real emergency. Charlie could cope in all situations - he was used to flying by the seat of his briefs.

 He closed his curtains on the day and night and entered the weird and wonderful fantasy world of Charlie Briggs.

Julie

Julie on the fourth attempt had managed to insert her key card into the moving slot in the moving door before opening the moving door handle and moving into her moving room.

She leant against the back of the door for a while, leaving the lights off and then headed gingerly towards the window on the far side of her room. She opened the window a few centimetres (as far as Health and Safety would allow) and stared out across the city. Below her were the blurred street lights and shop signs of a main high street populated by groups of revellers leaving the local pubs. Some of these youngsters were trying to flag down taxis while others were propping each other up as they walked along the pavement towards the next port of call – maybe a club, maybe a mate's house or maybe home.

Julie stood there on the other side of the glass slightly swaying as she watched their world go by - a world full of possibilities. Even in her liquid condition Julie was more than aware that she was alone in a hotel room and yet all of the people she was looking at below seemed to be in the company of friends or lovers, laughing and touching each other. Had her probabilities and possibilities of attracting a bed mate been reduced to a figure of next to nothing? She could strip off in front of the window and flash her body for all to see and no-one would notice or care or react.

Julie was not just alone, she felt invisible. If she was sober enough to use metaphors from her life as a Maths teacher, Julie would claim that she added little to anyone else's life; she just kept taking away and causing division. All she wanted was a plus one and the chance of multiplication in the near future before her body clock stopped ticking. It was no good, she couldn't carry on like his. She would have to change and have a different approach to life. From tomorrow she would get a grip on her life, stop drinking...as much, start to lose weight ...again, go on a few dating sites...again. Julie had heard it all before but this time she meant it. She was serious. She was serious and angry. She had let herself slide and her job was becoming too important in her life, at the expense of everything else. And now that her livelihood was threatened by budget cuts, Julie began to realise, that her two-bit job at Whatmore didn't matter anymore. In fact, none of this mattered.

She knew what she had to do. She couldn't wait until tomorrow. She would do it now. She grabbed her hand bag and key card from the bed and headed for the door.

PART 2

Passing Through

CHAPTER 4

Peter Burlington woke up and immediately regretted it. *Why, oh why do we all have to wake up every morning and leave behind a world of dreams and re-enter the dreary day-to-day reality?* Is the dream world created to punish us for being disappointing earthlings who have systematically ruined the big plan? So, each night our makers taunt us by showing us the world that we should be inhabiting. But, what about the dreams that turn into nightmares that seem worse than our own daily lives. What are they all about? Perhaps they show us that life can be even worse if we are not careful! Perhaps it is just better to sleep without dreams – good or bad – and never wake up.

Peter stopped trying to be a half-asleep, half-assed philosopher and started to get his bearings. He reached for his mobile on the bed-side table so he could check the time. He then reached for his glasses, also on the bed-side table to give him a fighting chance of reading the time on his phone. 6.34. Why does he wake so early at the weekend? It's Saturday. No work today. He can re-charge the batteries and lead a relatively normal life, if only for one day. Sundays were different; they were almost as bad as week days. Sundays were school days without even setting foot inside Whatmore. From the moment Peter was fully awake on Sundays he was thinking about school, working on school matters in his study and projecting his thoughts to the week ahead. But Saturdays were different. On Saturdays he tried his best to forget about Whatmore, forget about snotty, horrible, little school kids and the snotty, horrible, big school kids – the staff.

Peter had the whole day to relax, the whole time to think about other things, more important things like...football...ice cream and...Michelle Pfeiffer. He would wind down for the day after being wound up by all of the C R A P that went with running a school. He was definitely not going to mentally list all these things now as it would eat into his Saturday, his one non-school day of the week. His plan, therefore, was to try to go back to sleep for a while or just slob in bed pretending to go to sleep because he could. He snatched a quick look at the news app on his phone to check if the world outside his room was still as crazy and mixed up as ever and went to set the alarm for 8.00. He then changed it to 8.30 before having third thoughts and altering it to 9.00. He needed to get up then to make full use of doing nothing for the rest of the day. No point in wasting precious time. You need to be awake and alert when you're planning to pursue a day of sloth-like indolence.

And then he noticed it. Just before taking off his glasses and placing them back on the table. The mobile screen read 6.47 and underneath it was the word Friday. Not *Friday 13th*, not *Black Friday*, just Friday. Friday, as in a school day. A day when he had to get dressed in a shirt, tie and suit, had to look smart, had to act professional and be relatively nice to all of the kids and teachers...all day.

Peter's next twenty-three muttered words contained eleven inappropriate expletives that did not meet the high standards expected of a public servant charged with preparing young impressionable minds for a bright future. But Peter said them anyway and said them so loud that the bed stirred beside him. Below the duvet was his wife, Rachel. Peter's long time and long-suffering wife. He quietly and stealthily crawled out of bed, heading for the ensuite. While peeing and then showering, Peter tried to work out why he had thought today was a Saturday. Was it wishful thinking or was he trapped inside a film like *The Truman Show* or *Freaky Friday*? It was no good agonising over his miscalculation though, he'd just have to go to work and hope and pray that he wasn't starring in a re-run of *Groundhog Day*.

He was showered and out of the ensuite in minutes. Washing his hair didn't take long these days as most of it had disappeared down the sink hole several decades ago. He grabbed his clothes from various drawers and wardrobes and changed on the landing so as not to disturb Rachel any more than he had already. He made a cup of tea in a travel mug, picked up his car keys and briefcase from the hall and was out of the house by 7.13 am.

Peter reversed slowly off the drive to avoid complaints from within his own household or the neighbours and then put his foot on the accelerator as he left his quiet cul-de-sac which was occupied mainly by retired pensioners – lucky sods! He switched on the radio and listened to a double act of jovial presenters paid to try to make going to work bearable. He listened carefully for the time checks and more importantly the day checks. The over-paid, under-talented presenters confirmed that it was indeed Friday and that Peter was not still asleep and that this was his harsh reality.

Peter's journey to work each morning carefully avoided as many cars and people as possible. But as he approached the Whatmore catchment area it was inevitable that he would see children and some of their parents from his school. It somehow brought the beginning of the school day even closer. He tried to focus on the road ahead and not let himself be side-tracked by other people whatever their shapes and sizes. He hoped today would be a good day. A *Good Friday*. Well, it was close to the weekend and Saturday was just around the corner. As was Whatmore now!

He indicated, turned through the school gates and drove slowly towards his spot on the car park. The head teacher's space was close to the front doors of the school and as he parked up, he realised that a handful of staff had beaten him in this morning...including his ambitious, relatively new, deputy head teacher. Bless her!

Peter's working day officially started as he negotiated his way through the sliding doors into the atrium of the school. He could hear the noise of children in the canteen. He could also smell the delights of a lorry-load of toast, baked beans and eggs being heated up and served up to pupils free of charge. It was a costly but worthwhile initiative to offer all pupils some hot food at the beginning of the day regardless of their status or right to claim Free School Meals. The free breakfast was rationed to two slices of toast with an option of baked beans or eggs as long as they were in the dining hall by 8.15 am. The younger pupils almost all took up the opportunity - their parents delighted not to need to spend their hard-earned benefits on cereal for little Tameka or Shane - whereas the older pupils mostly opted for a few more minutes in bed and couldn't be bothered to get up slightly earlier to eat anything free and healthy. Peter had for some time been keen on this initiative. He was convinced that in the immediate area around Whatmore there were many parents who, for all sorts of reasons were not providing their children with an adequate diet. He was not judging the families, God knows they had enough to deal with, but if the school could provide two reasonable meals in a day for the kids then he was all for it. Not all of his senior management team were in agreement. Particularly his deputy and the Business Manager. His deputy would have used the money on more resources in the classroom while his Business Manager just wanted the school to spend less money. Every so often in an SLT meeting the issue would be raised by one of them and Peter would have to fight his corner to continue to serve free breakfasts for the sake of the health and well-being of the kids. He would usually have to stall the heated discussions with a pledge to review the benefits and costs at a later date. It a strange irony that Peter was so keen on the pupils' health and dietary needs when he had little regard for his own. He was over-weight and often went without breakfast himself while stretching his expanding waste line with top-ups of greasy or high-calorie food as the day progressed and the need to comfort eat became essential.

Peter knew he was looking his age these days and he was also feeling it. As he considered this, he tried to remember how old he was - he was either 56 or 57, which was it? After doing the maths in his old head he decided he was now 57. It seemed only a few years ago that he could run up the stairs and stand up throughout live concerts or football matches. Now, his body craved comfy chairs that didn't make his back ache. There was a time when he could drink until the small hours but now his body clock started shutting down half-way through the evening. And Peter didn't dare drink anything after 10 o'clock at night as it would mean extra nocturnal visits to the loo. Peter looked tired, pale, fat and old and very soon he wanted to give up this *working for a living* lark for a better life. On better days he felt like a ghost walking around the corridors of Whatmore but on the not-so-good days it felt his body had been inhabited by a zombie from the *Walking Dead*.

His Deputy Head, Kay Conrad, was his complete opposite. She was young, tall, thin, fit and healthy. She had jet-black skin, shoulder length braided hair and wore strikingly colourful clothes. She was a stunning looking woman with boundless energy and boundless ambition. On interview, almost three years ago, she was literally and metaphorically head and shoulders above the other three short-listed candidates. She impressed the whole interview panel with her speed of thought and attention to detail. The decision was unanimous to appoint Kay and there was a warm and confident feeling around the governing board that they had appointed not only an outstanding deputy but also an outstanding head teacher in the making.

Over the last couple of years, the governing board at Whatmore had not been disappointed. Kay had been given certain responsibilities to fulfil since the re-organisation of the senior leadership team and had taken on the key roles of monitoring Teaching, Learning and Assessment, ICT and Performance Management. Kay made clear at her interview her feeling that as the only deputy she wouldn't want to be allocated any classes to teach as she would be in and out of every other teacher's classroom all of the time. And she was and still was today. She supported and encouraged teachers and their teaching assistants, guiding and advising, sometimes criticising delivery and execution but always in a positive and considered way. The staff came to respect her almost immediately, accepting the hard messages that she gave from time to time. In almost every case, members of staff agreed with Kay's judgements when it came to their performance management review and appraisals were signed off without any blood being spilt on classroom carpets.

Peter was very impressed with Kay's professionalism, work ethic and attitude to the job but as his deputy, his number 2, his right-arm woman, he was a little less convinced. Peter did not feel as if he could relate to her on a personal level – she was a semi-closed book as far as her private life was concerned. He knew and understood that private meant private but on the many one-to-one meetings they shared it never seemed that she could move away from talking school business and that made long meetings quite intense. Kay was also lacking in the sense of humour department and found it difficult to poke fun at herself or indeed others. This was something that Peter missed and had been a serious void since his last deputy left.

Peter entered his office at 7.47 and powered up his equipment – his laptop, his printer and most importantly, the coffee machine. His office had been cleaned at about 7.00 by one of the cleaning staff. He wasn't sure if it was the same person each day who re-arranged his paper work and hoovered up all the biscuit crumbs off the carpet but he was very grateful that by the time he entered his office each morning his room was ready to be systematically untidied again.

He poured himself a mug of coffee and looked at his diary to remind himself what the planned highs and lows of the day were. A one-to-one with the Head of the English Department, a meeting on finance with his deputy and the Business Manager, the weekly phone call with his Chair of Governors, a twenty minute slot with a parent who needed to vent - plus learning walks, break and lunch time duties, end of the school day at the school gates duty and, if he was lucky, time to visit the toilet twice. How Peter yearned for a blank day in his diary. A day when no-one wanted to see him and he didn't want to see anyone. Chance would be a fine...

There was a brief knock followed by the door opening before Peter had chance to say either *Come in* or *Go away*.

It was Kay. In one hand she was carrying various folders, her diary and walkie-talkie and in the other held her mobile pressed to her ear. She carried on the last knockings of a phone call with someone as she sat down in her usual chair and placed her stationery shop on the seat next to her. "...OK...yeah...OK, look, I've got to go. I'll discuss it with you in my office after school... Bye."

"Everything O'Kay?" asked Peter with a smile on his face, amused and amazed at his own remarkable word play for this time of the morning.

Kay put her phone on top of the diary and folders and didn't register Peter's stunning sense of humour. "Yes thanks. No real problem. I'll sort it out tonight," she said.

Peter waited for further explanation but nothing was offered by Kay. Nor were any pleasantries like, *Good morning,* or *Can I have a word, please?*

Instead it was straight down to business. "I was working on the Year 11 progress data last night and I wanted you to have a head's up before I show the Chair of Governors." Kay reached for a folder, produced a spread sheet and passed it over to Peter.

Rather than him spending ten minutes trying to decipher the numbers dancing across the page and then making a generalised vague comment to disguise his lack of incisive analytical skills he went for the easy option. "So briefly tell me what your analysis indicates?"

"It's not good, particularly the English predictions. It looks like we're not going to improve our results this year. I know it's only February, but I've factored in the mock exams and teacher assessments and it looks like the school is going backwards this year," replied Kay, delivering a deadly serious message with a dead-pan expression.

Peter sat rigid in his chair feeling as if this was the beginning of an interrogation session in the secret underground basement of the Department of Education. Kay's breaking news of a gloomy forecast for the Year 11 exam results was not entirely unexpected but it was still unpleasant and uncomfortable to hear. Peter knew that if Whatmore's results were not better this summer then there would be questions asked and doubts voiced by various people about his leadership. These people would range from staff, parents, governors, Ofsted and members of his own senior leadership team. In particular one of his group would be disappointed to be part of the senior leadership team that seemed to be failing the pupils but Peter suspected that she would not cry too many tears in the hope of it creating an opening for her in the future. These downward numbers meant that Peter's number was almost certainly up.

He sat there contemplating his future while Kay delivered a condescending technical monologue which not only explained to Peter the system of assessing pupils' performance but how she went about calculating Year 11's projected grades. He didn't interrupt her; he just sat there, feeling like Homer Simpson at the nuclear power plant where he worked, scared to pull a lever or press a button for fear of being found out.

A new vocabulary tripped off Kay's tongue at a frightening speed. These acronyms, words and phrases were familiar to Peter but paralysed him and he began to feel as if he was trying to learn a new language in a foreign country. "EBacc...ASP...attainment threshold measure ...Five pillars... Progress 8... Confidence intervals...floor targets...coasting..."

It was the word *coasting* that got Peter's attention. This was a word and a world that he understood and could relate to. He wanted to coast towards the coast. Beach front hotels, amusement arcades and fish and chips wrapped in paper. He wanted to escape from this land of numbers and letters, a land of pluses and minuses, a land of up and downs. He wanted to sit on a bench with Rachel and look out to sea and turn his back on every school in the country.

But not today, unfortunately. Today he was glued to his office seat, stuck in this reality of underperformance. The metaphorical tide was turning and before long he could imagine that he would have to use a few salty metaphors to describe his own predicament. Words such as *drowning* and *sinking* quickly came to mind.

"So, the English grades are our major concern; Maths is still doing well?"

"Well, not brilliantly, but they are improving year by year," replied Kay.

"It's funny how things change. It was only three or four years ago that Maths was a real worry and English was one of the highest performing subjects in the school. Richard is doing really well now. It's been very satisfying to see how he's developed his skills as a leader."

"Yes, he has real potential. I don't think he'll be with us for very much longer. He's ambitious and will be looking to move on and upwards fairly soon. It's a shame that the Head of English is not looking to leave us." Kay's laser-like eyes directed themselves across the table.

"I understand what you're saying but our job is to continue to support the English Department and particularly Eve. She's finding it tough. She's had to re-build the department after Jo Slater left us a couple of years ago. Others left in her wake and the quality of the team dramatically dropped. I know you don't rate Eve but she is trying her best..."

"But her best isn't good enough. The data speaks for itself. The pupils are performing reasonably well in many of their GCSE subjects but not in English. Very few members of the English department are inspiring and motivating their classes. The behaviour in English classrooms is not always what it should be. We have given her time to try to turn things around but we need to act now."

"What are you suggesting?" asked Peter knowing exactly what Kay would say.

"Eve is alright as a person but she's not leadership material. She needs to be replaced as Head of English."

"Hold on Kay; you know and I know that it isn't as easy as that. We're not in the middle of an episode of The Apprentice. We can't drag Eve in here and tell her she's fired. We'll have to start competency procedures and prove that she isn't fulfilling her role. That will take time and will almost certainly cause even more turbulence within the English team. We've only got a handful of months before the year 11 pupils take their GCSE exams. We need to steady the ship..." Peter almost finished his explanation with ...*and not rock the boat*, but thought better of it.

"But by us not acting decisively, we aren't fulfilling our roles as leaders of Whatmore School. We have identified an issue...a problem that needs solving and we are just seen to be prevaricating. I certainly don't want to be associated with a plan to do nothing or at best wait to see if she improves." Kay leaned forward in her seat.

I bet you don't, thought Peter but said "I'm not suggesting that we do nothing. I'm not suggesting either that we just sit on our hands and wait for Eve to magically improve. We need to do something and, in the end, we may have to wield the stick but for now let's consider supporting her, the team and the pupils through this stressful run-in to the summer exams. What are your classroom observations telling you?" He was trying his best to take a little heat out of the conversation.

"Well, as I've already indicated, some English teachers' classroom practice requires considerable improvement. There's not enough pace and rigour in the lessons. The teachers aren't stimulating the pupils and that's when the pupils start misbehaving. The problem is that I've tried to coach the more challenging teachers but they also need Eve showing them and modelling how to teach great English lessons and unfortunately, she can't. She's not good enough herself and consequently there's no real improvement in teaching taking place within the department."

"And what's your view of Eve as a Head of English?" asked Peter next.

"Very little drive, energy and enthusiasm. Finds it hard to give tough messages. Very little ambition..."

Peter wanted to say something along the lines of *so she's the antithesis of you then* but held his tongue. "Let me get this straight, Kay. In your view, Eve is either a poor leader or a poor teacher or both?" he asked, trying to be clever but then regretted it as Kay responded in such a way as to make his question seem both ill-considered and lightweight.

"I can't see how you can be judged as a good leader but a poor teacher. As an effective subject leader, you have to show that you can deliver in the classroom first and foremost. I accept that there are some excellent teachers who are not interested or capable of leading others but a head of department must be good or better as a teacher. So, in my judgement, from countless observations, she is not consistently good as a teacher and therefore she is a poor leader!" Kay explained this triumphantly, as if addressing a child with learning difficulties.

"OK," said Peter, who was tiring of this conversation and the day even though it had only just begun. "We'll have to move quickly on this. I'd like the two of us to meet on Monday and put together a plan of action. Have a think over the weekend about what we can do to improve the English grades in the short term and what strategy would be most effective in the medium and longer term. But Kay, I won't entertain sacking Eve as a solution in the short term. We may have to take steps towards that outcome in the future but it will be gentle steps approved by the governing board and the local authority. We're not going to break employment law and I certainly don't want to impulsively destroy a teacher's career."

"I will give it some thought over the weekend. If only she was like the Head of Maths. Richard Perry is one of the best department heads I've ever worked with."

"Yes, he's very good...now." said Peter with a half-smile on his face.

"Am I missing something?" asked Kay, summoning up enough emotional intelligence to realise that Peter was holding something back.

"Well let's just say that Rick...I mean Richard...wasn't always the best department head in the world, but he had a little help from his friends along the way. Anyway, as luck would have it, I'm meeting Eve during period 1 this morning. She's asked to see me so I'll take the opportunity to discuss one or two things."

"Do you want me there?"

"No, I think I'll be OK, thank you," replied Peter, trying to disguise his total opposition to Kay's patronising suggestion. Thanks for dropping in. I'd better show my face at the school entrance and the canteen."

Kay gathered up her folders and they walked out of his office together, Kay heading for the staff room, Peter heading for the toast and fried eggs.

Peter's next half an hour consisted of the following:

1. Eating a fried egg sandwich at a table of delightful Year 7s in the dining hall while they chatted about teachers, lessons, homework and what they were all going to do over the weekend.
2. At the school entrance, telling older pupils who were wandering into school to pull up their ties, take off earrings, hide their mobile phones, lose their chewing gum, and stop swearing, all while smiling at them in a welcoming way.
3. Saying "Good morning" to any members of staff who walked close enough to him to hear.
4. Chatting with his relatively new PA who was friendly enough but not as efficient or effective as her predecessor who had retired six months ago.
5. Herding some reluctant pupils from corridors into their period 1 classrooms.

Peter then made his way back to his office, smiling at his PA and reminding her that Eve Thornton was popping in to see him, and put the kettle on, ready to make a drink when Eve arrived. He sat at his laptop and systematically read his emails, saving or deleting as he went, sometimes making a note in his diary or adding to his to-do list.

Eve arrived after about five minutes. She knocked on the door and respectfully waited for a response from her head teacher. Peter had experienced many different ways that members of his school had entered his office over the years, from scared younger pupils who didn't even want to knock to furious members of staff who barged through the door with steam escaping from their ears.

"Come in!" Peter half-shouted so Eve could hear him.

Eve Thornton came in, closed the door behind her and walked slowly towards Peter's desk. Eve, although admired by most of the younger men and older boys in the school, lacked confidence and often partially hid her eyes behind her long curly blonde hair.

"Good morning Miss Thornton, sit yourself down. Would you like a drink - tea or coffee?"

"I'm OK, thank you," said Eve.

"Are you sure, I'm going to have a coffee..."

"Well, if you're having one...may I have coffee as well... Just a little milk in mine, thanks."

Peter quickly made two coffees and placed one on each side of his desk. "How can I help you?" he asked.

"Pardon?" said Eve.

"You asked to see me, don't you remember, earlier this week. We arranged this time because it's a free period for you and my diary was free for this hour."

"Yes, yes that's right, sorry, of course..." Eve took a sip of her coffee.

"Are you alright, Eve? You seem a bit tense."

"I'm OK... It's just that...I need to talk to you about...my job...here at Whatmore." Having made her admission, Eve pushed some of her hair behind her ears and placed her hands on the arms of her chair, gripping the ends rather too tightly.

Peter sat silently and passively for a few seconds, his mind racing with possible scenarios that could have led to Eve sitting so nervously across the table from him.

"OK. Take your time, Eve."

"I've wanted to speak to you for a couple of weeks now but I wanted to see if things might improve. Firstly, before I tell you, I need you to know that what I'm about to say is in strictest confidence."

Peter started to get worried. His response was standard and text book. "Eve. If what you tell me is, in my opinion, a police matter, then it cannot remain private and confidential. It's the same as our disclosure policy for children. If it's just a work-related matter, then we can talk confidentially but I may have to stop you if the discussion strays into unprofessional territory. Is that OK?"

"It's not a police matter. But you need to be aware of what's happening."

"Right. Before we properly talk, let me just tell my PA that we don't want to be disturbed."

As Peter rang through, he wanted to scream *WHY ME GOD?* but didn't think it would be entirely appropriate. *What's she going to say?* he thought. His mind continued to race. Was it pregnancy? Was it an application for a new job? Was it a pay rise? Was it unpaid leave for a hen weekend in Majorca? His bizarre thoughts ceased as soon as his PA broke the spell. "No phone calls or visitors until Miss Thornton leaves the room," was the instruction.

Peter put down the phone and looked at Eve. "OK, that's sorted. Now what is it, Eve?" said Peter in what he imagined to be a fatherly fashion.

"I'm being bullied." Eve stopped speaking after that short statement.

Peter was not expecting this disclosure and the surprise and nature of Eve's statement almost made him involuntarily laugh in shock. He regarded the petite, youngish woman sitting uncomfortably in front of him. He was useless at guessing ages and from experience realised that *Guess the age of a woman* would always be a dangerous game to play but he could see that some of the Year 11s might view her as an easy target. She was small, one of the youngest-looking teachers on the staff, (although she was at least in her late twenties or early thirties, he guessed internally) and very attractive (he judged internally). This could certainly make her victim material in the eyes of older pupils in the school – boys or girls or both!

"Which class is it? Your Year 10s or 11s. Is it certain pupils? I just need a written statement and a list of names and it will be dealt with, I assure you," Peter said in his best decisively reassuring voice.

"No, you don't understand," said Eve, putting down her mug of coffee and reaching for a tissue from her bag beside her. She dabbed her eyes and tried to stem the beginnings of a flood of tears.

Peter's response was to wheel his chair to the other side of the desk so he was sitting closer to her and to ask if she wanted another coffee. She shook her head and apologised for the water works. Peter made all the right noises and waited for Eve to compose herself. "Would you like anyone else to sit in with us while you tell me what's going on? One of your colleagues in your department or a friend in another team or perhaps your union rep?"

"No thanks. I'm OK now. I don't want anybody but you to know at the moment. I need to tell you and get it off my chest before the weekend starts. I might feel a little better tomorrow if I know you're aware of this and are doing something about it."

"Of course," said Peter. "Just take your time and say whatever you need to say."

"It's Kay Conrad...Mrs Conrad is making my life a misery. She's picking on me and I'm sure she wants me to resign."

. . .

Thirty-five minutes later Peter had written more on his notepad than he had in the last month.

"Eve, can I say again how brave you've been to tell me all of this. I'm aware of the time; it's five to ten and period 2 is only five minutes away. Are you sure you don't want someone to teach your class now or you could go home and we'll cover your lessons for the rest of the day?"

"No, I'm fine. I'll be OK now that I've told you. I just want it to stop. I hate coming to school at the moment and I don't like feeling like this. I love teaching and the kids are great. I know the results last year weren't good and the predictions for this summer aren't that promising either but the department is starting to bond together and we're really beginning to improve," Eve said starting to move from her chair.

"Look, I'll talk to you next week and we'll take it from there. I need to think carefully about all of this but I assure you that I won't tolerate bullying by anyone in this school. Ironically, I have a meeting with Mrs Conrad and the Business Manager now so I think you ought to go so you don't have to face her in the corridor outside."

"Yes, thanks, Mr Burlington. I will go and I'll see you next week. Thank you for listening. I know this puts you in an awkward position but I had to tell you." With this last comment, Eve left the office, closing the door behind her.

After a few seconds of silence, Peter couldn't help himself. "THANK YOU GOD!" he half-shouted at the ceiling as he closed his note book and placed it in his briefcase. Anytime now Mrs Conrad, his trusted deputy and Gareth Dunne, his Business Manager, would be walking in to discuss school issues and problems of a different nature. Peter grabbed a couple of pain killers from the chemist's shop in the bottom drawer of his desk and swigged the last dregs of hour-long cold coffee. He was just considering taking another two tablets and perhaps doubling that when Kay entered the room without knocking followed by Gareth.

"Morning Peter," said Gareth. "You were expecting us, weren't you?"

"Yes, yes, take a seat around the table." The weekly Finance meeting was held around the round table near the windows of Peter's office. Gareth walked over to it laden with paper work.

Kay headed for her usual chair, texting as she went.

"Anyone want a drink?" Peter offered.

Peter made Gareth and himself coffees, poured Kay a glass of water and settled himself at his usual position so he could stare out of the window whilst pretending to listen. This meeting would definitely involve Peter thinking and dreaming outside of both the box and his office. He was already pre-occupied by his previous discussion with Eve and how he was going to tackle her issue. Peter stared at Kay's glass and wondered if she would notice the cocktail of spit and strychnine he'd diluted into her water while her back was turned. He was brought back to reality when Gareth spoke and Kay deigned to put her mobile phone down on the table.

"This week I want to talk about staff and teaching ratios," said Gareth keeping his eyes on the two children in his class – the able one and the less-able one. "As I've indicated on numerous occasions, we're over-staffed and our staffing budget is well over the recommended percentage of the overall spend of the school. We're moving towards a new financial year and need to have a plan of action to reduce costs since our reserve will quickly diminish and we'd then be in dire straits."

This was all the excuse Peter needed to teleport his mind back to the middle of the 1980s when Mark Knopfler was singing about *Money for Nothing*. His brain was consumed with the song for the next ten minutes. He was on stage, wearing a head band, strutting his stuff and strumming his Gibson Les Paul, a million miles away from spread sheets, projections and cost cutting. He was back in his dream world, the care-free days of rocking, rolling and having a good time. He came crashing back to earth when the conversation between Gareth and Kay turned to robbing Peter to pay Les Paul.

"I agree, Kay. One way we could save some money would be to cut down on the expenditure with regards to free breakfasts for all of the pupils. We could probably save one teacher's job if we charged the parents for breakfasts," Gareth was saying earnestly.

"I know I have a different view to you two on this matter," interjected Peter, "but this shouldn't be a choice between saving a teacher and pupil health and welfare because their parents can't afford to feed their kids properly. The trouble with your argument Gareth is that if we charged our parents for a school breakfast then most of our kids wouldn't have anything to eat until their free school meal at lunch time. Our duty of care is to the pupils first and foremost."

"So does that mean you'd rather reduce the work force and increase the teacher-pupil ratio in classes? We already have over 30 pupils in all of our Key Stage 3 classes apart from the lowest ability sets. Are you saying that we should tell the staff that they have to teach classes of up to thirty-four or five? Larger classes will clearly have an impact on performance and results." Kay was making a familiarly sound argument.

"And don't you think that empty stomachs will have an effect on our pupils' performance and results? I'm sorry but I'm not giving way on this. We'll just have to be more creative and find other ways to cut our staff spending budget for next year," said Peter.

Gareth stepped in at this point to pick up on Peter's point and to diffuse the debate. "So, here's some ideas. We could save money on staffing by dramatically reducing the number of teaching assistants we have on our books. We could re-structure the leadership positions within the school. We could ask for voluntary redundancies and then not replace or - and you won't like this either, Peter - we could systematically and surreptitiously rid ourselves of our poorest teachers through performance management."

While Gareth was reeling off his cost-cutting alternatives, Peter stared out of his office window again and was taken back to a time when he was almost sure that he'd been party to a similar conversation with past colleagues, some years ago. He tried to look both Gareth and Kay in the eye, but they were too busy looking at each other and avoiding eye contact with him.. On Sunday, Peter would find himself reflecting on this part of the meeting again. Was it a set up? Were Kay and Gareth expecting the minor explosion from Peter at the suggested underhand ways of reducing the budget? They certainly pressed his buttons and released a nuclear assault from the chief of staff.

It took about five minutes for Peter to calm down and feel remotely civil towards these two colleagues who, just at the moment, felt like the enemy.

"If we do anything, it will be discussed openly and honestly with the staff and the governors. I will not be associated with any devious or Machiavellian way of getting rid of colleagues. Is that clear?" To underline his strength of feeling, he spoke in bold type.

Kay and Gareth were clearly taken aback by their Head's show of strength and assertiveness. They weren't used to this and didn't know how to react. Should the response be – *Sorry Sir, it won't happen again* or *Take a chill pill before you have a heart attack, old man.* In the end, their reaction was the same, a silent stare at each other while Peter felt obliged to fill in the empty embarrassing gap by changing the subject.

Ten minutes or so later, the finance meeting finished. It was the end of period 2 and both Peter and Kay were needed on duty in two of the handful of hot spots around the school site during first break.

As Peter took his position of surveillance by the back doors leading to the main playground area, he found himself reviewing the morning so far. He had woken up thinking it was the weekend, had then been told in confidence by the Head of English that she was being bullied by his deputy and then in the following meeting, his Business Manager and the deputy head had tried their hardest to chip away at his way of working, his educational beliefs and his authority. It was fairly obvious to Peter that Kay and Gareth were in cahoots over spending and staffing and given the chance would run the school differently. They were biding their time at present but sooner or later there would be blood...a coup or a mutiny.

Peter was so absorbed in paranoid conspiracy theories that his eyes and ears ignored the many young adults standing or running around enjoying the break from lessons. Yes, there were some high jinks going on across the expanse of the hard-standing including the odd swear word, the odd prod and poke and the odd bit of teasing and banter, but generally the kids were alright. Peter could spend all day out in the concrete jungle observing the interactions of the Whatmore pupils, his pupils, in effect part of his extended family. He felt like David Attenborough in one of his documentaries, whispering a report on good-natured and caring animal behaviour from a deep, dark, remote part of the world and wondering why human beings believe they're the most intelligent of all creatures.

Peter did not feel that he saw the best in human behaviour from some of his adult family this morning. He was uncomfortable and disappointed by the tactics of his deputy and his Business Manager, two key members of his senior leadership team. He clearly could not trust either of them. He certainly didn't want to be in their company for the rest of the day. So, after Peter had spent a few minutes at the end of break scooping up a few reluctant older pupils from the far corners of the playground who didn't really fancy going to period 3, he decided to go for a learning walk to find some wonderful pupils and some great teachers and TAs who would restore his faith in human nature - small and big people who he admired and trusted.

. . .

After the learning walk Peter went straight to the dining hall to be on time for lunch duty. For forty-five minutes he patrolled and funnelled the pupils as they queued up for their meals and drinks. His reward at the end of the shift was a generous portion of fish and chips served by one of the canteen servers with a wink and a smile. He ate it at a table of five Year 8 girls who were explaining to each other who they fancied, where they should meet in town on Saturday to go clothes and make-up shopping and then back to who else they fancied. They lowered their voices, giggles and excitement as their ancient, fat, balding but nice head teacher sat at the other end of the long rectangular table and starting tucking in to his meal. The girls were very polite, said hello and responded to Peter's questions about today's lessons before they all stood up, said goodbye and left him, no doubt, to continue their grown-up girly give and take in the toilets or the playground.

Once replete, Peter headed back to his office. He had a parent to see in half an hour but first was duty bound to make his weekly phone call to the Chair of Governors. The informal telephone conversation was usually a fifteen-minute catch-up and up-date on the week's events at Whatmore School. Peter had instigated this scheduled conversation with his some years ago as a way to keep the Chair in the loop on school matters. Peter was now on his third Chair of Governors since he became head but all three were happy to take his weekly call. Nirek Dhawan had only been Chair since last September but had been on the governing board for three years. He was a bright, well-meaning, local man who was self-employed in the field of IT. He had a family and hoped one day that his two children would come to Whatmore for their secondary education. Peter didn't know much more about him than that but he was loyal to the school, attended all the meetings and chaired meetings in a professional and business-like way.

"Hello Nirek...how are you...good...have you got a few minutes to go through the week's events?" asked Peter.

"Yes, that's fine, Peter. Let me just get my notepad...OK...so how has the week been?"

"Overall, it's been a steady week. The pupils have been great generally. Their attendance and behaviour have been good although I'm still concerned about persistent absence levels from three or four of our families. We're going to talk to those parents over the next week or so and point out again the importance of getting their kids into school. One temporary exclusion for two days...a Year 10 pupil who lost it in a Science lesson and swore at a teacher. Otherwise, no problems with pupils," said Peter.

"Great...that's good to know...how about the staff...any problems?"

"The teachers and TAs are working hard; a couple of teachers have been absent with flu part of the week but we've managed to cover the lessons easily enough.

Year 11 teachers, particularly, are working their socks off preparing their pupils for this summer's GCSEs but all the staff are doing well."

"It must be a stressful time for teachers...and the Year 11s. Are we picking up any issues?" asked Nirek.

"How do you mean?"

"In terms of stress. I was reading in the paper last week that there are more mental health concerns in school now than there used to be because of the number of exams that the pupils have nowadays. It must take its toll on teachers as well."

"Well...we seem to be lucky here at Whatmore. The pupils take exams in their stride. If anything they're a little too laid-back about them. That's what stresses out the teachers more than anything."

"What about the staff? Are they all coping with the pressure and performing well? What do the GCSE predictions look like?"

It was at this moment that Peter's paranoia started to surface again. Were these just innocent questions or was it more than that?

"The staff seem upbeat. They're working really hard to improve on last year's results. As you would expect...some of our staff need a little more support than others. The...Year 11 predictions are...promising in most subjects...some departments seem to be making real progress. Again, one or two subject areas are still not quite performing as well as we'd like," Peter was aware that he was rambling and hoped Nirek would leave it at that.

"Which subject areas are we talking about Peter?"

It was no use. Peter would have to give details. If he didn't, he'd appear incompetent or, at best, uninformed. "Our major worry is English. The pupils find answering questions on unseen extracts really daunting. No matter how many examples they go through with their teachers, on the day of the exam some of our Year 11s don't seem to be able to do it for themselves when they read part of a text for the first time. Generally, they're better at the creative writing side of things rather than critical analysis." Peter hoped that some technicalities would ward off Nirek from asking anything else.

"I see. So, the English teachers are focusing all of their efforts on textual analysis from 19th, 20th and 21st century literary prose and non-fiction. Is that right?"

"Well...yes...to a large extent," replied Peter, wondering where Nirek's knowledge of the English course had come from.

"And is the Head of English…Eve…doing a good job in leading her troops?"

"We have some concerns, but with experience I'm sure she will be very effective as a subject leader."

"And is she a model teacher?" asked Nirek.

Peter wisely declined to make a sexist joke and responded in carefully considered stutters. "Miss Thornton will be a real…asset to the school…once she has built up her confidence. Unfortunately, there are some colleagues who…need convincing…and lack patience…"

"I'm sure you're right but unfortunately we don't have time on our side. Our pupils can't wait around for our teachers to become effective in a few years' time. Wouldn't you agree?"

"Yes, I take your point but we have a responsibility to develop our staff," responded Peter, trying desperately to make his case.

"I agree entirely, Peter - but only if the member of staff is worth developing. Anyway, I'll have to leave that one with you. Is there anything else we need to discuss?"

"No, I don't think so. I'll be seeing you next Wednesday for the Teaching and Learning Sub-Committee meeting, won't I?"

"Yes, I'll see you then. Thanks, Peter. Have a good weekend"

"And you Nirek - bye."

Peter put down the phone certain that this call was not the first conversation Nirek had received from Whatmore this morning.

. . .

It was Sunday morning in the Burlington household. Peter was in his study. It was the only room in the house that Peter called his. Rachel owned the sewing room. It was her arts and craft room. Rachel used this area of the house as her refuge where the use of sport on television was banned and Peter was only allowed in if he didn't talk about school. The rest of the house they happily shared and, for the most part, lived in happily enough. Over the last five years or so the front and back garden had become Rachel's domain but Peter was trusted to cut the lawns during the summer months.

Yesterday, Peter and Rachel had gone shopping and had lunch in the town centre before visiting the cinema and then in the evening watching a couple of episodes of a US crime show they both liked. Peter was glad to be reasonably active during the day but it didn't stop him thinking about Friday's events.

Rachel, as usual on a Sunday, had gone to visit their daughter's family. The weekly agreement was that Rachel would get the train to their daughter's house, Peter would get his school work done during the morning and early afternoon and then would drive down later to visit. It worked well for the Burlingtons. Rachel had quality time with their grandchildren, sometimes child-minding the two of them during the day, while her daughter and son-in-law enjoyed some precious time as a couple. It worked well for Peter too. He had some alone time to get his thinking and work done before joining them all for a few hours.

So, here he was, at his desk in the study, with his home comforts surrounding him – a travel mug full of coffee, a packet of biscuits, a laptop playing his favourite prog rock bands and a box of paracetamol. His main objective this morning was to make sure he consumed more biscuits than pain-killers but the way he felt after the Friday from hell was that if he ate all the biscuits and one less tablet then his worries would be over.

He decided to tick off all the other essential items off his to-do list before really considering the *Eve-Kay-Gareth-Nirek* situation. The next hour and a half were busy – answering emails, reading reports, planning agendas, eating biscuits, sipping coffee, refraining from eating pills and listening to two albums by Caravan. Now it was time to wrestle with Peter's immediate problems. Namely: Eve's accusations of bullying towards Kay; Kay's insistence that Eve was not an effective subject leader or teacher; Gareth and Kay's style of management in saving the school money, and their fairly obvious dislike of Peter's way of working; and last but no means least, the suspicious interest displayed by the Chair of Governors towards Eve.

Peter first reflected on what could be substantiated as against what was just gut feeling. Eve's tears seemed real but was she really being bullied by Kay? He needed to find proof. Kay's claim that English predictions were disappointing was beyond doubt, but should the blame be laid purely at Eve's door? Were Kay and Gareth gunning for Eve or just suggesting ways to cut staffing costs? Were they undermining Peter's authority? Did Nirek have prior knowledge of the earlier discussions on Friday or was he just fulfilling the role of critical friend? *God knows* was his answer to all of the above. He would have certainly scored lower than a 5 in a GCSE exam for such a vague and confused answer!

Eve was Peter's main concern. The other matters were important but were issues he could try to deal with himself. Eve was young, inexperienced and a thoroughly nice person. She didn't deserve to be made to feel like a substance clinging to the bottom of Kay's shoes. But that was how it had appeared after she opened up to Peter in his office. From Peter's reading of the situation it did sound as if Kay was targeting Eve but did that constitute being *picked on* and, for that matter, was there anything wrong with that if she or her team weren't performing as well as other areas of the school? Eve had explained how she was being observed teaching her classes far more than anyone else and that Kay was continually arranging to meet her to go through every detail of the English department. She'd claimed that Kay would also belittle her in front of other heads of subject in meetings when Peter wasn't present and that Kay was making her feel useless and worthless. Eve had also admitted that her treatment was making her doubt herself, was affecting her home life and her happiness and, in consequence, she was considering leaving Whatmore School if not the teaching profession in general. It was at this point in Friday's meeting that Peter had realised that he'd have to act decisively so that this potentially great asset would not be lost to the world of education.

It was clear that Peter would need to talk with Kay but it was also clear to Peter how bullies accused of bullying commonly react. He had talked to enough over the years outside classrooms and in his office. The automatic responses to such an accusation were along the lines of - *It wasn't me, Sir* or *It's not true, it's all in her head* or *She's a wimp that can't take a little constructive criticism*. Nobody likes to be called a bully and bullying in the workplace is often more problematic and difficult to prove than bullying in the playground. Kay would be bound to say that she was applying pressure on Eve for all of the right reasons. She was trying to get the pupils to do as well as they could in a key subject and that this would in turn help the school in league tables and with Ofsted. Kay would say that most subject heads would have had difficult conversations with her over the last couple of years because of under-performance but they wouldn't claim to be being bullied by the deputy head. She would then say that she enjoyed a positive working relationship with the staff and that she was just doing the job she'd been assigned by her head teacher. Kay would be quick and bright enough to steer her response towards suggesting that if she were a bully then her immediate line manager should also be tarred with the same brush.

Peter, sitting in his study, slouched behind his flat pack desk, stared into his beautiful back garden feeling as if he were trying to steer through a mine field. In his short-term memory, he was still staring into the eyes of a young woman on Friday morning who was crying out for help. He had to do something. He had to act in such a way that Eve would see and feel differently towards her job. So, he would have to talk to Kay on Monday. Would it be a formal or informal discussion? Perhaps something in between. He'd have to make Kay aware of her inappropriate behaviour and attitude towards Eve and that her methods were bordering on being unprofessional. All of this needed to be conveyed without pouring extra petrol on the fire and inflaming the situation even further. In Peter's experience bullies have a habit of bullying their victims even more once they've been found out.

Peter needed a plan of action. He also needed another re-fill of coffee and more biscuits. Five minutes later, after a trip to the kitchen and the toilet, he was back at his desk armed with further refreshments, a note pad and a sound track of progressive rock. He was ready to plot his battle strategy. He started jotting in his note pad:

Monday. Meet with Kay -

1.Start slowly and in general terms - discuss the overall English data and projections for the summer exams; discuss each teacher within the department – strengths and areas for development (finish with Eve as a teacher); discuss Eve's leadership – strengths etc.
2.Kay's view of Eve as a person, professional colleague – good and bad.
3.How do we make her a better teacher/leader? (no talk of dismissing her).
4.What can we do to help Eve? (positive suggestions only) Bullet point key positive supportive suggestions and set a time frame that lasts until the end of the summer term.
5.Who should support Eve through this period – Kay or me? If Kay ~ discuss how she should and shouldn't approach this mentoring role (stress to Kay that she needs to be sympathetic/empathetic – don't want any accusations of bullying! If me - discuss with Kay why she doesn't want to mentor her. Does she have a problem with Eve?
6.Draw up an agreed plan – no classroom observations for a week, then all recorded and fairly spread across the English team.
7.Plan begins on Tuesday. Peter explains to Eve on Tuesday what will happen. Kay not to approach Eve on Monday. Mentoring starts with Eve that night or as soon as possible.

Peter was quite pleased with his plan. It seemed to work on paper. By Tuesday Eve should know that he'd taken positive action to change things for the better, Kay would have hopefully adopted a *kinder* approach towards Eve or not be involved in her mentoring at all. Win, win!

After meeting with Kay tomorrow, Peter would see Gareth on his own and set him straight on certain things that he saw as reasonable and unreasonable when it came to cost cutting at Whatmore. Then he would ring Nirek and explain that he had come up with a new plan of support for the English department and the Head of Department, that it has been discussed with his deputy and agreed. He would see Eve first thing on Tuesday morning and give her some assurances about the future. Job done. Sorted. Nothing to worry about!

Peter sat back in his chair, put his hands behind his head and smiled. He could still do it! He could manage people and situations. He could run Whatmore while keeping all the school dinner plates spinning. Now all he had to do was execute his plan over the next two days. For now he could afford another hunt and gather trip to the kitchen for more sustenance. This time it would involve bread, cheese, pickle, crisps and more coffee. It was nearly lunch time after all!

Back in his man cave Peter ate and drank while flicking through his A4 envelope file filled with pieces of paper that appeared to be important but, in the big scheme of things, weren't. Most of these papers held little interest for Peter these days. He wondered how many important pieces of paper he had read or skimmed before recycling them over the years. Was he binning more and more as he got older, wiser and more and more cynical? Did he care less as his co-called experience increased each year? Was it his coping strategy to dismiss as many new initiatives as he could? He accepted that as he got older the thought of new became scary. He'd be happy to trundle along at the same pace along the same road until he reached his destination of retirement. Peter didn't want to change but he also accepted that everything around him was indeed changing. This job was not good for his health and sanity.

He looked at the clock hanging above the door. It would soon be time to leave. Time for his family. He'd eaten his early lunch and on a full-ish stomach, he was ready for the secret dessert he had after each meal. He reached into his trouser pocket and pulled out a strip of tablets. His anti-depressants.

. . .

At some ungodly time on Tuesday morning Peter decided to get out of bed. He couldn't toss and turn anymore without disturbing Rachel. He showered and dressed on the landing and then headed downstairs to the kitchen. It was 5.41 am. There was time for a leisurely breakfast before he had to leave for work. Tea was made, cereal poured and milked, two rounds of toast buttered and spread with marmalade. There would be no need to have breakfast at school today. This would keep him going until....later in the morning. Perhaps until after he'd seen Eve.

6.04 am. Peter sat on the settee with a second mug of tea and looked at the rolling news on a television channel. While keeping his eyes on the never-ending Brexit fiasco, the bizarre behaviour of the President of the USA and the severe weather in the East, West, North and South of the world, Peter once again reflected on Monday's events.

The conversation with Kay had been challenging to say the least. It took Kay quite a time to admit to Peter that perhaps she had been a little too *negative* in her dealings with Eve. As predicted, Kay's defence was that she was just doing her job which meant trying to drive up standards and keep Ofsted from looking too carefully at Whatmore's exam results this summer.

Predictably Kay had argued that she had a sound professional relationship with all subject leaders including Eve Thornton but in her one-to-one meetings, Eve didn't respond well to criticism and would get emotional and upset. Kay eventually conceded that she found it difficult to deal with Eve as Kay was not a *touchy feely* sort of person. Kay was used to telling people how to improve and then expecting them to follow her advice. After a few minutes of *touchy feely* conversation with Peter, Kay also conceded that in her career she had been known to be *impatient* on occasion.

These concessions were all Peter needed to begin a discussion with Kay on her potential to be a very effective head teacher in the future. Peter heaped praise on Kay, which she deserved for many of the great things she did, but he also managed to point out some of her failings. When she started to take issue and disagree, there was an open goal for the head teacher to compare Eve's response to Kay's criticisms of her and Peter's criticisms of his deputy. Peter then led the dialogue towards his conclusion that Kay needed to develop her emotional intelligence and empathetic skills. She needed to lead and manage her colleagues as individuals and individually. She needed to put herself in other people's shoes.

Finally it was agreed and accepted that Kay would adopt a *different* approach when mentoring Eve from today onwards. Peter would be looking to see this leadership skill improving in the next few months which would strengthen her reference when she started applying for headships.

7.11 am. Peter took Rachel a cup of tea upstairs and kissed her sleepy head, telling her that he'd be back by about six o'clock. He closed the front door and reversed his car slowly off their drive.

On his way to Whatmore, while half-listening to the news and sport on the radio, Peter replayed yesterday's conversations with Gareth and then Nirek.

Gareth's meeting hadn't taken too long. It was one-sided and lacked the emotional intelligence that Peter championed with Kay. Gareth was left in no uncertain terms that his role was to advise Peter on financial matters and not lead discussions on fiscal solutions. The Finance Meeting would look at all budget headings, consider spending and cost-cutting but then Peter alongside the governors would decide on how the budget would be apportioned. The meeting lasted less than thirty minutes.

Once Gareth had left with his tail between his legs, Peter decided to phone Nirek and appraise him of the situation with Eve Thornton and the English Department.

Once Peter explained how Kay would be working in a supportive and positive way to help the English department and the head of the team improve their skills and outcomes, Nirek seemed re-assured and expressed his confidence that the senior leadership had everything in hand. Peter couldn't resist leaving Nirek with the knowledge that Peter, and only Peter, would inform the Chair of Governors if there was any future change to this plan.

Peter parked up in his normal space and walked into school to settle into his office for another day of mayhem and madness. He looked in his diary and foresaw a day of problems that might yet turn out to be fairly positive and rewarding. He would see Eve as quickly as possible and explain to her what had been decided. He had crossed Eve's path in a corridor at the end of yesterday's lunch time but had not thought it appropriate to talk to her then, contenting himself with exchanging a half-smile and walking on. Now he would see Eve straight after the briefing in the staff room. He had arranged for another teacher to cover Eve's class and would tell her at the end of the briefing to start off her lesson with her Year 8 group and then after ten minutes another teacher would relieve her so she could come to his office.

8.30 am. Peter took the briefing in a full staff room. After going through his scribbled notes, he passed the baton on to Kay for her messages and then it was open to the floor for information updates. The meeting was not designed for discussion or debate; it was on its worst days, a torrent of information that Peter knew that most of his staff lost interest in. It was a useful meeting for Peter, however, because it prevented staff ever saying to him *I didn't know* or *That's news to me.* Seven minutes later Peter wrapped up the briefing with his traditional Hill Street Blues reference "Let's be careful out there" that probably only one or two of the aging staff still understood and appreciated. It was three minutes to the beginning of tutor period, so he could have a quick word with Eve about period 1. Peter looked around the staffroom but couldn't see her. Had he missed her leave? Hadn't she come to the briefing? Was she late into school?

Peter went to her tutor room but she wasn't there either. He quickly arranged for a TA to take her register and headed went in search of the member of support staff responsible for recording staff absence and organising cover on a day-to-day basis to ask if Eve had phoned in to say she was running late or ill. To his frustrated surprise it appeared that a voicemail from Eve had been left on the system earlier saying that she wasn't well and would need cover for the day.

9.32 am. Peter decided to ring Eve at home. It was not his usual practice to phone a member of staff at home, particularly after only an hour of absence from school. It could after all be interpreted as badgering but he wanted to speak to her just to put her mind at rest over the bullying situation. He also wanted to put his mind at rest that her illness was not a result of the way Kay had been treating Eve recently. He pulled her home number up on the screen in front of him but then became unsure that a phone call was wise. She could be asleep in her bed dosed up with goodness knows what. He decided to leave it for a few hours.

1.14 pm. Peter was back in his office after his lunch duty. During the morning he had casually asked a couple of English teachers independently if they knew where Eve was. They both said that she was absent today and one of them grumbled about the fact she hadn't set any work for her classes. It was fairly clear that they knew little or nothing about her reason for being away today. So again, Peter stared at the screen, took two of his anti-depressants with a swig of coffee and decided this was the time to ring.

"Hi, this is Eve..."

Peter was relieved to hear her voice until he heard "please leave a message and I'll get back to you..."

He had no choice but to leave a message. "Oh, hi Eve. Um...just phoning to ask how you are...I...just...found out that you're...under the weather...I also wanted to talk to you about...what we talked about on Friday... If you can...give me a ring at school...later on...when you get this message...or you could give me a ring at home tonight...if you like...OK. Bye then...take care."

It was not the most fluent message in the world but at least it got Peter's message across. He had demonstrated that he cared and that he wanted to follow up on Eve's complaint.

5.34 pm. Peter cleared his desk. He sent a text to Rachel saying that he was just leaving school and headed for outside. Other than his own car there were just two cars still in the car park. Kay's shiny sports car was there and so was the Head of Maths' car. Peter wondered if they would be still parking their cars at Whatmore next year. Probably not. They would both be off to higher pastures new. Did he envy them new opportunities? No. In fact he wished them both well. Good luck to them if they wanted to climb the greasy pole. They were both driven and ambitious. Unlike Peter. His only ambition now was to retire as soon as possible with some sanity left.

5.36 pm. Peter left the car park and joined the rush hour traffic. The stop-start journey for the first two or so miles slowly took him away from the high-rise community that Whatmore served. He spent most of the first part of the journey concentrating carefully on the rear bumper of the car ahead and the voices of the radio presenters and their guests. Once on the more open road, Peter could turn his mind and attention to planning his future. He could take early retirement. His pension would take a bit of a hit but he might be able to negotiate a hand-out if he played the right game. If he hinted to his masters that he was considering handing over the reins soon perhaps they would offer him an incentive. In his mind he was sure that no-one would be begging him to stay for another twenty years, or ten or even five. Rachel and he could live off a reduced pension and he could always top-up his incomings with a bit of invigilation or exam marking. Peter had decided some time ago that when he did retire, he would not be a supply teacher or have any real and direct responsibility for kids learning once he left the school gates. Not for love, not for money! He would do part-time bits and pieces to top up his pension and slowly ease into full-time retirement. Rachel had been happy with this plan. Peter knew that she would want him to have some distractions outside of the house that kept his brain ticking and kept him from getting under Rachel's feet. He would talk it through again with Rachel tonight and then choose his moment to talk to Nirek and the local authority and see how eager and generous they would be in saying goodbye Mr Chips.

The *when to retire* and *how to retire* could be decided by Peter, with advice from others. The *why retire?* question was much easier but took longer to answer. His own health and happiness were a primary concern. He took a tablet a day for high blood pressure and another couple of tablets for depression. Rachel knew about Peter's blood pressure but for the last two years he had been discreetly taking Amitriptyline to dull his senses. He hated not telling Rachel but he knew that if he told her how the job was making him feel she would worry and get stressed herself. He hated taking the anti-depressants but it did help him with sleep most nights and most school days were now bearable. He promised himself that as soon as he retired, he would ween himself off the tablets and lose some weight.

The other reason for retiring early was the job itself. He had had enough. Some time ago Peter had admitted to himself that although he liked the company of big and little people inside school, he hated the world of education. One day, he thought, once he had retired, he would write a book about what is wrong with our education system. As he drove along a dual carriageway, Peter randomly listed some of the topics he would write about:

1.Ofsted
2.League tables
3.Academies, MATs, Free schools, Fee-paying schools, Faith schools, Grammar schools
4.Testing and assessment
5.Assemblies and religious education
6.Uniform
1) 7.The decline of the Arts in the curriculum

8.The primacy of English and Maths
9.Under-funding of schools
10Homework and marking
11.British Values
12.Universities

Yes, Peter thought, there is a book there. He couldn't write it while he was still working inside the system, but once he retired, he could let rip on his masters in their ivory towers who thought they knew how schools should run while their heads were way up in the clouds.

6.38 pm. Peter turned into his cul-de-sac and parked up for the night. It had been a long journey. He often left school later, after rush-hour and somehow got home at about the same time. He would speak to Rachel tonight after dinner and finalise their thoughts about retiring early. He wanted to get her view on whether they could comfortably live off his pension and lump sum and how he could sell the idea to the people who might be agreeable for him to go. They would discuss tactics and agree on a way forward. They would also talk about what they would do in the future together. School-free and care-free. A future plan of action, or rather, a plan for inaction.

9.10 pm. Rachel and Peter sat on the settee. They had eaten and stacked the dish washer and had talked early retirement through. It was a unanimous decision- 2 to 0 - that Peter should put the wheels in motion tomorrow morning and hope for the best. If he could leave at the end of the year it would be a real bonus. Perhaps Kay would get his job? She would be good, in time. Good luck to her!

They had already decided to splash out on a biggish holiday with their daughter and her family as a way to celebrate new-found freedom. It would be a good end to Peter's career and the beginning of a new chapter in his life. A life without medication.

Peter sat sleepily on the settee, half watching a TV show, feeling as if a heavy weight and a long wait had just been lifted from his shoulders.

9.11 pm. The phone rang. Peter reached over to the small table by the arm of the settee and picked it up. After saying "Hello" and "Yes this is Peter Burlington" he was silent for the next fifty seconds or so before putting the phone down and staring at Rachel.

"That was the police. A young woman I know has just died on the way to hospital after swallowing some pills. A police detective is on his way round to ask some questions."

CHAPTER 5

For a few seconds Neil was not sure where he was, when it was and who he was. Only when he strained his eyes could he see the vaguely familiar stippled effect of his *Orchid White* painted bedroom ceiling.

He checked the alarm clock. 10.55 am. The clock had not alarmed him. Probably because he hadn't set it last night or in the early hours of this morning. Why would he? There was no reason to get up early. The alarm clock display told him it was a Monday morning and fairly soon it would be Monday afternoon. All he needed to do now was confirm his name. Was it Neil Armstrong? Had he had a late night after travelling back from the moon? Was he Neil Young? Had he just performed at the O2 Arena and slept in late after three encores? Or was he Neil Simon, screenwriter and playwright, after a long and successful late-night session at the laptop creating another comical masterpiece. Sadly not. He was none of these Neils. He was in fact Neil Nobody. Once known as Mr Turner or Sir, but now he just plain and ordinary Neil.

He eased himself out of bed. His head ached, his eyes ached and his teeth ached. This had to be the start of flu or was it just the early onset of old age? He seemed to recall that he was in his early thirties so he blamed his state of mind and health on the medication he'd taken last night. The medicine, as usual, was in liquid form and could be bought over the counter at any well-known supermarket or off-licence. He had definitely had more than the prescribed dose last night but it did help him sleep and more importantly, it helped him forget. Namely, his name and, to a degree, his life.

Neil made his way across the bedroom and walked towards the three-bedroom doors that kept moving and shuffling along the wall. He chose the middle door, opened it and walked towards the bathroom. As he approached, he could hear a noise coming from the bathroom which increased in volume with every slow step he took. Was it the sound of someone crying? It sounded like it. Neil stopped in his laboured tracks a couple of paces from the bathroom door. He could hear the sobbing of a woman. He needed to move forward and open the door, but what Neil really wanted, was to go back.

. . .

Neil loved the family holidays he had had with his mom, dad and sister. A week in Llandudno or Bournemouth, a long weekend in Weston-Super-Mare or Brighton, even a day trip to Blackpool. He and his family loved the sea, they loved the beaches, they loved the fish and chips and candy floss and most importantly they all loved the piers. There was something magical about a timbered structure that stretched out bravely and proudly into the incoming waves. You could happily stroll along a pier and you would be walking on water. As a child Neil would run around the wooden playgrounds with his head spinning and giddy, pretending to be a soldier or a sailor or a pirate on a gigantic gang plank. As he grew, the gang planks seemed to get narrower but Neil still enjoyed walking the piers. The main thrill now was discovering the hidden treasure at the end of each pier – the amusement arcades. He loved the bright flashing lights, the loud music, the sound effects and the thrills and spills of playing arcade video games. His younger sister was not as enamoured with the game machines. She would waste all of her money on trying to possess a cuddly animal that lived inside a big glass box using a small crane and a grabbing claw that never managed to grip on to any of the toys. She would end up being comforted and cajoled by her mom or dad but Neil was oblivious to her disappointment. He was in his own virtual world, a land of aliens and ninjas, where at the press of a button he could shoot them or beat them up. He was transformed into a super hero or transported to a different planet. If his mother and father would let him, Neil would stand and stay transfixed in front of an *upright* machine until the end of the world as he knew it. And while his parents and his little sister played Air Hockey and Penny Falls, Neil would perch precariously on his platform, a quarter of a mile out to sea, in his distant galaxy far, far away.

As much as Neil liked the other activities that were on offer on holiday, the daily trip to the end of the pier was the best show in town. It was the high point of every holiday in those pre-teenage years.

. . .

In the first half of Neil's teenage years, while he still went on holiday with his family, the video games at the end of the pier began to lose some of their appeal and fascination. He no longer needed to travel to the coast and walk into the sea to play Street Fighter, Mortal Kombat or T2 Judgement Day. He could play them and many more in the comfort of his own bedroom on his games console.

Neil still liked going to the amusement arcades at the end of a pier for his holiday thrills but his game play had changed now. Neil no longer collected lives with a speedy hedgehog or raided a bank with a stolen car. He wanted to collect real money for himself by beating the machines and the system. He started harmlessly with fruit machines, slotting money into the mouth of greedy bandits. His mom or dad would support him by donating a few pounds to change into ten pence pieces or tokens. Sometimes Neil would play for half an hour or so, winning and losing, it appeared, in equal measure. But by the time his parents told him it was time to go as his sister was getting bored, he had money left in his hand, but never quite as much as when he started. Still, the bandits never lost and they never lost their appeal to Neil, no matter how much they stole from him.

At school, away from his holiday piers, Neil was always fascinated with Maths and ICT above all the other subjects he studied. By the end of Year 11 Neil Turner had performed well in all of his chosen subjects but in Maths and ICT he was top of the class. In the sixth form he chose these two subjects as well as Pure Maths to study at "A" level.

The next step was university. He decided to move away from home to study Information Technology at degree level. Most people who went to university looked back on this time as the most memorable part of their lives. But not Neil. While it seemed as if everybody else was having a wild time, Neil was hating all the free time outside lectures. He found forming friendships and relationships difficult, so he kept to himself by and large. His only friends at uni were a handful of fellow nerds from the IT faculty who also felt more comfortable interacting with virtual people than the real variety. Neil's natural talent with programming and data systems did not transfer easily to the real world of people and peers. So, Neil spent a great deal of his *free* time in his own room working and playing on his devices.

His university room was full of gadgets and gizmos all run off one plug socket and three extension leads. From his room he delved into the lives of people from all over the world and across galaxies with a click of a mouse. But when it came to a Saturday night, he found it impossible to walk across the courtyard into the Student Union bar for a drink. And so, while the other students in his year struggled to stay sober enough to focus on their exam papers, Neil concentrated on his studies and gained a first-class honours degree.

He left with a scroll, but no real memories – no adventures, friends or sexual dalliances.

His mom and dad were proud of his achievements but had noticed that he was becoming introverted. An uncomfortable family meeting was called when he returned home. His parents suggested that he should have a year away from his beloved computers and trek around the world or work for a charity in another country, but Neil was not tempted, not at all. He wanted to earn big money in an IT company so that one day he could smugly show his fellow students that he was the successful one and they were the losers. In the next few months Neil applied for IT jobs far and wide, knowing that he would have his choice of an exciting position in a variety of forward-thinking companies due to his first-class degree.

Neil landed a few interviews but, for some reason or other, each company opted for someone else and did not offer him a job. As time passed, of necessity, he lowered his sights until he found a job. Just any type of IT job that paid enough so he could rent his own flat. He found a position that suited him and sounded impressive. It was not a high-powered job but it would be the first step on the ladder. A month later, after his DBS certificate came through the post, he started his new job as ICT Manager at Whatmore Secondary School.

. . .

Neil was made to feel welcome by the Head teacher, Peter Burlington and his senior leadership team. He was given an office and told to take his time to familiarise himself with the school and its workings. His role was to manage the ICT and data systems in the school, provide reports on Year 7 – 11 pupils' progress and upskill the teachers and support staff.

It didn't take Neil much time to work out that Whatmore School was a back-water and most of the staff were drowning. The teachers generally had not a clue how to use some of the IT equipment in classrooms and were constantly being bailed out by the pupils they were supposed to be teaching. The ICT kit was archaic and in an ideal modern world should have been recycled along with some of the older teachers. For the first few months Neil felt like a fire fighter, answering teachers' emergency calls in classrooms – "Mr Turner, I can't get my interactive whiteboard to work!" or "Neil, I can't access the network...system...thingamajig!"

With time and a great deal of patience Neil managed to *teach* most of the staff the basic rudiments of using a computer and an interactive white board and he was left alone in his office to work on systems. He liked being in his office, it was his safe, secure space, his peace and tranquillity only rocked by the phone ringing or the door being knocked. On a good day he would be left alone by everyone. On a bad day he would have to attend briefings, meetings and visit classrooms by walking along populated school corridors.

Occasionally, the head teacher would invite him to his office and talk to him about how things were going and each half term in the first year of his time at Whatmore he would join members of the senior leadership team in their weekly meeting. Neil found this daunting but soon realised that when it was time to speak, no-one else was really listening or understanding what he was talking about. There was Charlie Briggs, the deputy head teacher, who spent most of the meetings cracking jokes and being suggestive towards Julie Osborne, the assistant head. In Neil's view, Julie was the power house of the school; she knew her stuff and when she talked, people generally listened. Then there was Sobia Didially, the Business Manager, a rather serious and brusque woman who kept a tight rein on spending and her sense of humour.

In each of the SLT meetings Neil attended, the thread going through all of the discussions was Ofsted and were they still a *Good* school. There was a paranoia emanating from Peter that the next inspection team to visit might find that Whatmore was *requiring improvement* or worse.

One day, towards the end of his first year at the school, Neil was asked by Peter Burlington's PA to come to his office after lunch. Neil feared the worst, after all the systems were not effective yet and some teachers were still struggling and treading water. He was certain that he was going to be *let go*. On his slow walk to the head teacher's office Neil prepared reasons why things were taking longer than he hoped and that in the next year Peter would see real improvements in the skills of the staff and the data systems being employed. Neil, walking along the corridors, was becoming passionate about his role and his purpose at Whatmore. He wanted to keep his job. The job, a year ago, he felt was beneath him. As it happened Neil need not have worried. In the seventeen-minute discussion in which Peter talked mostly and Neil just listened, he was offered a rise in salary and a position on the senior leadership team.

. . .

With extra responsibility and accountability Neil was expected to *up his game* as Charlie Briggs put it one day. Neil had noticed over time that Charlie, an ex-PE teacher, couldn't stop making sports references. It wasn't that Neil had to work harder now that he had his promotion, but he would have to be more visible around the school. As a member of the SLT he would have to do the odd dinner duty and show up to all staff meetings and briefings, mix in the staff room and be *proactive rather than reactive.* Neil wasn't quite sure if this was a phrase that Charlie had heard recently on Match of the Day. Neil wasn't a sporty person and didn't know one end of a real football pitch from the other although he had played FIFA Soccer on the games console with his father some years ago.

Neil dutifully did his duty – in fact three dinner duties a week with Charlie. He became more visible and more accessible. His wage increase allowed him to re-invent himself and he took a little more pride over his appearance. He kept his hair shorter, smartened up his clothes and under the avuncular mentoring of Charlie started to go for a drink every so often with some of the staff on a Friday night.

On one such Friday night, Neil met Lucy Humphreys. Neil had gone out with a bunch of teachers and TAs from Whatmore and as often happened by about nine o'clock a good proportion of the group started to leave, giving legitimate reasons like tiredness and re-acquainting themselves with their partners. Neil also decided to leave as the only remaining drinkers were Charlie and the PE staff who would be still there until they were politely asked to leave when the landlord needed to lock up. They would be talking about sport exclusively from now on.

Neil headed for the door but before leaving just had to have one more go on the fruit machine. He usually punctuated his drinking session with a trip to this machine whenever he needed to escape from the tedious conversations about the behaviour of Year 9 Set 5 or the changes to the GCSE specifications and exam papers.

The fruit were spinning in front of his eyes for some time before he was aware that someone was looking over his shoulder at the four rotating wheels of fortune.

"Are you going to let anyone else have a go?" asked the voice behind him.

"Oh, sorry, I won't be long, I'm just on a bit of a winning streak," replied Neil.

"I noticed. It looks like the drinks are on you...or are you going to keep playing until you lose it all?" asked the woman, moving to Neil's side.

"I just put a fiver aside for a quick game but the machine doesn't want me to stop. I think I'm up by about ten pounds."

"Wow, you'll be a millionaire by this time next year!" She smiled and Neil looked at the woman properly for the first time and smiled back.

"I wouldn't normally let someone ruin my amazing winning streak but would you like a go at my expense?"

"Are you sure? I might bankrupt you. For all I know that might be your last five pounds and then you'll be selling the Big Issue tomorrow."

"I think I can survive. I have a piggy bank stuffed with pence pieces in my bedroom."

"Now that's a chat up line you don't hear that often!"

They laughed at each other and Neil stood to one side as this shortish, shapely long-haired brunette entered his life. After twenty-five minutes this amazing woman was still playing in profit while laughing and joking. To Neil it was the happiest time of his life since his days on the piers.

Instinctively they both knew when to stop and they made great play of trying to divide the money up fairly. Neil wanted to give it all to the woman and the woman wanted to give it all to Neil. It was only £32 but it was as if they were happily trying to share the spoils from a death in the family or a bank robbery. In the end they went to the bar and had a drink.

"I'm Lucy and I travel around bars looking for a millionaire to marry," confessed the woman. She had a wicked look on her face.

"Hi, I'm Neil and I lure women into my bedroom with my James Bond gambling skills." replied Neil.

"Well, well, Mr Bond, perhaps you should have ordered a martini, shaken not stirred, instead of a pint of lager at the bar just now."

"I'm off duty tonight, I'm only a spy on Saturdays and Sundays. I'm an undercover ICT manager in a school during the week. What about you? Surely you're not a Russian spy out to kill me with your poisoned stiletto?"

"No, but I do have access to poisons. I'm a nurse here at the general hospital. We've been out for a quick drink after our shift." Lucy turned her head and indicated three older women standing at the other end of the bar. The trio smiled at Lucy and then turned back to talk to each other in hushed tones over their drinks.

They found a table to sit at away from Lucy's work colleagues and Charlie and his cronies and got to know each other.

"So, what sort of nurse are you?" asked Neil.

"The brilliant kind. Caring, intelligent, with a sense of humour and all of my own teeth!"

"That's great for a woman of what...sixty or seventy? I'm not very good at guessing women's ages."

"I may have all my teeth but you won't for much longer if you don't guess again," Lucy retorted with a mock angry expression on her face.

"OK, fifty?"

Lucy shook her head.

"Forty?"

Another shake of her head.

"Thirty?"

"That's more like it. Thirty-one last week and never been kissed."

"Now that is hard to believe," said Neil.

"Well, perhaps once or twice, when I was twelve or thirteen. What about you?"

"I'm still looking for my first kiss."

Lucy had no idea how true that remark was. "I meant how old are you Mr Bond?"

"Oh sorry. Thirty-two. Nearly thirty-three."

Lucy looked across at her friends and decided that she really ought to re-join their gathering. "Here's the deal 007. I reckon you still owe me after I doubled your winnings. I'll let you off if you ask me out to dinner sometime this weekend. Unless of course, you're on spying duties?"

Neil was flummoxed, gobsmacked by this brazen suggestion. "Uh...No... Yeh...that would be great...how about tomorrow night...is that OK with you?"

"Why you smooth operator...are you asking me on a date after we just met?" Lucy was beaming coyly at Neil.

"Yes, I suppose I am...I don't know how that happened...Where would you like to eat. Have you got a favourite restaurant around here?"

"No. Surprise me as you surprised me by asking me out!"

"Do you know what...I think I've been pleasantly manipulated. Shall I meet you here tomorrow night at 7.30? I'll wear a red carnation in case you forget who I am by then."

"Is that all you'll be wearing? That's brave of you on a cold winter's night. I was thinking of wearing a wet suit." Lucy stood up.. "Oh, one more thing..."

"Yes...what's that?" asked Neil, standing up to face her. "Are you going to tell me that this is a set up or you're really an escaped mad woman from the local psychiatric hospital?"

"No on both counts. I just wanted to give you this." Neil was expecting a five-pound note as a jokey reference to the winnings but instead Lucy moved forward and kissed him quickly on his lips." Now we've both been kissed! See you tomorrow Mr Bond."

And with that she turned, heading back to her friends, and didn't look back.

Neil walked straight for the door and hit the cold night air. He was intoxicated and felt happily drunk as he walked back to his flat.

. . .

Neil had precious little sleep that Friday night. In one sense he didn't want to go to sleep in case when he woke up in the morning, he would discover the events of last night were only a wonderful dream. He was excited. A woman had approached him, chatted him up and kissed him. She was gorgeous with a wicked sense of humour and appeared to like him. He couldn't quite believe it. He couldn't really trust his memories of last night but he was certain that he had *upped his game* and been *proactive* for once. Perhaps not quite as proactive as Lucy but for Neil that was a giant step...a huge leap for mankind. He was growing up. He looked under the bedclothes. He was definitely growing up! Charlie Briggs would be proud of him. Charlie Briggs. Hold on. Had Charlie set this up? Was Lucy part of a practical joke? It must be a set up. Charlie...the bastard!

By lunchtime on Saturday Neil was convinced that last night had been a hoax. He would be sitting in the pub at 7.30 tonight and Charlie and his mates would burst in through the doors and laugh at him. By 5.30, Neil was even more convinced that Lucy would be a no-show. She hadn't given him her phone number and he didn't know where she lived. She was untraceable. But what if she was for real? He couldn't risk it. This wasn't his last opportunity for happiness. It was his first. He would prepare for the date. Hope for the best but expect the worst.

At 7.20 pm he sat at the same table as last night with Lucy. He nursed a soft drink as he was driving later, hopefully, to the restaurant he'd booked. He kept his eyes on the door fully expecting Charlie to appear at any moment.

At 7.29 pm Neil still sat nursing his drink. Other people entered the pub but not Charlie and not Lucy.

At 7.34 pm Neil promised himself six more minutes and then he would go back to the flat and try to forget the whole humiliating experience.

At 7.38 pm the door opened and Lucy walked in, on her own. She looked radiantly beautiful and made her way over to *their* table. He stood up and they kissed, this time much longer. It was a kiss of relief for both of them. They had both hoped but lacked trust the other would be at the pub.

"I'm so sorry I'm late, Neil. The taxi was late."

"Please don't apologise. I'm just glad you came. I was worried you might have had second thoughts."

"I was worried I might have frightened you off after my antics last night. Sorry, I was a little forward. Sometimes, when I'm nervous, I say and do things too quickly. I don't engage my brain." Lucy looked down at her lap momentarily, having lost her confidence for a moment. Then she took off her coat to reveal a very attractive, mid-length dress and placed the coat on her lap.

"Well, I think you have a very engaging brain as well as a very engaging...smile. Anyway, would you like a quick drink before I whisk you away to the local fish and chip shop?"

"Oh Mr Bond. Are you trying to woo me over a piece of battered haddock?"

"I'm hoping to. What would you like?"

I'll have a small glass of white wine, please."

Neil went to the bar and ordered her drink. He was still pinching himself. What did Lucy see in him? Was she trying to recover from a broken heart? Was she on the rebound? Was she visually impaired? Was she really a man?

Neil brought her drink back to the table and tried to get an answer to these questions without sounding rude. "I've got to ask, Lucy. Was it just coincidence that you wanted to play on the fruit machine last night?"

"No. I have to be honest with you. I'd been watching you out of the corner of my eye for about twenty minutes and I could see that you weren't comfortable in the company of some of the group you were drinking with. You looked a bit out of it...sort of lonely...so when you went to the machine, I thought I'd keep you company."

"OK, so it wasn't my stunning good looks and sex appeal that attracted you towards me?" asked Neil.

"That did come into play as well, I have to admit! But I had to talk to you when I saw that cute puppy dog look on your face."

"So now you're saying I look like an abandoned dog!"

"Ahhhh, but a sexy squidgy little dog," Lucy said and squashed Neil' face up in her hands before kissing him again. "Sorry...I'm being daft."

"Lucy, be as daft as you like," said Neil with an unforced smile.

. . .

At the restaurant they talked and talked, laughed and laughed and brushed each other's hands at every reasonable opportunity. Within a few hours they'd shared well-edited life stories and it was as if they had been a couple for years.

Lucy was an only child. Her mom and dad ran a pub in North Wales. Lucy had under-achieved at school, had spent too long with friends and not enough time studying. She had a serious boyfriend in her early twenties. They'd lived together in a flat not far from her parents' pub for three years and during that time she worked in a shop during the day and studied in the evening, having decided she wanted to be a nurse one day. When her boyfriend cheated on her, Lucy returned to the pub and saved for her own flat. She had had two more relationships that hadn't work out but she had eventually qualified as a nurse five years ago and started working anti-social shifts so serious dating became difficult. She worked and slept, slept and worked but discovered a real love for nursing. She liked looking after people and generally being with people. A few internet dates had ended up disastrously or worse and she admitted to Neil that she was starting to worry she'd soon become a single frump who would never meet her prince.

Neil was less detailed and honest with his potted autobiography. He talked about his family, his interest in Maths and ICT and his job at Whatmore. He skirted around his lack of girlfriends and friends in general deciding that he would make up some stories of failed romance if Lucy interrogated him at some point in the future.

The normally shy, guarded Neil relaxed into the evening. He felt so comfortable in the company of this sociable, self-assured and funny individual. Oddly Lucy reminded him of a female equivalent of Charlie Briggs.

Lucy was also relaxed in Neil's company. She was clearly not in the presence of an arrogant show-off, a bore or a letch. Lucy liked his smile, his sensitivity and vulnerability - the fact that he seemed to have a genuine interest in her.

At the end of the evening, Neil offered to pay for the meal and the drinks but Lucy insisted on going halves.

While Neil drove Lucy back to her flat, they continued to talk about their pasts, their presents and life in general. It was only when Neil parked up outside her flat that the conversation suddenly stopped. Neither Neil nor Lucy wanted to start the next part of the conversation. Both were thinking the following things:

Lucy: *Shall I ask him up for coffee?*

Neil: *If she asks me up for coffee what shall I say?*

Lucy: *Is it too soon to invite him up to my flat for coffee and sex?*

Neil: *What if she wants sex with me?*

Lucy: *Shall I ask him for a second date or shall I wait for him to ask?*

Neil: *I want to ask her for another date but what if she says no?*

Lucy: *God I really fancy him; I hope he makes a move.*

Neil: *I hope she can't see my raging erection under my trousers.*

"Well, thanks for a lovely evening, Neil..." said Lucy breaking the silence but then paused and waited for Neil to show some leadership and authority.

"Thank you, Lucy...I had a great time..." he replied sounding fat too formal, "I wonder if you..."

"What Neil? Spit it out, 007!" said Lucy energetically, letting her frustration get the better of her.

"I wonder...wondered...if I asked you out again, would you say yes?"

"If you remember, Mr Bond, I asked you out on this date, so it's only fair that you should do the asking this time."

"But you might say no."

"Well, you'll have to risk it. I am growing old here waiting for the question."

"You mean older, don't you?" said Neil and with that she pretended to be angry and tried to playfully thump him on the shoulder. At last Neil was too quick for her, grabbing her clenched fist and drawing her to him. In no time at all, they were kissing passionately.

They kissed many more times that night.

. . .

Over the next few months Neil and Lucy spent as much time as possible together. Neil's traditional 8 to 6 job did not synchronise with Lucy's shift pattern but that made their time together even more special and precious. During this getting-to-know-each-other-time friendships and pastimes were put on hold and as their dependence on each other grew, they felt stronger and more secure as a couple than as two individuals.

Neil's sexual inexperience was a distant memory and improved with every passing over night and sometimes even during the day with Lucy's guiding hands. If they were to self-evaluate their performance and progress in bed, they would have undoubtedly scored themselves as *Good* with elements of *Outstanding*.

Their relationship was so much more than just the horizontal pleasures of the flesh though – they laughed together – sometimes with each other and sometimes at each other. For a couple of thirtysomethings at times they acted as teenagers who believed they found the love of each other's life.

During those idyllic weeks of new found love some serious grown-up stuff was seamlessly introduced into the kissing, the cuddling, the laughter and teasing. Visits were even made to parents to introduce the other half and break the ice.

Lucy took Neil to her parents' pub for a weekend. She had not mentioned Neil to her parents over the phone for the first month. She didn't want to tempt fate. But by the sixth week of their relationship she found it impossible not to tell her mom that there was a man in her life. Lucy just hoped that sharing her joy with her mother would not be the kiss of death to the relationship and that the man would stick around in her life. She had a series of phone calls with her folks giving them the low-down on Neil and suggested that this one was *the one*. Lucy's mom and dad had heard this several times before during the last ten years. And at the end of each relationship that turned sour her supportive and comforting mom would always say things like "Well, I never really liked him" or "You're better off without him" or even "There are plenty more fish in the sea."

Lucy was apprehensive about how her mother and father would react to Neil. She knew that they loved her and, as their daughter, they wanted the best for her and certainly didn't want another user or abuser dating their only child.

Lucy needn't have worried. Neil was charming, respectful, considerate and on his best behaviour.

As they all went to bed on the Friday night having talked and laughed for hours about Lucy's childhood and teenage years, Lucy's mom secretly winked at Lucy and gave her daughter the thumbs up. Lucy smiled at her and mirrored the gesture to her mom. That two-way approval was as good as a legally binding contract.

Lucy followed Neil upstairs and indicated that they'd be staying in her old room. After both had used the bathroom they slipped into bed and waited for Lucy's mom and dad to also complete their ablutions and retire..

"That went well," whispered Lucy.

"I haven't started yet," replied Neil quietly.

"I mean downstairs, you idiot." Lucy gave her bed mate her traditionally playful thump on the arm.

"You want me to go downstairs, do you?" whispered Neil, starting to dive under the duvet.

"Neil, stop it!" said Lucy a little too loudly. "Behave yourself a minute will you. I meant meeting my folks. I think they approved of you."

"Well, I suppose I wasn't chased down the front path by your dad aiming a shot gun at my arse."

"No, I told him to keep his gun locked away on your first visit."

"Good thinking. I really like your folks. They're nice people with a good sense of humour. I don't know how they created you, Lucy Humphreys!"

"I must have been adopted."

The response was a suppressed laugh and then Neil continued. "Did you realise that other than your flat and my flat, we haven't slept together in another bed since we met."

"What are you suggesting, Mr Bond?" whispered Lucy in his ear.

"Don't you think we ought to mark the occasion in some way?"

"Possibly! Tell me more, 007."

"Well, my gun, unlike your father's is unsheathed and ready to fire."

Oh yes...and...?"

"I just wondered if I could, very quietly and with stealth, make a move on you..."

"OK, if you must. How about starting downstairs?" said Lucy very quietly as she lifted the duvet.

. . .

'*Meet the Parents 2*' was staged a couple of weeks later at Neil's house. Neil had briefed his mother and father about what to say and more significantly what not to say. He had phoned his folks while Lucy was at work and summarised their part of the script:

1.Don't tell Lucy I didn't have a girlfriend before she came on the scene.
2.Don't tell Lucy I didn't have any friends before she came on the scene.
3.Don't tell Lucy I was a problem child/difficult teenager/awkward adult.
4.Do tell Lucy I'm reliable, caring and considerate and have never caused you any worry or anxiety.
5.Do tell my sister that if she wants to see Lucy, she will have to keep to the same script.

Neil's sister, married with two kids, had been teasing Neil in emails since she found out he had at last got himself a girlfriend. She had threatened Neil that at the earliest opportunity she would tell Lucy all about her weird older brother.

When the evening came Neil's mom, dad and baby sister were golden. They stuck to Neil's script and embellished stories of Neil that gave Lucy the impression he was a normal healthy, sociable, desirable catch for any woman. His mom, dad and sis couldn't believe he had caught this big, beautiful fish. They all fell instantly for Lucy. She was smart, funny and clearly loved Neil. In Lucy, they would have a great addition to the family and their private worries about Neil would be eased by the influence of this lovely woman. In fact, their worries were already easing as all three of them had noticed a huge difference in Neil's personality. He seemed more confident, self-assured and generally positive about his future. His mother and father could relax now their son had a good, steady job and a good, steady girlfriend.

At the end of the evening, Neil's parents hugged Lucy and said that they would love to see her again. Neil's sister also invited the couple to come over to her house so she could meet her husband and the kids.

In the car driving back to Neil's flat, Lucy stroked Neil's leg.

"You know that's my clutch leg, don't you? I have a very sensitive clutch," said Neil.

"So all of your girlfriends have told me," Lucy replied, squeezing the top part of his leg.

"Cheeky! Well what did you think of my family? Did they pass the test?"

"I think they're great. I was a bit nervous about meeting them. I thought they might not like me."

"How could they not like you? There's nothing to dislike. You're a lovely person Lucy Humphreys and I'm the luckiest bloke in the country having you as my girlfriend."

Lucy looked over at Neil whose eyes were fixed on the road ahead. "Are you sure you're fit to drive? You sound as if you have had too much to drink or are you just saying nice things so you can get into my knickers?"

"I thought I'd drive home first before I put on your knickers, if that's OK with you. But seriously, I'm sober; just soft drinks all night, but I do want to say something serious, Luce."

"OK. What is it?"

"I want to say...that you're perfect, Lucy Humphreys and...I...love you..." Neil took his eyes off the road for a split second to stare into Lucy's eyes in the semi-darkness of the car.

"Sorry, my hearing aid just fell out. Could you just say that again slowly, Commander Bond?"

"I...SAID...I...LOVE...YOU..."

"Well that's OK then, because I love you too," said Lucy and squeezed the top of his clutch leg again. "Oh hello, James is standing to attention!"

"I know, said Neil laughing, "and I've still got another thirty minutes to drive!"

. . .

As the academic year moved towards its final term, Neil was happy and stable in his personal life but Whatmore was facing choppy waters, particularly in its senior leadership. Sobia Didially, the Business manager, had left suddenly earlier in the year. Julie Osborne secured a promotion as deputy head at a school in Lichfield and Charlie Briggs had eventually decided to retire. This was Charlie's third threatened retirement but this time he was committed to it and there was no turning back. Charlie had become disillusioned and cynical about education and although he was still an effective deputy, his sense of humour was slowly failing and being transfused with a daily dose of grumpiness. Charlie had said to Neil on one of his happier days that when he retired from the chalk face, he'd love to write a book about everything wrong with education, but he couldn't write and more importantly couldn't be bothered.

So, Charlie was going and a new leadership team structure was to be put in place by Peter Burlington and the governing board. The proposal was that there would be only one deputy overseeing an assistant head who would be responsible for ICT systems, pupil progress data and performance tables and a business manager in charge of all things relating to finance. This slimmed down SLT was a cost cutting exercise and only Peter and Neil would still be in their positions come the beginning of the autumn term in September.

On the day of the interviews to replace Charlie, Neil had hoped that Julie would walk through the school gates and be offered the job that everyone at Whatmore thought was rightly hers. But alas, she didn't apply and at the end of a two-day selection process, the successful candidate was announced as Kay Conrad.

Neil had had a conversation with Kay on day one of the interviews during lunch time and also saw her in action in one of her presentations she gave on her vision for the school. Neil found her a go-getting type with a big ego and an ambition to match. Neil thought that it wouldn't take Kay long before she had the measure of the head teacher and would soon be playing leap frog with Peter Burlington. It was a political battle that Neil wanted to stay well away from. He would do his job and keep his eyes firmly set on the screens in front of him.

Neil arrived home at 5.24 pm. His sometimes home. Sometimes his flat was home, sometimes Lucy's flat was home. They had toothbrushes and clothes in both flats. *This is a crazy arrangement*, Neil thought to himself, while trying to change out of his suit into casual clothes. He hunted through his wardrobe for his favourite pair of jeans and then realised that they had to be in the other flat. He talked to himself as he walked around the flat, "Why bother having two flats, we need to get rid of one, but which one? Would Lucy want to lose her independence? Is it too early to suggest this? I will mention it tonight, maybe..."

At 8.05 pm Neil received a text...

On my way home. Slippers by the fire. Tea on table by 8.40 x

Neil replied...

Yes ma'am x

Thirty minutes later Lucy opened the door to Neil's flat and shouted, "Hey hon!"

"Hi sweetheart, how was your shift?"

"OK," Lucy said, walking into the kitchen as Neil was making the final adjustments to an improvised pasta meal. "I hope my slippers are by the fire as well." She walked over to Neil, turned his head away from the electric hob and planted a big passionate kiss on his lips. "I needed that!"

"So did I. In fact, I need a lot more than that if it's alright with you?"

"Sure, let me just get out of my uniform and have something to eat and then we can have a cuddle by the fire."

"Ahhhh nooooo! We're becoming a middle-aged couple. What's happened to the rampant sex on the carpet in front of the fire in your naughty nurse's uniform?"

"Sorry but I've already done that today with one of the patients but I suppose I could do it again if the pasta's really good. If it's as bad as last week all you can hope for is a peck on the cheek, Mr Bond."

Lucy blew him a kiss as she disappeared into the bedroom to change. Neil tasted the pasta and smiled as he served it, confident that he'd get his just desserts after the main course.

Later, lying in front of the fire, surrounded by cushions, clothes and under a duvet that Neil had yanked off their bed, he decided to mention the subject of living arrangements. He kissed Lucy's neck as they snuggled together enjoying the glow of the artificial logs of the gas fire and the warmth of their closeness and broached it. "Luce, I want to know what you think about something...there's no need for an immediate decision but I'd like to discuss this with you, if you're up for it?"

Lucy turned her body around so that their noses were almost touching. She thought about making a wise crack but decided not to. "What is it love? Is there a problem?"

"No, not at all. I was thinking that we have two flats, your place and this one. Would it be a good idea to sort of...pool our resources...and just live in one place?"

"You mean properly move in together?"

"Well, yes. We could cancel the rent on one flat, or both and rent something different...or we could look at buying a property."

"You have been thinking, haven't you? Funnily enough I've been thinking the same thing but I didn't want to mention it just yet in case I scared you off."

"Luce, you won't scare me away. I love you and I want to live with you under one roof all the time if you think we've successfully got through the induction period."

"You mean, can I put up with all of your foibles and idiosyncrasies? The toothpaste left in the sink, the socks on the bedroom floor, the loud music while you're in the shower, the swigging from the milk bottle, the looking at your phone while I'm trying to talk to you. And then there's the conversations you have with yourself in front of the mirror in the hall..." Lucy said, reeling an impressive list off the top of her head.

"Excuse me," interrupted Neil, "if that's all you can think of..."

"No that's not all...there are the little notes you leave me around the flat saying that you love me, the flattering compliments you always make when I'm dressed up to go out; then there are those moments when you secretly squeeze my bum when we're out in public, the way you always manage to make me feel special and, of course, there's the wild animal sex that leaves me weak at the knees for days."

"Is that it, Ms Humphreys or can you add anything else to your list?" asked Neil smiling and kissing Lucy's bare neck.

"I can't think of anything else but give me five minutes..." she said placing a kiss on his forehead.

"Are you saying that my behaviour around most of the flat leaves a lot to be desired but you desire more of my bedroom behaviour?"

"Yeah that seems to be the long and the long of it...so to speak. I have to say, Neil, I do like your mind as well as your body most of the time. I like your mind when it's dirty or clean but I only like your body when it's clean."

"Hey, what are you talking about? I had a shower three weeks ago!"

After a short interlude of comical bare body wrestling under the duvet, Lucy kissed Neil again and put on her serious face. "I think your idea about living in one flat is a great idea. It would save us money and as you say we could save up for a deposit on a house. Most importantly it sort of signifies the start of the next phase of our lives together...God...does that sound too sickly sweet?"

"No Luce, it sounds great. So which flat shall we get rid of?" asked Neil.

"Well, before we make that decision, I need to tell you that my boss has suggested that I apply for promotion. It's a Band 6 job. More responsibility…"

"Wow, that's fantastic. I assume that would be more money going into the pot…"

"Steady on Neil, I haven't applied for it yet. That's what I want to talk to you about. The job is at another hospital about seventy miles away. I couldn't drive there and back each shift from here. So, if I applied for the job and got it, we'd have to move nearer the hospital. Is that OK with you? If it's not, then I won't apply. You're more important than my nursing career."

"Don't be daft, sweetheart; you must apply, nothing ventured and all that. And anyway, your job is important to you. You're a great nurse and it's really good your boss recognises that. I'm 100% behind you applying."

"But if I got the job, we'd have to move close to the new hospital because of the shift patterns which would mean that you'd have to travel a long way."

"No, I wouldn't. I could quit my job at school and get another job close to where we rent a new flat. I'm not enjoying working at Whatmore. Things have changed. It's time for a change…for me as well as you. I'll get another job easily enough," said Neil confidently.

"OK, if you're sure. But I don't want to force you into anything," said Lucy a slightly guilty edge creeping into her voice.

Neil decided to change the mood, partly for selfish reasons. "Lucy, it's not a problem I assure you. Now let me do some forcing of my own…wild animal style!"

. . .

It was moving day. It was moving on day. Lucy, to nobody's surprise, other than Lucy, got the promotion. She would start as a Charge Nurse in August. It was quite an achievement to be considered for the post with only five years' experience behind her but she was a natural organiser and leader.

Neil left Whatmore School at the end of the summer term along with Charlie and a couple of other teachers. Charlie would be replaced by Kay Conrad. A geography teacher was not being replaced and a full-time MFL teacher was being replaced by a part-timer. Neil's role was being absorbed into the new cost-cutting leadership structure that had been changed again after Neil informed Peter Burlington would not be coming back in September. Neil would be replaced by a remote IT company able to maintain the computer system in the school for less than half of Neil's wages while Kay had agreed to undertake data analysis. So, it seemed to Neil his presence at Whatmore would not be much missed and his absence soon forgotten.

Charlie Briggs on the other hand would be missed. But Charlie was pleased to be going. He was ready to start a new phase of his life with wife number three. He was surprised, however, when Neil caught him one day to tell him he was also leaving in July. Charlie was re-assuring that Neil would find a new job once he and Lucy had settled into their new flat. As colleagues, Charlie and Neil had been through some difficult times at Whatmore but on the whole had managed to keep a friendly working relationship at school. They had agreed they would keep in touch but as is often the case this was a vague gesture unlikely ever to materialise in the future.

On the last day of the summer term Charlie, understandably received a big send off. As the longest serving member of staff at Whatmore, he was showered with cards, presents, handshakes from the men and kisses and hugs from almost every female on the staff. The head teacher also gave a long and emotional speech that could have been delivered by Martin Luther King.

Neil got a few cards and presents, but no kisses and a two-minute speech from Peter Burlington. And with that Neil walked out of Whatmore for the last time with a few precious memory sticks and very little else.

Neil and Lucy vacated both of their flats at the end of July and moved into a slightly larger apartment just a few miles from the hospital. They were going to rent the property for an initial six months while Neil looked for a new job. Sitting on a two-seater settee in their new shared furnished flat surrounded by packing boxes, they had a mere three days to sort out all of their stuff before Lucy started her new job.

"Where on Earth do we start?" said Neil, looking around the chaos.

"You start by telling me that you love me, that this is the most exciting thing that's ever happened to you and that you know we'll be happy ever after here," said Lucy, holding Neil's hand.

"OK...love you...exciting...ever after... Now what?"

"How about making us a cup of tea? If you can find a kettle, two mugs, a tea bag and a spoon!"

"I can do that. Anything for my little pumpkin," Neil said and squeezed Lucy's hand as he got up to look for the box labelled *Kitchen*. "By the way, you know we have two bedrooms here...I was just thinking..."

"Yesssss?" said Lucy suspiciously.

"I was just thinking..."

"Yesssss?"

"Which one do you want?" he joked, pulling her off the settee to kiss and hug her in an embrace Rodin could have sculpted.

Eventually Lucy loosened her grip on Neil and looked at him with love in her eyes. "I thought the other bedroom could...may be...for...you know...the patter of tiny feet one day..."

"Oh no, not a dog. Please not a dog. I hate dogs. I hate dog owners. I've told you before that there are two types of people in the world - those who hate dogs and those who love dogs and think everybody else does too! Dogs smell and poo and make a noise...a bit like babies really! Anyway, the rental agreement says quite specifically no pets...not even a goldfish." Neil tried to deliver this mock tirade while trying not to crack his face.

"OK then," Lucy said, also trying to sound serious, "I suppose we'll just have to have a litter of babies instead!"

"One day...when we both have good jobs and we can afford our own house. Is that alright?"

"OK, master... So does that mean I don't have to have sex with you for another couple of years then?" There was an obvious twinkle in Lucy's eye.

. . .

By the end of November, Neil was getting frustrated. Their funds were running low and they were totally reliant on Lucy's wages. She liked her new job but it meant long hours and non-stop accountability for her team of nurses, leaving her exhausted when she got back to the flat at all times of the day and night.

Neil spent most of his time on his laptop looking for jobs and submitting applications. Over the last three months he had tried IT companies, schools and colleges, banks, marketing organisations. He wanted something where he could use his IT skills and not have to deal with the general public but was finding it hard to get an interview.

One night, in the first week of December, Lucy sympathetically and tactfully said that he would have to get any sort of job to keep his mind active and to help with their rent and living costs in the flat.

Neil didn't demur. He swallowed his pride and got a job on the high street as a shop assistant in a department store. His ICT skills were not needed as the only interaction with technology he was allowed was when he was assigned to the tills. The work was tiring and dispiriting but it did bring in the pennies - not a great deal and certainly a lot less than when he worked at Whatmore.

Lucy was pleased that Neil was working. It got him out of the flat for thirty-seven and a half hours a week. She didn't care about the low pay he was earning; it was contributing to their life together. She did feel guilty, however. Guilty that he had sacrificed a good job to move with her so she could pursue her career ambitions and that he so obviously hated this demeaning job, working and serving middle-class, middle-aged women.

Lucy sensed his growing frustration as Christmas approached. The work was frenetic and drained him. Neil also sensed that Lucy was finding her job taxing; the difficult and different shifts each week. And the flat turned into a place to eat and sleep and very little else. Their home became quieter, lacking the laughter and excitement. The thrill had not gone but it was going. This was the time when things started to change without either of them realising it.

The build up to Christmas was crazy. There was a shopping frenzy in the first three weeks of December and then there was a need to quickly re-arrange the store for the New Year sales. Neil was back at work on Boxing Day so he only had Christmas Day off. It was a very different festive holiday to Neil's school job in previous years when he had two weeks off. Then the rest of January was manic with obsessed punters buying up anything that had any sort of percentage knocked off the so-called actual price.

Lucy didn't even have Christmas day off. She had to work extra shifts over the Christmas period as she was one of the few nurses on the ward without kids and all the others wanted to share some of the festivities with their families. It seemed that when Neil was at home, Lucy was working and vice-versa. If they were both off work together, they would either be eating junk food and/or falling asleep on the settee or in bed. Their Christmas together was a token present, a card and a kiss at some point on 25th December and a promise to each other that next year would be better. Unfortunately, New Year's Eve and Day were just as bad with work and tiredness.

By the fourth week of January, the department store was settling down and Neil was feeling less frantic but Lucy continued to be busy at the hospital with the start of the annual flu epidemic which seemed to plague every hospital across the land. Each year politicians would promise solutions and every year the number of deaths increased.

Neil's working week was now 9-5 five days a week. He could guarantee that on three of those nights there would be no point in rushing home as Lucy would be at work or she would be fast asleep and not wanting to be disturbed. He would walk slowly down the high street, browsing the few speciality shops that remained on his way to the bus stop. There were charity shops, take-away shops, hairdressers, nail bars, a mini-market and a couple of pubs. Sometimes he would pop into the small supermarket and buy food for the two of them, knowing that there was every possibility that it would be eaten separately. Occasionally, if he knew that Lucy was not going to be at home that night, he would eat in the Indian restaurant before catching the bus home. Once or twice he had stopped off at *The Coach and Horses* for a quick drink and a packet of crisps to take the edge off the day. He hadn't been into a pub on his own for a while; the last time was when he was waiting for Lucy to start their first date. This time, he knew Lucy was just beginning an all-nighter, so he could start with a drink at the pub and then have an Indian meal before catching the bus home. A very pleasant barmaid poured him a pint of real ale and he sat down. He sat down, ate his crisps, slowly emptied his glass and texted Lucy.

> *Eating at the Indian. Hope you are not too busy tonight. Drive carefully on way home. Love you. x*

He knew Lucy would not be able to text back. He would be woken up from his slumbers in the morning by Lucy crawling into bed after a bowl of cereal when she got home at about 6.30 am. They would have a quick kiss and a cuddle and Neil would get up to have a shower while Lucy would fall asleep.

There was no rush to get home. Neil had another pint while he scrolled down his mobile's screen looking at meaningless news feeds and messages. He finished his second pint and headed for the door. It was then he ran into an old friend. He smiled and introduced himself to the fruit machine standing there, lonely and friendless. He reached into his pocket and found some loose change. He would just waste these few coins in the next five or ten minutes and then go for a meal. An hour or so later he had got through the loose change and two five-pound notes he'd changed at the bar. He hadn't won much or lost much but it had passed the time. He would just get an Indian take away at the end of his road once he had caught the bus. It was 7.45 pm. He ought to go. He pressed the spin button one more time, the game ended for the day and the wheel of fortune stopped.

. . .

Over the next few weeks *The Coach and Horses* became Neil's regular after work pub. After getting a pint from *George the landlord* or *Shiels* the bar maid, Neil would head straight for his friend in the corner. He would ply him with money and while Neil played him and his friend played Neil, the tedium of the working day dissolved. He was where he was meant to be. In the zone. Light years away from the old biddies in the department store pestering him for a different colour or a different size or an exchange. *Why can't they shop online like normal people*, he often thought whilst standing behind a counter. Counting the hours down to the end of his working day. Then, he could make a meaningful exchange with his friend. It was a business transaction with benefits. No need to smile or make polite conversation. For a few pounds, earned by this dead-end job, he could buy a thrill or two to alleviate the boredom and frustration of his new life. And at the end of the session he would wave at George or Shiels behind the bar and walk away, guilt-free, and enter his other life, living with a gorgeous nurse who loved him but recently was often too tired to show it.

To show Lucy that he still loved her Neil would happily do more of the cooking, washing and cleaning around the flat. He would cook meals for the freezer that Lucy could heat up when she wanted something different from the daily junk. Also, he would dutifully make sure there was an adequate supply of bread, butter, cheese and jam available to her for snacks. He would take the vacuum cleaner around the rooms. He would wash their clothes and iron them. At first, it was quite a secret novelty for Neil to wash Lucy's smalls. It had taken him over thirty years of his life to be able to legitimately handle a woman's underwear both on and off her body. He still wrote the odd note for Lucy. Sometimes it was factually informative, telling Lucy, for example, about the food available in the freezer or that her spare uniform was drying on the clothes horse. At other times it was more intimate or personal. He would leave a note by the kettle for her when she would return from a night shift hoping she was OK and saying that he missed her. One-time he left Lucy a post-it note on the bedroom door. *How about sex? x* When Neil awoke the next morning - woke up next to a prone Lucy - he discovered another post-it stuck to his forehead saying *Sure. Start without me but don't wake me up. Love you x.*

The times they were both conscious and at the flat together for a significant length of time were still precious and treasured. There seemed to be little time for Lucy's friends and their families so they stayed in and comforted each other and they talked and joked. On one such Sunday morning, with a whole free day stretching ahead of them, they chatted about what they could or should do...perhaps a walk, a drink in the pub, the cinema, a drive to see parents. They could not make up their minds. Behind the reluctance to make a decision was their tiredness and the prospect of having to get dressed. They were also quite happy to just be together.

"We ought to do something today. It's so easy to just slob all day in our pyjamas," said Neil, trying to be positive.

"Yes, you're right, but it's good just having some *us time* without other people pestering and demanding that we keep them alive or sell them socks," replied Lucy. "My job's time-consuming and stressful and yours is...well...is stressful in a different way. I know you hate it. It's not the sort of thing you want to do. It's not using your skills and qualities. I still feel really guilty you had to quit Whatmore to be with me."

"Luce, please don't feel guilty. It's OK."

"No, it's not! It's my fault that you're unhappy in this dead-end job. And this job I'm doing is crazy and we just don't have enough time together. We rarely see each other at the moment and most of the time we're too knackered to enjoy each other's company. I wish I hadn't taken this promotion. It's buggered up our chances of saving for a deposit for a house. I'll have to carry on working in the future even if we have kids. What was I thinking? We were really happy before we moved..."

"Sweetheart, don't upset yourself. We can get through this. It's just a blip. If we do love each other then we can survive this. I'll look again for IT jobs. I promise..."

"But you didn't find anything suitable last time. What makes you think you'll get anything now?"

"I don't know but I've got to be positive. I can't accept the fact that I could be a shop assistant the rest of my life."

Lucy started to cry. She cried for Neil. She cried about the lack of money coming into the flat. She cried about the decision to take her new post. She also cried about the future - the future that had seemed so rosy six months ago - and she cried about the present rut they were in.

"Luce, cheer up love. We'll be alright. Now let's get dressed and go to the pub. Let's drink too much and then come back here and fall asleep in front of the telly. I'll start applying for jobs again, starting tomorrow. We just need a bit of luck," said Neil consoling Lucy and, at the same time, himself.

. . .

Over the next month or so Neil applied for over thirty jobs he liked the look of and some he wasn't so keen on but that paid decent money. During that time, he spent each night trawling the internet for new openings and possibilities but his optimism diminished slowly and surely with the lack of positive responses from his applications. And, as is human nature, he became depressed and disillusioned with the process of job seeking and rejection. Gradually and imperceptibly, he started to distract himself from the boredom and despair of filling in application forms by using the internet for other purposes.

In Neil's case it wasn't porn. In his own mind, that was being unfaithful to the only girl in the world he loved and lusted after. No, it was the online version of his friend at *The Coach and Horses*. Only this time he didn't need any cash, he could use his credit card. He could sit on the settee or lie in bed and play. There was no need to buy any drinks or pass the time of day or night with George or Shiels at the bar. He could use his laptop, tablet or phone and while away some time waiting for Lucy to get home. Sleep was fine, Neil could dream of a hi-tech future with a high-paid job where he and Lucy lived in a four-bedroomed detached property and Lucy would be able to be a stay-at-home mom, looking after the children and the cat. The waking hours were the difficult parts of the day, particularly when he wasn't at work. These were the periods of time that needed stimulation.

It wasn't like watching porn but in some ways, it had the same effect. There was a thrill and a danger in playing online. It was a secret habit. It raised the blood pressure and heart rate. There was a climax and often a come-down after you made yourself stop. It was invisible and had no observable effects.

Neil changed his travel pattern after work each night. He would walk past *The Coach and Horses*, he would ignore George and Shiels and just pop into the mini-mart for food before catching the bus and quickly getting home. Sometimes he hurried home to see Lucy, but on other nights when there was no prospect of seeing her, he would make a meal and then reward himself with a half an hour or so on his laptop on the slot machines or poker games. He was careful. He knew not to be stupid. Small bets. Small amounts of time. And when the fun stopped, he would stop. Then he would look for those illusive jobs that were hiding from him.

Lucy didn't want to keep asking Neil about his job-hunting but she did want to encourage him and keep his spirits up. One night while half-watching the television, she found a way to introduce the subject that was often on her mind. "Love, you don't have to watch this rubbish on telly with me. I know you hate soap operas. I just need to watch something that doesn't require a brain for a little while. If you want to go on your laptop, it's fine, honestly," she said.

"No, I'm good. Anyway, I like cuddling up to you on the settee. All seems right with the world when we have a snuggle," replied Neil, kissing Lucy on the forehead and squeezing her shoulder.

"God, I love you Mr. Bond. We're so lucky to have found each other." Lucy pulled herself up the settee so she could kiss Neil on the lips. "Have you seen any interesting jobs advertised over the last few days?" she asked innocently.

"One or two. I've applied to a company that supply and maintain IT systems in businesses and schools. The headquarters are miles away but they're looking to recruit people to cover certain areas of the country in a sort of trouble-shooting capacity, sorting out issues and training the work force, that sort of thing..." said Neil vaguely.

"That would be perfect. We'd need a second car but we could get a loan...."

"Hold your horses, Luce. I haven't heard back from them yet."

"Sorry, I was just excited. I just want you to have a job you enjoy and I want us to have some money so that one day we can think about..."

"A house of our own and babies?" Neil finished Lucy's sentence. "Look, Luce, one day soon I will get a good job and we'll be able to have those things. I want them too, sweetheart. You must stop worrying about my job and money at the moment. You have enough stress at work. Promise me that you'll stop worrying. I tell you what I will do, I'll keep an eye on our accounts and our spending patterns. You just go out and earn the big bucks and I'll monitor everything and let you know if things get tight or if I'm unhappy. Is that a deal?"

"Yeah, that would be great. You know, this is the first time in my life I feel really settled with a man. The guys I dated before didn't make me happy and secure in the way you do."

"You mean I'm old and boring?"

"You're not old!"

"Oh, I see, you think I'm a middle-aged, middle-minded safe pair of hands!" Neil said, slipping his hand under her tee-shirt.

"Steady old man, you might have a heart attack!"

"I'd prefer a stroke if that's OK with you?"

. . .

As the weeks and months went on Neil became immune to the tedium of the department store. He worked his shifts and then came home and came alive. He upped his game by upping his game time. Half an hour became an hour. He was winning more than he was losing. He explained to Lucy that he was earning bonuses at work and showed Lucy the online account that evidenced more money in their main account than there would normally be. Over a few days he would incrementally add a hundred pounds or more to their house kitty. Of course, there were losing streaks but he kept calm and carried on gambling. If he had a series of lucky wins it prompted him to raise the stakes. £5 bets, became £10 bets and £10 bets became £50 bets and then when the series of wins became losses, he raised the stakes even more. And strangely the longer Neil played, hour after hour, it would take him less time, perhaps a few minutes, to lose a large amount. If he was unlucky on the roulette wheel, he would turn his attention to blackjack. On occasions, although not a sports fan, he would bet on football, cricket, rugby, tennis or the horses. He became an expert on the results or possible outcomes of sports matches without having a clue how the sports were played.

One night, Lucy came in late from work and found Neil *working* on his laptop. "Hi honey. How's your day been?"

"Fine Thanks," said Neil muting his gambling machine.

"Are you OK?"

"Sorry Luce. I'll be with you in a minute. Do you want to get changed and I'll heat up your meal?" replied Neil, his eyes on the screen facing away from Lucy.

"Alright. I'm starving. I won't be a minute..." Lucy's voice faded away in the distance as she entered the bedroom.

One more spin, just one more, Neil said to himself. He lost on both occasions before having to close the laptop as Lucy entered in her pyjamas.

Neil heated up and served her the meal he'd made earlier but he didn't ask about her shift or tell her he loved her or joke with her during the next few hours they shared in the lounge before going to bed.

Lucy found it difficult to sleep. Neil seemed distant to her. She was worried about him – *What's wrong with him? Have I done something wrong? I'll ask him tomorrow.*

Neil also found it difficult to sleep. He was worried about himself – *What's wrong with me? This is wrong? I've got to stop. No more. Starting tomorrow...*

. . .

Tomorrow became today. It was business as usual for both of them. Lucy had an early shift. Neil had a long boring shift. Then when Neil opened the front door of the flat, armed with some vegetables and a pasta sauce, he was met by the distinctive smell of cooking and the subtle odour of perfume and there was Lucy in the kitchen, looking glamourous.

"Hi Luce, what's the special occasion?" Neil was worried that he'd missed a significant date on the calendar. He quickly asked himself a couple of the obvious questions. *Is someone coming round for a meal?* and *Is it Lucy's birthday?*

"No, nothing special. I just thought I'd make an effort for a change. You do so much of the cooking and you hardly see me dressed in anything but my PJs, so I thought I'd treat you as a thank you present."

Lucy sauntered provocatively over to Neil and gave him a long and lingering kiss.

"Wow, I like it. It smells like chicken curry, my favourite, and what's for dessert?"

"I am," Lucy said with a wink.

"My all-time favourite pudding as well. Have I died and gone to heaven?"

"Not yet, but you might have by the end of the evening!" replied Lucy. As she walked back to the cooker she was deliberately swaying her hips in her figure-hugging dress.

Later that night in bed, after curry and two helpings of dessert, they had time to talk before they started to nod off.

"You know you don't need to thank me Luce," said Neil out of the blue.

"OK. Just leave the money on the bed side table when you go home to your wife," teased Lucy as she turned to face him.

Neil laughed, kissed her and stroked her hair away from her face. "You know what I mean, you dirty girl. I enjoy doing the cooking. It's the least I can do. You're the main bread winner. You have more stress in your job than I do. Cooking or preparing food for us makes me feel I'm doing something useful and creative at the moment. Working in the store is mindless and of no real value. Not like you... saving lives every day."

"Does your job really get to you? You mustn't worry about your wages. We can survive."

"But I don't want to just survive. I want to get enough money together for a deposit for a house and then kids," Neil said, the frustration obvious in his voice.

"I know sweetheart. One of these jobs you're applying for at the moment will work out for you. I know it will. In the meantime, we're OK." Lucy paused." We do have enough money to pay all the bills, don't we?"

"Yeah, we're fine. I'm checking the accounts every week now," Neil smiled at her in a reassuring way. Kissed her and said goodnight and tried to sleep with a clear conscience.

As Lucy drifted off to sleep, she made a pact with herself not to keep asking Neil about his job searching and their financial situation. It was not helping his state of mind. Lucy would also make sure that at least once a week she'd make an effort by cooking a meal. As her waking eyes closed and her reality turned to dreams Lucy thought about ways to re-invent their relationship, dressing up and going on date nights...sprucing things up a bit by having desserts more often and in different places...

. . .

Over the next few months Neil and Lucy looked forward to their "special evenings." During those nights they felt young and frisky again. Neil joked at the end of one of them that even the rabbits in their local park looked at them with wonder, amazement and jealousy.

But in between these special nights there were chunks of time when they didn't see each other at all, or when they were in the flat together, they didn't see each other as sexual objects because one or both of them were too tired or too pissed off with work.

Neil continued to earn money at the department store and to win and lose money online. Every so often the win was fairly substantial and helped with his losses. He decided to set up a separate account for his gambling. He transferred some of his earnings at the store to the new account to protect their meagre savings and day-to-day spending. He also wanted to protect himself from Lucy's watchful eye. He also stopped applying for jobs. He didn't tell Lucy this but fortunately she hadn't asked him recently about his applications. So, he spent longer online winning and losing money. And on good weeks when he looked at his private bank account Neil could see positives not negatives.

To Neil's eyes Lucy seemed happy and content. She was getting to grips with her role in the hospital and she loved the evenings when the two of them made a real effort for each other. His frustrations had faded. He sleep-walked through the day at work and waited in anticipation for the occasional thrill of the courtship rituals with Lucy and the dizzy spinning of lady luck when he was on his own.

They made an effort to see their families from time to time. They had gone out with Lucy's new work colleagues once or twice and managed to attend a couple of parties and a wedding of one of Lucy's oldest friends. It was her second marriage.

On the way home late at night, Lucy woke up in the passenger seat having drunk rather a lot of champagne during the wedding breakfast and the evening event. Neil was singing to himself while driving. Lucy squeezed his leg.

"Hi handsome. Who told you that you could drive me home and make mad passionate love to me?"

"I think it was the vicar or the bride's father," said Neil, smiling and squeezing Lucy back.

"You know I love you, don't you? Even when my vision's blurred and I have the start of a hangover," slurred Lucy.

"It's funny, most women find me relatively attractive when they have a blinding head ache or can't see properly! But, do you know what, I love you whether you're stone cold sober or blind drunk!"

"But why do you love me? I work long hours, I'm always tired and I can't cook..."

"Well, there are certain things that make up for that you know. You have an amazing mind and body; you make me laugh and you have an amazing body...or have I said that already?"

Lucy squeezed Neil's leg again and laughed. "Agh, it hurts when I laugh. God I can't take drinking like I used to. I must be getting old...and to top it all, my best friend from school is on her second marriage... We haven't had one between us...I mean, neither of us has been married...you know what I mean, don't you?"

"I'm not sure young lady, are you asking me to marry you before you get too old and wrinkly?" Neil glanced over at Lucy in the car's darkness trying to gauge her reaction.

"I...no...I...was...not...really...asking...I was just moaning about my friend and how she's been married twice..."

"I see. So, you don't want to marry me?" said Neil, trying to look serious and hurt.

"No, I didn't say that, I mean, you haven't ever talked about it or asked me what I would like to do...and also you haven't popped the question, have you?"

"Well, Lucy Humphreys, if I did pop the question, what would you say?"

"I suppose if you took me somewhere romantic and asked me when we were both sober, preferably in the next ten years and even more preferably in the next week or two I might be in a position to answer your question... If you want to ask it, that is?"

"OK then. That sounds quite specific. I take it you have an answer in mind?"

"I believe I do...but it will involve a lot of preparation work on your behalf before you ask the question,"

"What do you mean?" asked Neil, in his genuinely naïve fashion.

"Surely I don't need to spell it all out for you or plan my own proposal. Neil, sometimes I think you live in a different world to the rest of us! To give you a few hints...you might want to make a trip to a jewellery shop, you might like to work out which night we're both free next and perhaps book a table at a restaurant, say, for example the Italian on the high street."

"Blimey, you've thought this all through. I was going to wait until next Christmas and surprise you with a plastic ring from one of the crackers!"

"OK, but if you value your genitalia I would think again."

"But Luce, it feels a little staged, conventional and embarrassing doing the bending down on one knee and making a fool of myself while people are eating their pasta. Particularly, if you say no!"

"Alright, I'm being bossy, aren't I? I'm sorry love...I've drunk too much and I've just got a bit tired and emotional. God is this the first stages of being Bridezilla!" Lucy admitted.

"There's no need to apologise. I've told you; I love you drunk or sober...but particularly drunk when you suck my...earlobes in bed." Neil, receiving a trademark squeeze on his upper thigh, continued, "Leave the planning to me. I'll sort it out."

For the last five minutes of the journey Lucy was in that in-between state of wakeful sleep thinking/dreaming of engagement rings, wedding plans and happy-ever-afters.

Neil drove home slowly and carefully, thinking how the last part of the evening had taken a different route to the one he expected. It was not that he didn't want to spend the rest of his life with Lucy. He did. He would like to marry her as soon as he could afford all that went with it but... He asked himself a few questions *Proposing doesn't mean a quick marriage, does it? We could be engaged for a few years, couldn't we? Where and when shall I propose? Do I go for Lucy's idea or do I do something different? What sort of ring does she want – expensive or cheap?* These questions and more remained unanswered as he approached the flat. Neil's only decision was incisive and definite. He would ring his sister and hope that she could help him out.

. . .

The proposed day arrived. Lucy went to work early and had made a point of saying to Neil that she'd be back by 5'oclock. Neil was pretty certain that she suspected that today was the day but she didn't let on. He had booked the afternoon off work so he'd be back in plenty of time.

The first part of the *surprise* was to make it feel like it was not a surprise at all, just an ordinary night in the flat. Neil quickly cooked a pasta dish with plenty of garlic that would smell out the flat for when she arrived home.

Lucy, true to her word, arrived home even earlier than her planned ETA. Neil heard the key in the lock and pretended to be slaving away in the kitchen.

"Hi honey, I'm home," shouted Lucy. "Oh, you've cooked us a meal."

"Of course; always the dutiful boyfriend. I've just cooked a pasta dish, if that's OK?"

"Fine."

"Do I get a kiss?" asked Neil.

"Yeah," Lucy walked over to Neil and gave him a peck on the cheek.

"Are you alright Luce? Bad day?"

"You could say that."

"I'm sorry to hear that. Look, if you don't fancy pasta, I could send out for a take away?"

"No, I'm fine."

"I know, we'll go out. We haven't eaten out for a while. I might be able to book a table somewhere."

"Honestly Neil, I think I just want to have a shower and put my pyjamas on."

"OK sweetheart. While you're in the shower I'll finish cooking."

"Yes, you do that." Lucy could hardly conceal her disappointment and frustration. She walked off and headed for the bathroom.

When Neil heard Lucy in the shower, he turned off the cooker and found various bags he'd been hiding in the bottom of his wardrobe for a couple of days and placed them on their bed.

Lucy came out of the bathroom with a bath towel tightly wrapped around her. Her demeanour was such that she could have hung a large sign around her neck saying "DO NOT TOUCH."

Neil intercepted her as she came out of the bathroom. "I got myself some discount clothes and stuff from the store today. Want to see them?"

He walked her into the bedroom where she sat on the edge of their bed as he made great play in being excited about the top he'd chosen. "Here, have a look," he said and passed her the first bag. Lucy grudgingly took it and put her hand in to take out his cheap shirt. What her hand encountered was the most glamourous black dress that she'd ever seen. Suddenly her eyes were full of excitement. "What's this?"

"Oh sorry, that's the dress you're wearing tonight."

"What do you mean?"

"That's the dress and in the other bags you'll find some other bits and pieces I want you to wear tonight."

Lucy didn't know what to do first, kiss Neil or look through each bag. She went for the bags. Black high heels, sexy black underwear and a silver heart-shaped pendant on a fine necklace. She then kissed him long and hard.

"So, we're not having pasta tonight?"

"Well, you might want to order it from the restaurant, but it won't be as good as mine."

"You're a blagger, Neil Turner. I thought it was a pyjama night tonight. Thank you. When's the restaurant booked for?"

"Seven thirty. You've got enough time to get ready. The taxi's booked for seven."

"The taxi?"

"Yes, I thought I'd have a drink tonight," admitted Neil.

"Wow. I'd better get ready. Neil, this is brilliant. Thank you. You are a beautiful man. Do you know that?"

"I have my moments."

They both got dressed up. Neil, in his best suit that he didn't wear for work and Lucy, stunning in her expensive new clothes and jewellery. They were in the taxi on time, and travelled to the restaurant Neil had booked a week ago. Not the Italian restaurant on the high street that Lucy was expecting but an altogether different proposition.

Entering the restaurant, Neil smiled at the member of staff on welcoming duties. "Hello I've booked a table under the name of Turner."

"Oh yes sir, follow me."

Neil duly followed so Lucy followed Neil. To a large table in the far corner of the room.

"Sorry sir. We had to put you on this large table. All the other tables were booked. I promise you won't need to share it with anyone."

"That's fine. Is this alright Lucy?"

"It's perfect, absolutely perfect."

Even though the table would comfortably seat another six people, they sat next to each other and held hands.

"I love you, Neil."

"I love you too, Lucy."

The head waiter came over to them with the menus.

"This menu is for you madam. Take your time and consider it carefully. I will be back soon," the waiter said and retreated.

Lucy opened the menu and found an envelope inside it with the word "Lucy" on the front. She looked up at Neil.

"Open it," he smiled.

Inside was a note that said "Will you marry me?" Taped to it was a beautiful engagement ring.

Lucy shrieked and automatically put her hands to her mouth. "Oh God. Oh Neil. Yes. Yes. Yes!" and kissed him and kissed him again.

Only then was Lucy aware of the applause coming from the restaurant's waiters, who were clearly in on the set up. And out of the corner of her eye she spotted people she recognised coming towards them; her mom, her dad and then Neil's parents and Neil's sister and brother-in-law. She stood to hug everyone, tears of happiness streaking her cheeks.

That night was the happiest Neil and Lucy had ever known.

Neil (with the aid of his sister) had pulled it off.

. . .

Over the next few days Lucy and Neil slowly came down off their euphoric high. Lucy during that time had used every form of social media to relay the news and show pictures of her ring to anyone who was interested or not. She kept looking at the photos on her phone taken during and after the meal at the restaurant. The head waiter took endless pictures and videos for them. The cake with sparklers, the staff who sang Italian love songs to the happy couple and the impromptu speech Neil made, which made all of the women there cry, particularly Lucy.

Four nights after the *Proposal Night* as it was now known, the two of them sat on the settee for the first time together as fiancé and fiancée. They cuddled, kissed and watched TV, closer than ever.

"I'm so lucky to be engaged to you," said Lucy fiddling with her ring.

"I'm the lucky one," replied Neil, kissing the top of her head.

"Good answer. Brownie points later. But first I need to know how you planned all of that behind my back. You knew I'd been keeping an eye on you."

"Lots of secret phone calls with my sister. I have to say she was very helpful with everything. Most of it was my idea, but she was great with some of the organising. I chose the ring, the dress and heels online and I picked the restaurant, but she gave me suggestions and advice on everything apart from the underwear, I got that at the store. You know how much I love mooching around the lingerie department."

"Well you and your sis did me proud...I mean...us proud. But how could you...I mean us...afford it all?"

"Don't worry about that. I had a contingency plan in place, I've been saving some of my wages in a separate account for a while now. It's like a bottom drawer for blokes. It might mean that we'll have to tighten our belts for a bit but we'll be OK."

"I know we will be OK. I know it," said Lucy confidently, reassuring both of them.

. . .

Sleep was deep and contented for Lucy over the next month. She worked long hours at the hospital and then travelled back to her fiancé, back to their home. It was no longer a flat that Lucy and Neil shared. It was a stepping stone to their own house and their own family. Lucy's dreams were now incrementally and gradually becoming the reality that she'd always longed for. She seemed on the outside to be a wild child that would never be tamed - a party animal that could never be caged - but underneath the make-up and the fur, Lucy was a one-man-woman and a mummy in the making. She was ready to be an adult with responsibilities. She was ready for her happy ever after.

Neil slept fitfully. His dreams, when he did sleep, were similar to Lucy's. He wanted the house and children but only after the good well-paid job that he enjoyed. When he was lying awake in the middle of the night, listening to Lucy peacefully dreaming, he would worry about the money draining from their accounts. The proposal night cost a small fortune and the online gambling, that was supposed to claw some of that money back, was increasing their debt. Indeed the debt was spiralling as Neil tried to climb out of the hole he had dug for himself. The more he lost, the more bets he placed to recover his losses.

Neil was living three separate lives. He was a well-mannered mannequin of a man when he worked at the department store. He was a loving and caring fiancé when he and Lucy shared time together in the flat. And when he was home alone, he was a maniac trying to defeat games that were stacked against him. He couldn't live like this for very much longer. And he didn't.

Lucy arrived home one day, after a shift from hell, to find Neil was sitting on the settee looking at his laptop.

"Hi hon, are you OK? What's for tea? God I've had a crap day at work. Why does everyone get sick...it's so...Neil? What's wrong?" Lucy could sense that Neil was far from right.

"Oh, nothing much. It's just that the shitty job I do is no longer available for me. They've *down-sized* me. Apparently, the footfall is plummeting and they don't need as many shop assistants now. They're making more money online than at the store. So, ironically, the IT man is being sacked because everyone wants to buy online."

"Oh Neil, I'm so sorry," Lucy moved over to the settee and sat next to Neil. "It doesn't matter. You'll find another job. You'll have more time to apply for things now. If necessary, I'll work some extra shifts while you get something. We are OK moneywise, aren't we? For a while at least?" Lucy asked, wanting confirmation.

"Yeah, yeah, we're OK for a while. I'll have to get a job somewhere, somehow. We do need an injection of money. I spent quite a lot on the proposal night," admitted Neil.

"This is all my fault. I cornered you into doing something special when you proposed to me and now look what's happened, we're struggling for cash. And I took you away from a decent job at Whatmore School so I could chase a promotion and that left us broke as well... God Neil...what have I done!" Lucy started to cry.

"Luce, it's alright, honestly. It's not your fault. It's one of those things. I've just been unlucky. I'll sort it out. We can manage. For a while at least. You are not working any more shifts. That would be crazy. You're knackered with the hours you do now. I'm not letting you do any more and that's final!"

Neil hugged Lucy and in time the tears subsided and then stopped.

They ate an improvised meal and watched some television before returning to the subject.

"What will you do Neil?"

"I'll sign on tomorrow and I'll spend every day looking for work either online or knocking on doors if I have to. You mustn't worry Lucy. It will work out in the end. Just have faith in me."

"I do Neil, I do. I just don't want you to hate me for taking you away from a well-paid steady job." Lucy became tearful again.

"Luce, I love you, I could never hate you. Now let's get to bed. You have work in the morning and tomorrow I'll start another phase of my illustrious career."

After a cuddle and a kiss in bed, they wished each other a *Good night* and tried to sleep. The crying and tears were gone now, only to be replaced by silent worries and fears.

. . .

The next few weeks and months became a haze of humiliation for Neil. While Lucy earned the bread, Neil made the sandwiches and toast. He collected Job Seekers' Allowance. He applied for countless jobs. He kept lowering the bar on his expectations but he wouldn't accept any type of job. He needed decent wages so that they could keep the flat, so that they could eat and so that he could gamble to pay off their debts.

Neil had secretly borrowed money from his own parents and Lucy's parents without her knowledge. Both sets of parents willingly agreed to lend Neil money and understood that Lucy need not know at the present time because he didn't want to worry her too much. He was, after all, doing everything he could to get a job. The money from both families was transferred to his account and life carried on. He left the flat less and less – he went out only to buy cheap food and alcohol at the local supermarket and sign on at the Job Centre. He spent most of his time in the flat online chancing his arm on jobs and the wheel of fortune. He was slowly becoming a lazy, unfit couch potato, drinking a little too much during the day and snacking on sugar and salt. The pounds were creeping on to his waist line.

The pennies and pounds were flowing steadily and unhealthily from his account and away from the dream house and family. Neil was in a mess. Neil was a mess. So he did what any self-loathing addicted gambler would do. He bet more, drank more and tried to forget everything and deny it was as bad as he knew it was.

. . .

The fun stopped one afternoon when Lucy came home a little after four o'clock one day. Neil was asleep on the settee. Two empty bottles of beer beside him along with his laptop. The screen showed a fruit machine game.

Surprised by Lucy without time to cover his tracks, Neil claimed he wasn't feeling very well. He flicked the screen of his laptop to the Home screen and said that he'd just lie down on the bed for a couple of hours.

Almost three hours later, Neil emerged from a deep, alcohol-aided sleep from the bedroom to discover Lucy sobbing on their settee.

She had been busy while Neil had been asleep.

During that time; she had accessed their accounts, including Neil's separate account, she had spoken to both sets of parents on the pretext that she was worried about him and she had looked at his browsing history on his laptop. In a matter of a couple of hours Lucy's world had been turned upside down. She was now processing the fact that they were not just broke but owed a fortune to the bank and their parents and that Neil had irresponsibly gambled away all their hopes and dreams for the future.

After a one-sided blazing row that lasted an eternity, Lucy packed a small bag of clothes, grabbed the car keys and stormed out of their flat. She had to get away for a while.

She was gone in sixty seconds. Fast and Furious.

. . .

He stood outside the bathroom door. He tried the bathroom door. It was locked.

"Lucy. Open the door. I want to see you. You've been gone almost a week. I know you're still angry with me but we can get through this. I've been stupid but I can change. I will spend the rest of my life trying to earn your respect again. I'll find a job and start repaying the debts. I'll go to a gambling addiction clinic...anything. I just need you to stay with me and help me through this...please Lucy, please..." Neil started to cry in desperation.

After what seemed like a lifetime, Lucy replied in a sad, resigned and defeated tone.

"Neil, I'm pregnant..."

CHAPTER 6

Saltburn-by-the-Sea

Sobia opened her eyes. A new day. In the last four years her eyes had been opened far more than during the time in her life when she was a wife and mother. In those old, distant days her eyes were shut to new possibilities and adventures. Her closed eyes didn't see how other people lived their lives but now she could see that many people were free; free from fear, rebuke and judgement. Her eyes back then were stained with tears of despair and bruised with surrender and defeat. Her 20/20 vision was clearer and more focused than her short-sightedness of 2015 and before.

Her new life, however, was far from perfect. She missed a great deal of her past life.

Firstly, her twin boys. They would be eight years of age now. They were very similar in their appearance and in personality and looked and took after their father. They screamed and shouted and played rough with each other. Sobia often felt that her home resembled what she thought a communal changing room would be like after one football team had beaten another. But she loved her boys and she missed them every day.

Secondly, her job as a Business Manager at a secondary school. She had respect and authority there and was appreciated by both women and men alike on the staff. She particularly missed two people – the head teacher, Peter Burlington and his PA, Penny Hinks, who were kind and generous to her in some of her most difficult days. They were the only ones back then who understood her double life, that at work, most of the time, she gave the impression of being an able, strong and confident woman while in her other- existence at home, she was passive and submissive.

Functioning in these two worlds had become more and more problematic and exhausting for Sobia. It was even more tiring to convince herself and others that she was alright. Changes had had to be made and almost four years ago, they were. Some of the changes were of her own making and some were made for her.

And so Sobia now woke up in her small single room with a very small bathroom. She had cooking facilities in one corner, she had a two-seater settee, a TV and a very small table with two chairs, and she also had access to laundry facilities. What more could she need or want? Well, she could do with a more sympathetic landlord and neighbours who were less noisy. But other than that, she was doing fine.

She had a quick bath, dressed for work and made herself some breakfast – tea and cereal. Her new day had started and yesterday was committed to the waste bin. However, yesterday wasn't completely wasted because it was another step on her journey towards a new future - her previous life and memories were gradually diminishing in her rear-view mirror.

Sobia closed the front door behind her, walked along the short landing, down one flight of stairs and out of the bedsit. It was a bright day and the early morning sun made it necessary for Sobia to wear her sunglasses. It made a change to be wearing them for the right reasons rather than to protect herself from the glares of people looking at her puffy eyes and the surrounding parts of her face. She walked along the street and smiled at the occasional familiar face.

"Hi Sara!"

Sobia looked across the road and spotted a friendly face, a woman she had often spoken to who worked in the local Spar. She waved in acknowledgement. "Hello Brenda, how are you?"

"Fine thanks. I'll see you later," replied Brenda as they passed going in opposite directions along Windsor Road, the main road into and out of Saltburn-by-the-Sea.

Sobia continued walking towards her place of work, reflecting on the random nature of choosing Saltburn as her new home town and also the selection of her new name. When she eventually left the family home close to Whatmore School, she had packed her car with a few precious possessions and headed north and east. She had left her old self behind and decided on a new first name to go with her fresh start. Even now, three years later, she felt that someone from the past might recognise her from across the street and yell, "Hi Sobia," even though she had shorter hair now and much slimmer, having lost about twenty-two pounds in the last couple of years. She worried that she might spontaneously respond "Hi there" but in fact no-one she met seemed to know or care about her old life. She was Sara to most people who cared to know her, and to her surprise many people did care.

Just before one of her favourite shops, she stopped at a pedestrian crossing and waited for the lights to turn green. She momentarily glanced towards Chocolini's, a shop of delights, specialising in anything and everything chocolate, before making herself look at the road and cars to stop herself being tempted. She walked to the small traffic island, turned left and almost immediately crossed Station Street to her destination.

She fussed through her handbag and found the keys which opened the door of the Elderflower Charity shop and café, a place she now managed. She was in fact the only paid worker. She had volunteers to help, but she was responsible for the stock, the finances and organising the helpers. The charity targeted its support on the aged and consequently a considerable number of Saltburn's elderly inhabitants made a point of frequenting the shop.

Sobia loved working there. She loved the people and they loved her and appreciated her efforts. It was so different to her other jobs where she had had to be an evil bitch to earn or save money for an organisation. In managing the charity shop, she could do her best to raise money for people in their twilight years without too much pressure and very few targets. Her monthly salary wouldn't make her a millionaire but she could survive from week to week, which was a relief as the first few months in Saltburn were tough and hand-to-mouth. Fortunately, Sobia did have some funds as back-up - the residue from the marriage. But during those first few months in Saltburn her savings quickly disappeared while she struggled to find a roof over her head and a job.

In time, after she found the bedsit and was appointed manager of the shop, her new life steadied and stabilised and then became enjoyable and rewarding, free from the stresses and strains of her previous existence. Free from the arguments and judgements, of never being good enough. Her husband and his family had looked down on her, treating her like an inadequate housemaid. She was forever being criticised for her deficiencies as a wife and mother and accused of dedicating too much of her time to her paid job. What a difference now, her operational manager, who oversaw Elderflower charity shops and care homes across the country, was delighted with Sara's work and efforts. He would ring her once a month to hear how things were going, and on two or three occasions had arranged a visit to the shop to see for himself how things were. Each time he had taken Sara out for lunch to talk shop and cafe, to praise her and to tell her, as he left to head back to his office in Birmingham, that she was one of his best and smartest appointments.

Sobia shut the main shop door behind her and left the CLOSED sign up. Two of her volunteers would be arriving at 9.00 but she could start preparing the light breakfasts they offered from 9.30 until 11.00. She fired up the urn, took out three sliced loaves from the fridge for toasting and set up the eggs and bacon to be cooked as and when required. She laid out the four circular tables with table cloths, place mats, cutlery and salt and pepper. Her regulars would usually request tea or coffee with toast, egg on toast, beans on toast, bacon or sausage breakfast baps. There were no lattes or cappuccinos on offer, no full English plates of grease or mega stacked burgers – this was a menu for a small appetite.. This was not food to go, or food to eat while staring at a smart phone – this was social dining where older people craving company could mix and be catered for. Sobia had no problem with younger people eating in the cafe but most of the younger clientele came to browse for bargains in the shop rather than to eat slow food. Lunch time was also usually busy, offering the same fare as breakfast with the addition of sandwiches and home-made soup. The volunteers generally prepared the food and drink and Sobia served the customers. But Sobia was not just a waitress, she was a friend and confidant, who would sit next to anyone in need of company.

The shop and café on Station Street were adjacent but separated. There were two doors between them. These doors were the access points to the offices upstairs. One belonged to a solicitor and the other was rented out to an artist and photographer who Sobia rarely saw. The Elderflower shop and café were linked at the back and Sobia could access both units using back door keys. This meant she had her own short-cut between the two sides of the business.

The Elderflower Charity Shop was an Aladdin's cave of cast-offs. Clothes, shoes, jewellery, bric-a-brac, books, toys, games, LPs, CDs and DVDs. Most of the items on offer had been treasured possessions but were now cluttering up houses and needed to be jettisoned. The shop was full of people's memorabilia and old keep-sakes that had faded and diminished in sentimental value. The shop had a moral obligation to make sure that items on sale were of decent quality and in good working order but no-one shopping in Elderflower expected pristine or perfect.

Sobia had a separate team of volunteers who looked after the shop. Usually one person on the till and another volunteer keeping the goods tidy and labelled. She tended to be in the café more during working hours but she was well aware that both sets of volunteers needed to see her presence fairly equally during the day. Sobia was always amazed how many locals would give up a full day or a half day a week to help out. Two of her volunteers, bless them, did two full days a week! This was a world away from hard-nosed business, penny pinching and profit. This was about caring for people, all people, and helping the wider and older community by raising money. Sobia's business plan differed from most shops - she wanted people to have a good experience at a low price. Profits on food and drink could have been higher but she refused to mark up the costs. This meant that local people used the café, not just tourists. And the same business plan applied to the shop. Sobia always kept margins down. After all, the goods on sale were donated, free of charge, so why make the prices unreasonable? Her business plan worked because people in this small, seasonal coastal town generally couldn't afford a lot and they used her shop to buy cheap and cheer themselves up.

It was almost nine o'clock and she had just finished laying the tables when Sobia heard a knock on the front door of the cafe. She went over to let in the first of her volunteers.

"Morning Sara," said Graham.

"Good morning Graham. How are you today?"

"All the better for seeing you this bright and beautiful morning," beamed Graham.

"How's Thelma?"

"She's in a good mood this morning. She has the day to herself without me getting in her way. Although she said she might pop in at lunchtime and have a sandwich and a chat."

"Ah, that will be nice. She clearly misses you, Graham."

"It's not to chat with me, it's to see you! Do you want me on breakfasts?"

"Of course, there's nobody better at bacon and sausage baps!"

"How would you know; you're vegetarian!"

"I know, Graham, but I still like the smell of the meat cooking."

As Graham moved behind the counter to put on an apron, there was another knock and Sobia opened the door to two more of her helpers.

"Hello, Janet. Hi, Tom. It's good to see you. Come on in."

"Thanks Sara. How are you?" Janet asked on behalf of both herself and her husband.

"I'm very well. It's a lovely morning isn't it? Are you both well?"

"Not bad. Tom's leg's playing up a bit...arthritis."

"Sorry to hear that, Tom. Are you OK to do this today?"

"Yeah, I'll be fine. I might just need to sit at the till for a bit."

"If you're sure. Janet, are you OK working in the shop with your husband this morning?"

"If I must!" said Janet squeezing Tom's arm, so Sobia gave her the shop keys.

"Great, I'll pop in once breakfasts have got under way. Thanks both, I really appreciate your help." As Janet left the cafe with Tom hobbling behind her, Sobia thought, *Just Nina to come.* She had no sooner thought it than the woman was there.

"Hi Nina."

"Sorry I'm late, Sara. I couldn't get off the phone with my mother."

"It's fine; no problem, Nina." In a previous life Sobia would have torn a strip off anyone who was late, but not a volunteer and not here and now. "Are you OK helping Graham in the kitchen today?"

"Yes. He's good company. He makes me laugh. I could do with cheering up after listening to my mother for half an hour."

"Is she still getting confused and upset?"

"Yeah, most of the time. Old age is so frustrating She's not coping and neither are the rest of the family," admitted Nina.

"I'm so sorry. Why don't we catch some time later today and have a chat?"

"That would be nice. Thank you," said Nina and headed into the kitchen.

It was 9.30 and they were ready for business. Sobia pulled up the café blinds and flipped over the sign on the front door. She knew that within seconds Janet would be doing the same for the shop.

Within a few minutes half of the café's seats were occupied and Sobia was taking orders. One or two of the men had brought newspapers to read but before long they abandoned the news for the daily gossip and moans. The woman they all knew as Sara was somewhere between a friendly landlady in a pub and a zealous proprietor of a bed and breakfast. She chatted with the regulars and the not-so regulars while Graham and Nina cooked and plated up the cuisine. There was nothing on show that a TV chef with an inflated ego would praise but it was hot food lovingly prepared by volunteers doing their bit for the elderly residents of Saltburn.

By 10.30 the café was full, some of the old folks perhaps overstaying their welcome but Sobia did not mind. What else would they be doing? Sitting on their own eating Meals on Wheels. She was providing her own service. A catering service. This was a different offer to fast food burger bars where the customers just played musical chairs morning, noon and night. The slow charm of the café also had its benefits - often people spent money in the charity shop waiting for a table to empty in the café while some café customers finished their food and headed three doors up the street to the shop. But most importantly of all, the shop and cafe served a real purpose for the local community.

Sobia, in the time she had been in Saltburn-by-the-Sea, had become a well-known and well-liked member of that community. This had not been her intention when she moved there. She had wanted to disappear from sight in a smallish place where smallish people could hide and not be sought. She had had enough of the big city life. She had wanted peace and quiet. A resting place at a slower pace.

Saltburn was that place. Somehow the relaxed town managed to maintain its original charm as a Victorian seaside resort and destination even during the summer season when it was invaded from Easter onwards by visitors and holiday makers. Tourists came for the pier, its balanced cliff tramway taking people from the shops and hotels down to the long sandy beach with its surfable surf and its amusement arcade. And for the less adventurous holidayers, Saltburn had its formal Italian gardens and cliff walks and was in easy reach by car for outings to the North Yorkshire Moors, the larger town of Whitby and the city of Middlesbrough.

Sobia loved Saltburn in the holiday season but she also liked the quiet autumn and winter months when the town took on a different personality. Many of the shops temporarily closed, bed and breakfast accommodation was vacant and at times Saltburn-by-the-Sea felt like a windy and wet ghost town. But Sobia's loyal local residents still braved the North Sea winds and sea fret to visit her café and charity shop, open as it was all year round for the town folk who bravely resided there permanently.

Sobia sat and chatted to all of her guests while they sipped their tea and chewed on their toast. She had a word or more for everyone - even the grumpy ones. She made them all feel welcome and worthy human beings who still had something to offer. Sobia would smile with them, tease them, reminisce with them and sympathise with them. She wasn't afraid of giving them a hug as well. For some of these elderly citizens it might be the only physical contact they had with another human being that day. But these weren't one-way relationships. Sobia enjoyed and valued the conversations around the café tables. She learned a lot about the *Old Days*. The simple days when the clock ticked at a sensible speed, days that started and ended without greed, hatred and fear, days of stable families and upstanding citizens. And as Sobia talked to these gentle men and women, she could see that they were slowly shrinking and disappearing from view. They had a great deal to offer society but it seemed that no-one of working age was looking for a cast-off bargain. The retired had outgrown their usefulness, they were a drain on the resources of the country, a nuisance and an embarrassment. And yet all of these people in Sobia's café were once young rebels who, on one hand, thought they were immortal and yet on the other hand had wanted to die before they got old. And now, years and years later, they held on to life as firmly as they could. And because they could not contemplate much of a future, these grey and golden oldies recalled and regurgitated the past, while some who might be in the first throes of dementia were living part of those past lives in the present. Sobia often had the same conversations about the war, about manners, about being neighbourly and about living on a pittance over and over again. The needle on the record was stuck on the same song, *Those were the days my friend, we thought they'd never end...* and the stylus jumped from the end to the start each day. And as Sobia gradually started to move through the middle- age gears herself, she related and sang along to the refrain of the song.

Once most of her breakfast guests had drunk enough tea from their bottomless cups to sink a battleship (no mugs at Sara's *caff*), Sobia left Graham and Nina in charge so that she could support Janet and Tom next door.

From the back of the shop she could see Tom behind the counter, labelling up some of the donations ready to go on sale while Janet was chatting to a couple of ladies who were regular browsers. Janet would take time to engage anyone who ventured into the shop without making them feel as if they were under the microscope. There was no "May I help you?" or "Are you looking for anything in particular?" It was more "Hello, how are you?" or "A bit chilly out there today." Janet and Sara had agreed some time ago that people's motives for entering a charity shop were slightly different to a regular high street store. Shoppers saw Elderflower as an indoor car boot sale or jumble sale. No-one had a particular purchase in mind when they entered the shop; they were looking for bargains that were in reasonable condition. They walked in with an open mind and often walked out with a few useful bits and pieces. So Janet didn't swoop on potential customers but like Sara she liked a chat. Unlike Tom whose skills lay in the effective quality assurance of the second-hand items to go on sale. He would check that all the CDs they received for re-sale were playable and had their plastic cases intact. He would see that the books were complete, without missing pages or graffiti. The only handwriting he would accept was on the dedication page where people would write their name or the name of the person that was going to receive the book as a gift. Clothes were inspected; they had to be clean and immediately wearable – no tears or ripped seams and no indelible marks. Ornaments had to be dust free and unchipped. Anything donated had to pass the *Tom Test* before they were labelled for sale. Occasionally, Tom would be able to rescue an item with a needle and thread or a surgical strike of a cleaning product but if they were beyond repair, they would be re-cycled or skipped.

Sobia paused for a moment in the dark stockroom at the back of the shop which was full of donations that needed processing. It was one of her roles in the shop to assess if the goods should see the light of day or not. It was also her job to see what sorts of items should be displayed and when. Certain items might be judged more saleable in the winter or to coincide with a particular festival or bank holiday period. The stockroom was heaving with anonymous past props waiting to feature in the show of someone else's life. These discarded items at one time or another told stories of expectation and excitement, regret and neglect and eventually sadness and waste. This dusty room stored away the detritus of lives trying to be forgotten. Sobia felt sad but at peace in this space. A great deal of her past life had presumably been deposited in a stock room similar to this in a different part of the country.

"Are you OK, Sara?" asked Tom from the open doorway.

"Oh...I didn't see you there... Sorry I was miles away."

"I didn't mean to make you jump. You looked sort of sad, which is unlike you."

If only Tom knew how often I had looked sad and jumped at the sound of a male voice in the past, thought Sobia and then said, "I'm fine, Tom. I was just thinking how sad it is that all of these things are no longer needed."

"Well, hopefully we can give them new homes. This stuff will be useful again."

"Let's hope so. It's good to know that we are keeping things going and the shop keeps us going too."

"Yes, it is. This shop certainly keeps me going. It gives me something to do. It keeps me feeling useful."

"Tom, you and Janet are more than useful, you are vital. I couldn't do this without you two."

"Bless you for saying that. And what about you, Sara? Do you feel happy and useful here in Saltburn? How long have you been here? A few years now. Is this what you want? This place can feel dead at times. Don't you want more? Do you know what I'm saying?"

Sobia did, but she chose to answer his questions with deliberate vagueness. "I really like Saltburn. It's different from big city life but I needed a change. And I have you guys to keep me company and keep me on my toes."

"But you're years younger than Janet and me and, to be honest, younger than most of the people who work here or use the café or shop. Have you got any...friends...your own age here?" Tom was probing as delicately as he could.

"Yes, I've got a couple of friends I see in the evenings occasionally. I'm often too tired to socialise during the week. I speak to family members and visit friends on a Sunday..." Sobia hoped that this would be sufficient to stop the polite questioning.

"Sorry, it must sound as if I'm prying. I don't mean to."

"Honestly, Tom, it's OK. I'm OK. I have everything I need here. You're not going to get rid of me that quickly."

"I'm glad to hear it. Well, I'd better get back to the counter. See if Janet has stopped talking those poor ladies to death. By the way we're going to shoot off as soon as the afternoon shift arrives as Janet wants us to do some shopping in Whitby. I'm just hoping my leg is too stiff to walk and drive." Tom was smiling as he hobbled back to the counter to sit down.

Sobia gathered her thoughts for a few more minutes in the stockroom and then surfaced to joined Janet in the shop talking to the two ladies who were not planning to buy anything today but were going next door to have tea and a piece of cake each.

By 11.30 Sobia had made her short way back to Graham who was busy behind the café's counter slicing tomatoes and onions, grating cheese and chopping some more vegetables for the soup of the day leaving Nina cleaning plates, cups and saucers, crockery and work surfaces. They were talking, laughing and joking with each other and with a few customers who had come in for a snack.

At the click of Sobia's heels, Graham looked up. "Oh, here comes the boss, Nina. Make out you're doing some work or we'll lose our jobs!"

Nina laughed and Sobia gave Graham a mock stern stare. " I may have to dock you three months' wages for gross insubordination. And don't expect a good report in your next performance management review!"

"Sorry boss. I tell you what. I'll work for free for the next six months to make up for it. Hold on a minute, I do work for free!"

"Do you?" chipped in Nina. "I wouldn't stand for that Graham; I get paid a good salary every month plus bonuses."

"Ssh, Nina," whispered Sobia loudly, putting a finger to her lips," I told you to keep that arrangement a secret between ourselves."

Behind Sobia's smile was a shadow of guilt. She was the only person working for Elderflower in Saltburn who drew wages and yet she was definitely not the only one working hard who deserved payment. "What's the soup today?" she asked.

"It's vegetable with the emphasis on tomatoes that are a little too ripe to go on cheese sandwiches."

"It smells delicious," said Nina, the tea-towel in her hands busy on a frying pan.

"I think you'll find that's me," said Graham. "It's my new after shave *Eau de Tomato*. I thought I'd splash it on this morning to impress you ladies."

"Graham, that's very considerate of you," said Sobia. "We are intoxicated by the sexy scent of ripe garden vegetables, aren't we Nina?"

"Very much. It's making my head swoon." Nina put the back of her hand to her forehead.

"Steady girls, you know I'm already taken and any time now Doreen will be coming through the door. I can't let her see me succumbing to the advances of my adoring fans behind the counter. Also, she'd have my guts for garters!"

"I know she would, Graham. We'll just have to wait until another time to be inappropriate in the workplace with you," said Nina with a smile.

"OK, but don't wait too long. I'm Seventy-two next month. I think my sexual drive is starting to run out of petrol."

"Do you think so? Well, when Doreen pops in, I'll ask her. You said she wanted a chat with me," said Sobia, trying to sound serious.

"Blimey, let me know if your conversation goes in that direction and I'll make myself scarce!"

"Will do."

Sobia headed to one of the tables to talk to a man of about the same age as Graham who was just finishing his tea and biscuits. After that it was conversing with a group of three woman and taking their lunch order. Within another fifteen minutes all but one of the chairs around the café tables were taken. The soup was the most popular choice although a few of the regulars went for their habitual cheese and tomato sandwich or bacon butty.

The lunchtime period lasted until 2.30 but Doreen arrived well before that and after speaking to Graham at the counter for a few minutes parked herself at a table that was now vacant and waited for Sobia to join her.

"Hello Doreen. How are things?" asked Sobia.

"I'm fine thank you. I've just been over the road to the library and got a few bits and pieces from the chemists. How is the old codger doing? Is he giving you any grief?"

"Well, we just about keep him in check. He tells me his birthday is coming up soon. Seventy-two next month?"

Doreen nodded. "Yes, that's right. I'm a bit younger than him but he's still going strong, physically."

'Oh no!' thought Sobia, '...it seems as if I am going to have that conversation after all!' She felt she wanted to say to Doreen, *It was just innocent fun. We were all just fooling around at the counter.*

Doreen continued in a hushed tone, keeping one eye on her husband working away behind the counter. "It's just that lately he's been a bit forgetful. He laughs it off, you know. Everything's a joke to him but just recently he's been having the odd memory lapse. I wondered if you'd noticed anything when he's here?"

"No I haven't, Doreen. He seems to be his usual self. He's worked here for...a year or so now and he's just the same Graham every day he comes in. A good laugh, a good worker and a good guy. We all love him to bits. We're lucky to have him."

"So am I, Sara. Perhaps it's my imagination or maybe at home he just relaxes and can't remember certain things or loses concentration. I'm just worried about him. You can understand that, can't you?"

"Of course. Perhaps if he keeps busy then his mind won't wonder so much. He can always do some more shifts here, if you both think that it's a good idea."

"It may be I suppose. But I do like to have him at home. He isn't as fit and healthy as he lets on. He does like the odd nap in the afternoon."

"I suppose we all need one as we get older. Do you do much together, hobbies and such like?"

"We do some things together with the *University of The Third Age* and then we do some things apart. I have the W.I.; Graham likes to watch sport on the box and sometimes he has a drink with his mate at *The Victoria*. We both like our own space from time to time. That's what keeps us together if you know what I mean?"

Sobia did know what Doreen meant - she had never been allowed space or freedom to do what she wanted in her own marriage.

"Yes, I understand Doreen. If you like, I will let you know if Graham doesn't appear to be himself but I don't want to spy on him. I wouldn't feel comfortable keeping an eye on him all of the time. Has he said anything himself about the memory lapses?"

"No, when I've mentioned it from time to time, he says that he's fine and to stop fussing." Doreen was beginning to sound a little sad.

Sobia made a move to stand up and said, "I'll see what I can do. Try not to worry."

"Thanks Sara. Thanks for listening to me. I bet you think I'm going mad."

"Not at all."

Doreen stood and hugged Sobia. Then looking over to the counter said in a loud voice to Graham, "Don't be too long. You have my tea to cook when you get home!"

"You women are slave drivers!" Graham smiled at his wife. . "See you later, love."

"Bye, sweetheart," said Doreen as she left..

Sobia went back to the counter to checked on Nina and Graham. They were cleaning and clearing everything away. Most of the heavy traffic had gone and there were only a few afternoon teas to make and serve from now on.

"Was Doreen OK, Sara? Only she didn't order anything to eat or drink," asked Graham.

"No, she was fine. She just wanted a chat."

"Oh yes. What about?"

Sobia thought quickly on her feet. "Never you mind...it was just something about... someone's...impending...birthday...perhaps..." she said, sounding both embarrassed and guilty.

"OK, say no more. Mum's the word."

"Anyway, I better head next door and see how the shop's getting on," said Sobia. She had decided to lay low in the shop for an hour or so.

Janet and Tom had been replaced by the afternoon shift, two very reliable ladies who volunteered together two afternoons a week. Sobia worked with them in the shop for more than an hour making sure everything on the shelves and hangars was looking presentable before returning to speak to Nina and Graham who were by then busy cleaning the hob, the work surfaces and the empty tables for the last time that day.

"Hi you two. What do we need from Sainsburys for tomorrow?" asked Sobia.

"Not too much," Nina said. "I've made a list."

"Great, how do you fancy helping me with the shopping? Are you OK for half an hour, Graham?"

"Yeah, that's fine," replied Graham as he systematically cleaned the rest of the pots and pans he'd used.

"Do you want to put the closed sign on the door?"

"No. If anyone pops in, I'll just say we're only serving hot drinks, cakes and biscuits from now on."

"Great, as long as you are OK with that," said Sobia, a touch of concern in her mind following her earlier conversation with Doreen.

Nina grabbed the shopping list off the counter, Sobia grabbed a few bags for life from the store cupboard and they left the shop and headed to Sainsburys, a journey which on foot took less than two minutes; down Station Street, across the road at the side of the traffic island which housed the Saltburn town clock, through the arches at the station and there they were at the supermarket gathering the supplies they would need for tomorrow – three sliced white loaves, three semi-skimmed milks, tea bags, sausages, bacon, margarine, jam, marmalade, brown and red sauce, salad and vegetables.

By the time Sobia had paid for the trolley of goods with her Elderflower card, she and Nina had extensively discussed Nina's mother and growing old. Nina was feeling guilty because she and her husband had moved to Saltburn almost ten years ago when her husband secured a job at the estate agents on Dundas Street which had meant leaving her mother who had for the last six years been living alone after Nina's father had suddenly died. She had coped well at the start supported by Nina's older brother and sister who lived closer and could pop in more regularly. Nina's journey to see her mother was a couple of hours each way on the train. On some Sundays when her husband wasn't working, they would drive to her mother's, but that would take the whole day, her husband's only free time in the week. Nina felt guilty about that, she felt guilty that her brother and sister were doing most of the necessary caring and she felt guilty that she was neglecting her mother as she became older, lonelier and at times confused.

It was not only Nina's mother who was confused. So was Nina. She wanted to do the right thing for her mother but her husband was needed at the Saltburn office. He would work as long as he could until the internet fully replaced high street estate agents which was a slowly growing threat to his job but in Saltburn there were still renting and buying opportunities for people wanting to live on the coast without paying silly prices. Still, Nina felt it should be her turn now to take greater responsibility.

Although she didn't want her mother to live with them, she was toying with the idea of suggesting to the family a move to a care home in Saltburn where she could visit her more frequently. Her mother had some savings and pensions to pay for care and her house could be sold to free up even more funds. She just needed to sell this proposal to her brother and sister and most importantly her mother. She already had her husband's support but she didn't know if her motives were selfless and well placed. Did she want to move her mother to Saltburn for her mother's benefit or for her own convenience?

Sobia listened to Nina and for a few minutes on the way back to the shop they sat on a bench by the station to finish the conversation so they wouldn't be distracted by Graham. Sobia didn't feel it was her place to give advice. She knew that Nina just needed a sounding board so she sat and listened while Nina sat and talked as the world passed them by. A couple of bag ladies of a certain age. Both of them with families on their minds.

Back at the Elderflower Café they found it clean, tidy and ready for re-opening in the morning. Sobia collected the takings and receipts from both tills and put them in the safe in the shop's stockroom. She would sort the receipts out tomorrow, log all of the incomings and outgoings on her laptop before walking across the road to the bank with the last few days' takings.

Once everything was safely put away other than a small float for each till, Sobia rounded up all of the volunteers and thanked them for their efforts. The shop was locked up first and then the café. The four volunteers all went in their different directions. The two shop helpers joined the small queue to catch the next bus home while Graham headed up Albion Terrace to cook Doreen her tea and Nina walked back towards the station and then along Dundas Street to call in on her husband who would drive them home. Sobia herself walked back along Windsor Road, past her flat and stopped off at the Spar to buy some milk and other essential supplies for herself. By 6.00 pm she was home, if she could call this home. She kicked off her shoes and made herself a mug of tea. She would make herself something to eat in a while. She just needed half an hour or so staring at the television while thinking about the day, her past and her future.

Her day had been busy and rewarding. Both the shop and café were doing well in terms of foot fall and making money. The Elderflower brand had twenty or so shops and cafes across the country and a percentage of the profits went into subsidising the care homes that also came under the same brand. Each working day had been satisfying – Sobia liked living and working in Saltburn-by-the-Sea, the locals were welcoming and friendly and the volunteers who gave up some of their own precious time to help out in the shop or café were warm and generous folk. The sometimes sunny and funny days in Saltburn had over time gradually replaced the dark days of her previous life.

She had worked hard at being successful as a business woman, a mother and a wife. If she had been rated on these three categories by a panel of judges consisting of her husband's family, the scores would have averaged out as follows:

Business Woman - 7.00, Mother - 6.25, Wife - 3.75

However, if Sobia had self-evaluated her own performance in each category on effort, commitment and sacrifice, she would have given herself much higher scores:

Business Woman - 8.00, Mother - 9.75, Wife - 9.75

She was still angry and upset at the way that so many members of her husband's family had turned against her once she had become a wife and then a mother. His family had become hyper critical of her every action. Every little thing needed improvement and nothing was ever good enough. It had been too much to bear. Over the years she had tried so hard to make it right, to be positive and to pretend that everything was fine. She had tried to cover up the cracks in her marriage, the bruises on her body and to block out the daily verbal abuse. Only once had she let her defences down when without realising it she had inadvertently let it slip to her head teacher at Whatmore School and his PA that she was being bullied at home. They were, of course, very understanding, sympathetic and concerned but after a few days she had resumed the façade that everything was OK and it had just been a storm in a teacup.

The stage play of a happily married couple, performed by Mr and Mrs Didially, had changed over its three acts and ended as a tragedy. The stage directions had described voices and hands raised by the husband and tears falling to the floor from the wife's eyes. He had been angry, she had been sad and the young twins had suffered in silence.

One day, without warning, decisive action was taken. Sobia returned home after work to find an empty house. Her husband and her two precious children were gone and so were the majority of their possessions. Each day Sobia had hoped that two of her three boys would return but with each day that hope slowly turned to certainty that they were not coming back. No-one else in her husband's family would talk to Sobia or help her in any way. Backs were turned on her and in time even the police gave up looking. Sobia became resigned to the awful and undeniable truth that her husband had made it impossible for her to see her children ever again.

Sobia could not function in the empty house or at work. Her performance as School Business Manager had deteriorated to such a degree that Peter Burlington had come close to starting capability procedures against her. Sobia had not been surprised. However understanding and sympathetic to her plight Peter might have been he had to put the interests of the pupils first. And so one day, Sobia had done what she felt she had to do. She had walked into Peter's office to hand in her letter of resignation and had walked away from the school for the sake of all concerned.

Some months later, Sobia had left the house that used to be a home and moved to another place. A place where she could, on the outside, start afresh. A place where she could be somewhere else and someone else. Her doctor and counsellor had advised it. Time would start to heal; time would help some of the worst memories to fade and a new location would stop the terrible reminders of the past.

So here she was, sitting on the settee, on her own in Saltburn a long way from that home.

And what about the future for Sobia? Her immediate future was to stand up, replace her work clothes with comfortable trousers and a long tee shirt and then make herself some tea. She made her way to the bathroom, wiped away the make-up she had applied that morning and then took a moment to stare at herself in the bathroom mirror. "What do you look like?" she asked herself. She didn't really need to answer her own question. For some time, the mascara, eyeliner, concealer and foundation had held back the years and tears but there was no fooling the woman in the mirror. She examined the crow's feet, the blemishes, the nooks and crannies around her face and particularly her eyes and sighed. "Is this it?" she said to the mirror. "Is this what I have to look forward to from now on? A face that stares back at me getting older every day and a one-sided conversation with a pale reflection of what I used to be? Sobia, you are pretending. You are a liar. You are being Sara, the wonderful boss who is lovely to everyone. Always happy and helpful. Never in a bad mood. Everyone's favourite...apart from her twin in the mirror."

"But if you were yourself," replied the mirror, "no-one would like you here in Saltburn. They might pity you if they knew the truth or some may even hate you for letting go of your children. Then you would be abandoned again by the few friends you've in this friendly seaside resort. And for the second time, you would be left empty and desolate."

"Stop it, stop feeling sorry for yourself. Would you still rather be married to that monster?"

"No, clearly not, looking at the expression on your face. So get a hold of yourself, keep up the pretence, try to keep smiling, keep hoping that the boys will be back soon. You are Sara, for now."

She turned away from her close closet friend and changed into her civvies. to make herself an evening meal. Soup from a can, toast and two jam tarts that she had picked up from Spar. After watching TV for a couple of hours, hers eyes began to lose the battle to stay awake so she washed up at the sink, used the bathroom and took to her bed.

She was asleep before her head hit the pillow.

If her mirror could look at Sobia now, hiding beneath the bed clothes, she would probably tell her that she hadn't been awake for a long time and had been sleep-walking through her days for years.

The next two days the shop and café opened and closed in the familiar routine, the only difference being among the volunteers helping her out. Sobia kept herself busy. She banked the takings, arranged and served at tables in the café, steamed some clothes in the back of the shop and talked to customers and helpers, always with a smile on her face. The evenings were much the same too. She ate food from Spar, talked to herself in the mirror and sleep-walked her way to her empty bed.

On Sunday morning she woke early with mixed emotions.. She was pleased that the shop and café were closed for the day. She needed a rest. On the other hand that meant that a day without much purpose. For many people a day off work was freedom - family and fun time -but not so for Sobia. Her day stared back at an image of her which did not know whether to laugh or to cry.

She made herself a cup of tea, had a longer bath than she would do on a working day and decided to break out of her four walls for at least some of this cool but sunny September morning. It was back to school for children in England this week so the composition of Saltburn's holiday makers would now take on a slightly different complexion. Families would be replaced by retired people or working people who chose to wait until the school holidays were over before experiencing the resort without the *joys* of children. September was the start of calmer months for Saltburn as the laughter and tears of children disappeared. That didn't mean that the North Sea would be calm. The wind and the waves would start to pick up now.

After putting several layers on Sobia left the flat, walked past Elderflower and turned up Dundas Street towards the road down to sea level. The funicular railway was still being serviced so she walked down the windy road to the pier and beach. She stopped for her breakfast at *The Surfs Up Café*, situated right by the pier. She talked for ten minutes or so with the friendly young lady who served her tea and toast. It amused her to think that on any other day of the week she would be the one doing the chatting to someone who had ordered their breakfast but today, Sobia was the lonely old lady who needed a friendly word.

After breakfast she headed for the pier. It was only a matter of yards away. But in those few steps her excitement grew with every stride. She loved the pier and it had become the favourite place in her small world. The pier, a simple and plain structure, had defied the North Sea for a hundred and forty years. In that time it had been battered and bruised by the elements and wayward ships and been reduced to half its original length. She had read that on eight different occasions a storm off the North Sea had taken its toll on the pier and a hundred years ago a ship, fighting the wind and waves, had smashed into the middle of the structure slicing it in half. But after many re-constructions, the pier's cast iron trestles still propped up its wooden decking and it still stood proud and defiant against anything that could be thrown at it.

Like many piers, an amusement arcade had been built on the pier but Saltburn's pier was quite unusual in that the arcade was on the shore end. Sobia walked through the gaming machines and the Penny Falls out onto the pier proper, walking until she reached the end. She was not alone. There were two others standing there, one staring out to sea and one fascinated by the surfers. While waiting for these people to leave her alone on her pier, she watched the enthusiastic surfers trying their luck to ride a North Sea wave. She admired their determination and willpower as they continuously fell off their boards and then immediately paddled back out again to hitch a ride on another wave. The men and women in their wet suits were in their own worlds – being spun around and thrown into the deep but enjoying every second.

After five minutes or so, Sobia was the only remaining person at the end of the pier. This, then, became her moment. Sobia had said to Tom a few days ago at the shop that on Sundays she often contacted her family. Well, this was indeed what she did, every Sunday, the North Sea permitting; she would walk to the end of Saltburn pier, face the sea and talk to her children.

"Hello boys. I hope you are both OK. What's your week been like? I hope you are safe and well. I don't know where you are but you must be at school somewhere. The children in this country have gone back to school now after the summer holidays. I hope you are at school learning lots and enjoying yourselves. I'm sure you are both behaving yourselves and are impressing your teachers. I wonder if they can tell you apart. What are your favourite subjects? Do you like Maths, like I did when I was at school? I hope you are still learning English wherever you may be. The head teacher I used to work with used to say that a good knowledge of Maths and English is a solid foundation for building a life and a career. And I want you to have happy lives and successful careers. When I see you next, I will be proud of you both no matter what age you are and what you have become…"

Sobia wiped away the salty tears from her eyes. She looked behind her to see if anyone was close by. There were a couple of small figures walking towards the end of the pier but she still had a few more precious moments alone with her boys.

"I'm sorry. I let you down some years ago but I never stopped loving you. It was your father that I didn't love. And he took you both away from me without asking and without my knowledge. I will never forgive him for that. I hope you don't think that I wanted you to leave. I never ever did. I was unhappy, but not with you. I was unhappy with the way your father treated me. But I'm not unhappy now. I feel much better but I miss you both terribly every single day and I know I won't be really happy until you are back with me. One day, hopefully soon, we will be back together, the three of us. Please remember me and don't let anyone tell you that I don't love you, because I do. Please remember the fun we had. The cuddles you gave me. Remember the songs and stories at bedtime. Please keep those songs and stories in your hearts. I must go now but I will talk to you next week. I love you both now and always."

Sobia stared out across the sea looking for two boys somewhere in the world. She did not know where they were, most likely on a different continent, far, far away from Saltburn-by-the-Sea's pier. She sighed and reluctantly walked back along the pier, pausing briefly in the amusement arcade to see some families possibly enjoying their last day of their holidays before returning to work and school; today they were making the most of their time together, spending coins without a care in the world, hoping for a jackpot win of £1 or if they were really, really lucky, £5! In Sobia's eyes they were all winners. They were all safely together and having fun.

She left the arcade and headed back up the road towards the town centre but at the top of the hill she turned left along Marine Parade, Glenside and Albion Terrace. On the way she passed the quaint band stand and the sign for the Halfpenny Bridge. The six hundred and sixty-foot-long, hundred and fifty -foot-high toll bridge, had spanned the Skelton Beck, linking Saltburn and Skelton, since 1869. The bridge meant that travellers did not have to descend down to sea level and then tackle the arduous ascent up the other side of the glen. Sadly, the bridge took lives in its construction and continued to take lives until it was demolished. Unfortunately, not only did it become unsafe in high winds over time but became a popular place for visitors with suicidal thoughts. And so in 1974 under close supervision and a conflicted audience the bridge was razed to the ground by explosives in four seconds flat.

On one or two of her darkest days since moving to Saltburn, Sophia had wished the Halfpenny Bridge was still standing.

Sobia walked the last few hundred yards along Victoria Terrace before she came to the foot path down to the Italian Gardens. The secluded small gardens were a hidden gem and next to the entrance was one of Sobia's favourite cafés. It was sheltered from the breeze and was a safe, quiet space to enjoy a slice of freshly made lemon drizzle cake and a cup of coffee. If the weather allowed it, she would sit outside and re-configure her life. On the pier each Sunday she was Sobia with a family in a different time and place, but now, an hour or so later, she was Sara from Saltburn, the lovely lady who ran another café and shop in the town.

The rest of Sobia's day consisted of trips to Spar and the laundrette to wash and dry her clothes for the week before ironing them while watching TV. Her evening was devoted to a simple meal, sending a few emails to far-flung places and gorging on a family- sized chocolate bar with a cup of tea before retiring to bed. As she drifted off to sleep, she thought about one day being re-united with her boys and tears began to well in her eyes. She rubbed her eyes and decided to re-focus. She thought about tomorrow. She had her dream team of Nina and Graham back with her in the café and she had two new volunteers who were going to help out in the shop. Sobia would have to spend quite a bit of time with the new couple but that was OK as Nina and Graham could run the café perfectly well on their own. And with that self-assurance, Sobia's mithering slowly turned to slumber.

The morning ritual started with a cup of tea, a bath, breakfast and a walk down Windsor Road, Station Street and into the café. Sobia checked that all of the bread, butter, margarine and milk were in date and filled up the urn and turned it on. The tables were laid for breakfast and then Sobia popped next door to check that everything looked fine in the shop for the new volunteers. The tills in both units had a float in them and so all that was needed was her kind and generous helpers to arrive and then she could switch the signs to OPEN.

Graham arrived first and having fired up the hob and grill was ready for the first order.

Nina smiled as she was let in, eager to tell Sobia that her family had agreed to look at the care home in Saltburn. It had apparently taken a great deal of persuasion but now everyone was in agreement about the move, if they liked the look of the care home. Sobia was pleased for Nina and told her so. She knew they'd have a proper chat later but knew Nina would understand that she was needed in the shop for most of the morning.

The new shop volunteers were a delightful pair of retired ladies who needed something to fill their new-found time and Sobia gave them a quick guided tour of the shop, showed them how to use the till and how the shop was laid out. They seemed competent and confident but she had already decided to stay with them for at least a couple of hours to support and train them up on their un-paid jobs.

By 11.45 Sobia felt confident to leave them to look after the shop until the afternoon shift of old hands arrived at about 12.30. She told them to pop into the café once their shift was over. Not that they knew it but Sobia was going to treat them to a cup of tea and a cake as a thank you for joining her team.

Sobia re-joined Graham and Nina for the lunch time rush. Of course, everything was already completely under control. A soup was being prepared by Graham and Nina was slicing and dicing salad for sandwiches and garnish so Sobia picked up a cloth to wipe down the few spare tables and say hello to a few customers who had pretty much stayed put in their seats from a late breakfast and were now waiting for an early lunch.

Over two hours' worth of soup, sandwiches and cake washed down by tea and more tea zoomed by with the three of them preparing food, clearing tables, washing up, chatting to customers and exchanging jokes and opinions on anything and everything. There was no need for background muzak to create an ambience or atmosphere; it was the people inside the café who made it a pleasant place to relax and while away the time.

As the afternoon unfolded, Sobia was able to have her promised chat with Nina who was plainly feeling much better. It now seemed very likely, according to Sobia's understanding, that Nina would feel less guilty and have peace of mind if her mother accepted the move to the Saltburn care home Nina had in mind.

Sobia had a real soft spot for Nina. She was a good, kind-hearted soul and was undoubtedly a fine daughter and a considerate member of her extended family. Graham, also one of Sobia's favourites, kept out of the conversation while he was cleaning and drying some plates and pans but eventually when the café was all but empty, he joined in the discussion. "Doreen's a bit like you, Nina, always thinking of other members of the family. Perhaps it's a woman thing?"

Sobia paused but fortunately Nina jumped straight in. "Well we can't trust you men to think about anyone else other than yourselves now, can we Sara?"

"Not at all," replied Sobia, half-smiling to keep her dark, past experiences at bay.

"What is it with you men anyway? You're all single-minded and focused on work, sport, cars and...nothing else!"

"Steady on, Nina," said Graham with a smile on his face, "there's more in a man's mind than you think. We're very complex creatures. There's no end of things spinning around in our heads and you women think we just have one-track minds. But we can multi-task just like you. Look, I'm talking to you and drying a plate at the same time. That takes real precision and skill. You women would have to put the plate down for ten minutes while you talked." Graham looked at Sobia. "That's right isn't it...um...er..."

"Sobia," said Sobia quickly to stop Graham's embarrassment and then realised what she had said. "I mean...Sara...Sara..." Sobia laughed as Nina and Graham stared at her in a bemused and confused state. "Listen to me, I'm forgetting my own name now...I was just thinking of an old friend of mine called Sobia a few minutes ago. Silly me!"

"You two definitely need a rest," said Nina. "Graham can't remember Sara's name and Sara gets her own name mixed up with her friend's. Perhaps we should all wear name badges and then we wouldn't get mixed up!"

"I suppose we're all at that stage in our lives when we forget the odd thing. Perhaps we have got too much going on in our lives," said Sobia aiming the reassurance at Graham.

He looked a little embarrassed but re-joined the conversation. "You're right. I know my memory isn't what it used to be."

"The trouble is," said Nina, "how do we know what our memories were like if we can't remember?"

"Goodness, that's a bit deep and philosophical for me," said Sobia.

"And me. And anyway, you two can't use old age as an excuse. You're both a lot younger than me."

"Perhaps a few years, Graham, but working with you has aged me dramatically," said Nina.

As Sobia and Graham chuckled, the front door to the café opened and a middle-aged man in a smart suit carrying a briefcase walked in. He was clean-shaven, and tallish with a stomach in the first throes of threatening his trouser belt. He was impressive to look at and certainly a good deal fitter and healthier than the normal customer walking in the door for tea and cake on a late Monday afternoon.

Graham and Nina stared, Nina perhaps for a couple of seconds longer than she should have done, before turning to look at Sara and discovering to her surprise that whilst they might not know this man, Sara certainly did.

Sobia said "Simon, this is a surprise. I wasn't expecting a visit. You normally text me or ring before you drop in."

They hugged awkwardly and then broke apart.

"Well, I was in the area...well about fifty miles away and I thought I'd pop in to the café and see how you're getting on."

"Oh, that's really nice that you stopped by particularly if it was out of your way... Sorry, where are my manners? Simon, this is Nina and Graham. They volunteer here two or three times a week. I don't know what I would do without them. Graham, Nina, this is Simon Kirby. He is the operations manager for Elderflower UK."

Graham came forward and shook Simon's hand, "Good to see you. Fancy the big boss coming to Saltburn to check up on our Sara."

"Well, it's not the first time I've been here. I think Sara and I have had lunch two or three times in Saltburn since you were appointed as manager here. Isn't that right...Sara?"

"Yes, that's right," Sobia said, blushing slightly.

Nina was quick to pick up on Sara's embarrassment and as she shook Simon's hand she innocently asked, "So, you came fifty miles out of your way to see Sara?"

"Yes, I'm visiting one of our new care homes in Middlesbrough tomorrow and I thought I'd have a pit stop in Saltburn before carrying on my journey."

"Can we make you some food or a drink perhaps?" asked Sobia.

"No, I'm OK for the moment. If it's alright with you guys, I'll just sit down in a corner and make a couple of phone calls first and then perhaps I can have a chat with you Sara before I head off."

"Of course. We're just finishing up anyway. It's quarter to five now," said Sobia. "Are you two OK finishing off here and I'll pop next door and close up the shop?"

Ten minutes later, the shop was closed, Graham and Nina had said their goodbyes and Sobia had shepherded them to the door. As Nina left the café, she squeezed Sobia's arm and winked at her while Sobia did her upmost to remain expressionless.

"Sorry about that Simon, I can't just rush my volunteers out of the door. Graham and Nina have been with me for a long time now. They are great people and good friends. They have made me very welcome since I came up here."

"That's fine. They clearly like working with you. Aren't we lucky in this country to have so many lovely, well-meaning people who give up some of their free time to help others?"

"Yes we are and it makes me feel guilty that I get paid and they don't!" Sobia said.

"How do you think I feel? I earn more than anyone at Elderflower but I probably don't work any harder than Nina and...er..."

"Graham," said Sobia smiling at another memory lapse.

"Yes...Graham. Anyway I'm sorry I just turned up here without any warning but I'm on the road quite a lot these days, keeping an eye on the shops and care facilities we're managing. So I try to see some of the managers at any and every opportunity, if I'm close by."

"It's nice that you visited us. Shall we sit down? Are you ready for a coffee or would you like me to make you a sandwich or something?"

"No, it's fine, Sobia... I can call you Sobia...as we're now on our own. No, you don't need to make me anything. I'm taking you to that Indian restaurant across the street. We tried to go at lunchtime about a year ago, do you remember? But they only open in the evening so we went to a café round the corner. I think you felt a little uncomfortable meeting and having a sandwich in your own café."

"I did. That's a lovely idea, eating there. Do you know, since I have been here in Saltburn I have not set foot inside that restaurant? I have often wanted to but it's awkward eating out on your own. And of course you can use my real name...it's weird having two first names. I think you are one of only a handful of people who know me by both names. Before I moved here, I was Sobia to everyone and now I'm here, I am Sara. Funnily enough it hasn't ever been a problem until this afternoon. Before you arrived, I was chatting to Graham and he forgot my name for a second - I think he is having some memory issues - so I tried to help him out but instead of saying Sara, I said Sobia, which confused both him and Nina. And then a few minutes later you walk through the door, the keeper of my secret. It's been an odd afternoon all in all."

"Well it's not really a secret is it? I thought you just wanted to change your name when you changed location so you could start a new chapter in your life. I only needed to know so your DBS application was legitimate and for the sake of bank details. It's not as if you're a fugitive from the police!"

"Not as far as I know," said Sobia, smiling and much more relaxed now it was just the two of them. "I've kept my married surname. But up here I'm just Miss Didially not Mrs. No-one knows I was married although in the eyes of the law I suppose I still am. It may help in getting my children back in the future. I'm not planning to change my name by deed poll or anything. It's just the new me...for the present."

"OK then. Why don't we walk over the road, order some food and talk some more?" said Simon picking up his briefcase.

Twenty minutes later they were sitting in the corner of "Spices" having ordered.. Sobia had been expecting to have eggs on toast for her meal tonight swilled down with a cup of tea so this was an unexpected treat. She was also pleased that she had on a rather stylish suit with a smart blouse she had washed and ironed yesterday.

"This is my treat, Sobia," whispered Simon. They were the first customers in the restaurant and they both felt a little conspicuous under the gaze of the three waiters anxiously awaiting more custom. "Mind you, the food is really cheap here compared to restaurants I've been to recently down south, so it's not that much of a treat. But anyway, it's a thank you for what you're doing for Elderflower here in Saltburn. It must be about three years now? How are you doing?"

"I'm OK. Better with each day that passes in one sense but sadder in another way. I stayed in the family house for a while after my husband left me and took the twins and then I decided to move. I thought I would get some funds from the house but it turned out that the house was paid for by his parents so when I came up here I had very little surplus cash. It's ironic, isn't it that I used to be a hard-nosed business manager at a secondary school overseeing millions of pounds and yet I wasn't allowed to run our own house's finances. I left it all up to him. What a fool I was, in all sorts of ways," said Sobia, aware of the risk that her initial laughter could easily turn to the first sign of a tear.

"Well that was then and this is now," said Simon leaping in with the first platitude he could think of to stem the tide. "At least you're away from him now...I know that means that you're away from the boys but that will change, I'm sure."

"I hope and pray that is the case. I really do. I sometimes consider what I would choose if I had the choice between living with my controlling, abusive husband and my two beautiful boys or life without any of them. And I always decide on having my children by my side."

"I know you would, but I hate the thought of you being bullied and hurt by your husband again. You deserve better than him. You deserve a better life. One day this will be resolved," said Simon. He desperately wanted to take hold of her hands across the table to re-assure her.

"Thank you for saying that. I hope to get the boys back someday soon. But it's been hard." Sobia changed direction slightly. "I want to thank you for having faith in me when I moved here without money and a job."

"Please don't thank me. I still remember talking to you a few years ago after you applied to run the café and shop. I'd read your application and arranged an interview with you at a café by the pier. You told me all about your experience in business and at the school, explained your family situation and your change of name and how you wanted to be a better person. It was as if you thought you were being punished for what had happened to you and that it was you that needed to change. I always remember that. It affected me. Then we took a stroll along the pier and I offered you the job with the waves crashing under our feet. It wasn't the most professional moment in my career but I won't ever regret giving you the job."

"Thank you, Simon. That means a lot to me. I still walk along the pier every week. It's a ritual I have got into. I talk to the twins and hope my voice is taken out to sea, like a message in a bottle they will hear one day."

"Talking of piers – you'll never guess – I was in Invergordon about two months ago...we're opening up a care home close by. And I stopped in the port to have some lunch. I picked up a guide for Invergordon and there, at the side of the port is another Saltburn pier. It's very different to your one. It used to be a working pier taking smelt to the ships. It's really long but not as pretty as the one here."

Simon blushed as he finished off his short anecdote. For some reason they both decided to look down at their food and take a bite off their plates for a moment before Simon continued. "Anyway, I want to talk to you about something else, if that's alright. You know the UK is struggling to house all of our elderly citizens in care homes as the population is generally getting older. Well, Elderflower is trying to build or refurbish care homes the length and breadth of the UK at the moment. We have four refurbishments that are almost ready to open and we have a new build in Birmingham that should be open next summer, in Sutton Coldfield to be exact. Do you know the area north of Birmingham?"

"Vaguely. I used to know someone in Tamworth, which isn't far away."

"No, it's not far at all from Sutton Coldfield. Anyway, as I said I'm hoping that it will open in the next nine months or so, if the construction keeps to schedule. I need to get a manager in place very soon to oversee the final stages of the build and to appoint staff and then run the care home...and...I was wondering if you would be interested in doing the job?"

"Pardon?" Sobia stuttered a response. "Me, why me? I don't have any experience in care homes. I am not a nurse or medically trained. I wouldn't know what to do."

"Sobia, you would be managing the care home, you wouldn't be directly caring for the residents or attending to their medical needs. That would be for others to do. You would lead the staff who do the caring, you would manage the finances, run the senior team and report to me and the Elderflower board."

"But...but there must be better qualified people out there that you could appoint. I would be out of my depth. And anyway, I would have to leave Saltburn, and leave my life here running the café and the shop. I couldn't do it. It's a lovely suggestion. I'm really flattered but I couldn't apply. I would have to return to city life. I escaped from that a few years ago. I like living in a small town where I am Sara. I care about the people here; I couldn't desert them..."

While Sobia fired off this volley of random reasons for not applying Simon sat there placidly with a hint of a smile in the corner of his mouth. "And that's why I want you to run the care home in Sutton, Sobia, because you care about people. That's the essential quality I'm looking for in the job description. Everything else is secondary."

"I'm sorry. It's a great opportunity but I can't let the likes of Nina and Graham down. I love Saltburn and I am beginning to love the person I am here."

"OK. OK. Point taken but promise me that you will give this some thought. I can't promise you the job today, not like the time we were walking along the pier, but I'm sure if you applied I would look very favourably at your application." Simon smiled knowingly as he said this. "Let me have your decision in a week's time after you've had a think about it."

"I will and thank you for thinking about me but I won't change my mind."

Four Oaks

Sobia was interrupted from her dreams when she felt a peck on her forehead.

"Good morning, sweetheart. There's a mug of tea by your bed."

"Thank you," Sobia managed to say to the shape who was moving into the ensuite. Within seconds she could hear the running shower accompanied by a range of badly sung Beatles songs. Sobia propped herself up in bed, adjusted the straps of her night gown and sipped her tea. She surveyed the bedroom. It was bigger than the whole apartment she had rented in Saltburn.

Simon came out of the ensuite with a towel wrapped around his waist, perched on her side of the bed and gave her the sort of long and loving kiss that she had only recently discovered existed.

"I have a meeting in Birmingham this morning and then I'm visiting a care home in Warwick and a shop in Coventry, so I should be home about seven. Is that OK?"

"No problem. I'll cook something when I get home. Unless, of course, you have plans to take the manageress for an Indian meal and then talk her into sharing your bed with her in the future," said Sobia smirking.

"No, I'm sorry to disappoint you, but that was a one-off deal. I'm afraid you're stuck with me if that's OK with you?"

"That's very much OK with me. Can I make you some breakfast before you go?"

"I'll tell you what, I'll make you breakfast. You spoil me too much. Why don't you jump in the shower while I sort out some breakfast? We can share a piece of toast before we go our separate ways today."

"Are you sure you know how to make toast? There's a recipe book by the toaster if you need help. I'll be down in a minute or two." As Sobia walked past Simon towards the ensuite she stroked his arm.

"Would you like me to.....scrub your back?"

"You'll get your clothes wet and anyway what about this toast you promised me? Perhaps we could share the shower water over the weekend?"

"That's a date for my diary," Simon said and disappeared downstairs to the kitchen.

Sobia showered and washed her hair quickly so she could spend a few minutes with Simon downstairs before he headed off for work. He had to be on the road early most mornings whereas Sobia didn't have to leave the house until 7.40 as it was only a five-minute drive to work. A drive in the car that Simon had bought her. As she dried her hair looking at her reflection in the dressing table mirror, she couldn't believe how things had changed for her in just over a year. She was a lucky lady compared to the woman staring in the mirror in Saltburn-by-the-Sea.

After much thought and conversations with her Saltburn volunteers, Sobia had decided to apply for the post. She still didn't give herself a chance when she travelled down to Birmingham for the interview. Simon had met her at New Street Station and taken her for a pub lunch before the interview in the afternoon at the main offices of Elderflower UK but Sobia found it hard to eat anything and even harder to contemplate that she was being interviewed for a high-ranking job she was neither qualified nor equipped to be considered a serious candidate for. Simon spent most of their time at the pub and walking to the offices reassuring her that she should just be herself and if she failed to impress on interview it didn't matter because she still had the life and job she loved in Saltburn.

Sobia had to wait outside Simon's office while the interview panel convened. She wanted to run back to the station but just as she was going to stand up and put her outdoor coat on, the office door opened.

"Ms Didially, would you like to come in?" said the rather austere woman who would have been at home leading Ofsted inspections. Sobia was shown to the Mastermind chair on one side of a circular table in the corner of the office. Opposite her were Simon and the woman from Ofsted; no-one else. There were a couple of empty chairs and Sobia imagined there would be an awkward few minutes while the rest of the panel assembled but within seconds Simon started asking serious and searching questions that Sobia did her best to answer. Both Ofsted and Simon made notes. Thirty minutes later, although it felt like, thirty hours, this part of the interview was over and Sobia wondered what would come next; psychometric tests, an assault course or role play. Instead she was dismissed and told to wait outside by Miss Austere or whatever her name was; Sobia couldn't remember. Five minutes later, Sobia was summoned back in by the woman who now called her by her first name and even appeared to be displaying a slight smile.

Sobia sat down opposite Simon and was waiting for the woman to sit down when she heard the office door close. She had not sat down; she had left the room.

Sobia took the opportunity to speak freely while she was alone with Simon. "Oh, I'm so sorry Simon, I let you down. I was a nervous wreck. And that woman from your board, she was so intimidating and scary. She hardly said anything or looked at me during that first part of the interview." She was teetering at level 10 on the Fluster Scale.

"Do you mean Sheila? She's not a board member. She's my secretary. I asked her to make some notes. She really likes you. And what do you mean – the first part of the interview? Were you expecting more? That's it, I'm afraid. No more to do."

"But I thought Elderflower would have all sorts of ways to embarrass and humiliate me this afternoon. So, is that it? Do I just wait to hear from you while you interview other applicants?"

"Well yes," said Simon, "but I can tell you now to put you out of your misery that we considered several people but only interviewed you and I'm delighted to offer you the post of Manager at Mercy House, Four Oaks." Simon smiled, stood up and walked round the table to shake Sobia's hand.

"Hold on Simon, I don't understand. You are telling me that I am the best person for this post?"

"Yes, the board looked at all applications, references and recommendations and they decided yesterday that you were the person we wanted to manage Mercy House but that we should still conduct the interview fairly and properly, the interview would be recorded by my secretary and I was given authority to offer you the job if you coped well answering all of the questions."

"But...but...I won't be any good, I haven't got the experience...I can't accept it..."

Two hours later, back in the same pub and at the same table, Simon and Sobia sat looking at each other. She was feeling far more relaxed. She was now breathing properly and able to eat something. She was also getting used to the idea that she would be on a very good salary although that was offset by having to consider the things she would have to leave behind.

A fortnight later, Sobia had told almost everyone that she was leaving the shop and café but she had persuaded Simon to give her job to Nina, who would do it splendidly. Two more weeks later she had agreed to temporarily use a spare bedroom and bathroom in Simon's house while she looked for somewhere to rent and the following Sunday, Simon drove up to Saltburn to help empty all of her possessions into his car.

They had a farewell lunchtime party with buffet food in the café for all of Sobia's volunteers which Simon paid for and then the two of them took one more stroll along the pier before heading to Sutton Coldfield. Sara was left behind at the end of the pier and Sobia was, to an extent, re-located and re-born.

Simon's house In Rosemary Hill Road was massive compared to anywhere Sobia had ever lived. He had been living on his own in the house since his last live-in relationship failed about three years before. It appeared that Simon's last partner took advantage of his generosity and sought the company of others while he travelled around the country for work. Sobia didn't like to enquire any further than that, but, unlike her own, it appeared the break up was relatively clean after he discovered his partner's dirty tricks.

Sobia was offered the big bedroom at the other end of the landing to his. The *family* bathroom was hers as Simon had his own ensuite. And she promised Simon that once she had found her feet in her new job and saved up a little bit, she would find her own place.

Simon had also bought her a small, second-hand car for her trips to and from work every day. Sobia had not even thought about travelling to work and back in amongst all of the other things she was worrying about. The car was a God-send and she assured Simon she would pay him back as soon as she could.

Sobia soon discovered that the pre-opening phase of a new-build care home was full on and for months she had no time to look seriously for somewhere else to live. She felt guilty but Simon kept telling her there was no rush and he liked her company in the mornings, evenings and for those parts of each weekend when both of them were in the house and not asleep on the settees or in their beds.

After a few weeks both Simon and Sobia began to enjoy living together. They ate breakfast together more and more and sometimes cooked an evening meal together. On Sundays they both looked forward to time away from their busy jobs. They would sit in the conservatory and read sections of the Sunday paper before going out for lunch at a carvery. Afterwards they would come back home and watch a movie together on separate settees and fall asleep every so often. They made a pact that on Sundays they would try to keep work out of the conversation but occasionally Sobia needed Simon's advice on care home matters. Equally, Simon found he liked to hear Sobia's views on his work.

When Sobia's first monthly pay cheque came through, she talked to Simon about the house-sharing arrangements. She insisted on paying for her room and keep. She also decided that it was only fair to clean the house and wash their clothes as a way of paying her way and showing her gratitude. The last thing Sobia wanted was for Simon to think she was taking advantage of his generosity. Simon, of course, couldn't stand by and let Sobia do these things on her own so he helped out with the chores and they worked happily together as a team.

It wasn't that long before they had worked out a more satisfying way of living together. One Sunday after their lunch they sat on a settee together while watching a film and fell asleep on each other. By the next Sunday's film session their heads rested on each other and they held hands enjoying the movie. The following Sunday on the settee they gently and cautiously kissed.

Understandably, the two of them took a little while to develop their relationship further. They both worried that that this new arrangement could be misinterpreted. Would Simon think that she was exploiting his good intentions? Would Sobia think that he had moved her in to his house to ease his loneliness as a live-in cleaner with benefits? So it took some time before they both assured themselves and each other that each felt a strong and powerful bond and they should slowly take the next steps. One Saturday night Sobia shared Simon's bed and from that point onwards she didn't return to her bedroom at the end of the landing.

Their gradual relationship grew into a secure and safe love match. They were both happy and had, after many years, found a soul mate. Sobia's life would be complete if she could just bring her boys home. It was the missing piece in her jigsaw and now it was a puzzle that they both would work on together. Simon assured Sobia that once the boys were found and returned then their home would be in Rosemary Hill Road. They would live as a family, a proper family.

Sobia threw on some underwear and a dressing gown and hurried down to the kitchen. Simon had a cup of coffee waiting for her and two rounds of toast with marmalade. She sat across the breakfast table from him, held his hand and said "Thank you darling, you are spoiling me."

"You deserve to be spoilt. If you're cooking the meal tonight, this is the least I can do!"

"So are you OK with toast tonight then?"

"Well I was hoping for a little more – but I'll take what I can get!" He said it with the cheeky grin she already loved.

"I think you did that last night as well!" she said Sobia.

"I don't know what you mean? Anyway, I'd better get on the road. I'll text you during the day when I can."

"I know you will and I love getting your messages. Promise me that you'll never stop sending them, even in our dotage."

"I promise, but hopefully we'll never be that far away from each other when we retire from the rat race."

"That's true."

Simon stood, moved around the table and kissed Sobia on her marmalade lips. "That tastes nice. Can I try a Marmite one tomorrow morning?"

"Over my dead body. How do you eat that stuff anyway?"

"It's the food of the gods!"

"Your god may be!"

"Oh no, are we having our first disagreement?"

"We sure are but I think we can handle a difference of opinion over what is better to spread on our toast in the morning," said Sobia with a glint in her eye.

"As long as you're sure. I don't want to get home tonight to find you've left me for some guy who also hates that terrible yeast-based product!"

Sobia laughed and smeared another marmalade kiss on Simon's lips.

"Van Morrison," said Sobia.

"Van Morrison," replied Simon and he picked up his suit jacket and briefcase heading for the front door. Sobia followed and waved him off as he drove down the driveway.

Sobia slowly closed the front door and started to hum their song "Have I told you lately that I love you" by Van the Man as she climbed the stairs to the master bedroom. She brushed her teeth again, applied a little make-up and sorted out a blouse and a two-piece suit that would look appropriate for work.

She was missing Simon already but knew that as soon as he got to his office, he would text her. He would also text her when he was leaving his office and after each visit he made during the day. It was a lovely feeling that someone, somewhere was thinking about her from time to time. Sobia also noticed that he stayed away from home less and less. His monitoring visits to Elderflower shops, cafes and care homes were being spread across his senior team and recently he had pulled rank and said that he would now concentrate mainly on the East and West Midlands so that he was closer to the main office. Sobia knew the real reason was that Simon wanted to be closer to her. She loved his unwavering devotion without it finding suffocating and it made a happy and healthy change from feeling literally suffocated as she had by her husband. Her family was now almost complete. She just needed her boys to return home.

Sobia checked her hair and make-up briefly in the mirror in the hall and set the house alarm. She threw her handbag and work bag on the passenger seat of her car and set off to work. In next to no time she had arrived at Mercy House well in advance of the eight o'clock change.

The care home was a three-storey building with rooms for sixty-eight residents. The ground floor could accommodate up to twenty-four elderly people with minor ailments associated with old age, who for one reason or another, could no longer live independent lives. The first floor had twenty-four rooms for residents suffering with dementia and the top floor had rooms kitted out for residents who needed full-time nursing.

On the day that Simon drove Sobia down from Saltburn with all of her possessions on the back seats and in the boot of his car, she had made him drive past the care home that would be entrusted to her. At that stage, the building was a sealed shell and was only partly furnished.

Her office was finished though and for the next few weeks she was based in there while all manner of tradesmen went about their business. A small team of specialists from Elderflower worked with Sobia to get her up to speed and to advise her on the way that a care home should be designed and fitted. In those first few months while teams of workers were wiring, plumbing, decorating and laying carpets Sobia learnt a huge amount about how things should and shouldn't be done.

At the same time a couple of staff from Simon's team at the main office in Birmingham came over to Mercy House to help Sobia with recruiting the first cohort of staff necessary to operate the home in its infancy. Within five months, Sobia had a staff team waiting to be trained and inducted in advance of the first wave of residents to arrive when the doors finally and officially opened.

Simon had explained to Sobia that recruiting residents was initially a slow process. His philosophy was that a new care home's reputation would in time speak for itself. The staff numbers would grow as more and more elderly people made Mercy House their home. Sobia, along with her senior team, would still have to market the home and run Open Days for the local community but there were no make or break targets to be met and no accountants from Elderflower suggesting that old people should be abducted off the streets to massage the figures. Simon assured Sobia on several occasions that her aim should be to slowly grow the intake alongside the reputation of the care home. When Mercy House finally opened, two elderly people were helped through the doors, one in a wheelchair and one with a walking stick.

Now, as Sobia locked her car and walked through the two sets of sliding automatic doors, Mercy House was almost half full. Almost all of the rooms on the ground floor were occupied, over half on the first floor and presently rooms were in use on the nursing floor.

"Good morning, Sobia," said the receptionist.

"Good morning, Judy," replied her boss. "How's the family?"

"Not too bad thank you. My youngest is still recovering from the flu but he's going into school today. No more time off."

"Quite right. You don't want him to develop man flu too early in life. Not until he has left home and is someone else's problem!"

Judy smiled. "Too right!"

"Judy, I'll be in my office for a few minutes and then I'll be out to oversee handover."

"OK," Judy replied and Sobia headed off down the corridor to her office.

Her office was fitted with a desk with a comfortable chair each side and a small round table in the corner with another four chairs. The chosen furniture meant Sobia could accommodate one-to-ones or discussions with several members of staff or residents or their families. For larger gatherings she would use one of the two meeting rooms situated on the ground and first floor.

She unpacked her work bag including her laptop which she plugged in and checked the messages on her landline. She grabbed her mobile from her handbag and quickly sent Simon a text and returned it to her bag, before picking up her work mobile and heading for the Nurse's station. She punched in the same access code through a couple of doors which led into the main living areas of Mercy House. Most residents on the ground floor were still in bed and the wide cheerful corridor was empty. She squeezed into the back of the room smiling and nodding at a few carers who noticed her entrance. The short hand-over meeting involved the Clinical Lead, two lead nurses, one about to clock off and one who had just clocked on and a carer from each floor who were also about to finish their night shifts. The hand-over meeting was so efficient that it didn't really need the Clinical Lead to chair it. Information of concern regarding the health and welfare of any resident was passed on to the day shift representatives. The lead nurse or carer would quickly summarise any actions taken and any changes to the care plans.

They would then check the master diary and outline any hospital appointments or GP visits scheduled for the day. In a matter of minutes, the meeting was over and the nurses' station was clear of staff – some going on duty and some making their way to the staff room to collect their coats and then head home for a well-deserved rest.

Sobia, instead of returning to her office made her way around the three floors to say good morning to as many members of staff as she could find and also to pop into the rooms of residents.

On the top floor one of the residents was still fast asleep but the other two were awake enough to say a few words. On the first floor one or two of the residents with dementia were up and about and ready for their breakfast. Others were receiving help with their personal hygiene and some were being reminded about where they were and how they needed to take their medication. Sobia would often help the staff out in the dining area on this floor by serving the residents food and chatting to them while they ate. This short ritual each morning reminded her so much of her time working in the café in Saltburn.

Her last stop was back down to the ground floor. She would knock quietly on each resident's door to see how each of them were. Again, some were still fast asleep while others were awake enough to have a chat. The elderly residents on this floor were generally sound of mind but their bodies were failing them. Some of these residents would try to persuade the carers that they needed to stay in bed all day but Sobia had quickly worked out who was capable of leaving their beds and stretching their legs and who was just being a little lazy. While Sobia was sympathetic to the residents who were tired of life and just wanted to see out their time watching TV in bed, she was continually reminded of a GP who visited one day who told her "If they don't use it, they lose it!" So, from then on Sobia would encourage her staff to encourage the residents to leave their beds for some of the time, using a Zimmer frame or a wheel chair if necessary. It was a difficult course for the carers to navigate because they could not be too forceful in their persuasive techniques as they could be accused of bullying. On the other hand, some of the elderly residents, if given the choice of their three meals in bed or in the restaurant would opt for bed with breakfast, lunch and dinner.

After chatting to over half of the residents and most of the staff on duty Sobia looked at her watch and realised she was running late for her 9.30 meeting.

"Sorry folks," she said as she entered her office and took the empty chair by the coffee table. "I got caught up in one of Ray's wartime stories, laced with his wicked sense of humour and innuendo."

"He's a real star, isn't he? For a ninety-eight-year-old, his mind is so agile; it's only his legs that are showing signs of ageing. Which is lucky for the women on the staff, if you know what I mean!?" said Maddy Hobday, the Deputy Manager of Mercy House.

The other three in the office chuckled at the observation. Around the small table with Sobia and Maddy were Razia Butt, the Clinical Lead and Murray Jones, the Finance Administrator.

"OK, first things first. Let's get everybody up to speed on the residents. Raz?"

Razia spent the next fifteen minutes or so going through some of the issues and problems that the nurses and carers had been having with certain residents. Razia, a trained nurse with over ten years in hospitals highlighted the main causes for concern – one lady was hitting out at the carers, a ninety-two year old on the first floor was trying to leave Mercy House at every opportunity - because she was late for her tea that her mother had cooked for her - and a man on the ground floor wasn't eating or drinking enough. Razia quickly went through the advice she and the lead nurses had given to the carers before outlining the various medical appointments in the diary for the day including a GP visit to see three residents and an optician and a chiropodist who were scheduled to see residents.

After Razia finished her summary of the pressing medical issues, Sobia thanked her and asked Murray to give the assembled group an overview of the current finances.

Murray passed around copies of spreadsheets that showed the state of the finances of the home. He took his time, without patronising his audience, to explain the inputs and outputs and the various bottom lines. The spreadsheets showed a relatively healthy position for Mercy House but Sobia was always one to point out at these meetings that finances in a care home were determined by health inside the home and in the local community. Early on Sobia had used her school experience to show the fragility of budgeting in a care home. A school, give or take a few children, had a fixed number of pupils each academic year and on that basis could forward plan spending on staff and resources. In a care home the numbers of residents fluctuated on a monthly basis. Sometimes, unfortunately, residents suddenly left the care home for distressing and sad reasons while in other cases they returned to their own homes as they were only in short-stay respite care to begin with. And although every effort was made to keep all rooms occupied, life and death was not always that simple. A caring care home was costly to run. Even though residents paid a considerable amount of money for the privilege of staying at Mercy House, the outgoings were even more considerable. Staff to resident ratios were low and the residents needs were expensive and fluid.

Murray's role was to monitor spending, focus on value for money but under the careful watch of Sobia to never let the high-quality standards of care slip.

Murray, at thirty-six years of age, was the youngest person around the table but he had over ten years of experience in public sector financing. Sobia, had been on the small interview panel that appointed him before the home was ready for business. She discovered post-interview that Murray and his boyfriend had been living in Glasgow until his partner had secured a highly-paid promotion in Walsall with a marketing company and Murray decided to follow his heart. He, came over as a somewhat shy and serious young man but was astute and reliable. Sobia took to him on interview and her decision to appoint him had never wavered since she'd started working with him. As Sobia's background was in finance, they would often have a friendly chat about money matters over a cup of coffee whereas most normal people would rather talk about the weather, current affairs or, in fact, anything other than finances!

They didn't always see eye to eye, however. Murray, occasionally, would suggest that Mercy House could save money by reducing staffing or putting up the monthly charges for residents. He would remind Sobia that the terms and conditions stated that charges could be raised each year by up to 8% but Sobia would not countenance any rise unless he could prove to her that the costs of running the home were increasing. Murray was persistent and convincing in his *discussions* with Sobia and she admired his tenacity, enjoying the cut and thrust of the dialogues. It reminded Sobia of another life in which she had argued long and hard with Peter Burlington about his over-generous position on budgeting. In those days she was the demon slasher of finance whereas now the soft shoe was on the other foot.

When Murray finished his exposition, the baton was passed on to Maddy, the deputy manager at Mercy House. An ex-PE teacher who had been Sobia's first appointment, Maddy was literally and metaphorically head and shoulders better than the other candidates who applied for the job. A tall, striking blonde woman with a kit bag full of personality and passion but little experience of working with the elderly. Sobia had no doubt that Maddy would be perfect for the role and after some healthy debate and some forceful flexing of her newly found managerial muscles managed to persuade the interview panel of Maddy's potential in the role. She knew that her passion, personality and sense of humour was an ideal fit for Mercy House. From her days at Whatmore, Sobia had always harboured a quiet and secretive respect for those teachers who could keep smiling no matter what faced them. And Maddy Hobday was the sort of person who could turn glum into glad in seconds.

Maddy's role, as well as substituting for Sobia, was customer relations, publicity and marketing. She was the main interface with the care home's residents, their families and friends. Maddy was the go-to person that residents' families would seek out. They might approach her with a grievance or gripe about how their elderly relative was being treated but by the end of a chat with Maddy all was OK with the world. Maddy had a way with people and, along with Sobia, was the heart and soul of Mercy House. She also led a small team of staff in organising daily events for residents and managed and publicised open days and other activities that would market the care home and hopefully attract new residents. Mercy House was, after all, a private, money-making organisation and the care home lived or died by the number of bums on seats or in beds. Maddy was constantly taking prospective residents and their families on guided tours of the home; she would continually take photographs of every event and occasion at Mercy House before posting them on Facebook or on their own website; she would spend time going out into the local community to forge connections with charity groups and search the West Midlands for inexpensive appropriate entertainers who would spend an afternoon entertaining the Mercy House troops. Although Maddy had, by her own confession, put on weight and was less fit as when she taught, her energy levels were still remarkably high and she would sometimes come in on one of her days off at the weekend to show off her two primary-aged daughters and the family dog to the residents.

Maddy, at speed, summarised the organised events for the week including a training session for staff, her off-site local community work and she notified the group about the two potential new residents who were due to have a look around Mercy House later in the week accompanied by their families.

"One day fairly soon," said Sobia, "it would be good to be in a position where we have a waiting list. Thanks Maddy and thanks Murray and Raz for your contributions. I just want to finish by talking about staffing. As you are all aware one of the main issues of running a care home is recruiting quality staff and retaining them. In the first months of opening we had real turbulence with staffing and I still wouldn't say we are in a position to claim we have stable staffing yet. There are several significant factors why carers, in particular, have left us within a few weeks or months of joining us. You all know the reasons," Sobia looked around at three of her senior and stable colleagues as she invited confirmation. They all nodded.

"Low pay is a major factor; you can earn more per hour working in the local supermarket stacking shelves than you do here caring for the elderly. The hours are challenging, particularly if you have a young family or any desire to have a social life. The work itself is difficult, caring for aged people is not easy at the best of times, but when you throw into the mix, residents with physical issues or dementia, then any care home is a tough place to find job satisfaction. And then you have the bureaucracy we all have to contend with. The never-ending paper trail of form-filling to cover our backs. It sometimes stops our carers from doing what they enjoy, which is caring for people. And most of this is not our fault. We have to dance to the same tune for our masters..."

There was a murmur of agreement but no-one was going to interrupt Sobia while she was solidly entrenched on top of her soap box. "Maddy, you and I have worked in schools so we know what it's like with Ofsted inspections, endless forms to fill in and boxes to tick - well it's the same with the CQC. We are bound to be inspected soon by the Care Quality Commission and so all of the daily drudge of paper work has to carry on regardless, and of course, the caring of our lovely residents must remain paramount while holding all of our staff to account. But we have to make the working lives of our carers and nurses feel appreciated and valued. I want the staff to want to work here and like working here. It's only then that we can retain the best members of staff."

Sobia paused for breath and gave way to a colleague on the floor of the house/home.

"I agree with you entirely," said Maddy allowing Sobia to take a sip of tea and relax for a moment in her seat after her stint at the dispatch box, "but sometimes it's difficult for our staff to enjoy work while they have to fulfil all that is required and expected of them. The CQC, through us, is asking more and more of its care home workers every month. But we can't keep asking our staff to go the extra mile and work above and beyond when they are just about on a living....or should I say surviving... wage. They are over-worked and under-paid. Some of our workforce could probably earn more by not working here and staying at home. There are limits to good will and the days of public service and treating work as a vocation are long gone. I totally agree with you Sobia, we have to make the job enjoyable and show the staff that this is...I was going to say *one big happy family* but that sounds trite, if that's the right word."

"I'm sure it is, but since when are families always happy," remarked Murray. "What we can't do though is give out pay rises or bonuses as we're not in a stable position yet and we are bound by Elderflower directives on pay."

"The nursing staff are more stable though. We have only lost one nurse since we opened, I think," said Razia. "Is there any reason for that?"

"Well, apart from the obvious one that they get paid more, I suspect it's because they come from hospital backgrounds and they generally prefer the life in a care home to that inside a hospital," replied Sobia.

"So what can we do?" asked Maddy to those around the table. "Is recruitment and retention always going to be an issue here? Perhaps the architects should have designed the reception area of Mercia House differently, instead of two sets of sliding doors we should have had one giant revolving door!"

"That would cost a lot more money," chipped in Murray.

Sobia let the amusement die down before admitting, "Look I don't have a magic wand to solve the issue of retention quickly but I do have a few ideas and I hope that if you give it some thought, more ideas will come from you! I'd like to talk about this in some length at our Friday meeting. Is that OK? Thanks everyone. Let's be caring out there."

Maddy, Murray and Razia stood up and left the office. Sobia returned to her desk. She opened her drawer and looked at her mobile. There was a short but sweet message from Simon.

Love you too xxx

The phone returned to its proper place, she headed off to the Reception Area smiling at the sliding doors.

"Judy, I'm just going to speak to chef for a few minutes. Give me a ring if you need me."

"Will do," said Judy who was immersed in admin work on her computer.

Sobia made her way to the first floor where the main kitchen was situated. Although breakfast was generally over for the residents, apart from a few very late risers, the kitchen was a hive of activity. Pots, pans and plates were being stacked in the dishwashers, cakes were being made for visitors to enjoy in the café and the residents' lunch was being prepped.

The head chef had only recently joined the home and Sobia was keen to keep him. He was good, he treated his team well and catered well for the different culinary needs of the residents. Sobia made it her job each day, until he had really settled in, to see if he was enjoying his role and if there was anything she could help him with - other than cooking!

After positive feedback Sobia left the chef to get on with his many plate-spinning jobs. She made her way back to her office which took over twenty minutes by the time she'd talked to more staff and residents on the way back to her desk but she couldn't put it off any longer - electronic paper work beckoned.

Over the next six hours Sobia's open door meant that her desk work was punctuated with incoming and outgoing phone calls, informal and formal conversations with staff, chats with residents and their family or friends. She stretched her legs by having lunch on the first floor with a small group of ladies who didn't really know who she was. It suited Sobia to be out of the real world for twenty minutes and to be invited back in time by the ladies' conversation into a simplified world of their past childhood in the present.

Sometime after five o'clock Sobia started the process of packing up and leaving work. At about ten to six she had finished ticking off the essential elements on her to-do list and spoken to the lead member of staff who would cover until the night shift arrived. Sobia, of course, was always in charge, but this week Maddy was the first to be called at night if there was a problem. Sobia and Maddy alternated this responsibility, but thankfully for both of them, there was rarely a problem that couldn't be dealt with by the staff in-house.

Sobia headed home and while driving decided what meal she could make for her and Simon. It had to be something that could stay on a low heat in the oven or on the hob as Simon could never be precise about the time he would arrive home.

In fact Simon arrived home only a little after seven-thirty and by nine, they were relaxing together on the settee, having eaten too much risotto, followed by the joint activity of stacking the dish washer and tidying the kitchen.

They were drinking their mugs of coffee and Sobia was lying across Simon's lap when she suddenly said, "I was thinking."

"Oh no! You've been thinking. That only means one thing...I'm in trouble somehow," said Simon stoking Sobia's cheek.

Sobia smiled. "Haven't you realised by now, you're always in trouble; it's just matter of how often I point it out."

"And I thought I was perfect. I can't think how I could have caused you any concerns or problems when all the other women in my life have always said I was a wonderful human being." Simon tried and failed to look earnest.

"Of course you are my darling," Sobia said sarcastically, reaching up and patting him on his head. "If you will let me tell you what I was thinking, Mr Perfect, then I might let you show me what a wonderful kisser you are. Deal?"

"Deal."

"I was actually thinking that neither of us have had a real break from work. How do you feel about taking a holiday somewhere?"

"Sounds good to me. It's funny you should mention holidays. I was saying to someone in the office the other day that I ought to have a holiday soon or I'll miss out on my entitlement and then of course I forgot all about it. Work stuff just gets in the way."

"I know. The same at Mercy. I make sure everyone else takes their holidays and I haven't really had more than a couple of days off here and there since I moved down here from Saltburn."

"That's decided then. Let's book some time off and go somewhere. Where do you fancy?" asked Simon.

"I really don't mind as long as Elderflower can't contact us."

"That's settled then. I'll book a flight on the next Space Shuttle. Seriously, do you want to go abroad or on a cruise or somewhere in the UK? I really don't mind."

"How would you feel about a driving holiday around England and Scotland? Staying in some nice hotels along the way. Or is that too much like your day-to-day job?"

"No, not at all. I love driving. And you can share the driving if you want. Have you got any ideas where you might want to go and what you'd like to see?"

"Well actually I have. You know me, I always have a cunning plan. I'd really like to see some more piers. I'd love to tour some areas of the coast and walk along some piers. I know most of them won't be as beautiful as Saltburn's but I would like to compare them. And if we can I'd like to see the pier you talked about in Invergordon and also spend a day or so in Saltburn-by-the-Sea," admitted Sobia sheepishly.

"Wow, you've got it all worked out, haven't you?" said Simon. "That sounds like a great deal of organising and driving and time off work."

"Not really. I have sort of done a bit of research already. I bought this book on *Amazon* called *Walking Over The Waves* and if we had a fortnight off work we could easily do five or six piers in that time and see some interesting places along the way. What do you think?"

"What do I think? I think you should have been a secret agent or at the very least a travel agent! You're a sneaky little so and so. You've had this in mind for a while, have you not?"

"I might have," Sobia said, a guilty grin on her face. "And I am now in a position to pay my way. We can go half and halves on the holiday. Well? Shall I carry on planning our grand tour or would you rather slob about on a cruise ship for a couple of weeks?"

"As much as I like the idea of slobbing, I think I'll opt for peace and harmony with a pier-to-pier vacation. I'm good to go. We need to look at a couple of weeks we could take off."

"How about in September, when all the children are back in school? Most of my staff with school-aged kids will want August off so I can't really take leave then. How about you?"

"That's not such a factor for me. September is fine. It gives us a few months to sort the itinerary out. Let's do it then," Simon said and gently brought Sobia's head up from his lap to kiss her."

"Not bad, Mr Perfect, but I think you need more practice!"

On Friday morning the senior team met in Sobia's office. The intention was to discuss the retention of staff but as with every Friday meeting the four of them started by reporting to each other their progress with their own key performance indicators. Each week Murray, Razia, Maddy and Sobia would have to send a report to someone in head office showing if they were meeting their targets against their key performance indicators. Once a fortnight they would be rung up by their external line manager to discuss their reports and presumably each of those external line managers would have to report on their own KPIs to someone even higher up the chain of command. Even Simon had his own KPIs and his own line manager. No-one in the Elderflower organisation, that Sobia or Simon had ever talked to, could see the benefits of this weekly time-wasting exercise, but there became a blind acceptance that this was the most efficient and effective way to keep everyone on their toes. Simon had flippantly said to Sobia one Thursday night while they both had their laptops on their laps filling in their progress forms, half-watching the television at the same time, that he suspected that although the CEO of Elderflower had all of these spreadsheets regularly sent to his computer, that his first and only response to all of this performance data was to press DELETE.

Sobia asked the small group to quickly run through their targets and progress to see if there were any red flags in amongst the eighty or so KPIs. Sobia's purpose was not to put her team members under the microscope but to ensure that no one person could be criticised. They had decided early on as a team that they would sink or swim together and not be picked off by people who didn't understand the workings of Mercy House. It made Sobia despair that the managers right at the top of the organisation just wanted *positive data* produced by its worker bees and didn't seem to care how long it took to generate it or if it was at the expense of the time that should be given to the elderly people they all worked for. Once or twice when they closed down their laptops for the night Sobia had expressed to Simon her discomfort at the way the senior, senior, senior management of Elderflower worked and Simon, as a senior, senior manager had to agree. Recently, when moaning about the way things were done, they had ended up talking about doing a better job themselves, the two of them running an independent care home and then as the conversation continued, they would back off the idea when they considered how difficult and infuriating it would be.

On other evenings Simon and Sobia would snuggle up on the settee without laptops and agree that they were both very lucky. Not only had they found each other but both had rewarding jobs. However, this made them feel very guilty at times. Sobia and particularly Simon, were on good money, lived together in a relatively fancy house with two cars and yet many of the staff who worked for Elderflower were not able to save any money from one week to the next. Sobia found it hard to justify her comparatively high wage compared to many of her staff at Mercy House and she felt a little embarrassed that the residents at the home were not only paying for their bed and board but making a healthy contribution to her wages too. Simon tried his best to assuage Sobia's guilt but it had been a devil on her shoulder that she couldn't shake off since the time when she was the only paid employee running the café and shop in Saltburn.

Sobia was uneasy when it came to seeming inequalities and unfairness. Even though she agreed with the notion of meritocracy she felt that these two jobs had been gifted to her. Whenever she expressed this to Simon, he would always say that it was good karma after the years she suffered with bad karma. He would also remind her that her life was far from perfect and complete because her boys were missing and that was the worst karma of all. Sobia had to agree. Without her earnings, she couldn't afford to fund the search for her boys.

"So, who wants to start?" said Sobia.

"I will if you like," said Maddy. "I know you guys will take the micky when I start to talk about my days teaching sport but here goes. Everybody likes to feel as if they're noticed at work, recognised for what they do well and rewarded..."

Murray started to shuffle in his seat at the mention of reward. Sobia saw him about to speak and with her eyes she silenced him while Maddy was in full flow.

"I know we can't shower everybody with extra pay but we can give a weekly or monthly award to a member of staff who has performed well or done something above and beyond the norm or the expected..."

"So how do we decide?" asked Raz. "Won't it look like a fix if Sobia just gives out an award every so often?"

"Well I think it shouldn't be Sobia or us who decide. It should be the staff themselves. Anybody on the staff can nominate anybody else."

"And what do you have in mind for prizes?" asked Murray trying to sound non-committal.

"If everybody on the staff tells Sobia what they would like as a prize, up to say £20, however that does not include cash, then the person with the most nominations each week or whatever is bought and awarded the gift. Some examples could be two tickets for the cinema or a food voucher from M&S or a really nice box of chocolates. They could also get a certificate and we could put their photo on the main noticeboard each time....we just need a bunch of nomination forms and a drop box for staff to post their nominations in."

"Sounds good, Maddy. Murray, Raz, what do you think?"

"I like the idea. It's a small thing and, let's be honest, it won't be the answer to retaining staff but it is a step in the right direction."

"I agree," said Murray. "How often do you want to give out *Above and Beyond Awards*?"

"I would suggest monthly. It gives everyone a chance to nominate and be nominated," said Sobia. "Thanks Maddy. Anyone else?"

"My suggestion is similar to Maddy's and is again a way of staff feeling valued, said Razia. "We expect our carers and nurses to sit with our residents while they eat in the café or restaurant and either watch or help them eat while chatting with them. Then we give the staff half an hour off during their shifts to escape to the staff room and eat the sandwich that they made at home. Well, why doesn't Mercy House pay for meals for its staff? If they have to eat with the residents let's create a situation where everybody is enjoying a meal together. The staff should still have their own breaks but they are still working while they are in the eating areas. It's just a nice way to reward our staff."

"I agree, but do you think some staff would take advantage of the idea of free food?" asked Sobia who had already warmed to the idea.

"No, I don't think so and any way, there's always food left over. We just have to make sure that the residents are served first and the staff can choose from what's left. I hate seeing food wasted and it may be that some of the staff don't want to eat very much but at least we're offering them something and again they may feel a little more valued," replied Razia.

"Murray," said Sobia, "are you OK with this?"

"As long as we can't be accused of eating the food that the residents are paying for, I think it would be a good way to create a better atmosphere in the dining room. I might even take advantage of the deal myself."

"Oh blimey!" joked Maddy. "The bean counter is going to eat beans with the rest of us!"

They laughed and then Sobia brought them to semi-order with her suggestion for five-minute one-to-ones each week with staff. The four of them would divide up the staff each month and create an informal time when the staff had time to talk to one of them about anything connected to Mercy House. Sobia emphasised that this was not to be part of the performance management or appraisal process; it was not to be led by management; it was a chat and a way for staff to vent or point out if they had any issues or if Mercy House could do anything better. The conversations would not be recorded but if members of staff wanted anything to be fed back to Sobia, then it would be.

They all agreed with Sobia's idea and divided up the staff in readiness for a Monday start. Sobia would send an All Staff email later this morning outlining the changes.

The meeting finished; Murray went back to the office he shared with Maddy while the three women went walkabout.

Sobia managed to get back to her office by the middle of the afternoon, phoned her line manager at head office to quickly give an update on the week and then spent some time assessing her performance against her targets. There were, of course, several interruptions during that time, which always started with "Can I have a quick word?" or "You haven't got five minutes have you?" She gave herself an ultimatum that she would leave by six o'clock and be home before Simon. She had enough time to finish a couple of emails and say her goodbyes and good lucks to her staff before having a free weekend. She looked up from her screen to see Maddy in the door way.

"I'm off Sobia. I need to familiarise myself with my family. With a bit of luck, I should have a husband and two children waiting for me at home. And I hope you enjoy your weekend." Maddy had an amused expression on her face. "Oh, by the way I found this dodgy individual in Reception. He claims to fancy you and wants to sleep with you." She moved aside and let Simon poke his head around the door.

"Hello, fancy meeting you here at this time of night. I've been at home for ages so I thought I'd come and see if you were alright."

"Hello, sweetie. That's very nice of you but you could have called. I've been in my office for the last few hours. I thought you were working late tonight."

"There was a change of plans," said Simon, turning to Maddy and they both grinned.

"Well, I'd better go and leave you two love birds alone. I have my own nest to find. By the way, remember I'm on call. I've got the Mercy House mobile so you don't have to worry about this place at all. I'll see you next week," Maddy said to Sobia and then turning to Simon half-whispered "bring her back safely, we need her here."

And with that Maddy was gone.

"That was odd. I don't know what she means," said Sobia, packing away the mess on her desk.

"I do," admitted Simon. He sat down opposite her. "I'm afraid our plans for a quiet relaxing weekend have been changed!"

"Why, who's changed them? Have you got to work this weekend?"

"No, neither of us are working this weekend. But we do have to jump in my car very soon and get moving," said Simon looking serious.

"Sorry, I don't understand. Where are we going?"

"Oh, didn't I tell you? We're going to Saltburn for the weekend." Now Simon had a broad grin on his face.

"But...but..."

"It's all sorted. We're going right now. I've packed all of your clothes, your make up and your other bits and pieces. We're leaving your car here. I'm driving us up to *The Brockley Hall Hotel* for a few days. Don't panic. Maddy knows all about this. Tomorrow I've arranged for some of your old work colleagues to join us for dinner in the evening at the hotel. I don't know about you but I think it's time to be re-acquainted with Saltburn, the pier, the funicular railway and above all, some very important people from your past that you haven't seen for a while."

Sobia didn't know what to say, the only thing she could do was start crying with happiness and love.

Saltburn-by-the-Sea

Simon parked up in the hotel car park a little after nine o'clock. There had been no need to have the radio on or play music on the journey as Sobia was so excited that she wouldn't stop talking about Saltburn and her old friends. Every so often she would squeeze Simon's clutch leg and tell him how much she loved him. She admitted to Simon at one point on the journey that she couldn't remember anyone ever surprising her with anything as thoughtful as this ever before.

They left their luggage in the car and made their way to Reception. Simon booked them in and they were led straight to a table for two in the conservatory area of the dining room. The manager on duty made a point of introducing herself while they were considering what to eat from the plush menu.

"Mr Kirby?" said the well-dressed, well-fed lady. "We've spoken on the phone at various times during the week. Everything has been sorted and we hope it's all to your satisfaction. And you must be Sobia?"

"Hello," said Sobia shaking the manager's hand." Yes Simon...Mr Kirby surprised me earlier on this evening with this lovely break. I used to work up here a couple of years ago."

"Yes, I know. I really hope you enjoy your trip down memory lane." With that she summoned a waitress to take their order.

They were hungry and thirsty after their long and excited journey. They pretty much licked the patterns off their plates and dishes and managed to consume a full bottle of red wine. Sobia was high on life before she started to drink and as their heads were already swimming, they decided to take it steady and enjoy a coffee in the lounge area of the bar before taking their suitcases up to their room.

Sitting by the bay window in the lounge on a two-seater settee Simon said "How do you feel?"

"Happier than I have ever felt and drunker than I have ever felt. I really didn't drink alcohol until I met you. You have had an effect on me, Simon Kirby. A really good effect. Since I met you I have felt differently about things. Sometimes I can't stop smiling. Sobia said it slowly, conscious that she was at risk of slurring her words in a public place.

"I hope it's not just the alcohol that makes you smile?"

"It's not. It's you. You have been so kind to me, so loving and patient with me. I know I have a lot of baggage but you never complain. I am a very lucky woman," Sobia took Simon's hand and squeezed it hard.

"I'm the lucky one. But I do agree you have some baggage. Do you know how long it took me to pack your suitcases this afternoon? Mind you, one of the suitcases is just full of sexy underwear!"

Sobia smiled, "talking of suitcases and underwear shouldn't we get the bags out of the car and find our room. I am interested to see what else you have packed for me. I hope there are at least some sensible clothes and shoes for us to go walking tomorrow."

"Oh, maybe we'll need to find a clothes shop tomorrow morning. I didn't think sensible - only thought sexy!"

"Don't worry. I know just the place to get some good quality inexpensive clothes!" said Sobia.

Simon and Sobia woke the next morning wrapped in each other's bodies. Their room was evocatively decorated and fitted with period pieces from a time before flat packs and MDF. It had an old-fashioned scooped bath in the corner of the room with a folding screen. Sobia plumped for the bath while Simon opted for a shower in the ensuite. Of course Simon had packed plenty of sensible and practical clothes and shoes for any and every occasion and it felt as if he had packed for a two week vacation rather than a two-day visit.

After a generous breakfast they were set up for a morning of re-discovery. Sobia had the morning planned and Simon let her lead the way. She was desperate to see the shop and café but decided to wait until lunchtime to hopefully see more staff then. They first walked the short distance to the funicular railway that took them to sea level. They walked through the amusement arcade along the pier to the end. Simon took a few photos of Sobia staring out to sea and smiling at the camera and then he looked back at the town and took some shots of the railway and the huts and cafes along the sea front.

Simon diplomatically left Sobia on her own for a few minutes to let the memories come back and to summon the ghosts from her past. He re-joined her after a while, wrapped his arms around her and told her he loved her. Sobia wiped a few tears from her eyes and kissed him. They walked back along the pier in silence, holding hands and thinking of their futures that would, from now on, be one future together.

They strolled along the sea front and back up to the main street. Sobia gave Simon a guided tour of her past haunts. The laundrette she used, the local supermarket she visited almost daily, the apartment building she lived in, the chocolate shop, the library and the cash machine she used. Simon loved to see Sobia happily re-living some of the good memories she had from her Saltburn days although he knew it hadn't always been a joyous time for her, particularly at the beginning. He was hoping that this would be a cathartic and cleansing weekend for her.

"Are you ready, Sobia?" Simon nodded towards the café and shop she had managed in a previous life.

"I'm ready. I'm ready as Sobia. I'm no longer Sara."

As Sobia led the way into the café, she saw Nina, now the manager, smiling from the counter. Sobia found out later that while she was talking to the shop assistants in Chocolini's Simon had texted a pre-warned Nina to say that they were on their way.

They hugged in the middle of the café and shed a few tears of joy in seeing each other again. Then Sobia became aware that standing behind Nina were Janet and Tom who also demanded lengthy hugs and kisses. Nina had also organised other staff who were working in the shop next door or who weren't on volunteer duty to come and say hello. For the next half an hour or so Simon let Sobia be shown around the two units by Nina and make conversation with some of the old regulars who had popped in to see her.

Eventually, Sobia and Nina sat down with Simon at a table and drank tea and consumed pieces of buttered toast that tasted as good as ever.

"Is Graham OK?" asked Sobia.

"He's not too bad," said Nina. "He comes in to the café with Doreen from time to time but he's getting quite forgetful now. Doreen stopped him working here about six months after you went down to Four Oaks. He and Doreen are coming to the meal tonight though, so you'll see them then."

"Oh that's good. And how is your mom? Has the care home in Saltburn worked out?"

"Yeah, really good thanks. She's as happy as Larry...and so are the rest of us. It's given the whole family peace of mind."

"That's what a good care home should provide," said Simon.

Nina nodded and then asked Simon, "And how is Sara, or should I say Sobia, getting on down at Mercy House?"

"Sobia is doing a brilliant job, just as Sara did here!" said Simon.

"I'm so sorry, Nina," said Sobia. "I know I emailed you after I left to tell you about my real name and my old life, but this is the first time we have seen each other face-to-face. I hope you have forgiven me for lying to you."

"It doesn't matter and it doesn't matter what you're called, you're a special person to me."

"And to me," chimed in Simon.

Sobia started welling up again. She would have to pop into Boots to buy more mascara at this rate.

After more hugs and kisses Sobia and Simon said their au revoirs and headed for the next part of the tour – a few shops where she hoped the people who used to run them would still be behind the counters, followed by a quick visit to the Italian Gardens and finally the site of the Halfpenny Bridge.

Sobia had packed the day with sight-seeing and some of it felt a bit rushed but she knew that tomorrow they would have another chance to experience her past at a slower pace. But now they needed to get ready for the get-together. They went back to their room and Sobia had another soak in the bath while Simon showered and then scrubbed her back. He toyed with the idea of joining her in the bath but was worried that if he got in, the water would get out. So he lay on the bed, watched the football results and *Pointless*. It would have been so easy to fall asleep but he stayed awake and every so often found himself grinning inanely to himself.

By seven they were dressed in smart outfits and they went downstairs to welcome their guests and direct them to the long table in the conservatory reserved for the Kirby party. In an undertone Sobia asked uneasily if Elderflower were funding this weekend in any way but Simon reassured her that the hotel and the meal tonight were on him and she should not fret about the cost again while they were here.

The table for twenty was one shy of full. Sobia later reflected that it felt like a wedding breakfast but with Simon and Sobia sitting in the middle of the table facing one another. To one side of her was Nina, with her partner sitting by Simon and on the other side of Sobia was Graham with Doreen across the table. Sobia was delighted that Graham was not only able to come to the meal but seemed able to remember so much about the time he worked at the café. It confused him a little that some were calling Sara Sobia but she didn't try to explain for fear of confusing him even more.

The evening was a wonderful success. Successful for Nina and Simon who had organised it but even more so for Sobia. Simon noted that Sobia had never looked so happy. He was hoping even happier times would be just around the corner.

The evening came to an end with the inevitable hugs and kisses, thank yous, the exchange of contact details and more kisses and hugs.

Sobia and Simon rolled into bed at about one-thirty very late for them. They both agreed that they wanted to round off the evening in sensual fashion but had to admit they had eaten and drunk too much and that although their stomachs were full, the rest of their bodies were running on empty.

They woke late from their slumbers not feeling much like breakfast but went down to the dining room intent on drinking a vat full of coffee.

"What would you like to do today, sweetheart?" asked Simon.

"Well, I would really like to do my old Sunday morning ritual if that is OK. Go down to the sea front and then have a stroll along the pier and…"

"I know, speak to the boys. That's fine. I'll walk down with you and then I'll give you some time to be on your own with the boys."

"Thank you, Simon. I love you so much," said Sobia, squeezing his hand for the twenty third time that weekend. "Is it OK if I just powder my nose before we go down to the pier?"

"Of course, I'll wait here for you, I'm going to have another coffee and I've a couple of texts to send. Would you bring my coat down when you come? Thanks." He passed her the room key. He poured one more drink, sent a couple of short but vital texts and waited for the day to unfold.

By a little after eleven o'clock Simon and Sobia were at the amusement arcade end of the pier. Simon hurried Sobia through the families playing on the gaming machines and on to the pier. Ten yards up the pier, he stopped and told her that he would wait in the arcade for ten minutes or so and then walk down to her.

Sobia hugged him. "Thank you. You know this means a lot to me."

"I know. I love you. I always will. You know that don't you?" said Simon welling up.

"I do." She kissed him, turned and made her way up to the end of the pier.

At the end of the pier she was alone. It was an ideal opportunity to speak to her boys across the seas but five minutes later her mobile rang.

She took it out of her handbag. "Hello?"

"Sobia, it's me, Ajay. How are you, Sis?" said Sobia's brother.

"Hi Ajay, I thought you were going to phone me next week?"

"I was, but we've had some developments in the last week or so and I wanted to keep you up to date. We tracked down the boys."

"Oh my god! Oh my god! Are they OK? Are they alright? Did you get to speak to them? Did he allow it?" shouted Sobia down the phone.

"Yes, we did and they're fine. They wanted you to know that they both love you and really want to see you."

"Oh Ajay, you have no idea how long I have waited for that news. Thank you so much. Thank you for never giving up in your search for them. I love you brother…what did you mean WE?"

"Oh just some friends and me. We found him and the boys in a little village after a tip off."

"Will he let them see me? Can I get out there to see them?" Sobia was sobbing and screaming with elation.

"Sorry, Sis, I can't make out what you're saying?"

"Sorry Ajay, I said will he let me see the boys."

"Long story short, Sis. He had no choice. We managed to persuade him to let the boys go. He won't be bothering you ever again. The boys are coming back to you. They're coming home to you."

"Oh god, I can't believe it! But...but how did you make it happen?"

"It's amazing what a few threats and a chunk of money can do!"

"Ajay, you didn't hurt him, did you?

"Just about as much as he hurt you; maybe a little more!"

"But how did you get the money to pay him off? You don't have much yourself!"

"Ah, well, that would be another friend who helped you. I think you know him quite well. Simon Kirby...I think you have heard of him, haven't you Sis?"

"My Simon?"

"Yes, your Simon. Sorry, Sis. I must go, I have a journey to make with the boys."

"I don't understand. What journey? Where are you? The phone call...it sounds so clear...it usually sounds much worse than..." The phone went dead.

Sobia stared at the phone for a second and then shoved it in her pocket. She needed to speak to Simon. Thank him for everything he had done for her.

She spoke to the sea one last time and said "I will see you soon my lovely boys. One day soon."

She turned and walked briskly back down the pier to find Simon. To thank him. To kiss him. To tell him that she loved him.

From a distance as she walked towards the amusement arcade, she could see four figures half-running towards her. Instinctively, she knew who the shapes were - Simon, Ajay and her two precious boys.

She started running towards them, crying with happiness and love.

CHAPTER 7

Charles Briggs was lying in a strange bed. Nothing new there. Charlie was no stranger to lying about in a stranger's bed. He was slightly aware of his surroundings as he drifted in and out of consciousness. He'd had a rough night but soon would feel like getting up, having a drink and some breakfast. His half-opened eyes closed again.

He woke again sometime later. His mouth was really dry. He must have the flu or something. He couldn't keep his eyes open. He would try to sleep it off.

Sometime later he tried to open his eyes again. He felt hot. He must have a temperature. His bedroom ceiling looked strange.

He woke again when he started to cough. His chest hurt. He thought he could hear other noises. His bed started to tilt upwards. A cold flannel was wiped across his face. In time the coughing stopped and he fell back to sleep and continued to live this scary half-dream that seemed half-real.

"I'll be back later," said a woman in the room.

. . .

Charles woke up one fine day many years before that and lived his first recorded and remembered memory. It was his seventh birthday. His folks had bought him a football strip. Not just any old football strip but his favourite team's home strip. The team he had supported from when he was in the womb. The team his mom and dad supported. The team he later went to see with his dad while his mother looked after his younger sister. Birmingham City. Later he would curse his father for taking him to St. Andrews to see a Birmingham home match. Why couldn't he have taken his son to see Manchester United or Liverpool? But no, Birmingham City became his team and their nickname – the Blues – became an apt description of the pain and suffering he would endure for the rest of his life supporting a team of mediocre footballers who at best overachieved occasionally and at worst were an embarrassment to watch. Admittedly, the family home was closer to Birmingham's ground than pretty much every other professional team but Charlie's dad could and should have given him a choice between the Blues, the Villa and West Brom to support. Looking at their success rates and trophies won over the years it became another reason to resent his father.

But back then, captured on video, was Charles ripping away the wrapping paper to discover the full home kit - the blue shirt, white shorts and blue socks. He beamed with joy. Within ten minutes he was being filmed by his dad in the back garden playing centre forward for Birmingham City, dribbling and scoring amazing goals between a couple of cricket stumps. His mother and sister watched Charlie from the kitchen window as they prepared the family lunch. Egg and chips was what the birthday boy had asked for. His mother had made a birthday cake but that would be unveiled at the party that started at three o'clock. Charlie had chosen ten friends to share in his celebrations. He had invited all boys, and all of those boys were keen footballers. It was fairly clear to Charlie's mom and dad that most of the afternoon the party would be taking place in their back garden and that it would be the flower beds that would be damaged rather than the wallpaper and furniture.

Over the next few years, Charlie became a sports fanatic, he loved not only football, but any sport that involved a ball or any competitive activity that involved running, jumping, throwing or hitting. Throughout his primary and secondary school years he coasted in most of the academic subjects. He could do reading, writing and arithmetic, he could do geography, history and science but he could really do sports, sports and more sports at school. He also played for teams outside school – football and rugby during the winter and cricket and tennis in the summer. His parents, but particularly his dad, was Charles' number one fan and his number one taxi driver taking him and supporting him on the side lines on a Saturday and Sunday morning. He was watched and scouted from time to time by professional teams but sadly he was never given a chance to sign a contract for any one sport. He was and eventually accepted the fact that he was a good all-rounder but not a shining star in one particular sport.

By the time Charlie started in the sixth form studying sports sciences, biology and psychology, his body and looks had developed and he soon became one of the popular members of his school year. The other boys in his classes and teams secretly wanted to be him and most of the girls were less secret about being with him. Charlie spent his two years in further education being physically exhausted balancing the exertions of a hectic sport and sex life. Somehow, he managed to scrape good enough grades that would get him into a Teacher Training College. His 'A' level results were not high enough to go to university so he decided one night that he would be a PE teacher. After all, PE teachers didn't have to do any marking, all teachers had about a quarter of the year off work and the Girls' PE teachers were often fit in every sense.

It was only when he started teacher training than Charlie realised that it might be a harder job than he'd thought. There were things to learn, essays to write and a considerable amount of seriousness and maturity was needed. These were two words rarely used to describe Charlie. Within weeks of starting at college his peers had nicknamed him "Good Time Charlie" and when they thought about him what came to mind were images of him streaking across a football pitch wearing only a traffic cone or in the student bar drinking his friends under the table while dressed in a wet suit.

Charlie was also quick-witted. He was the first to come up with a joke or a daft remark, but to his credit, he was always first to make fun of himself. He was ideal company, in lectures, in a bar, in a library or in student accommodation. The only company he wasn't keen on was his own. He made every effort to be with others so that he could be the class clown, the joker and the star of the show to hide his own self-doubts and insecurities to the point where he didn't know what they were anymore.

To everyone else Charlie was the person to be with. When he undertook his first teaching practice, when most of his friends were worried about teaching kids only a few years younger than themselves, he had won his classes over in the first few moments. The teenage boys thought he was funny and *safe* while the teenaged girls viewed him from afar and fell under his trance. He passed all three teaching practices with flying colours and was told by two of the schools that they would be interested in offering him a permanent job once he had finished his course. He was flattered but as with everything in Charlie's life he found it difficult to plan that far ahead. All he wanted to know was when and where was the next party or match and who was he going to spend his time with.

Good Time Charlie, was not entirely hedonistic, not that Charlie knew or cared what the word meant. He made some of his *good time* to be with his parents and sister when he could. He loved his mom and dad. They were like chalk and cheese but complemented each other well. His father was an engineer who left school at sixteen and joined a large car company on the shop floor, rising through the ranks to manage that shop floor. He was a practical man. A man of few soft words but the words he spoke were sensible and measured. His mother, on the other hand, was all words and smiles. She was first and foremost a wife and mother but she also found time to work part-time as a secretary. Charlie had always regarded his mom and dad as having traditional almost old-fashioned parental roles. His father was the serious bread-winner and his mother the primary care and love giver. He knew they both loved him and his sister but showed it in different ways. What was certain was that they were fiercely protective of their children. Woe betide anyone of any age saying a bad word against either of them. This was of course commendable, but it did lead to Charlie, in particular, getting away with murder. He could always convince his mother that he was led astray by school friends and that he was not the only one in detention, whereas the reality would often be that he was the lead protagonist and that he was in solitary detention for his misdemeanours.

As they both went to the same secondary school, his sister knew the real Charlie, but was always loyal and backed up his stories to his parents. Elizabeth, or Lizzie as she liked to be called from a young age was three years younger that Charlie. She was a very bright girl, a little more serious than her big brother but a good mate to Charlie all the way through school. Even though both had their own friends, nothing could break the bond they had with each other. Charlie was protective of his *little sis* and Lizzie worshipped *big bro*. When Lizzie started dating boys in year 10 while he was in the sixth form, he would keep a watchful eye on her boyfriends' motives and hands. Lizzie, though, found it difficult to keep track of Charlie's relationships but in their private moments together, out of ear-shot of their parents, she would sit him down on his bed and recap on the sex education lessons he had fallen asleep in at the back of his class.

When Charlie left home to go through the motions of training to be a PE teacher at college in Bristol and Lizzie was in the sixth form, they would speak on the phone at least once a week. Charlie would adopt the role of parent occasionally telling her to not get distracted by boys and that her A levels were more important than anything. Lizzie would spend her time on the phone telling Charlie to go steady on drink and women and to phone mom and dad once they had hung up. They would laugh and tease each other because they were perfectly at ease with each other. It often felt that if they had not been brother and sister they would have made a perfect couple.

Charlie grew up quickly after college when he realised that he needed to earn money which meant he had to get a teaching job in a school. Lizzie was now away at university and going back to live with his parents felt like a backward step. He accepted a position in a large secondary school in Derby and rented a room in a run-down outskirt called Normanton. He could drive back to see his folks in the second-hand car his dad had generously bought him. It took less than an hour and he could visit his sister at Cambridge University in about two hours.

Charlie with all the arrogance of youth believed that life as a teacher would be a breeze and, on that breeze, it would be plain sailing. He imagined that every teenager at the school would like exercise, they would like being taught how to play sports properly and they would like him. To be fair, it turned out that quite a few pupils did, but there were a significant number who didn't want to play ball. Some of these lads were fine in other lessons and with other teachers but for Mr Briggs they were not having it. These lads tested Charlie to the limit most weeks and enjoyed playing the only game in town - taunting the new PE teacher.

Charlie would retreat to his digs most nights and want to cry, scream and write a letter of resignation. He planned his lessons differently; he tried a different behaviour management system and he got teaching advice off anyone in the school who would listen to him. The trouble was that most of the classroom-based teachers thought that teaching PE in the gym or outside on the playing field was a doddle and couldn't quite sympathise with his situation. They were stuck trying to get thirty teenage boys and girls concentrating on Maths or History in a confined hot bed of testosterone and hormones. The Maths, History and other teachers of academic subjects couldn't believe that teaching PE was on a par with their work or that the pupils might not be motivated to do it.

Fortunately, a couple of experienced PE teachers did remember when they were NQTs and did sympathise. Charlie's Head of Department, who had all of the pupils eating out of his hand, was his greatest help and eased Charlie's first year by taking some of the reluctant and recalcitrant pupils out of his groups and into his own. He also kept giving Charlie pep talks, as if he was his own personal trainer, which motivated him and made him believe that he could be successful at the school. It paid off and by the first week in Charlie's second year of teaching at the school, he was no longer the new teacher to test. Mr Briggs, according to the pupils was *solid* and *a laugh*.

By the third year Charlie had got a decent flat in Littleover and was Mr Popular with pupils and staff. He organised Friday night sporting and drinking sessions with some of the staff and was well-liked and appreciated in the staffroom for his personality and commitment to the school.

One aspect of his life that had not progressed as well was his personal life – namely women. He had not wanted to pursue a relationship with any of the women on the staff as he felt it may be awkward and he didn't have many friends in Derby that he could go out clubbing with. So, every other weekend Charlie would go to visit his sister in Cambridge. He would sober up on Saturday morning and then drive down. The routine was that he would treat Lizzie to a three-course meal and then they would go drinking with some of her friends in a local pub, he would sleep on her floor and then take his sister for breakfast before making his way back to his flat.

"So, what do you think of my friends?" asked Lizzie tucking into the full Brexit.

"They're a good bunch," said Charlie. "Are they all on your floor in the halls?"

"No, some have rooms along the corridor and some are studying science with me and I met them in lectures. A couple of the guys play squash with me on a Wednesday night but we all somehow just started hanging out together on Saturday nights."

"Isn't it awkward having your big brother tagging along when you have all of your mates with you?

"God no! I like it and so do the others. You keep us grounded talking about the real world of work and you keep us entertained with your sports and teaching anecdotes. I like seeing my big bro from time to time."

"Especially if he pays for your drinks and food!" Charlie retorted, a glint in his eye. "Don't some of them want to be with their girlfriends or boyfriends on a Saturday night?"

"Well, there are a few of them that have a regular partner. There's one couple who come out together with us on a Saturday night but you wouldn't know they were any more than friends. Some have boyfriends or girlfriends back at home but most of them are too busy studying to have serious relationships and on a Saturday they just like to taste freedom and alcohol! Remember Charles, we're Cambridge students and we didn't come here to enjoy ourselves. We are this country's future!" Having to wipe strawberry milkshake from her lips rather ruined the serious note she was trying for..

"I see. I feel comforted in the knowledge that the world is going to be in safe hands when you and your mates inherit it. It's just that last night you all looked like the sort of deadbeat boozers I used to hang around with at college."

"Maybe, bro, but my friends have got a few brain cells floating around in their skulls whereas your old mates just had beer in and on their brains."

"True, very true. But I'm a reformed man now. I'm an upstanding citizen. I set an example to our children. I teach the future."

"You mean you show kids how to kick a ball or run around a field!" Lizzie teased.

"Vital skills nowadays for any future politician or CEO!"

"I hated PE when I was at school. I didn't see the point."

"But you play squash now. You're clearly a late developer."

"I only play squash because I fancy one of the guys in the club."

"Sis, that's outrageous. You swan about the squash court in your skimpy shorts and tee-shirt using an Olympic sport as an excuse to pull men. I disown you as a sister!" Charlie was trying not to smile. "Has it got you anywhere yet?"

"No, I'm afraid not. I may have to play naked next Wednesday to get him to notice me."

"Never mind, at least you're developing strong wrists. That's a quality most men like in women!"

"I don't know what you mean, bro. Anyway, talking of the opposite sex, how's your love life?"

"It's rubbish. I made a decision a year or so ago not to date any women on the staff and I'm just not meeting anyone outside school. I'm developing very strong wrists too!"

"Ugh! Thank you, bro, that's an image I won't be able to shake off for the rest of the day, if you see what I mean." Lizzie screwed her face up managing to smirk at the same time. "Well, fear not, my big brother. I have some good news for you. One of my friends fancies you!"

"OK. I'm intrigued. Is it the girl who drinks pints and wears rugby shirts?"

"Who said it was a girl? I didn't! As it happens, it's one of my girlfriends."

"So, which one?" asked Charlie, his interest piqued.

"I'm not telling you. Next time you come down you'll have to work it out for yourself."

Two weeks later Charlie visited Lizzie again.

The same schedule. Saturday morning Charlie recovered from the night before. Drove down to Cambridge in the afternoon. Treated his sister to a meal at his expense. Went to the pub with Lizzie's friends. Lizzie slept in her single bed. Charlie slept on the floor.

At some point during Sunday morning, the two of them were lying on their backs looking at her room's ceiling.

"Ugh, I drank too much last night," Lizzie moaned.

"Likewise. You and your friends are a bad influence on me. I would have drunk soda water all night if you hadn't introduced that drinking game," said Charlie. The words coming out of his mouth were as dry as a bone and needed toothpaste and water desperately.

"You fibber! I've never seen you take a soft drink in a pub in your life. You regard a pint of shandy as a non-alcoholic drink! Anyway, big bro, have you worked it out yet?"

"Worked what out? I haven't got any sober brain cells to work anything out just now."

"The friend of mine who fancies you," said Lizzie turning sideways in bed and staring down at her prone brother.

"No, you know me. I'm not great at reading signs, in fact, I'm not good at reading, compared to you. You'll have to give me a clue. All of your girlfriends on campus are really nice and a good laugh. They all seem really friendly. But if you mean, did I go around the group and ask them one by one if they fancied me, no I didn't. Even Good Time Charlie couldn't do that. Maybe I'm getting more reserved in my old age."

"You poor old man. What are you, twenty-four and you've lost the art of chatting up women? There's no hope for you. A singleton for the rest of your life."

Just then there was a knock on the door.

Lizzie shouted "Who is it?"

From the other side of the door they heard "It's Claire. Do you want to come for breakfast?"

"Yes, give us ten minutes and we'll be ready."

"OK."

Lizzie let Charlie use her tiny ensuite first. He took his overnight bag with him. First, he drank a gallon of water from the glass that Lizzie used to hold her toothpaste. Then he got rid of a gallon and a half of urine from last night. Finally he had a good wash, changed and brushed his teeth using his own brush and Lizzie's tooth paste.

Charlie lay on the bed and waited for Lizzie. She was half way through her ablutions when there was a knock on the door again.

Lizzie opened the ensuite door and shouted for Claire to come in.

"Oh, hi Charlie," said Claire.

"Good morning," said Charlie moving from the horizontal to a sitting position on Lizzie's bed. As he did so he quickly realised that Claire was, even through beer-goggled eyes, looking stunning for a Sunday morning. Her long brown hair looked perfectly brushed, her tight jeans and top were colour co-ordinated and she had recovered from last night's drinking to apply make-up accurately in all of the right places. Charlie, on the other hand, looked his usual rugged mess.

Lizzie came out of her bathroom also looking glamorous. "Hi Claire, shall we go to the Tasty Café on the high street for a bite to eat?"

"Sounds good," said Claire.

"Lead the way you two, I'm dying for a hot drink and a bacon butty," said Charlie.

As Lizzie locked her door, she paused and addressed Claire and Charlie. "Is it OK if you two go ahead, I just want to talk to my boyfriend first."

"Boyfriend! I didn't know you had a boyfriend, Sis?"

"Neither does he yet, but he will soon!" Lizzie, Claire and Charlie smiled. "I'll see you in a bit." As Lizzie turned to walk up the corridor, she winked at Claire who faintly blushed under her newly-applied blusher.

Two and a half hours later, Claire and Charlie were finishing off their third coffee having eaten their way through enough breakfast for six people. There was no sign of Lizzie as yet. After an hour or so Claire had received a text from Lizzie that supposedly told them she was still with the bloke from squash she fancied and would meet up with them soon. In reality the text from Lizzie had just said *How are things going?* Claire told Charlie that she would just say OK to Lizzie but instead replied *Great!*

Claire and Charlie sat across from each other at a four-seat table next to the window of the café on the high street but didn't notice any of the passers-by. They didn't notice or care about the other people in the café having a late breakfast or lunch. Instead they looked at each other, talked, smiled and laughed, drank coffee, ate food and looked at each other some more.

During this all-day breakfast, Charlie learnt that Claire was raised in Wythall in South Birmingham, she was one of three children, she didn't see her parents that often, she was in her last year studying criminology and her goal was to be a crime investigator in a police force somewhere in the country. She loved the outdoors, keeping fit, played various sports and liked listening to and watching live music. Charlie also learnt, but not from Claire herself, that she was very attractive and that he wanted to spend more time getting to know her. Claire, on the other hand listened to Charlie and gave the impression that she was learning a lot about him, when the truth was that she already knew a great deal about him from various conversations she had had with Lizzie over the last six weeks.

Eventually Lizzie arrived at the café. Charlie and Claire's natural conversation and their supernatural magic was broken temporarily by the third party but for the next hour or so the three of them managed to talk, laugh and drink more coffee. Lizzie explained how she got talking to a group of squash players, including the one she liked and that she had lost track of time. Claire couldn't look at Lizzie as she spun this yarn but Charlie seemed to believe it all, hook, line and sinker.

Back at Lizzie's room, Charlie collected his overnight bag, kissed his sister goodbye and then awkwardly kissed Claire goodbye saying that he would see them both again in a fortnight. Charlie left the two girls and headed to his car with a warm smile on his face.

Claire and Lizzie, on the other hand, spent the next hour in Lizzie's room talking about Charlie. Claire regressed to a fourteen-year-old excitedly telling Lizzie about her time with Charlie at the café. She outlined all of his positives and her feelings towards him while her cheeks burnt and other parts of her body stirred. Lizzie, diplomatically, refrained from giving Claire a slightly more realistic picture of her brother which would have included several areas of immediate concern and areas for future development. Instead, Lizzie listened and continued to offer help to her good friend in the tricky process of ensnaring her big but unaware brother. They planned the tactics for Stage Two of *Capture Charlie* in a fortnight's time. They would meet up alone in Claire's room next Sunday to refine the man trap as Lizzie was hoping to arrange a date for herself with the unsuspecting squash player.

As arranged, on the following Sunday morning, at a reasonable hour, Lizzie knocked on Claire's door to discuss *Capture Charlie Part 2*.Lizzie heard a muffled reply and walked in to find Claire still in bed looking flushed. Was her friend ill? She hadn't seen her last night. Lizzie had been out having fun with the squash player while her close friend was lying sick in bed on her own. Lizzie immediately felt concerned and guilty until she saw an upward movement from the lower half of the duvet culminating in a head poking out at the top. It was Charlie's head. His cheeks were also rather flushed.

"Well, well, well! What have we got here?" said Lizzie, sounding like a cross between a disappointed mother and a police detective. She found it hard not to smile at the two guilty red faces with the duvet covering their modesty. All that was on show was their heads, their hands grasping the duvet right up to their chins and their feet sticking out the bottom of the single bed.

"I was sure we arranged for you to come down next weekend. Did you get the date wrong?" asked Lizzie playfully.

"Sis, I got the date exactly right," Charlie said. "I didn't come early at all or did I Claire?"

"I don't remember you coming early all night," said Claire starting to laugh which opened the flood gates of mirth for them all.

After calming down and adjusting to the situation, Lizzie sat at the end of the bed amongst the feet and said to her brother, "Charlie, if you mess my best friend around, I'll find the sharpest pair of scissors in Cambridge and cut your dick off!"

"Oh, please don't!" said Charlie.

"Yes, please don't!" agreed Claire, blushing again. Inevitably they all burst out laughing again.

Over the next six months a new social schedule emerged for Charlie. One weekend he would visit Claire in Cambridge and alternate weekends Claire would take the train up to Derby. When Claire finished her finals, she moved up to Derby incrementally and by the time Charlie broke up for the school summer holidays they were officially living together. During the first six months as a couple they visited and enjoyed the approval of both sets of parents and became acquainted with each other's friends. Claire would start her police training in Nottingham in September which gave them several weeks off to go on holiday together.

The two Cs had discussed all sorts of possible holidays, from adventurous to exotic to lazy but they eventually decided and planned to do a four-week road trip mainly based around the north east of America. They would visit places and sights starting at Boston, Albany, Buffalo, Niagara Falls, Cleveland, Pittsburgh, Washington and finish off at New York.

Charlie funded the majority of the trip but Claire insisted that once she started earning she would pay him back. Charlie had teased her that he wanted re-numeration in various other ways and true to her word Claire obliged him in the build up to the holiday and in almost every motel room during the vacation. The road trip cemented their relationship, they talked and laughed, laughed and talked and even when they were both quiet, which was not often, they seemed to be tuned into each other. They took hundreds of photos of buildings, landscapes, American football and baseball stadia and of course the Falls. It was a tiring trip but when they handed back the hire car in New York they promised themselves a few days of relaxation before they caught their flight back to Gatwick.

They had managed to book a room in a hotel just off Times Square, close to Central Park. They shopped for presents and souvenirs for their families and close friends, took in a show on Broadway and rounded off their holiday with a trip to the top of the Empire State Building.

"Thank you," said Claire holding Charlie's hand tightly as they marvelled at the vista of New York City from the viewing tower.

"What for?" asked Charlie, although he thought he knew what she was getting at.

"For being you, for taking me on this amazing holiday, for making me happy," she said, feeling quite overwhelmed by her emotions.

"You don't have to thank me anymore. You've thanked me enough since I said I would pay for the trip," said Charlie.

"Does that mean I don't have to have *gratitude sex* with you from now on?"

"No. You'll just have to call it something else."

"Like what?"

"How about...*preparation for marriage sex*?" Charlie said.

Claire looked into Charlie's eyes to check if he was about to spoil this moment with a joke, but no punch line was delivered.

Charlie continued. "Just supposing...what would you say if I asked you to marry me? Would you consider it...seriously...don't laugh...I'm trying to be serious here!"

"If I said yes, does that mean I don't have to pay you back for the holiday?"

"Yes...but you'll have to wear your sexy police uniform in bed and let me use the handcuffs!"

"Any other small print before I consider your offer, Mr Briggs?"

"No, I think that's it for the moment," said Charlie.

"Well, in that case, weighing up the evidence and personal sacrifices I will have to make keeping you in order, after due deliberation, I will accept your offer of marriage if it's on the table."

"I can do tables as well as beds!"

They hugged and kissed and laughed. Compared to other marriage proposals delivered at the top of the Empire State building it would have to go down as the least romantic and serious verbal contract ever agreed but it typified the two Cs. They had met their match and their match was made, not necessarily in heaven, but over three hundred metres closer to it.

Claire, as well as becoming Mrs Briggs, completed her two-year basic training as a police constable and was fast-tracked onto the CID programme. It was clear that with a few sacrifices along the way she had a real future in the police. She was far more focussed and dedicated about her career than Charlie was and with the long shifts there was little time in her time off for her to get broody or even randy. Once in a while the two of them had quality time together. They would visit both sets of parents and once in a while they would make the trip to Hastings to see Lizzie. She had in her last year of university managed to hook up with the squash player and now they shared a house together.. They both had good jobs and were planning to marry and have some kids in the future.

On the long drive home to Derby one Sunday afternoon Charlie brought up the subject of children with Claire.

"It's just not the right time Charlie. It's not that I don't want children but I can't afford to let pregnancy and motherhood get in the way of my plans at the moment. It's a difficult career path within the police force, particularly for women, and having a child would scupper my chances in the future."

"Well it shouldn't. We're not living in the 1950s for God's sake. I know we're still relatively young but it would be good to have a few kids don't you think?"

"A few. Blimey Charlie! How many were you thinking we would have?"

"I...I...thought it would be good to have two or three. You know, have at least one brother or sister for the first one."

"Christ. And how long would that take out of my life...my career? Any way, it's not the right time for even one now. Let's not talk about it anymore. If you're OK driving I'm going to shut my eyes for a while, I'm knackered." Claire tilted her car seat back. It was a long drive home giving them both time to think.

It proved a defining moment in their relationship. They never really talked about starting a family again. They never really talked again. They spent the next year being outwardly happy with each other. They still visited friends and family who would still see them as a lovely and loving couple. But Charlie and Claire were far from happy. Their hopes, dreams and futures seemed to lie along different paths.

Charlie, became frustrated at work. Although less ambitious than Claire, he realised he was ready for a new challenge and more responsibility in a school. The obvious promotion would be Head of Boys PE but the current incumbent was not moving on as he only had about five years to go before retirement, so Charlie would have to look at vacant positions in different schools.

One Friday night Claire came back to the flat late after a long and stressful shift. Charlie was out drinking and having fun with friends from school. She found the Times Educational Supplement lying open on the settee. There were a few adverts for jobs circled in different parts of the country. It was Charlie's way of saying one of the following: *I've had enough of my job; I need a change; I've had enough of this life with you.*

It didn't matter to Claire what Charlie was trying to say. Claire was too tired to be worried or annoyed. She certainly needed a change in her life too. She preferred the company of her police colleagues who were generally more interesting and mature than Charlie. Their marriage was a convenience that didn't suit either of them anymore.

Charlie woke mid-morning when Claire brought him a mug of tea to help with his hangover.

"Thank you. Did I wake you when I got in last night?" asked Charlie sheepishly.

"No. I must have been fast asleep."

"As usual."

"Yeah, as usual. I saw you're looking at new jobs. A promotion somewhere?"

"I need to find a new school. I'm ready to run a department."

"That's good. Any school in particular?"

"There's one I liked the look of; Whatmore. In a challenging area but it sounds my sort of school."

"Where is it?" asked Claire knowing full well where it was as she'd looked carefully at the three adverts Charlie had circled.

"It's some distance away. I haven't applied yet. But if I apply and get the job we'd have to talk about what we do," replied Charlie.

"Do you think so? Don't you think that we both know what we ought to do?"

Four months later Charlie moved into a flat near Whatmore School. Claire kept their flat on and paid the rent on her own. They were still married in name for a while but their amicable divorce was processed within a year. Although Charlie became single at the end of that year, he did become an uncle. A distant uncle who found it quite difficult to visit his sister. Lizzie struggled with the reality of her best friend and her brother breaking up. She didn't blame Charlie entirely but he felt her quiet anger when he met up with her. Although he enjoyed seeing Lizzie play happy family, Charlie was a little jealous of his sister. It was a reminder of what he had hoped for with Claire. As time went on, Charlie found the long drive down to Hastings very difficult and as a result his visits were more sporadic. However, he kept in touch by phone and sometimes saw his sister at their parents' house.

Charlie took to Whatmore very quickly. It was a challenging school but the pupils, by and large, were OK and the staff generally a good bunch. Charlie, although arriving as Head of Boys' PE, was mentored by the very experienced deputy head, who would take time each week to speak to Charlie and check that he was confidently swimming and not sinking.

His team of two other male PE staff, one, Jamie, in his second year of teaching, and other, Dave, with over ten years of teaching, were capable and solid members of staff. Jamie was still learning his trade but was willing and energetic. Dave was reliable but not ambitious. He had had no inclination to apply for the job that Charlie got. Dave was a *good/outstanding* teacher but his paperwork and record keeping required improvement. It was Charlie's belief that Dave would grow old teaching and playing sport until his knees gave up. Charlie, on the other hand, could see a different career path ahead of him. Although he loved his sport and loved teaching pupils, he fancied, in the future, having a whole-school management role. Perhaps one day he would be a Year Head or an Assistant Head teacher, who knows.

Within a couple of years Charlie was a star at Whatmore. He was popular in the school gym, on the playing fields and in classrooms. The senior management of the school also rated him. He brought in new initiatives and encouraged boys and girls to play together in the same teams. Whatmore had mixed teams for football, cricket, basketball and netball. This also meant that the Boys and Girls PE teachers were working closer together. The Head of Girls' PE, Sandra Wilson, was happy to help Charlie to encourage boys and girls to work together in after-school teams but logistically PE lessons were still segregated. Sandra, although about eight years older than Charlie, had a soft spot for him. Charlie, yes, even Charlie, became aware that Sandra had a spot that was growing softer and hotter. But he was not inclined to squeeze any spot of any female staff at Whatmore. That was a personal pleasure that would almost certainly turn into a professional pain.

By the end of his second year Charlie was setting up team sports with some of the feeder primary schools. He would take groups of Year 7 boys and girls to compete with some Year 6 pupils. One of his favourite primary schools to visit was Bennett's Well Primary which was just a short crocodile walk from Whatmore. Almost all of the Year 6 pupils at Bennett's Well came to Whatmore. The head teachers of both schools felt that it was a really effective link to help the transition. It also meant that Charlie, in particular, got to know the staff at Bennett's Well. Charlie's main point of contact was the deputy head who was, along with many other duties, in charge of transition. Her pupils knew her as Mrs Phillips, but to Charlie she was Helen. An attractive woman, perhaps two or three years older than Charlie, Helen had long blonde hair that she put in a pony-tail most days at work and she often wore a track suit as she took most of the PE classes in the school.. She was a busy deputy head with a whole host of responsibilities given to her by the head, including safeguarding, discipline, attendance and pupil data and in the afternoons, she would take PE classes on their small playing field or in the hall, once the lunchtime debris had been cleared away.

Charlie would each week bring a selection of his pupils over to Bennett's Well in the afternoon to have a joint PE session with Helen's pupils or after school when mixed teams in Years 6 and 7 would play competitive sports as an extra-curricular activity. The purpose of these get-togethers was for the children to mix, have fun and also get heathy. Helen and Charlie made these sessions good fun by goofing around with the children and it was often reported back to the respective head teachers from the pupils that this was the high point of the week.

It soon became a high point in the week for Charlie. Helen was funny and enjoyed Charlie's sense of humour, she was good looking from her head down to her toes and she was a fitness fanatic. It soon emerged from their conversations that they both enjoyed tennis, badminton, squash and running. Before either of them had had time to think about the consequences, they had arranged a Saturday morning five mile run together around a local park. Within weeks the run was extended to six miles followed by coffee and then eight miles followed by lunch in a pub.

After one such lunch Charlie invited Helen to his sports club one night for a game of badminton followed by an evening meal. It was following the hot and sweaty encounter on the court and the three-course meal in the restaurant and after they had both taken showers and changed, that Charlie and Helen for the first time drifted away from the topic of sport and schools and got personal.

"Well Charlie, I thought you said you could play badminton. I've had closer games with some of my Year 4 pupils!"

"I thought I'd let you win this first time. Lull you into a false sense of security before I raise the stakes next time."

"Oh yeah. What are you planning?"

"OK, so we agreed that the loser would buy the drinks with the meal this time. And next time I thought I'd suggest that the loser buys the meal and then I would thrash you."

"Oh Mr Briggs. Are you going to thrash me with your racket during the meal or after the meal? Have I been a very bad girl?"

"Mrs Phillips! What do you mean? I'm sure you've got hold of the wrong end of my stick...or racket!"

"Maybe or maybe not. But either way I'm not Mrs Phillips," said Helen.

"So who are you then? Have I been losing to Mrs Phillips' twin sister?"

"No. I was Mrs Phillips until about eight months ago. That's when the divorce came through but at school, I've just let the kids keep calling me by my married name. It's just easier at the moment. In September I'll start afresh with my original name."

"So, go on...spill the beans...Helen...?"

"Brooks."

"Well, nice to meet you Helen Brooks. Are you any better at badminton than Helen Phillips?"

"Oh yes. Much better. In fact, I'm better at everything."

"Really? Like what?"

"Well if you stick around, I'll show you...I'm better at tennis, squash, leap frog, tug of war and many other things."

"OK then I might just do that if you can take the humiliation of losing and paying for all of the meals. But seriously for a second, I ought to tell you that Briggs is my married name before I got divorced well over a year ago. Luckily though, my original name was Briggs, so that worked out OK."

"That was convenient. Do you still keep in touch with the then Mrs Briggs?"

"No. She and I grew apart. She's in the police. She was one of my sister's closest friends and I gather she's doing well. She lives in Derby. What about you?"

"My ex cheated on me over a few months. A woman at work. I never saw it coming until I read a couple of texts that pinged on his phone when he was in the shower. That was it. Bye-bye. Five years of marriage down the drain. I suppose I'm finally just getting over it. But it's been tough."

"It sounds as if it was harder for you than me. We just gradually fell out of love without realising it."

"It's still sad though. You enter into marriage believing you're going to grow old together..."

"Yeah. I have to say that I can't get my head around your husband wanting to trade you in for another model."

"That's just it. I don't think that was his intention. I think he just wanted the other woman on the side as a bit of variety and fun."

"How could he do that to you? You're beautiful and funny..." Charlie realised as he was delivering this that he was blushing. And making Helen blush.

"Charlie, that's very nice of you to say but don't pity me. I'm sure I was to blame to some degree for him straying."

"Well, I can't believe that. And I can't believe any man wouldn't want to be faithful to you."

"Thank you, Charlie. That's really sweet..."

"Helen, how can I put this? If and when you're ready, I'd like to ask you on a date. I just want you to know that I really like you. I know it's early days after your divorce but I can wait. What do you say?"

"How about tomorrow night?" asked Helen. The glint in her eye was patently obvious to Charlie.

The following night Charlie arranged to pick up Helen from her small block of flats and offered to drive them to an Italian restaurant a few miles out of town. Both of them had agreed to make an effort and not wear their track suits. Charlie had brushed off his suit, re-ironed a white shirt and dusted off his lucky tie. He looked good and his bedroom mirror approved. He drove to Helen's place and pressed the intercom button for her flat. Helen told Charlie she'd be down in a moment and when she opened the external door Charlie had to fight hard to stop his jaw dropping. She was wearing her hair down to a strappy little black number with various pieces of jewellery adorning the outfit. He also had to control himself from executing a hop, skip and a jump towards her dark red lipstick. After both of them complimented each other on the doorstep, Charlie escorted Helen to his car both of them looking and feeling like teenagers on a nervous first date.

At the restaurant they relaxed and began to re-set their relationship as teacher colleagues, teasing and joking with each other, sharing stories about school and family stuff. They laughed more than anyone else in the restaurant, much more than the four or five married couples who stared at them from time to time with looks of annoyance and jealousy in their eyes. Helen and Charlie however, only seemed to have eyes for each other. Their waiter had to keep coughing to get their attention during the evening. Charlie insisted on paying for the meal saying that he was clearly earning more than Helen because his job was much more responsible and valued by society and also if he lost his next game of badminton he would not be in her debt.

"What makes you think there'll be a next game or a next meal?" asked Helen.

"I can't be certain but I'm sure you'd like to hear more stories about my past...climbing Everest, meeting John Lennon and writing a best-selling novel."

"That sounds amazing. And did all of this happen at the summit of Everest?"

"Well, I'm not telling you tonight. It's a very long story. I'm hoping that you'll share another evening with me when I can expand...so to speak," said Charlie trying hard to keep a straight-ish face.

"Well Mr Briggs. I would hate to stop a man expanding at my expense."

Charlie drove Helen home and they stole glances at each other in the darkness of the car and their own thoughts raced faster than the car.

Charlie offered to walk Helen to her door but they both knew that late on a Sunday night it would not be a good idea for Charlie to approach Helen's threshold which might lead to coffee and more...coffee.

"Before you go," said Charlie, "could I possibly taste your lipstick? I've been wanting to all night."

"I suppose that wouldn't hurt," said Helen and reaching into her handbag and passed Charlie the glittering tube..

They both laughed and then undid their seat belts so their lips could meet in the middle. The kiss lasted longer than it would have taken Charlie to run four hundred metres. It was a gold medal kiss. It was the sort of kiss that neither of them had experienced for a very long time. They both secretly knew that this was the start of something special but they shouldn't rush things.

It was agreed that they meet up again on Friday night and during the week they would just act casually and professionally with each other.

The week dragged for both of them. They managed to send professional messages to each other by text or email. Some of the arrangements for Friday were firmed up. Charlie was to drive over to Helen's flat, pick her up for a game of badminton, a shower and change into smarter clothes, a pub meal and then the plans for the evening fizzled out. Charlie could see a gaping hole in the arrangements at the point when Charlie drove Helen home from the pub. He hoped that the evening would not stop there. He also hoped that Helen would also hope that the evening would continue but understood that she might want to take things slowly. They had shared a passionate kiss which must mean something, Charlie thought, but he didn't want to assume Helen would be ready for the next stage. They had only had one kiss, for goodness sake. Helen may have been under the influence of alcohol and in the sober light of day thought better of it. Charlie was confused.

What should Charlie do? Should he pack an overnight bag and leave it in the boot of the car? Should he just put a toothbrush and an extra pair of pants in his sports bag? Should he just assume that there would be just another kiss or no kiss at all and that he would be driving back to his own flat alone? Decisions, decisions!

Friday night came. Charlie packed the boot of his car for any and every eventuality and drove over to Helen's place. He pressed the intercom and Helen ran down the stairs from her third floor flat to open the external door. This time she was wearing her track suit and carrying a sports bag. But unlike last time she moved straight towards Charlie and kissed him on the lips.

"God that feels good. I've waited five days to kiss you again. I'm sorry Charlie, I can't wait that long again. I'm a woman and I have needs."

"Well, I don't know if you've noticed but I'm a man and I have very special needs. I need to kiss you and then kiss you again."

As they walked to his car Helen came up with a suggestion.

"OK Charlie. I tell you what. If you can beat me at badminton tonight, I'll pay for the pub grub and then you can kiss me again and again."

"Where exactly?" said Charlie as he started the car.

"On the lips naturally," replied Helen.

"No, I meant in the car when I drop you off or in your flat?"

"OK. I'll raise the stakes," said Helen smiling. "If you beat me by three points in all of the sets we play, then I'll let you kiss me in my flat and not just on the lips."

"Oh God, you're a tease, you know that, Helen Brooks. The way I'm feeling down below right now I can't promise that I'll be able to walk let alone run on the court."

"Well if you can't move on court, then you're not going to win and my lips will remain sealed!" said Helen provocatively and gently stroked his leg.

"Helen, if you carry on doing that I won't even get to the club!"

They laughed most of the way to the sports club. They became serious as they played badminton. Charlie became frustrated as he lost all three games of badminton to Helen. They then got changed and headed for the pub for a meal, both of them smart-casual in jeans and tee shirts.. They ate a hearty two-course meal and shared a bottle of wine with Charlie only having a smallish glass as he was driving.

As Charlie poured the last remnants of the bottle into Helen's wine glass, she touched his hand. "Are you trying to get me drunk Mr Briggs? It won't work you know. You lost all three games. You know the deal, no kisses etcetera until you beat me at badminton," said Helen.

"I don't remember the deal being that specific or lasting that long. How about if I pay for the meal and the drinks? Would that help to sway your mind?"

"What sort of girl do you think I am, Charlie? You offer to pay for a meal and expect a kiss in return. I'm not that easy!" said Helen, trying to look stern and offended while her lips looked warm and inviting to Charlie.

"How about the meal, drinks, a lift home and all the toffees in the glove box of my car?"

"No. Nice try. I do like your toffees but you'll have to wait I'm afraid. A woman can't be rushed when it comes to courting."

"Well, you can't fault my efforts so far. I'll clearly have to have an intensive course in improving my badminton skills this week. I'll be ready to whip you on the court next weekend."

The rally of teasing and joking continued all the way back to Helen's flat. This time, though, Helen let Charlie walk her to the external door of her flat, kissed him unexpectedly and then opened the door to say her goodbyes but as the door closed again on Charlie, she pushed it open, grabbed his hand and pulled him through it. "I've a confession to make Charlie. I'm afraid of the dark. I need a real man to lead the way up the stairs, open my door, guide me through the hallway and into my bedroom. Can you think of anyone who might help me out?"

"Funnily enough, I have a rather large torch in my pocket that might come in handy!"

"Is that what it is! I wondered what it was when you were driving me home just now."

"Don't be alarmed. Hold on to my hand for now and I'll take you up your passageway to your bedroom." Helen held Charlie's hand and they remained in very close proximity for the remainder of the weekend. The only time Charlie left the building was to bring his overnight bag in from the boot of the car.

For the next twelve months or so Charlie and Helen co-existed in one or other's flats. The staff at both schools soon became aware of their relationship but the children seemed oblivious to their sporting relationship even when Charlie took his teams over to play at Bennett's Well. Helen and Charlie always managed to brush past each other in the hall, playground or sports field while they were coaching or encouraging the pupils. When they passed the referee's whistle from one to the other, their hands would linger for a split second and their energy and love would be transferred. At the end of each joint sports session they would make a point of saying goodbye loudly to one another in front of the children, pretending that they would see each other next week when in reality they would be *seeing each other* later on that afternoon and all night.

And so it went on. They were introduced to each other's families. Helen was an immediate hit with Charlie's parents who could see that their son was happy with the new woman in his life. Charlie's sister Lizzie took a while to accept that Charlie could be happy with this vivacious bombshell compared to her university friend but Helen knew how to win Lizzie over and sometimes when the whole family met at Charlie's house, Helen would drag Lizzie out to the pub for several drinks while Lizzie's husband, Charlie and his folks looked after the kids.

Occasionally Charlie was taken to see Helen's mother. She lived on her own in the outskirts of Manchester in a small terraced house. Helen's father had disappeared off the grid some ten years ago and was not referred to by Helen or her mother. Charlie found it difficult to talk to Helen's mother as she was quite odd and unpredictable. She could be engaged in conversation with Helen or Charlie one minute and then without warning lose her thread and begin talking about a different topic. Helen had explained to Charlie after his first meeting with her mother that she had always been that way and that in time he would get used to her manner but Charlie found it hard to understand how Helen, who was so funny and focused, could be so different from her mother.

On the second journey home from Helen's mother's house the two of them had a serious conversation about a different matter. By the time they had arrived back at Charlie's flat they had agreed to look for a property to live in together. They would get rid of their flats and go half and half on a deposit for a house. A small house, three bedrooms perhaps and possibly a garage. There was agreement on this and also the need to live away from the catchment areas of Whatmore Secondary and Bennett's Well Primary schools.

Within five months they were living in their own house. Some eight miles away from the schools, safe in the knowledge that there would be no children recognising them as they jogged around their neighbourhood or went to their local shop for a loaf of bread. Life was good for them. They joined a local gym together and made friends in their cul-de-sac. They were delighted that their new friends were not involved in teaching at all and they could share an existence and related stories outside of education.

They decided to keep two cars and drive into school and back home again independently. Not because they were embarrassed about being seen together, it just made sense not to rely on each other for lifts when each school had its own meeting schedules before and after school, sports events and parents' evenings that weren't synchronised with each other in any way.

On Wednesday afternoons Charlie would still take Year 7s over to Bennett's Well. On one of these afternoons Charlie was at the side of the football pitch cheering on Whatmore's team while Helen was refereeing the game. Helen had stopped the game while one of the Year 6 pupils replaced a boot that had flown off when she shot at goal. Charlie used this opportunity to get one of the Whatmore substitutes to run on the pitch with a note for the referee.

The year 7 boy handed the referee a note from Mr Briggs. The small sheet of paper folded in half said *Mrs Phillips* on the front. Inside there was a short question.

Helen, will you marry me? Charlie x

The boy came hurrying back to Charlie.

"Well?" asked Mr Briggs to the boy." What did she say?"

"She just said *Yes*."

And a smile was conveyed from the touch line to the centre circle and back again.

As weddings were not novel experiences to Charlie or Helen, they decided on a quiet celebration in a registry office. However, their stag and hen do's in two pubs close to each other were a lot louder. Both Charlie and Helen ended up drunkenly unconscious wearing daft apparel in their double bed after being escorted home by Charlie's best man and Helen's bridesmaid.

A week later they were sober and married.

In the next few years they settled into a comfortable routine. Charlie and Helen became house-proud, they kitted out their house with good quality furniture and mementoes from some of the foreign holidays they enjoyed together. Every other Saturday was ear-marked for families. They decided that Helen would visit her mother while Charlie would travel in the other direction to see his folks after the Saturday morning football matches that he ran at Whatmore.

Helen and Charlie would get back from their family duties to the cul-de-sac late on Saturday evening and meet up in bed. They were comfortable, open and honest with each other but there was never any mention of babies of their own and as the time passed, they both began to operate on the assumption that they would be living together in the house without children. They used the gym twice a week in the evenings, and every other weekend on a Saturday they would enjoy a run in the local park followed by a pub lunch, the cinema or seeing friends while their Sundays would be taken up with food shopping and school work.

At work Charlie started to feel a little stale as Head of Boys PE and wanted to try other things either at Whatmore or in another local. He met with the head teacher at Whatmore one day to say that he needed to re-invent himself and was considering moving into the pastoral system at a secondary school. The head was very understanding but could not offer him a Year Head position until a vacancy occurred. Consequently, Charlie started looking carefully at the Times Educational Supplement for relevant posts in the local area. Unfortunately, very few were advertised because they tended to be offered to internal candidates who had shown an interest in the pastoral system.

Charlie was feeling stuck in a rut.

One evening Helen and Charlie talked about both of their jobs. Charlie explained that he did not want to carry on in PE until the day he retired and Helen sympathised and told him to look for jobs a little further afield if that meant getting a Year Head position. Helen was happy enough being a deputy head at Bennet's Well. She had no ambition to be a primary school head teacher but she was prepared to travel longer distances from a different house if she could keep her existing job. She suggested looking at schools and moving north a little because it would be easier to see her mother whose mental health was slowly becoming a worry to Helen.

Charlie started to check out secondary schools that were advertising Year Head positions and were a little further north. He found the ideal position in the ideal school in the *Times Education Supplement* in Coleshill. According to AA Route Planner, It was still only a fifteen minute drive from Bennett's Well which suited Helen and it would not be much further for Charlie to drive from their home.

Out of courtesy on the following Monday morning Charlie sought out his head teacher to tell him he was applying for a job and ask if he could use him as his first referee. Charlie was given the head's blessing and backing to apply. Details were sent for and then with Helen's help Charlie started to fill in the forms and create a letter of application and an updated curriculum vitae. He intended to finish the application and send it off by the weekend but when Friday came Charlie had a message from the head teacher to see him during period 2 when Charlie was free.

"Charlie, take a seat. Thanks for coming to see me. How's that application going that you mentioned earlier in the week?" asked the head.

"Almost done, I'm just checking it through this weekend and I'll send it off on Monday."

"That's good, that's good...but before you send it off, I just wanted to mention something to you I'd like you to consider..."

"OK," said Charlie sounding and seeming puzzled.

"I've been talking to some of my governors at a staffing meeting this week and it has been agreed that we need to expand our senior management team with a new post. We'll be looking for someone in an assistant head role to help out with the pastoral system, to build further links with our feeder primary schools and oversee trips and visits. My deputy in charge of the pastoral system has admitted that she wants to retire in a couple of years' time and needs to train someone up. The Chair of Governors and I wondered if it might be a position that interests you?"

"Yes, of course. It sounds perfect for me, but I'm sure there'll be other members of staff who'll be interested in the post when it's advertised."

"I'm sure there will be some interest inside and outside the school for this important role and, of course, if you apply you'll have to be interviewed alongside other potential candidates."

"Yes, I understand."

"A question for you Charlie. When are the interviews for this Year Head post you are going for?" asked the head trying to look as if he was asking this in all innocence.

"Oh, it's ages yet, middle of next month. I can't remember the date exactly. I didn't want to count chickens if you see what I mean?"

"I quite understand. This is good from your point of view then because the Chair of Governors would like to get this appointment done quickly so it's going in the TES this Friday and will be advertised internally also on Friday. And we hope to make an appointment after interviewing people on the 11th or 12th of next month. By all means carry on with your application for Year Head. That's your prerogative, but I trust you will consider this post as well...it's a bigger pay jump and it really is a good step up the ladder. Thanks for coming to see me Charlie. Have a good day."

"Thank you, you too," said Charlie as he turned around and headed for the door. Neither could see the other's face but both bore a slight smile..

By the beginning of the next academic year Whatmore had a new Head of Boys PE and Charlie was Assistant Head. Although Charlie Briggs leap frogged two good Heads of Year who applied for the senior management role in order to get the post, no-one inside school seemed to resent his climb up the greasy pole. It was Charlie after all. He was great with the kids, a superb teacher, a reliable colleague who would always have your back and he was a good laugh.

Helen was delighted for him. There was no need to move house now. They went away for a two-week sunny holiday in Spain where they played golf of the serious and crazy varieties, swam in the hotel pool, snorkelled in the sea, drank far too much and misbehaved in their hotel room on a regular basis.

Charlie loved his new role in school, but it was time-consuming, particularly since the deputy head, who was supposed to be retiring in a year or two's time, was taking the opportunity to view her retirement from the back seat while Charlie drove the car forward.

Within the first six months, his extra-curricular routine with Helen had changed. Monday to Thursday evenings were taken up with pastoral matters – filling in forms, writing letters, sending emails etcetera. Sunday was the same and Charlie and Helen managed to preserve and protect their Friday nights and Saturdays together on alternate weekends but sometimes Charlie was too busy to see his family and his sister.

On those weekends when they were supposed to see their folks, Charlie and Helen decided that Helen should spend two nights with her mother in Manchester. She was getting a little more confused and Helen needed to check on her more and more. By the end of the year, with Charlie's blessing Helen was seeing her mother for part of every weekend. Charlie offered to go with her to her mom's but Helen said that she was happy to go on her own as long as they had Sunday afternoon and evening together.

As the academic year was in its last two months Charlie was even busier visiting feeder primary schools, helping to induct the new Year 7s and pretty much doing all of the leg work for the deputy head who had told Charlie that she was retiring at the end of the next academic year. Charlie wanted to tell her that he was under the impression that she'd already retired but thought better of it. If he played his cards right for one more year then he could be deputy head.

One Saturday evening, driving back from his parents' house where he'd had a great time playing with Lizzie's kids before they went to bed in his old room, Charlie decided to phone Helen. He stopped in a lay by and phoned Helen's mobile. It went to voicemail; she must have it on silent. He then tried her mom's house. It was a good time to ring. Just before Helen took her mom to bed. No-one answered the phone for a while and then Helen's mother came on the phone:

"Hello, who is this?"

"It's Charlie, Mrs Brooks, can I speak to Helen?"

"Who?"

"Helen, your daughter, can I speak to her?"

"Who's this?"

"It's Charlie, your daughter's husband, can I speak to Helen?"

"No."

"Why is that Mrs Brooks? Is she there?"

"No she's not here."

"Do you know where she is?"

"Yes, I think so."

"Where's she gone, Mrs Brooks?"

"She's gone out with her husband."

"No, I'm her husband. I'm Charlie. I'm married to Helen."

"No, you're not. Helen is married to Jeff. They've gone out somewhere. They said they would be back soon."

"OK. OK Mrs Brooks don't worry. I'll speak to you soon. Bye."

Charlie laughed and shook his head. 'The poor dear,' he thought.

Charlie drove home and tried Helen's mobile again. No reply again. He would wait until the morning and try her again.

"Oh hi," said Helen. I was going to ring you soon after I got mom her breakfast. Sorry I missed you last night. I was in the bath when you phoned the house and I had my mobile turned off; God knows why!"

"Are you OK? I was worried about you. I hate it when I don't know where you are."

"I'm sorry. I bet my mother wasn't much comfort either."

"Not really, she just gets confused."

"She's getting worse. I don't know what to do about her."

"Well, let's talk later. What time are you setting off?"

"Later, if that's OK with you. I want to spend the morning and some of the afternoon with her."

"OK. We'll talk when you get back. Love you."

"And you."

That evening when Helen got back to the house, exhausted from her weekend with her mother, Charlie tried to persuade Helen to think about a care home for her mother, or getting her to stay at their house for periods of time or letting him take some of the pressure off his wife by joining her for at least some of the weekend visits. Helen wouldn't agree to any of his suggestions for different reasons. Money was an issue when it came to funding care for her mother and Helen felt that it wouldn't be good for either of them if she came to live with them. Helen also felt that it was unfair to expect Charlie to use up his spare time with her mother when he had his own family to see and all of the work to do at home for his job.

It was the next Saturday evening when Charlie rang Helen that he started to worry again. Her mobile went to voicemail and the mother's land line didn't ring at all.

Helen eventually phoned Charlie on her mobile at about 10 o'clock as he was settling down to watch Match of the Day.

She was OK. She was fine. Helen's explanation was that she'd had to unplug the phone as her mother kept trying to make random calls. Helen hoped it was just a phase as during the week she needed to phone her mother using her land line.

The following Saturday afternoon, Charlie made a decision to stop working on a new school behaviour policy and drive up to Helen's mother's house to lend some support for Helen. He didn't phone Helen; he didn't try the landline; he just jumped in the car with an overnight bag.

Charlie knocked on his mother-in-law's door some two hours later.

Helen took a while to come to the door. She opened the door slightly. "Charlie, what're you doing here?" she said loudly.

"I've come to give you a hand and to see your mum, I haven't seen her for ages."

"I was just getting in the bath," Helen said clutching her dressing gown to her and opening the door to let him in. "Come on through and say hello to her." Helen gave Charlie a kiss and led him through to the lounge where her mother was watching some sort of game show on the TV.

"Mom... mom, you remember Charlie, don't you? He's come to visit you. I'll just turn the TV down a bit while you have a chat. Charlie, I'll just throw my clothes on and I'll be back down in a jiffy." Helen looked at the flowers and wine he had stopped off to buy on the way up and then she noticed his overnight bag. "Are you staying overnight?"

"Yeah. I thought we could take you mother out somewhere tomorrow morning if she'd like to." Charlie looked at Mrs Brooks senior as he said it but Helen's mom did not reply.

"OK. That would be lovely, wouldn't it, mom?" There was a slight grunt from her mother. "I'll just go upstairs and I'll be back down soon."

"Shall I bring up my bag?"

"No," said Helen forcefully. "I'll take it up. You stay here and talk to mom."

Helen disappeared and Charlie was left with her mother.

"So, how have you been? Are you enjoying having Helen stay with you at the weekend?"

"I suppose so. I don't see her that much."

"What do you mean?"

"She's out with her husband Jeff most of the time or upstairs with him making a bloody noise."

At this moment the penny dropped. After a minute or so of realisation and seeing penny after penny dropping in front of his eyes, he asked Helen's mother if he could turn the TV down even further. Charlie quietly left the lounge, stood in the hall and listened to his wife whispering and then a low male response. At that point he knew his second marriage was over. He opened the front door, slammed it behind him and drove home.

The following day Helen drove home. She had aged overnight.

Charlie stayed calm as he asked for the truth. Helen tried to go on the offensive through a series of denials, lies, more denials, accusations, heart-felt apologies and reassurances but Charlie had already made up his mind. His marriage, marriage number two, was over. Whereas Helen's first marriage had never really ended. She had been in touch with Jeff, husband number one, a few years' back and their relationship had re-kindled and was now a hot, burning affair. Helen had used her mother's illness as a way to spend most weekends with her lover.

Within a year Charlie was legally single again. The house was sold. The money was split and Helen left Bennet's Well primary school as quickly as she could. She was now living with Jeff, again, close to her mother's house.

No More Marriages was Charlie's new motto as he tried over the next couple of years to forget about Helen, dating and sleeping with as many women as would allow him easy access. He even started occasional flings with younger female teachers at Whatmore but that was as far as it went. No falling in love, no marriages.

He threw himself into his work. He taught a few periods of PE a week but his time was taken up with being in charge of the pastoral system. He was respected by the staff and by the vast majority of the kids at Whatmore and their parents even when Charlie was left with no alternative but to exclude a pupil for misbehaviour. It was no surprise, when the deputy head handed in her resignation in May, that the next day Charlie was asked by the head teacher to apply for the position.

By September, Charlie had managed to climb the ladder to deputy head of a large secondary school without having to move schools more than once. He was in his low forties but according to most of his girlfriends he was in his mid- thirties and still felt like a twenty-year-old in both senses. He was living in a rented one bedroom flat and had no intention of buying a house and making it a home. He had had his fingers burned with wife number two. So he managed to save a fair amount of money with his increased salary and although he still played his sports and spent money on wine, women and more women, he was still quids in at the end of each month.

He managed to see his folks every two weeks and met up with his little sister at least once a month. Her kids were in their late teens now which made Charlie feel old but he loved seeing Lizzie's family and her children loved their Uncle Charlie. Charlie, although he would never say this aloud to Lizzie, was really proud of his sister and loved her to bits. She remained the one constant woman in his life, other than their mother, who was a good, kind and caring friend to him.

After a while Charlie noticed a slight shift in his relationship with the staff at the school. He was no longer *one of the guys* but a member of senior management and consequently not entirely to be trusted. He still went out on a Friday night with *the lads* which included lasses, but his drinking pals skirted around school issues and he started to feel as if he was tolerated and no longer a member of the staffroom. He accepted this difference in the way people saw him, as he would have felt the same if as a young teacher he was getting drunk next to one of the senior team on a Friday night. The younger women on the staff were also becoming more sensible and mature and not joining Charlie for *after drinks* back at his flat. There was, however, a married woman in the PE department that liked to join him for a bit of exercise once or twice a week. However, at times, Charlie was beginning to feel a little isolated, lonely and old.

It was on one of those days, a Saturday morning in the local park, after Charlie had tried to run off his alcohol intake from the night before with a few laps around the pool, that his mood was unexpectedly changed. He trundled around the hard standing trying to keep his speed below 3 mph in case he got breathalysed by a park warden. In amongst the duck feeders, the teenagers in love and the mobility scooters that were overtaking him he noticed a woman jogging in the other direction. On his first passing of her he just looked at her face and rather smart track suit. On the second passing he noticed the body that was covered by the track suit, on the third passing he smiled at her and she smiled back. On the fourth passing he said "Hello again" to her and was sure she said "We must stop meeting like this." By the next lap he had thought of a good reply "Do we have to?" and on the fifth circuit she said "Not really." At that point both Charlie and the woman instinctively stopped and walked back to chat.

"I'm so glad you stopped," said the woman." I'm knackered. I only kept jogging around this park the last three times so that I could see you again!"

"Me too. I'm feeling the effects of a heavy night last night but you kept me going so to speak."

"Can we sit down on that bench over there before I collapse on the floor?"

"Sure. My name's Charlie by the way."

"Hi Charlie, I'm Pat. Patricia really but most people call me Pat."

They sat at the bench and talked and talked and then went to a café by the park and talked some more. It was a warts and all conversation. Charlie described his job and his two failed marriages. Pat described her job in a bank and her one failed marriage. They were both single, both childless, both in their forties (the first time Charlie had admitted to this to anyone outside of the family) and were both looking for some company with someone from the opposite sex. Pat was on a fitness drive because she had put on a few pounds recently and Charlie, on cue, said the right thing to a woman he fancied and had just met.

Consequently, later that night having eaten at a Chinese restaurant together and Pat having accepted the invitation to come back to his flat for a drink or two, he could categorically make a first-hand judgement that she didn't need to lose a few pounds.

Pat was a different type of girlfriend for Charlie. She wasn't that interested in sport; she didn't know much about education and she wasn't as sparky as Charlie's usual women. However, she was a thoughtful, beautiful and a generous woman. She was altruistic and liked to please others but had self-doubts occasionally and felt insecure. The more Charlie got to know her, the more he realised that she was a caring, sincere person he could trust completely. She just needed a partner who made her feel loved and safe. Charlie was certain that she was genuine and faithful. He really liked this about Pat. It was what he needed. There were times over the months that they got to know each other that Charlie wondered if Pat had perhaps been taken advantage of by her ex-husband or others in her life. If this relationship was going to continue then he would look after her, not take her for granted and one day he would love her, in the real sense of the word.

There were many positive things about Pat that Charlie did love from the outset. She was very practical and sensible with money. She helped Charlie get his finances in order and assisted him in putting his money in high interest savings accounts. She helped him make his flat look respectable. She was an amazing cook. She was very funny at times and got on really well with his mates at the gym. She was a real hit with Charlie's parents and Lizzie and her family. And she adored Charlie. She was very keen to please him and she spent most evenings pleasing him at either her house or at his flat. There was never any mention of trying for a family and they seemed perfectly happy to be a couple without any further responsibilities.

A year after they met for the first time in the local park Charlie and Pat sat down at her dining table eating one of her signature dishes and drinking some cheap plonk she'd bought. She broached the subject of Charlie saving more money in a way that would also help her out. She suggested that he gave up his flat and moved into her house. He could pay her a minimal rent and do some DIY around the house and then, if it worked out, they could consider going halves on the mortgage. It was a win-win situation for both parties. The house was a lot bigger than the flat, Charlie would be paying less rent for the time being, and have a very attractive house mate who cooked for him and satisfied all of his other appetites. Pat would have a man to look after, a sexy fit bloke who would look after her, she would not be lonely anymore and one day she hoped that they would be together in the eyes of the law.

The flat was sold. Charlie moved in. Pat cooked. Charlie wallpapered various rooms. Pat joined Charlie's gym. They made time for each other, looked after each other and life became good and comfortable for both of them.

Pat continued to work in their local bank as a sub manager. Charlie soon found his feet as the deputy head at the school. Eighteen months after Charlie moved in, they decided to get married. It felt natural and the right thing to do. It was a quiet ceremony. Charlie did not want to go overboard with a wedding celebration after his two previous failures. Pat was fine about that but she was delighted that she and Charlie had made a commitment to each other. They honeymooned in Marbella on the Costa del Sol in a hotel and apartment complex that just happened to be on a golf course and not far from the beach. This suited the two of them fine and they quickly settled into a routine. Charlie taught Pat the rudiments of golf for an hour or so early each morning and then he was allowed to have a serious round while she sunbathed and developed her tan. He would then meet her on the beach for a swim and something to eat at a sea front bar before enjoying a late siesta followed by a meal and several glasses of wine. For fourteen days they were happy to stay in Marbella, potter about in the evenings and not bother with a hire car.

Pat and Charlie fell in love with Marbella and talked about one day buying a property out there once they had retired. But for the foreseeable future each year they would spend two weeks during the school summer holidays improving their golf, their knowledge of Spanish wine and their tans. Charlie and Pat's plans were now stretching into the long term. There would be no children, however, as Pat began the menopause, but that did not worry or affect either of them.

In his early fifties when Charlie's parents died within a year of each other, Pat became a real support to her husband and also to Lizzie's family. She became almost like a big sister to Lizzie. The two of them would regularly meet up at a restaurant for a natter and once every two months or so Pat would cook a meal for

Lizzie and her husband. Charlie was always given the task of choosing and pouring the drinks as he wasn't trusted to even assist the chef.

At the end of one of these drunken fun evenings Lizzie and Charlie were loading the dishwasher in the kitchen. Earlier, Lizzie's husband had been helped up to bed in the spare room by Charlie and then Pat, who had succumbed to the generous glasses of wine Charlie had poured, apologised that she too would have to take to her bed.

"Charlie, don't muck this up," slurred Lizzie.

"I have loaded a dishwasher before you know. I think this is the fourth time I've done it in my life. I'm getting quite good at it, but don't tell Pat or else she will want me to do it more often."

"You mean you've loaded the dishwasher only one time more than you've had wives?"

"I was only joking Liz," said Charlie defensively.

"I know that, but it's your present wife I worry about. She's bloody lovely. Too good for you. So, don't cock it up!"

"It wasn't my fault with Helen," said Charlie.

"No, I know it wasn't, but Pat is different. She loves you, adores you and I'm not sure you feel the same way about her."

"What are you talking about Lizzie? Of course I love her. I'm married to her, aren't I?"

"Yeah, but being married to someone doesn't always mean that you love them. Take Helen for example..."

"OK. Let's not dwell on that. But I do love Pat. She's great. I'm really happy! I promise you," said Charlie with a smile on his face.

"Well... make sure she knows that you do! Look after Pat and don't start looking elsewhere. Pat's the right one for you. Grow old together."

"It's late and I'm off to bed. Good night, my special agony aunt." He kissed and hugged her and they helped each other up the stairs to their respective snoring partners.

The memory of that conversation would re-surface in Charlie's brain in the years before he eventually retired.

During the next ten years or so Charlie became the brightest star at Whatmore. He was the go-to guy for help on most things inside school. His one failing was ICT but other than that he was Mr Whatmore when it came to handling pupils, parents and staff.

Then a new head teacher was appointed, Peter Burlington, a little younger than Charlie. Fortunately, they got on extremely well. Peter was a good guy and although he seemed to worry about everything, Charlie knew he was to be trusted.

Charlie also got on well with the other members of the senior team – Julie, Neil and Sobia.

Julie was a star in the making. She would be a head teacher one day. She was talented and driven. Charlie, from time to time, would secretly admit to himself that although Julie was twenty years younger than he was, he would quite like to test out the generation gap.

Neil was a techy nerd but he was also a good guy he could tease. Neil, mostly, hid himself away safely in an underground bunker full of gizmos and gadgets where teachers found it difficult to track him down in person, so Charlie had taken him under his wing and over time Neil started to become more confident with real interactions with real people - even if they were teachers!

Sobia, the business manager, was a more difficult person to work with. She was quite serious and at times direct with people which meant that Charlie found it harder to have a laugh and a joke with her. She was, however, very good at her job in making sure that Whatmore remained solvent and independent of the vulture-like academy chains waiting to swoop down and consume the school.

The school was generally in a good place during those years. There were times when Ofsted called and the school managed to stay out of the red zone. There were times when Peter Burlington appointed a duffer to lead a department or funding became tight and redundancies loomed but the school stayed standing and no-one died metaphorically or literally. Charlie was now somewhere along the first stretch of the last lap of his career. He was not sure when he would retire but retirement started to feature in his distant thoughts.

Inevitably, Charlie started to feel old. He noticed that very few women on the staff flirted with him in a serious way. It was definitely a case of *Good Old Charlie* now. A bit of harmless fun but no more than that.

At home Charlie was still treated like a prince by Pat. They enjoyed each other's anecdotes from their work days. They went for walks and talked. They made time to go to the cinema and have a meal out once a week. And on occasions they would go to a football match, a cricket game or even get tickets for Wimbledon. Pat eased off going to the gym and the sports club but was happy for him to go by himself so that he could have some fun with the lads. It wasn't as if Pat was left on her own. She would go out at least one night a week with work colleagues or her girlfriends and would often go shopping on a Saturday afternoon with her best friend while Charlie played golf or tennis at the club.

For reasons best known to Charlie, he was still dissatisfied with his life. It was not that he was a restless soul, but he did miss the thrills and spills of his earlier life. He needed an extra ingredient to spice up his life. So, with the aid of the Head of Year 11, he started an extra-curricular activity that was not open to the students. There was no specific timetable for this activity. It was unplanned, spontaneous but mostly based in Charlie's office in the Pastoral Area of the school. The activity would start when all of the other staff had left the building and the coast was clear. Charlie, in his head, rationalised cheating on Pat as acceptable for a variety of spurious reasons - ranging from "It was not serious", "I still love Pat", "Pat wouldn't really mind if she knew", " It's probably helping the marriage", "I can stop this at any time" and " It's just sex" through to " It means nothing."

Unfortunately, the Head of Year 11 didn't feel quite the same. She was in a loveless marriage. She needed Charlie. She wanted Charlie and would quite like Charlie for herself. It reached the point where Charlie needed to act. A few decisions happened within a few days. He decided that at the end of the school year he would take early retirement. He also decided that the affair should be terminated with immediate effect and that he and Pat should live in Spain for at least some of each year.

Peter Burlington and the Chair of Governors at Whatmore graciously accepted his resignation, the Head of Year 11 accepted the decision of stopping the extra-curricular activity ungraciously but without any significant fall-out and Pat agreed to Charlie's idea that they both retire at the end of the academic year and create a base in Spain.

Charlie Briggs, who had never previously stuck to an action plan in his life managed to lead his way through his own exit plan. That August Pat and Charlie headed for an open-ended vacation to find a suitable villa to buy. By the next year they had settled into a routine of spending half the year based at their house in England and the other half in their villa in Marbella.

For the next three years or so they enjoyed the sun, sand and sea in Marbella. They made good friends, they ate good food and drank too much. Retirement was idyllic. Charlie and Pat fell in love with this way of life. They both deserved it. They had both worked hard during their working lives and now it was pay back.

. . .

Charlie woke up again. Pat was sitting by the bed holding his hand. She looked worried.

"Hi Charlie," she said gently.

"Hi sweetheart...God I must have had a skinful last night... I feel really rough."

"Do you know where you are, Charlie?"

"Of course I do... We're in the villa... Can you get me some pain killers and then I'll get up...? We're going out for a meal tonight with Martin and Jacky."

"No Charlie, we're back in England. We're at The Queen Elizabeth in Birmingham. You had a sudden heart attack on the golf course at the club in Marbella. We had to fly you back home for the surgery."

"What...you're joking... I don't remember anything. But I...how long ago was this?"

"Three weeks ago. It's serious Charlie. We thought we'd lost you."

"Am I... on the mend now? What have the doctors said? I feel bloody awful."

"It was touch and go but..." Pat Briggs started to cry.

"But what Pat?"

"I don't know. No-one is telling me much... they just keep telling me to be hopeful. You've had a lot of visitors but you've not been...awake. Lizzie has been here every other day. Some of your gym club buddies have visited and several of your old colleagues from school. In fact, there's one down in the canteen, she's having a coffee just now."

"It must be Julie...She was assistant head at Whatmore."

"No, I've forgotten this woman's name now but she said she used to work closely with you. She was Head of Year 11 at your school. I'll just get her."

Charlie tried to stop Pat leaving him. He tried to call her back but his mouth was too dry and he couldn't speak.

Charlie closed his eyes as a very sharp pain hit his heart again. There was no time to see any more women. A flat line had been drawn.

CHAPTER 8

Julie should be getting up. She shouldn't be staying in bed any longer. It was a Saturday, however. No work today or tomorrow. She ought to be making the most of the weekend. But if she got up she would want breakfast and after that she would want more breakfast. She had promised herself that she would not eat anything after six o'clock last night. The weigh-in was at midday today.

Julie had joined Slimming World a week ago. She had paid her money, been weighed and been set a target for today. She should try to lose two pounds in the first week. Unfortunately, she had to attend on Saturdays as she was too busy to get to the Lichfield Guild Hall during the week, either during the day or in the two possible evening slots. So she plumped (if that was the right word) for a regular Saturday lunchtime session. It sounded good in theory when she committed to it but then realised that Saturday morning followed Friday night and that was a real problem. Friday nights at her flat almost always consisted of a take-away delivery from somewhere in the world and a bottle of red wine, usually from France via Aldi's. If, on the rare occasion these days, that she went out, she would end up eating the same type of food but not in cartons and drinking the same wine but in a glass not straight from the bottle.

Now, Julie realised, she would have to be disciplined and only eat unhealthily from Saturday afternoon onwards and start being sensible from about Wednesday. This week, her first week, had been a killer. Particularly from Wednesday onwards and specifically on Friday night. If it wasn't depressing enough to spend the whole night in her own company, she had starved herself of comfort eating and drinking. This was self-inflicted torture. But she had to do this. It was time to do this. She was fast approaching her forties in both age and waist size. She was still single, despite some ships and shits that had passed her in the night and she was childless. It was becoming more challenging to filter her face and body on Instagram and then put the modified versions of herself on dating sites. She would be found out as soon as the first face-to-face date took place. So Julie decided to take real action rather than virtual action. She would go to Slimming World and lose weight. She would buy an exercise bike and get fit. And she would stop drinking so much and getting even more depressed.

Julie kidded herself that these drastic measures were to make herself feel better about herself. If she could lose a couple of dress sizes she would be at peace with the woman in the mirror. But she knew in her heart of hearts that this wasn't the case. Primarily, she was going to do this so she could find a man. She didn't want to be on her own anymore. She would make sacrifices and re-discover her slimmer body that had lain hidden under some extra skin and fat, for a man who, at this very moment, did not know she even existed.

Last Saturday, the prospect of a week of semi-abstinence was terrifying. She was dreading all seven days. Fortunately, she was given some advice from a colleague at work who had survived the initial stages at Slimming World. The advice was simple: whatever the weather, be it hot or cold, wear plenty of clothes, preferably heavy clothes and keep as many layers on when you get weighed for the first time. So last Saturday when Julie went along, signed in and became a member of Fat Club she was weighed down with this good advice. She knew it would be a real shock at first when they told her how much she weighed but each week after that she could incrementally wear fewer and lighter clothing for the weigh-ins. This way she could lose weight gradually over the first month or so without really having to do much serious dieting. Of course, unfortunately, there would come a point in the future when this undercover tactic would have run its course as removing any more clothes would lead to an arrest for public and pubic indecency.

So Julie, last night, tried to remember what she wore last week so that she could wear something slightly lighter for the second weigh-in. She couldn't remember even though she was stone cold sober. She had purposely not weighed herself all week hoping that it would be a big small surprise when she was told that she had lost a couple of pounds. Then she could celebrate the win of losing by buying and eating a pasty before shopping for a couple of hours and then having lunch somewhere after convincing herself that the pasty was her late breakfast. She had it all figured out.

Julie made a mental note to write a written note on her fridge magnet calendar what she wore today so that she could shave a few more ounces off next week.

Shaving! That was another tactic to use on the day of Fat Club. If she waited until a Saturday morning to do her legs and arm pits it might well help.

She dragged herself out of bed, stood in front of her wardrobe and stared at her rather sad array of clothes. Hanging up were her work and social clothes. There was an unintentional method of hanging her clothes on the rail. On the right hand side were outfits that she wore for work – formal and semi-formal, in the middle were casual clothes that could be worn to go shopping or meeting friends and on the left hand side were the clothes that were gathering dust because they were too tight to wear at present. That would change though, with time and application.

She chose a pair of jeans to wear. She would transfer to leggings in a few weeks' time. She went for a chunky woollen roll neck jumper with a tee shirt underneath. She threw them on the bed and had a quick shower. After drying herself she went to her chest of drawers and fumbled around in the top two drawers for her underwear and socks. Thick socks, naturally, a bra with metal cup supports and a Bridget Jones style pair of pants. Again there were modifications that she could make to reduce her weight in the next few weeks. Sockless, braless and a thong. Her small selection of sexy underwear consisting of lace knickers, stockings, suspender belts and half-cup bras had gradually been neglected for months and now resided at the back of the top drawer - collecting dust rather than admirers.

After applying a little make-up Julie stood in front of her mirror and gave herself an inspirational talk. "Come on, you can do this. Six months and I'll be at my target weight. I'll be able to wear some of my clothes again. I'll feel much better about myself. I'm not going to get to this weight ever again. I'm not going to eat and drink for the sake of it. I'm going to get healthy. And pull yourself together Julie and stop talking to yourself."

Julie grabbed her shoulder bag, checked the contents for essentials – mobile, purse, Slimming World diary and keys to the flat. There was no need to get in the car, it was ten minutes' walk into town.

She locked her ground floor flat behind her and soon realised that the day was brighter and sunnier than she had thought it would be for a January morning. After walking for a few minutes up the main road Julie started to regret wearing so many clothes. She was sweltering with her coat on over the thick woollen jumper. She took her coat off and walked on towards her destination. Saturday morning shoppers were busying themselves. She automatically bowed her head to avoid eye contact. It was not because she was a wanted criminal or anti-social but she would inevitably be recognised and people would want to say hello or chat. She just wanted to be anonymous for the next few minutes. It would be even worse if people saw her going into the Guild Hall. There was a big sign outside the main doors advertising Slimming World and the times in the week you could come along. How would she explain that?

As expected, it was not long before she heard the first "Hello Miss!" from a Year 7 girl out shopping with her mom.

"Hello there," replied Miss Osborne with a smiley face but carried on walking determinedly. This was the problem with being a deputy head teacher in a small city and living close to the school where you worked. Anytime Julie ventured out of her flat she would be recognised by her pupils and their parents. Fortunately she was well liked by 99% of the pupils and their parents so the acknowledgements and conversations were pleasant and friendly.

"Hello Miss Osborne," shouted a couple of nice boys from Year 10 who were sitting on a bench in the market square as she walked past. They were eating fast food.

"Do you want a chip, Miss?" one of them said with a smile on his face. Any other time she would have gone over to the lad and taken him up on his offer. But not today. Well not for the next thirteen minutes. Not until she has been weighed.

"No thanks, Jordan. I'm just about to have some lunch myself. See you on Monday, boys." She smiled and continued on her journey.

It then dawned on her that there could be some pupils' parents at Slimming World. That would be a little awkward and embarrassing. She just wanted to get weighed anonymously without any fuss and then get out of there quickly until the next week. Well, she would find out in the next few minutes.

Julie arrived at the Guild Hall and joined the fat queue. To be honest, when Julie looked up from time to time she saw much bigger bellies and bottoms than hers. In fact, she felt rather pleased with herself that she would not have to diet quite as hard as some of these other women would have to. She could not see any men in the queue, it was just middle- aged women who were wearing pretty much the same things. Long black tee shirts, leggings and slip on and off shoes. These women had clearly been coming to Slimming World for a while now. They were down to their thinnest and lightest clothes so now, no matter the weather, they had to keep wearing their Slimming World uniform each time.

When they were let in at midday exactly, a thin woman with a loud booming voice welcomed everyone. She was friendly and chatty to most of the regular fatties as they queued up to pay for the privilege of being humiliated and shamed. Julie joined the line and stood out like a sore thumb. She was wearing twice as much as anyone else and she was the only person not talking to someone else about their week of slimming or eating too much.

Julie paid her subs and then followed on to the next line to be weighed. It took a few minutes of processing and recording before Julie handed over her booklet and she climbed on to the scales after kicking off her shoes.

"Well done Julie, you've lost a pound this week. That's a good start," said a patronising woman at the table who filled in her weight in the booklet. Julie thought the woman sounded like a condescending teacher talking down to a low-ability child who had just won a prize for effort in class.

"Thanks," was all that Julie could say and took back her booklet, put her shoes on, grabbed her coat and left. She was not staying for the session that followed where most of the members of Fat Club talked in a circle about calories, sins, vegetables, chocolate and stretch marks.

Julie smiled when she left the Guild Hall. She had lost a pound. She had not seen any parents inside and she could now eat a pasty.

She headed for Greggs, just off the main square in Lichfield. The place was fairly busy, but most of the customers were just buying food to take away. Julie waited in another queue which was very different to the last line she was in. This time she was waiting to pay money to put on weight. She paid for her pasty and bottle of fruit juice before sitting at a table for two. She would not be here long. Just long enough to eat her late breakfast and provoke a flurry of short texts.

> *Lost a pound. New woman. Lol*
> *Congrats. Fancy a drink later?*
> *I'm supposed to be dieting!*
> *You can watch me get pissed then.*
> *CU outside the Horse and Jockey at 8.*

Julie smiled as she put her mobile back in her bag. She was in a good mood. She had been dreading the weigh-in and now it was over for a week. And not a bad result. A pound off. Now it was time to lose a few more pounds by buying a bargain or two in one of the clothes' shops. The trouble was that she didn't know what size to go for. Clothes for today or for six months' time? Decisions, decisions! But it wouldn't stop herself browsing the bargains. She was the Discount Diva of Lichfield. Any rails with 10% - 50% off and she was there at the front of the scrum.

Two hours later, carrying a couple of bargains, Julie was hot and bothered and needed to sit down and have a drink. She was wearing too many unnecessary clothes and carrying too many unnecessary clothes. She headed to the Faro Lounge, found a table for two and plonked her bags down on the one chair and sat on the other to consider the menu.

She needed a drink. A long cold drink. She started her decision- making with a large diet coke before succumbing to a lager. She was not going to eat but she remembered that she had only had a pasty all day and it was now three o'clock. It wouldn't hurt to have a bowl of soup. In the next thirty seconds this turned into a salad sandwich, which then transformed into a heated cheese baguette with a side of chips. This would definitely be her main meal of the day. She had made the decision and would stick to it.

Julie put her coat on the back of her chair and went to the bar to order. She joined the fifth queue of the day. One Slimming World, two for clothes to celebrate losing a pound and two for food to celebrate losing pounds at the other queues. The only thing Julie didn't like at the Faro Lounge was that as a person on her own you had to find a table, leave some possessions on the table to reserve it, then leave the table to order. It was so much easier as a couple or a group going to eat in a place like this. Julie thought it was easier all-round being with someone else. Someone to really share the success of today, someone to talk to other than a few kids saying hello. At least tonight she would have her new best friend to talk to and a laugh with.

Julie met Naomi at a school partnership meeting about eighteen months ago. They discovered when they sat next to each other that they were both deputy heads, both had only been in post a year or so, their schools were sited fairly close together, they were similar in age and, remarkably, they both lived in the Lichfield area. Julie had a one- bedroomed apartment in the north of the city, Naomi a large house in the south that had been split into flats. Naomi and another woman had separate rooms in one of the two upstairs flats while Naomi's older brother, Curtis, lived in one of the downstairs flats.

Naomi and Julie hit it off well from the beginning. They shared the same sense of humour and due to their unfortunate histories with men were both presently single, Naomi by choice. Julie, not so much.

Julie's understanding of Naomi's back story was that she'd been married up until four years ago. She had dated her teenage sweetheart and their relationship grew stronger and more secure. That was until Naomi went to university and her boyfriend did not. According to her friend, he didn't apply himself to get the necessary qualifications to go into higher education.

As happens, their lives took different paths and he became jealous of Naomi's life at Manchester University while he worked all hours in a local pub. They did continue their relationship after she qualified as a teacher but he was envious of her superior salary. They married and set up home but Naomi's husband remained jealous of her career and her friendship groups.

For some years they argued, they made up, and he made promises to change but, in time, they argued more, followed by more making up and un-kept promises. One night, some six years into an unhappy marriage, Naomi admitted to herself that she'd had enough and moved out of their flat to found some peace, quiet and career success in another part of the country. She became Head of Science and then Assistant Head teacher at a small secondary school in Chester. During that time she was granted a divorce and then moved to Lichfield when she was successful in her first application for a deputy headship. During this difficult time Naomi's main support was her older brother, Curtis. Both of their parents had died when Naomi and Curtis were in their twenties. And despite living some distance from one another, they were very close as siblings.

When Naomi moved to Lichfield, Curtis decided to move closer to his sister. It turned out to be very close! Naomi shared a flat with a girl on the first floor of a large Victorian house and before long a vacancy occurred in one of the two ground floor flats in the same house and Curtis took it. Curtis was able to follow Naomi to

Lichfield as he was single (much of the time) and his work as an independent graphic designer relied only on fast broadband and strong Wi-Wi reception, not a particular location.

Since her divorce, Naomi had not seriously dated anyone. In the heart-to-hearts between Julie and Naomi since they became *besties*, Naomi had not mentioned dates with men or men that she fancied. Julie knew that Naomi's confidence in climbing back on her horse had been rocked after falling off and failing at the first hurdle. So now, for the moment anyway, Naomi was happy to be single.

Julie, on the other hand, was looking for a mate. A mate to share her life and have babies with. Her yearning to be loved by a man and wanting children of her own had grown more intense as each relationship with the opposite sex ended in misery. Added to her desperation was the thought of the menopause lurking somewhere around the corner and the prospect of becoming a sad, old, childless spinster. The overwhelming desire to share her life with someone else had become obsessional. It sometimes kept her awake at night and at other times would invade her thoughts during the day. She always tried to rationalise her predicament when she felt like this. She would try to convince herself that she was attractive and intelligent with a good sense of humour. Yes, she had put on a bit of weight recently, but she was still desirable and a good addition to any hot-bloodied man's bed. Perhaps not any man though. She had had a couple of devastating experiences with married men that ended badly for her, rather than the men.

One experience lasted eight months where Julie tried to become a better long-term prospect than the oblivious wife but in the end Julie was awarded the consolation prize. The other experience lasted one night in a hotel with a man she loved and hated at the same time. Within twenty four hours of the deed Julie hated herself as much as the man she had slept with.

Julie had enjoyed the company of several single men as well. A couple of men that were younger than her, one or two that were older by several years but there was no-one she managed to convince that she was right for them or vice-versa.

It had been several months now since she had enjoyed a series of dates with a guy who might be the one. The dating sites Julie had signed up to had cost a fortune in money, time and energy for very little reward. No princes, just a procession of slimy toads carrying excessive amounts of carry-on baggage through the check-in and check-out.

The only prince on Julie's horizon and in her dreams was Curtis, although Julie would never admit this to Naomi. He was a stunningly attractive man, with a fit, muscular body and dark chocolate skin that Julie often dreamt of licking through her sleeping hours. One morning, after a particularly vivid dream, Julie had wondered if this was another reason why she could not lose weight!

For some time now, during the waking hours, Julie had stopped trying to find the perfect mate, or for that matter, any mate. She would take care of herself. She would look after herself. She would worry about herself. She was, after all, a modern independent woman, with a highly responsible job and she had made it on her own so far.

After leaving school, Julie had studied Mathematics at university, completed a PGCE course and started teaching Mathematics at a secondary school. She had worked herself up to Head of Maths within four years and five years later went to Whatmore Secondary School as Assistant Head. She taught a few Maths lessons still, but her main responsibilities were sorting out the timetable and cover lessons. There was talk of her becoming deputy head but it didn't materialise so she had applied for the post at Netherton School in Lichfield and became one of two deputies at the school. It was a great school with both staff and pupils well motivated and a pleasure to work with. It was different to Whatmore. She was now in her third year there and if she stayed until she retired, she'd be perfectly happy. It was just her private life that needed some changes.

Julie walked home saying hello to more pupils and parents from Netherton. She had added probably two or three pounds since she left the flat this morning. Not to worry - she had plenty of time to lose those pounds before next Saturday and she'd be able to reduce her layers of clothing, no matter what the weather.

Once she was home Julie kicked off her shoes and took off her thick jumper. She made herself a mug of tea and resisted the urge to go to the biscuit tin by the toaster in the corner of the kitchenette. She looked at the clothes she had bought a few hours ago. Perhaps she would wear the blouse she bought tonight? She looked at her watch. Over two hours before she would have to get ready to go out. Should she do some school work, watch something on Catch Up or close her eyes for ten minutes?

Two hours later she opened her eyes and regretted giving herself three multiple choice answers to choose from but she could spend tomorrow on school work and watching TV and of course using her exercise bike.

Julie didn't take too long to get ready. She would leave her jeans on, wear her new blouse and a short jacket that just about still fitted. She didn't spend too long on her make-up as she wasn't looking for a man tonight, just a natter session with Naomi. There would be no room for blokes on the prowl tonight. Julie and Naomi both wanted safe and happy company with a trusted friend.

Their normal protocol was to make their own way to The Horse and Jockey, meet outside the pub and at the end of the evening either beg a lift home from Curtis, if he was available, or go halves on a taxi if he wasn't. These arrangements made them feel like young teenagers having parents taking them to and from a youth club. But Naomi and Julie were uncomfortable walking or staggering back to their respective flats alone late at night, even though Lichfield was a pretty safe place to live.

"Hi Ni," said Julie as Naomi came into view.

"Sorry, Jules, I didn't recognise you after all of that weight you lost today."

"Very funny. I thought you were my supportive friend?" Julie hugged her friend.

They entered the pub and found a small table in the corner of the far end. From their previous experiences at *The Horse and Jockey* on a Saturday night, they could usually find a table quite easily until about nine o'clock when the place started to fill up. They both liked *The Horse and Jockey* for a variety of reasons. Firstly, the pub was equi-distant from their flats, secondly, they served good bar snacks and thirdly, they liked the main barmaid who tended to look after women who were struggling to get served when groups of men were jostling for attention at the bar.

Naomi and Julie settled down at the table.

"What's your poison?" asked Julie.

"I'll start slowly," said Naomi. "I'll have a pint of lager. I hope you're going to join me?"

"I'm on a diet. I'm off alcohol. Do you know how many calories there are in a pint of lager?"

"Three hundred thousand and twenty-six?"

"OK, OK. Not that many admittedly, but I know where this is going. You're not going to let me drink orange squash all night are you? And if you get me drunk tonight I'm officially going to unfriend you, do you hear?" said Julie laughing and getting her purse out. She went to the bar and returned minutes later with two lagers and two packets of crisps.

"Thanks. I thought you were on a diet?" said Naomi.

"I am. I'm going to drink this pint very slowly and the crisps...they're to soak up the booze!"

"I like the sound of this diet, Jules. I might try it!"

"God Ni, you don't need to lose an ounce. You're the perfect shape and size. Whereas my body definitely requires improvement. For some reason over the last year or two I just stopped looking at myself in the mirror and my weight's crept up."

"Honestly, Jules, you look fine. Don't start getting freaked out about your body and hating yourself. We're all different. We all come in different shapes and sizes. Inside the packaging we're all different too. And I can tell you that no-one is better than you when it comes to what's inside. You're a great teacher, a successful senior leader and you've been a really good friend to me since we met. That's what's important. You can always lose the odd pound over the next few months if that makes you feel better but you don't need to change for the sake of it and certainly not for any blokes. You're a really nice person and the men you date should see below the surface."

"The trouble is that the men I've dated have just wanted to look below the surface of my clothes, if you know what I mean?"

"Yeah I do. But that doesn't mean that you have to lose weight to satisfy what they want. It should be what you want."

"I know," said Julie, looking down at her lager and unopened crisps.

There was a moment or two of silence when Naomi realised that she'd started preaching at Julie. "Babe, I'm sorry. I didn't mean to go off on one like that. It's entirely up to you what you do. I'll support you whatever. Just as you've helped me in the last two years. You know I just have this thing about some men's motives and I don't want you to get hurt. I know you want to find a good guy to love and have a family with and if you think going to Slimming World will help, then go for it."

"I know what you're saying, Ni. I suppose I'm looking to get fitter and slimmer so I can start liking myself again and hopefully get liked by someone else. I know most men are shits but I do want a family. I really like kids, not just to teach. I'd love to raise one up myself."

"Well, you don't need a bloke nowadays. There are ways you can have a baby without the direct input of a man, if you know what I mean?"

"Yeah, I know, but it's quite nice to have a quick direct input on the kitchen table every so often."

"Ugh! I've eaten takeaways at your kitchen table in the past!" said Naomi feigning disgust.

"So you have, but I've always given it a good wipe down before you've arrived!" Julie laughing finished off her first lager of the evening.

Naomi got the next round in. More crisps (to soak up the lager) and more lager (to soften up the crisps).

The women sat there undisturbed in the corner of the pub exchanging stories about their schools, their colleagues at work, their families, their friends, politics, music and TV. After five or six more drinks they came full circle and talked about the opposite sex. By last orders Naomi and Julie were well on the way to being a disgrace to the teaching profession. Their tongues were loose and their minds were candidly brazen on the subject of their sexual preferences and fantasies. Every whispered sentence was rude and met with a fit of the giggles. Julie was left in no doubt despite her foggy brain that although Naomi was still reluctant to trust men after her failed marriage she was still very keen to enjoy some passing side benefits if and when the occasion arose.

Almost every whispered word that came from their mouths had a dirty double meaning and both women's stomachs were hurting from laughter, drink and snacks.

When they noticed that most of the other customers had vanished into the night, Naomi phoned her brother to see if he could pick them up. Ten minutes later they walked slowly and unsteadily out of the pub, towards Curtis standing by his car.

"Good evening ladies, your personal taxi is here. You were lucky to catch me on my mobile. Another twenty minutes and I would've been in bed."

As Julie climbed in the back seat she couldn't stop herself picturing things about Naomi's bother that were rather unseemly for a deputy head, no matter how drunk.

Both women spent the journey to Julie's flat apologising to Curtis and saying what a wonderful human being he was. He took it in good spirit and laughed at their drunken mutterings. He parked up outside Julie's flat and Naomi tried to string a few words together from the front passenger seat which incorporated a vow that Julie was her best ever friend and that she'd ring her tomorrow. Curtis, being a gentleman and sober, helped Julie out of the car and walked her to the door. He helped her find her keys and opened the door as Julie could not quite work out which of the many key holes dancing about in front of her eyes was the correct one to slot her key into. Julie gave Curtis a kiss on his cheek, said thanks and good night and went in.

When Julie's eyes began to sober up the next morning, she tried to read her radio alarm clock. She could just about see that it was eleven something. She knew it wasn't a school day as she was hungover and she had some memories of her evening in the pub with Naomi. However, she couldn't remember much about being in her flat late last night although she had vague flashbacks of using the toilet in the traditional way and then in a kneeling position to recycle some of the crisps and alcohol she had consumed. She had also managed to take off her new blouse and jeans and one of her socks before slumping on her bed.

She was deeply aware that she had a blinding headache and looked a complete mess. Her hair was all over the place and smelt of sick. She staggered towards the bathroom and examined herself in the mirror. She had put very little make up on last night but what she had applied had taken its revenge on her face this morning. It was a smeared mess. She was a mess. She stood there in her bra, big knickers and single sock and looked as if she could scare any scarecrow in Lichfield or the surrounding area.

She sat on the loo and felt sorry for herself for a while. While seated, she gave herself another talking to. Not in front of the mirror this time. She couldn't stand up for any length of time and didn't want the monster in the mirror making eye contact - it was too scary.

"Right. For the rest of this week I am not drinking alcohol. I will have a drink on a Saturday only. That's if I've lost some weight. I'm going to eat sensibly and I'm going to use my exercise bike every night...starting tomorrow."

She made herself a black coffee, drank it, had a shower and washed her hair. Then she had another mug of coffee while she watched an episode of *The Big Bang Theory*. By lunchtime she was feeling human again. She was feeling normal because she was craving something to eat. In her fridge and freezer was a collection of food ranging from sensible to naughty but nice. She wouldn't eat much now, just a small snack and then have a salad for her meal tonight.

She sat on her settee, ate her lunch and watched more TV until guilt took over. She needed to do some school work. She had a lot to catch up on and the sooner she got her laptop out, the easier it would be not to think about having anything fattening to eat to compensate for the tasteless crap she had just eaten.

She was soon engrossed. Her role at Netherton School was varied and interesting. At Whatmore she had been responsible for timetabling and cover for staff as well as teaching Maths to various classes. At her current school, the other deputy had those leadership roles while she was appointed to focus on data analysis, performance, staff and pupil welfare and behaviour, and Safeguarding as well as parental and community engagement. She was really pleased to have relinquished the roles of sorting out the day-to-day cover of teachers and timetabling the curriculum, two roles which often led to conflict with the teaching staff. She was less pleased that she didn't teach Maths as much as she used to. She taught a high ability class in Year 10 and another in Year 11, but that was it. The rest of the time in school was spent dealing with individuals or groups of pupils or parents and holding meetings with staff. During her evenings at home, when she wasn't in governors' meetings, parents' consultation evenings and other school events, she would plan her Maths lessons, mark the pupils' books, write policies and reports and spend much of her time recording performance data and analysis. This was her main job this afternoon.

The Heads of Department for English, Maths and Science had sent Julie their internal progress data for the pupils in Years 7,8 and 9. She wanted to copy this information onto a spreadsheet in order to analyse each classes' performance over time and then track individual pupil's progress from the previous point in the year. This was time-consuming but had to be done for internal purposes, the governing board and external agencies such as Ofsted.

Three hours later she had analysed the data and written and emailed her report to the head teacher and the other deputy for their perusal before discussion at Monday's senior management meeting.

She then prepared her lessons for the week. This did not take her long as she could teach Maths standing on her head even if her head was still sore from an evening out with Naomi. Julie, although she would never claim it out loud, was the best Maths teacher in the school. Her head of department, who ran her a close second, also knew this and was happy to let her boss teach her lessons without any interference.

She was considering marking some pupils' books when her mobile rang and lit up informing her that Naomi was now sober enough to chat. "Hi Ni," she said.

"Don't talk so loud, Jules. My head is still rather delicate. You're a bad influence on me, you know that don't you?"

"ME! Sorry...me,." Julie said, the second *me* half the volume of the first. "You were calling the shots last night. In fact you were calling the long drinks as well!"

"I don't remember it that way, girlfriend. I'm sure that you said you'd have a drink to celebrate then went for it big time."

"I think what you're trying to say is that we're as bad as each other."

"OK. Perhaps we were a bad influence on each other last night."

"Agreed. Maybe we ought not to see each other while I'm trying to lose weight. Why don't I give you a call in about twelve months when've lost a few pounds? How does that sound?"

"Or perhaps we could meet up next Saturday?"

"OK then. Sounds good to me," said Julie trying to laugh quietly for the sake of both (deputy) heads. "What shall we do? *The Coach and Horses?*"

"I think Curtis's flat mate is having a few people round to celebrate his birthday. He said we're OK to come along."

"Sounds good. Can I crash over at your place? Then I can drive back to my flat on Sunday morning?"

"Yeah, of course. Does that mean you're going to get embarrassingly legless again?"

"You cheeky bitch. I'm an upstanding citizen of the local community. I am highly respected in Lichfield."

"Not if the Netherton parents and pupils saw you last night."

"God. I hope no-one saw us at the pub last night or getting into Curtis's car."

"So do I!"

"Anyway. I've made a pact with myself that I'm only going to drink on Saturday nights if I've lost a pound or more at Slimming World."

"Well, that's an incentive to lose weight if ever I heard one. I suppose you can always take the thick jumper off next week and wear leggings."

"I could, but I'm actually going to try to lose some actual weight during the week. I'll have you know that all I've eaten today is a couple of crisp breads with cheese spread. And tonight I'm going to have some salad."

"Wow. That's good. So you're going to take it serious then?"

"I've got to, Ni. I want to feel better about myself."

"OK. If that's what you want and need. But remember what I said to you; do it for yourself, not for anyone else."

"Alright. I promise I will."

"Anyway, you might meet a single bloke next Saturday at the party who has a fantasy about a strict deputy head teacher with an ample pair of boobs and a generous booty. Then you won't have to lose any more weight."

"Yeah. Some hope. Anyway, what's your week looking like?"

"The usual really. Hectic. A parents' consultation evening on Thursday. Curtis and I are going to visit our aunt on Saturday morning but we'll be back during the afternoon. I can call you when we're back and then you can come over for a sober catch up before the party. What's your week like?"

"I'm seeing my folks on Tuesday. A governors' meeting on Wednesday evening. I'm doing a presentation on pupil progress. Should be fine."

"I'm sure it will. You'll be able to bluff the governors with your facts and figures. Well, have a good week, Jules. I'll see you sometime on Saturday afternoon, thinner and sober."

"Will do. Thanks, Ni. Last night was fun, even if this morning was awful."

"Take care, Jules."

Julie finished off her exercise books before sorting out some salad for her tea, swilling it down with a large amount of orange squash. She was still feeling a little queasy and tired from last night's escapade but before slumping on her bed with a couple of paracetamols, there was a Sunday night ritual she had to fulfil. She picked up her phone.

"Hi mom. How are you?"

"Oh hello dear. We're fine thank you. Your dad's knee is still playing him up a bit but he's coping. How are you?"

"I'm OK. I've been really busy at school but I did see Ni last night for a chat, which was nice."

"How is Naomi? I expect she's as busy as you are. You must bring her over for a meal again soon. She's good fun."

"Yeah she is. How's your week been?"

"Well, we went into town the other day and joined the University of the Third Age. We're going to join a few groups. Your dad wants to get involved with some writing and reading groups. He's still promising to write a novel now that he has more time on his hands. I want to join a group on gardening and go to some presentations on history."

"That sounds good. You need to fill up your days now after working at the chalk face for all of those years. I know you wanted to put your feet up for a while but you need to keep busy in your retirement. Have you decided on the cruise you want to go on yet?"

"Not yet love. We're going into the travel agents in Solihull next week, but we can't make our minds up yet. We'll find something soon, I'm sure."

"If I were you I'd start with a short one, maybe a seven or ten day cruise, just in case sailing doesn't suit you."

"Yes, that's a good idea love. Apparently the Bay of Biscay can be quite choppy but it might be quite exciting to ride the waves. Anyway, we're quite happy just pottering about. It's much better than working. Neither of us miss teaching at all. It's a young persons' profession now. You and Naomi are fine at the moment but in another fifteen years you might both be feeling the same as we do."

"I feel like that now, mom. I'm tired all of the time and I don't teach that many lessons. I'm certainly not going to work in education as long as you did. I'd like to do something different at some point."

"But you could be a head teacher in a few years. Wouldn't you like that?"

"Perhaps. I don't know, mom. I do like Netherton School. I like the head and the staff and the pupils are fantastic by and large. I'm not sure I want to go to another school to get a headship in the future."

"Well, if you're happy, then stay where you are. If you can put up with the tiredness. What else do you fancy doing anyway?"

"Oh, I don't know really. Perhaps I could be a movie star and move to Hollywood? Would you be alright with that?"

"I don't mind you being a movie star as long as you don't move to another country. We need to see our only child every week or I suppose you could buy us a house out in Beverley Hills. Any other thoughts about the future? Finding a husband and having children perhaps?"

"Mom, don't start that again. I'll tell you if and when I find Prince Charming. I'm not looking at the moment. I've stopped using that dating site I told you about. Most of the men I got talking to online turned out to be liars and were nothing like their profiles. So I'm taking a break for the moment. I'm going to get fit and healthy. I'm going to lose some weight and then try again in six months' time."

"OK. So how did you get on at Slimming World? Did you get weighed yesterday? Was it...alright? I wanted to text you but I thought I would wait until we spoke tonight."

"Well the good news is that I lost a pound. But the bad news - I probably put it all back on afterwards when I met up with Ni."

"Never mind dear. It's a good start and it will slowly come off. It takes time to adjust to a new way of working. Are you still coming over on Tuesday?"

"Yes, I'll be there. I'll leave school as early as I can, go home, get changed and make my way over to you for about six-ish."

"Do you want me to make you something that's…healthy?"

"Mom, you don't need to worry. I was looking forward to your shepherd's pie along with rhubarb crumble."

"OK then. I'll do that for us all. But there's a few calories in that pudding you know."

"I'll have a good day tomorrow and from Wednesday onwards I'll watch the sins."

"Fair enough sweetheart. We'll see you on Tuesday."

"Give my love to dad. Love you."

"Love you too."

Julie smiled as she put down her mobile. She loved her conversations with her folks. Her mom was the one to pick up the phone but she knew her dad was close by listening to one side of the conversation as best as he could. On Tuesday, dad would be the one talking, usually moaning and groaning about anything and everything but always with a twinkle in his eye. Her mom and dad were lovely people. Julie's mom the worrier, the carer, the shoulder to cry on and the listener, her dad more practical, giving good advice when called for and the quick-witted joker. They made the perfect combination. They were dedicated to their only child and at no point in her life did she ever feel an occasion to hate them. They were supportive, encouraging and gave her just enough freedom so that she would stay on a straight and narrow path.

She knew that her mom, in particular, was worried about her not finding *Mr Right* and putting on weight. But she also knew that they loved her unconditionally and just wanted her to be happy. They were very proud of her achievements and were thrilled to bits every time she was promoted. Julie's father had made his way up to assistant head teacher in a tough secondary school in Chelmsley Wood and her mother had been a primary teacher in various schools in Castle Vale, ending her career as a SENCO. Julie had managed to leap frog both of their careers in the last few years before they retired. Partly because, until recently, she was a little more ambitious than her mom and dad and also because her subject specialisms - Maths, Statistics and ICT - made her a desirable prospect in any school and in any senior leadership team.

So here she was, the only daughter of kind and loving parents, with a great job and a particularly good friend close by, and yet she was quietly sad and uncertain about her future. She was unhappy about her body, her lack of a man she could trust and settle down with and she didn't know if she'd reached as high up the greasy pole as she wanted to go. She could manage to disguise her sadness most of the time, but occasionally, particularly when hung-over, she felt a little sorry for herself.

She distracted herself as quickly as she could, finishing the marking of her pupils' books for tomorrow's lesson. Once completed, she packed them in *a bag for life* and then had a quick look at her week-to-view diary one last time to see what tomorrow had in store for her.

Monday was a mixture of meetings, teaching a Year 11 class and two lesson observations. During each academic year Julie would observe every teacher at least once. Less experienced teachers she would observe at least twice and the teachers experiencing difficulties for one reason or another would get regular visits until they were performing well enough. No matter who you asked in the staffroom, the teaching staff and the teaching assistants were positive about Julie's approach to lesson observations. She was regarded as constructive, encouraging and fair. Even if a lesson observation was not up to standard, Julie always left the teacher knowing how the lesson could be improved and made the member of staff believe she or he was capable of that improvement. Every term of the school year at a staff briefing, Julie would openly invite any member of staff to observe her lessons and point out improvements she could make to her own teaching. Teachers appreciated the offer but few took her up on the offer. There was so rarely anything to criticise and they all knew it.

Julie's separate meetings with the Heads of French and Geography were health checks on the performance of both departments. The meetings would focus on pupil performance data across the year groups with a special focus on the Year 11 mocks that took place just before Christmas. They would also discuss the performance and well-being of the staff in each department and any personal or professional issues the middle leaders might have with their teams.

At the end of the school day, Julie would be involved in the senior leadership team meeting which could last anything up to three hours. This meeting involved the head, his two deputies, the assistant heads and the Business Manager. These weekly Monday night meetings were purposeful and focused but lacked the banter and humour of the Whatmore SLT. From time to time Julie would sit in a meeting and remember the good old days when Peter, Charlie, Neil and Sobia would stray well away from professional conduct and descend into a world of childish stupidity. She missed those times.

Julie had started at Whatmore believing that Peter Burlington and Charlie Briggs were ineffective buffoons but as time went by she had begun to realise that both men, in their different ways, were a delight to work with. Firstly, they knew their stuff, secondly they cared about all the pupils and staff at the school, and thirdly, they never took anything too seriously.

Peter Burlington had mentored Julie, had encouraged and praised her and made her believe in her own abilities. He was the first person to indicate to her that she was a head teacher in the making.

Charlie Briggs had offered Julie other things along the way. He could be annoying at times, inappropriate even, but most days at work Charlie made her smile and feel valued. She knew that on a personal level Charlie could not be trusted; he was a cheat, cad and stud rolled into one good-looking bloke with the eye for any woman. Even so, Julie really liked him on the whole although there were times when she had hated him and one time in particular.

Julie was not sure what the two of them were up to these days. Was Peter still at Whatmore or had he retired? She felt bad for not keeping in touch. She knew that Charlie was retiring the year after Julie found her deputy head position at Netherton. What was he doing now? Who was he doing now? And what about Neil and Sobia. Were they still at Whatmore?

Julie picked up her mobile from the coffee table in front of her and searched for the latest staff list at Whatmore. From her old senior leadership team, only Peter was still there. Charlie, Neil and Sobia had left. Julie promised herself she would give Peter a ring to see how he was doing and then try to track down the other three. Peter would surely know where they were now.

Julie put her phone down, picked up the remote control and watched the TV for an hour or so before getting ready for bed and trying to get to sleep before the hunger pains got too bad.

Julie's Monday morning started at 6.45 am when her radio alarm woke her up with the usual news of conflict, greed and starvation. Just another day in this mad world.

On Tuesday evening at her parents' house she ate far too much of her mom's home cooking which meant an enforced period of starvation for the rest of the week.

At Thursday night's Year 11 parents' consultation evening she was called into action to quell a couple of difficult situations involving parents disappointed with their children's mock exam results. The parents wanted someone to blame other than their kids and took the opportunity on an evening like this to attack their teachers. As intermediary in these situations, Julie was highly skilled in the arts of diplomacy, deflection and diffusion learnt from the head and deputy at Whatmore. She remembered how furious parents would storm up to Whatmore School ready to tear a strip off a teacher and yet after meeting with the deputy head for five minutes they would be eating out of Charlie's hands before apologising to him before they left. Julie had modelled her way of working with parents on Charlie's style and it worked. Maybe she could become a diplomat or a politician when she'd had enough of teaching or perhaps she was too honest, empathetic and caring for that sort of role. But if she was really being honest with herself, the only sort of roll she was ready for now was a baguette filled with grated cheese, sliced tomatoes and salad cream. It was not going to happen though - it had to be pieces of cardboard with thinly spread low fat cream cheese smeared over them.

By Friday evening Julie was cream-crackered after a busy week. She had experienced her own moments of conflict, greed and starvation. And now, as she lay down on her settee half-awake, half-asleep, all she think about was Saturday lunch time. In a little under eighteen hours she would be weighed at Slimming World and could then go to The Tasty Café in Lichfield to order a nice long white or brown six inch roll, thick with real cheese and dripping with salad cream. She pictured herself stuffing the roll in her mouth. *Oh God, talk about naughty but nice.* When she recovered from the experience Julie started to worry about this weird fantasy replacing her *normal* desires. This was definitely neither normal nor healthy! *Is this a symptom of dieting?* Perhaps she could ask one of the women at Slimming World tomorrow if it was perfectly natural when dieting to have erotic yearnings for certain food items. Perhaps not!

Come to think of it, she had not thought about normal sex for a while now. Was she hallucinating about other things because she was dying of starvation and consequently, losing her sexual desires? Was she going mad? Julie could not keep this up for six months. She just couldn't.

She started to feel weak but knew what she had to do. She went into her bedroom, took off her school work clothes and stared at her naked self in the mirror on the dressing table. That was all the incentive she needed to carry on dieting. *Why hadn't Sid James and Barbara Windsor made a Carry On Dieting movie? It would have been funny and perhaps a little sad,* Julie thought. She pulled on her dressing gown and went back into the kitchen and made herself an inedible looking tea.

She sat on her settee, stared at the uninviting food in front of her and fought back a tear of depression and loneliness. This was her Friday night. Sitting in her bedclothes, eating cardboard, drinking orange squash and watching *The One Show*. It couldn't get any worse than that. She couldn't do this, could she?

She woke up on Saturday morning to the noise of her stomach rumbling. Her tummy was telling her to eat unhealthy food and forget about Slimming World. But she couldn't afford to listen to her gut. She showered and got dressed in the next phase of her clothing action plan. A thinner jumper and leggings. She made sure she had her purse and her mobile with her and headed off to the Guild Hall.

After a couple of "Hello Miss" comments and a "Hi, Miss Osborne," she arrived at the front of the Slimming World queue of fatties ready to be weighed and humiliated. She slipped off her shoes, handed over her diary and stood on the scales. Had this week's torture been worth it?

It had.

"Three pounds off, Julie. Well done!"

"Thanks," she replied with a smile and a blush on her face. It was as if she'd been awarded a certificate by her head teacher at a prize giving ceremony. "It gives me great pleasure to award the *Best Effort in Class Award* to Julie Osborne for her perseverance and resilience. Well done, Julie."

She left the Guild Hall almost expecting the paparazzi to be waiting to interview her and take photos of the *New Julie* but no-one noticed her relieved smile or saw her make a dash for the nearest café specialising in tasty sandwiches and rolls.

Half-way through her grated cheese, tomato and salad cream roll she took out her mobile and texted the two women who mattered most to her.

> *Hi mom. Lost 3 pounds this week. Speak to you tomorrow night. Love you and Dad x*
>
> *Well done love. Keep it up. Proud of you. Always. Love Mom xxx*

> *3 pounds off, Ni*
>
> *Good stuff*
>
> *Might have a drink tonight*
>
> *Just one?*
>
> *One at a time!*
>
> *Should be back in a couple of hours from my aunts*
>
> *I'll text you before I drive over. CU later x*
>
> *Well done you. CU soon x*

Julie smiled her way around some shops, stopping for coffee and cake at another café before walking back to her flat with a couple of bargains – a blouse for work and a top she might wear tonight.

At home, she took off her jumper and stretched out on the settee for half an hour with yet another cup of coffee and a chocolate bar. She then spent another half an hour selecting a short list of party clothes. She packed an overnight bag full of clothing combinations. She would change at Naomi's when they had jointly agreed on the right style of attire for the party. Her bag was brimming with clothes, make up and a bottle of wine.

She texted Ni and was given the thumbs up to drive over.

Not long after that Naomi was teasing Julie about the size and weight of her friend's overnight bag.

"I didn't know what to wear, so I brought everything appropriate that fits."

"Are a lot of your clothes too baggy now you've lost all this weight?"

"Very funny. What are you going to wear?"

"I haven't really thought about it yet; probably some jeans and a top."

"You see. I can't compete with you in your skinny jeans because I've got a fat ass, so I'll have to wear a dress or a skirt and a long blouse or something."

"Don't be daft. Your ass isn't big."

"It's a lot bigger than yours!"

"Perhaps one size or two at most, but you've got bigger boobs than me."

"I'll swap my boobs for your ass!"

"But your bum is three pounds lighter than it was last week and talking of that we ought to have a drink to celebrate."

"Why not," said Julie.

"Wine or lager?"

"I'll have wine if that's OK. Actually, I've got a bottle of white somewhere in the bottom of this bag."

"Don't worry. We'll take that one to the party."

Naomi headed to the fridge for a chilled white wine and re-joined Julie on the settee with the bottle and two glasses. They talked through their respective experiences of the last few days and Julie extended an invitation to Naomi to have tea at her folks' house in the next couple of weeks. While they were talking and into the second bottle of wine, they heard the front door open.

It was Naomi's flat mate..

"Hi Beverley," said Julie.

Beverley, a good few years younger than the two women slumped on the settee, was dressed hippie-style with a bright and multi-coloured maxi dress and a head band tying back long curly ginger hair away from her pretty face. Not only was she attractive, but intelligent and talented. By day, she was a copy and proof reader for a medium-sized publisher and by night (at the weekends) she played local pubs in a folk group. To cap it all, she was a lovely person and an ideal flatmate.

"Oh hi, Julie. How are things?" said Beverley putting down her shopping bags.

"Good, thanks. How about you?"

Before Beverley could answer Naomi chipped in. "Bev's in luuuuv." Can't you see that warm glow emanating around her?"

"Stop it, Ni. It's early days, Julie. I met him at one of our gigs a few weeks ago but I really like him. He's staying over tonight after coming to see us play with a bit of luck."

"Well if you get back to the flat before us we'll be very quiet so as not to put you off your stroke," promised Naomi.

"If you drink anything like as much as you did last Saturday, the whole of Lichfield will hear you get ready for bed."

"Sorry, mum."

"And no listening through my bedroom wall with those wine glasses!"

"We promise Miss, Sorry Miss." Naomi and Julie were now laughing spontaneously.

"You teachers, honestly. If only your kids knew what a pair of drunken tarts you were!"

"Hey less of the lip, young lady. Anyway, haven't you got to get ready for your gig and hot date? You're not going out dressed like that are you?"

"You sound like my mum! No, actually I have just bought a few things at the shops to keep him interested." Beverley opened a bag and pulled out a dress that Julie could only wear in her dreams.

"Wow, that's fantastic. You'll look great in it. I wish I could get into a dress like that," Julie said..

"One day, Jules," whispered Naomi encouragingly.

"Well, I'd better get ready. See you two later." With that Beverley collected up her dress and bags and headed for her room.

"See you."

Naomi and Julie spent the next hour or so finishing the remains of the second bottle of wine while giving each other a fashion show. By the end of the show there were clothes strewn all over Naomi's bedroom but they had finally agreed on their choices of outfit for the party. Naomi would be wearing a purple blouse and black jeans and Julie her new black top, a dark blue knee-length skirt and black tights. They then tried applying makeup while starting a third bottle of wine.

"God, I feel pissed already," admitted Julie.

"Me too."

"I think I've put those three pounds back on already. Who's going to be at this party tonight?"

"I've no idea. I don't really care as long as there's more booze. This is the last one in the flat." Naomi was pointing at the nearly drained third bottle.

"I've got the one in the bottom of my bag and there'll be some alcohol there already. Isn't it a birthday party? Curtis's flatmate you said."

"Yeah that's right."

"Shouldn't we get him a card or a present?"

"Just our presence should be enough!"

"D'ya think there'll be some fit blokes there?"

"God knows, Jules. All I know is Curtis said James had invited some of the people he works with round to the flat and that Curtis could bring his girlfriend along with the two of us."

"Sorry...Curtis has a girlfriend?"

"Yeah, this one is only recent. They met online. He's only gone out with her a couple of times."

"I take it you haven't met her.

"No, tonight will be the first time. She works in IT, so she'll be a bit nerdy."

"Hey, I work with IT!"

"You're not a nerd though. You're a teacher during the day and a drunken tart in the evenings."

"Well I try, but no-one wants to pay for my services in the evenings." They were finding it hard to stop themselves laughing now.

Once their make-up was applied reasonably accurately they headed down to the ground floor, coping precariously in high heels on the high seas of a barrel of white wine. They made their entrance to the party which comprised a grand total of three people; James, Curtis and Curtis's new girlfriend.

James was pleased to see them. If truth be told he was pleased to see anyone. He was clearly panicking that no-one was going to turn up. He had met Naomi on several occasions but in his current state still felt the need to introduce himself. Julie then felt the need to introduce herself to James, hand him a bottle of wine, wish him happy birthday and explain her connection to the select group of people standing around uncomfortably.

Curtis's new *nerdy* girlfriend didn't look like a nerd to Julie. Angela was a slim, attractive woman who looked at least ten years younger than Julie who hated her on sight. "Call me Angie. You're the drinking friend of Naomi's aren't you?"

"Friend of Naomi, yes. We sometimes have a drink. Sometimes we can manage a whole evening without alcohol," said Julie, spiralling down into sarcasm.

"Right. Only Curtis said you two were quite drunk last weekend."

"Yes, I just about remember that don't you, Ni?"

"I'm not sure. I had a lot of cocaine that night before we started drinking." Naomi was also beginning to hate Curtis's girlfriend.

"It was last Saturday, because we were watching the end of a film at my flat and you rang his mobile and then he jumped up, got in his car and drove you both back from the pub. He's a good brother to you, isn't he, Naomi?"

"Yes, he's wonderful. All of his girlfriends agree," said Naomi with a false smile. It was a toss-up which of the drinking friends was going to hit Angela first. Fortunately, Curtis came back to rescue the situation. He handed out fresh glasses of wine and in spontaneous synchronicity Julie and Naomi raised theirs in Angela's direction. "Cheers!"

"Aren't you drinking Angie?" asked Julie.

"No, I don't drink. I like to keep a clear head at all times. I'm trying to persuade Curtis to reduce his intake if he wants to look after his body."

Julie could feel her hands tensing into fists but this was not the place to cause a scene. *What a bitch,'* she thought. *I might not be able to compete on age or looks but I'd be a much better girlfriend to Curtis than this cow.*

While Julie was deep in that thought, Angela was holding court telling them all how she and Curtis had clicked online and then in real life and...blah, blah blah.

In the next fifteen minutes or so other dull and boring friends and work colleagues of James arrived.

After another twenty minutes and two more unfit blokes arrived.

Another thirty minutes brought two couples arrived who looked as if they were just old enough to vote.

After another ten minutes and a series of superficial conversations it was clear that for Julie and Naomi the party was going nowhere.

"We should have gone to *The Horse and Jockey*," shouted Naomi into Julie's ear. "This music's giving me a headache."

"Not to worry. At least the drink is free!"

"I don't think you're going to meet the man of your dreams here. The blokes are too young, too dull and too beardy."

"Don't you like beards then?"

"Never have. Your brother's the only decent bloke here. What do you think of Angela?"

"She seems a real judgemental cow to me. I want to slap her," admitted Naomi.

"Yeah, that was my assessment and also my plan of action. I wonder how long before Curtis ditches her."

"I don't know. Maybe he likes the snotty stuck-up bitch type? Maybe, just maybe he likes her because she's into IT and...quite attractive?"

"Do you think she's fit then?"

"Yeah, she's good looking but a bit thin for my liking."

"So you like a larger woman?" teased Julie.

"God yes. I like a bigger ass, like yours!"

The volume of their laughter was causing heads to turn and within a few minutes they agreed it was time to go. They said their goodbyes to everyone, thanked James for the invite, hugged Curtis and made a point of emphasising their goodbye to Angela, fully expecting and hoping this would be their first and last meeting.

The two women staggered drunkenly back to Naomi's flat. It was quiet and in darkness. No sign yet of Beverley and her new boyfriend.

"Do you want a drink?" asked Naomi. "Coffee or whisky?"

"I'm not sure I can drink anymore – I'm trying to keep my body fit and healthy like Angie's!"

Naomi found the whisky bottle after groping around the kitchen cupboards. "There we are. There's not much left but enough for a glass each. She poured out the remains of the bottle into two tumblers.

Julie said, "I hardly drank at all until I met you."

"I hope we're more than drinking buddies though."

"You know we are. You're my best friend. You've kept me going over the last year or so."

"I feel the same."

"To friends – drunk or sober then."

They knocked back the scotch.

"I need to get some sleep. I've got quite a bit of school work to do when I get home tomorrow, I mean later this morning," Julie said

"So have I, but it'll probably take me until after lunch time to be able to focus on my laptop screen."

"Ni, I was thinking. You know I was going to crash on your settee tonight."

"Yeah. You're not thinking of driving home?"

"No but Beverley and her boyfriend aren't back yet and it would be a bit weird sleeping on the couch when they get back. Can I sleep in your bedroom?"

"Sure you can. No problem. We can share the bed."

"OK. If you're sure you don't mind. I'll just get my toothbrush and use the bathroom, if that's alright?"

Five minutes later Julie made her way back to the bedroom encountering Naomi slipping a long T-shirt on over her half-naked body. "Oh, sorry."

"Don't be daft, it's fine. I'll use the loo while you get ready for bed.".

Julie looked in her overnight bag. She had three choices, a pair of pyjamas, a T-shirt like Naomi's or a black semi-see through garment for those just-in-case occasions. She opted for the T-shirt and lay down on top of the bed clothes waiting for Naomi to return. When she did, Julie said, "This feels a bit weird. Like we're a couple of sisters having to share a bed."

"I suppose so."

"Apart from the fact that we'd be very weird sisters - one of us thin and black and the other fat and white!"

"Will you stop going on about your figure. You look great and you know I think your booty is beautiful." Naomi laughed. She turned off the bed side light and the two women lay there staring at a ceiling that was slowly spinning.

After a moment Julie broke the silence. "I'm afraid to say that was a terrible party. I'd have preferred to stay in your flat. Some of those people were so boring."

"I know what you mean. No-one could keep up with our sparkling wit and intelligence. We are, after all, educators of future generations."

"I don't feel like one right now'"

"So who do you feel like?"

They both giggled.

"I'll settle for my battery-operated friend," said Julie.

"So you have a friend like that too?"

"Yep, after you, Nigel is my closest friend."

"Jules, you've given your vibrator a name?"

"It seemed the right thing to do. I felt he should have one. He's loyal, trustworthy and always there when I need him. Hasn't yours got a name?"

"You mean, haven't they got names? No, I like to keep them guessing. I like to play one off against the other. They get quite jealous of each other and then they try a bit harder to satisfy me!"

They fell silent again for a short while.

"God, listen to us," said Julie. "Both reasonably intelligent women who have good jobs and are quite good looking and yet using vibrators because we can't find happiness with a bloke."

"I told you, Jules, I'm off men. I'm quite happy as I am. At least I can trust my boyfriends in my bedside drawer."

Jules turned onto her side to face Naomi. "Sorry, I shouldn't go on about men. I must sound obsessed."

"A little bit." Naomi could just about see Julie with the light from the lamp post outside permeating the thin curtains.

"I'm sorry. From tomorrow men are off the agenda. We'll just get on with our lives without them. Deal?"

"Deal."

"Good night, Ni. You're the best."

"Good night, Jules. I love you," whispered Naomi and leaning over kissed her briefly on the lips, softly and sweetly.

Julie froze for a second but she didn't say anything or try to move away. After a long moment she moved her head towards Naomi and kissed her back. This time the kiss lasted longer. Both women moved a hand to the other's head and pulled their lips harder onto each other. Neither Julie nor Naomi said anything in between breaths. In time their tongues began exploring each other's mouths. In time they began to explore each other's bodies and then they fell asleep without saying anything else to each other.

Julie was woken by a hand gently caressing her bottom.

"Good morning," whispered Naomi in her ear.

"Good morning." She turned to face Naomi but didn't know what else to say until Naomi kissed her again.

Julie pulled away a little, staring at her friend. "My God, Ni...I don't know...I can't believe...what happened last night?"

"You mean what happened through last night and into the morning?"

"Yes... I was really drunk...I still am...I'm so sorry."

"What're you sorry about? You seemed happy last night."

"I was...I mean I am, but we're not lesbians; we're both into men and...are you OK with this, Ni?"

"Yes. Blame me; don't blame yourself. I've wanted to kiss you and hold you for some time now. You're beautiful, Jules. I think about you all of the time. I love you. I'm the one that's sorry, Jules. I thought...I hoped...that you might feel the same. It's not your fault, Jules. I led you on. I'm the one that needs to be sorry..."

"Ni, it's not that I don't like you, love you even, but I wasn't expecting this. Can we can talk about this when we're both sober. Next week. I ought to go." She tried to take Ni's arm from around her waist.

"Jules, if you want to go, that's OK...If you want to leave and not speak to me ever again, I'll be heart-broken but I'll understand in time...I'm so sorry that I mucked up our friendship...I don't want you to hate me, Jules...Please tell me that we can survive this?" Naomi was weeping quietly now.

Julie stared into Naomi's tearful eyes. She knew in that moment that she couldn't leave Naomi like this. In fact she couldn't ever leave Naomi. She moved her head towards Naomi's and kissed her. It was the most honest kiss she had ever given to anyone in her life.

"Julie, well done. Congratulations. Here is your award. You've lost fourteen pounds in just over six months. Only another seven pounds and you'll have achieved your target weight."

"Thank you. I'm so chuffed with myself. I never thought I could do this."

"Well, you have. See you next week."

"Oh, I almost forgot. I won't be here for the next two Saturdays but I'll be back in three weeks' time."

"OK. Bye then."

"Bye."

Julie put on her sandals and walked out of the Guild Hall in tee-shirt and leggings into bright sunshine. There was a broad smile on her face.

On the other side of the Market Square Naomi was waiting for her.

"Well?"

"I got my *One Stone Award*," said Julie waving a piece of brightly coloured paper at Naomi. In front of all the Saturday lunch time shoppers, Naomi hugged her and kissed her.. "Well done babe. I'm so proud of you. That's fantastic. Let's celebrate."

"OK but diet soft drinks only for me. I know it's a special occasion but I haven't touched a drop of alcohol in four months and I'm not going to start now."

"Perhaps we could push the boat out and have a small slice of low calorie cake and a cup of tea?" Naomi smiled as she squeezed Julie's bottom.

"OK but no cream on the cake and no sugar in the tea."

"You're so strict, Jules. I don't get any pleasures in life anymore."

"Are you sure about that?"

"Well, perhaps a few."

Julie looked at the bag that Naomi was carrying. "Is that food? I thought we were going out for a meal with my mom and dad, Curtis and his new girlfriend tonight? What's her name again?" asked Julie.

"Rochelle, I think. Yeah, I'm pretty sure it is. The trouble is that he keeps changing them. This one's three weeks old which is a long time for Curtis."

"That's the fourth different girlfriend he's had since we've been together, isn't it?"

"I think you're right."

"So what's in the bag, hun?"

"It's a little present for you. A *congratulations and I'm proud of you* present." Naomi handed Julie the bag and Julie pulled out two small pieces of black material.

"It's a small sexy bikini for a small and thin sexy lady for our Turkish holiday next week," said Naomi.

"That's lovely of you, Ni. How did you know black's my favourite colour?"

"Just a guess."

"It's a bit daring though. It doesn't leave much to the imagination."

"That's the point!"

"Let's go home and I'll try it on for you."

"Sounds good. You never know, by next summer you might not be able to wear it. Your belly'll be too big if the IVF works."

"Let's hope so." Julie squeezed Naomi's hand.

They began the walk home to what had once been Julie's flat but was now their shared love nest.

"Hi, Miss," said two Year 9 girls who were walking towards them into the city centre.

"Hi, girls. How are you?"

"Fine thanks, Miss. See you after the summer holidays. We're in your Maths class in September."

"I know. I'm looking forward to teaching you. Girls, this is my fiancée Naomi."

"Hi."

"Hi, girls."

"When are you going to get married Miss?"

"Well, let's just say that at some point during next year you may have to call me Mrs instead of Miss."

"Wow!"

"See you soon, girls," said Miss Osborne for now.

"Bye," said the girls.

PART 3
Back To Front

CHAPTER 9

Peter

Peter Burlington had eaten and drank far too much last night. His head and stomach could testify to that. He'd slept fitfully due to over consumption and the need to burp, fart, pee and poo, but thankfully not all while he was lying in bed. He'd also spent a significant proportion of the night thinking about the future and worrying about his team. Considering they were all supposed to be celebrating a *Good* Ofsted judgement – his four senior team members had spent a considerable chunk of the evening bickering about the school, the Ofsted inspection and its implications along with the budget. Strangest of all, they had behaved so oddly with each other. Over the years there had been odd quarrels and spats but last night had felt unpleasant and quite personal at times. The humour was missing. Was it post-Ofsted tiredness? Was it the alcohol? Whatever it was, it worried Peter. It worried him considerably - the future of the team, the future of the school and Peter's own future.

Peter did not like conflict. Ideally, as headteacher he would like every pupil and teacher at the school to get along with each other and live in a world of peace and harmony. But unfortunately, Peter was not answering questions in a 1960s Miss World Competition - this was Mr Realism of the 2020s. He wanted his last five years or so in education to pass trouble free. He would have liked a period of time where everything stayed the same – no new initiatives and no staff changes.

Until very recently Peter had thought that Julie, Neil and Sobia would stay at Whatmore until he retired. He had thought Charlie would also commit to at least one more year, if not two. But budgetary constraints and team disharmony might now mean that things would have to be different. In Julie's case she might look for a deputy headship, now she could record that she was an excellent assistant head who had helped steer a school through a positive inspection on her application forms. In Peter's mind Julie was clearly ready to climb the greasy pole but the budget meant that he couldn't offer her the second deputy role which was no longer a viable option at Whatmore in the current climate. Not unless Charlie wanted to get out this year. Charlie might just stay on and wait until the next Ofsted was due and then bail out just before it. Who could blame him?

Sobia and Neil could get jobs elsewhere – bean counters and geeks were always in demand. They could get good, well-paid jobs anywhere. In fact, Julie, Sobia and Neil could decide to go very quickly. Charlie was the sticking point in all of this.

Peter started to make plans in his sore head. If Charlie stood down, then Julie could take his place at a reduced salary as she'd be younger and less experienced. She could front up teaching and learning and one of the Year Heads could step up and take charge of the pastoral system if a few quid was thrown in his or her direction. That would save money and keep most of SLT happy. Charlie was key to his plan. But he needed to go of his own accord. Peter couldn't badger him into retiring before he was ready. Knowing Charlie, he would keep talking about retiring but never make the decision. Charlie was the healthiest and happiest person that Peter knew – so why would he want to leave the job he loved. Even though he was older than anyone else on the SLT, Peter was sure Charlie would out-live the rest of the team.

It slowly dawned on Peter as he lay in bed that his SLT would probably look very different in a year's time. That really bothered him. As he got older, he accepted the fact that he struggled with change although appreciating its inevitability. Just as pupils and policies came and went, so did staff. But he was pretty powerless to stop the wheels of motion and emotion from causing turbulence.

With those thoughts spinning in a head which felt like a fully-loaded tumble drier on speed, he decided to shower and go down for breakfast. His SLT had agreed last night that they would meet up at 9.00 am. He would try to be the first one down and set a good example. He just hoped that everyone was in a better frame of mind this morning.

He knew a small buffet-style breakfast would be set up waiting for them in the private room they had used during the previous evening. He seemed to remember the manager saying that cooked food was also available to order but the very thought of a full English this morning sent him hurrying to the ensuite toilet.

Neil

Neil woke up for the fourth time just before the alarm on his mobile phone rang. It was time to get out of bed, eat some breakfast and then make a quick get away from the senior leadership team for the rest of the weekend. He wanted to spend his time until Monday morning not thinking about the events of last night. He'd had enough of Whatmore. Particularly of certain SLT members.

He had woken up first at 3.17 am still furious with Charlie Briggs for spreading lies about his sexuality. He had wanted to break into Charlie Briggs' room and throw a bucket of ice-cold water over his sleeping body. But although he was angry, he had thought better of it. The shock could give Charlie a heart attack...if he possessed that organ.

Why had Briggs thought it amusing to spread rumours about him? It was not that Neil found it a slur to be regarded as gay but he objected to being wrongly labelled by someone who didn't really know him. Why did Briggs think it acceptable to pigeon-hole other members of staff and categorise them in a certain way? He would admit that he was not a man's man but just like Briggs he certainly liked and was attracted to the opposite sex. The big difference between the deputy head in charge of the pastoral care of pupils and himself, a number cruncher, was that he treated women with respect and as equals whereas Briggs saw females as numbers on his bed post.

At 5.42 am he woke up again fuming about Sobia wanting to cull staff in order to save money.

It seemed to him that the head teacher was being manipulated into making decisions that were not in the best interests of the school. He wasn't worried about his own job – he could take it or leave it – although it was useful to have a steady stream of money rolling in. But he was worried that if Whatmore was forced into making staff redundant the wrong people would end up leaving and pupils' education would suffer. He was no teacher. He couldn't do it. He didn't have the confidence or outward personality to command a class of children, no matter what age the pupils were. But he did care about the pupils and Whatmore deserved the best teachers they could get in order for them to succeed.

He believed that his job as IT manager at the school played a significant part in getting the pupils the qualifications they needed to go on to further and higher education. His primary task was to keep all of the tech working and making sure that the staff could use it to teach their classes. He also had the responsibility to support the senior staff with data recording and analysis on pupil assessments, behaviour and attendance. These roles were key to the success of the school and he doubted very much that his job could be lost to save money. No-one else in the school had the capacity or spare time to fulfil this position. So, he assumed his job was safe but he couldn't be certain. In one sense, after what had happened last night, he wasn't sure he wanted to stay at Whatmore any longer. Perhaps he would spend some time looking for jobs when he got home later in the morning.

At 6.38 am he woke for the third time, releasing himself from a painful dream where he was a young child in a playground being called names by so-called friends. The bullies were shouting at him "Your mom's a slut" and "You're a bum boy."

He sat up and drank from a bottle of water on the bed-side table. He should have been relieved to be away from the dark days of his childhood where his peers were, at times, so cruel. Schools were supposed to be different now, twenty years on.

But, sadly, some of those children as they grew up remained cruel and thoughtless.

And as for Whatmore, perhaps it hadn't yet grown up and matured when one of its elder statesmen was not setting a good British example of tolerance, understanding and respect. Briggs would no doubt think that labelling a colleague was acceptable or funny. But he didn't find this acceptable or funny. He was disappointed and disillusioned. He was angry and upset.

He knew what he had to. He found his phone which was re-charging on the floor by his bed and entered a virtual world of safety. This world had its thrills and spills, its ups and downs but he could control these moments. After half an hour he had won and lost in his unreal world. But more importantly his anger had subsided. So he closed his eyes again and drifted away to a deserted island somewhere in the Pacific Ocean which had food, drink and free Wi-Fi.

At 8.28 am he woke up properly. He woke up to his reality and situation. He would have a shower and wash away yesterday. He would play the game and have some breakfast with the leadership team. He would face his friend and foes. And then, Game Over.

Sobia

Sobia had slept well in the knowledge that, for the first time in years, she was away from family life – even if it was only for one night and a morning. She had had an evening without cooking a meal, loading the dishwasher, giving the twins a bath before putting them to bed with a couple of stories. An evening without listening to her husband moaning about how hard he worked each day. And this morning she would not have to get the boys their breakfasts while her husband had a *well-deserved lie-in* after his busy week at work. Well, just for a change, she could lie-in and have someone else prepare a breakfast for her.

She had slept soundly all night. Not even the difficult discussions at the end of the evening could interrupt her dreams of a different life. Her conscience was clear. As Business Manager, her job was to give the SLT and governors the financial facts, no matter how unpalatable. Her job was to report on past spending, likely incomings and give advice and steers on spending going forward. She was not, however, in the business of blaming anyone for the financial predicament Whatmore was in. Nor was she in a position to make decisions on how the school spent its money. But Peter had always appreciated her way of laying out possible options on spending and saving with the accompanying pros and cons. It was unfortunate that staffing costs in real terms were increasing and pupil numbers, if anything, decreasing. It was an equation that led to a negative answer.

In a cut-throat world without any sort of loyalty, an organisation would get rid of all of its highly paid experienced workforce and replace them with young inexpensive employees. But although this tactic could save Whatmore many thousands of pounds, it was never going to happen. She understood that a school in a tough catchment area needed its experienced and effective teachers. However, some savings and cuts would have to be made. She had spent several one-to-one sessions with Peter, before Ofsted called, explaining the predicament. It was Peter's decision to tell the rest of SLT last night. In hindsight, it was probably a bad decision. Last night was supposed to be an evening of celebration after the success of the inspection and yet it had turned into a difficult evening of bitter quarrels fuelled by alcohol and personal issues. The reality was that it needed to be said and discussed by the team and then the governing board.

She hoped the bitterness would not continue over breakfast. She could do with a pleasant and civil meal before going back home. Even if the twins had been perfect for their daddy last night and this morning, her husband would still make it clear that he had been a martyr in having to fulfil her role and that this would not be happening again. She could hear, see and feel it now. His anger, his threats, his control. She would put up with it because she loved the boys and needed them. And she kept them safe, safe from him. So, she would drive home after breakfast and take the boys for an afternoon at the adventure park so her husband could have some peace and quiet in the house. This would hopefully compensate for being away last night and this morning. It would also mean she would have some quality time alone with the boys she loved with all of her heart. She wouldn't change being a mother for the world, but everything else, yes, she'd consider it.

She decided to have five more minutes lying in bed on her own. It was quiet and peaceful. Then she would have to ring her husband and check that he was alright. Of course, he wouldn't be. He would be unpleasant but at least she would have rung him. She would wait for the real backlash when she got home.

She lay there thinking of some of the decisions she had made years ago when she was single. There was a piece of her heart, mind and soul that envied Julie.

Charlie

Charlie was no stranger to waking up in a strange bed. There was, however, a big difference today to the many other occasions he could recall. This Saturday morning, he was lying in bed on his own. And yet when he finally nodded off at some point in the small hours, he was sure that he hadn't been alone. Very strange!

In fact, the whole evening had been odd to say the least. The evening had started well with the celebrations and a fairly decent meal at the school's expense. But then it all went rapidly downhill from the moment Peter had proposed a toast in recognition of the Ofsted inspection. Julie was clearly in a bad mood from the start and slowly became a pain in the arse the more she drank. Although Charlie had a lot of time for Julie, he was surprised to see Julie reacting badly to his jokes and banter. She normally took it in good spirit but last night, well, she was drinking pretty much any spirits.

Then there was Neil. He wouldn't normally say boo to a goose, but last night he was being a bit of an arsehole. Charlie couldn't stop himself smiling a little when he realised his choice of description for Neil considering the subject that caused Neil's annoyance in the first place.

It had been quite a revelation at the bar last night when Julie and Neil had admitted to having an occasional fling. Charlie was not convinced by their story. He was sure that they were messing about and trying to cover up their real-life stories. The weird thing was that Charlie didn't really care if Julie was or wasn't single or if Neil was or wasn't gay. Usually they were good people to work with and generally have a laugh with – that was what really mattered to him.

What also really mattered was the conversation about the school's need for spending cuts and savings. It didn't take him long last night to realise that he himself was part of the financial problem and could be part of the solution.

He lay in bed and tried to work through various scenarios.

Firstly, Peter Burlington was safe. He was now a *Good* head teacher and the school would not have to be *academised*. Peter could see out his last five years or so until he retired. Yes, he was bullet proof.

Then there was Sobia Didially. She was the Business Manager and as such her job was to recommend ways to save money. Unfortunately, he had to admit, that she was the only person on the staff who had the skills and experience to do this job at the moment. So, ironically, she was safe in her well-paid job trying to make everyone else's job unsafe.

Neil Turner was next in his thoughts and consideration. He had never really regarded Neil as a senior leader at the school. Like Sobia, Neil was not a qualified teacher and not a real presence around the school. He had been catapulted into the position of an assistant head because he had a skill set Whatmore lacked at the time – a knowledge of IT systems and data. To a large degree this was still the case. So even though Neil talked a strange language that was all geek to Charlie and most of the staff, his post was undeletable.

This left Julie. Julie was a deputy head and a head teacher in waiting. A very talented member of staff with all of the right attributes. As he lay in bed he wanted to think about those attributes even more but for the moment he returned to his game of thrones. If Julie was not rewarded internally soon then she would quickly get a deputy head position in another school. Julie was the next generation and she should be given a chance to succeed. Julie would be very effective as a deputy at Whatmore. She could support, even prop up, Peter in his last years as head teacher. But if Charlie went and Julie took his place there would be a need to fill in the gap of running the pastoral system. One of the Year Heads would have to step up and that wouldn't save much money. Perhaps it would be better if Julie went. She was young and single and could find a deputy head post anywhere in the country. Charlie would then be in a position to stay until he felt it was time to retire. That would save money or would it? If Julie left, who would look after the teaching and learning side of things?

It was confusing. His brain was beginning to ache. He realised that whatever was decided would not be popular and that was why he had never contemplated being a head teacher.

He continued to lie in bed and tried to change the subject in his mind. His mind wandered and then settled on the two women on the staff who could be part of this game of musical chairs – the Head of Year 11 and the Assistant Head.

The Head of Year 11 would make a very capable head of the pastoral system. She was firm but fair with the pupils and she dealt with even the most difficult parents in a polite and professional manner. As a colleague she was reliable and trustworthy. She was also flexible and accommodating. For some time now Charlie had believed this to be the case, particularly since they had entered into the mutually rewarding arrangement they had both enjoyed in his office from time to time at the end of the working day over the last year or two.

Then there was Julie Osborne. She would make an excellent deputy head. She was competent, hard-working with a good sense of humour, normally. If she wanted a deputy post elsewhere he would be more than happy to write her a glowing reference if she wanted it. His only issue with Julie was that recently she seemed to lack stability and was becoming rather unpredictable. Last night after the meal was a case in point. But also, in the early hours when Julie had banged on his door and then on his bed.

Julie

The marching band in her head eventually woke Julie up. The continuous banging of drums had become louder as she gradually opened her eyes and tried to focus on anything in front of her. She tried to raise her left hand. She was sure there should be a watch on her wrist but she could not see it. Normally, when she had drunk too much, she would just close her eyes again and try to sleep it off but the band would not stop playing. She needed to consume a serious number of pain killers and at least two gallons of water. Julie eased herself up the bed and discovered she was still wearing her evening clothes from last night. She must have been so drunk that she couldn't face finding her small suitcase and changing for bed.

After a while she managed to focus on the suitcase and then her handbag that was next to her bed on the floor. She leaned over and searched for her life-savers. Next she slowly and unsteadily inched her way to the bathroom and grabbed a small glass on a shelf and proceeded to have three maximum strength pain killers and seven or eight shots of cold water. She hoped that soon the band would beat a hasty retreat and she could hear herself think without having to endure the sad soundtrack to her life playing in her head.

She looked at herself in the mirror. Not a pretty sight. Her hair was a mess. Her face was smeared with makeup and her eyes were red. She could look at herself no longer so she took off her clothes and eased her way into the shower.

Sometime later she emerged. She still looked awful but now it was a wet version of awful. The band was still playing but thankfully slightly softer. She started to remember key facts. She was Julie Osborne. A full-time teacher and part-time drunk. She was single. She was sad and angry after last night's meal with the senior leadership team. And although she looked like a survivor off The Titanic, she felt as if she had drowned in the freezing Atlantic water while the band played on.

As she drank more and more water some other details became a little clearer. The meal and drinks. Charlie being horrible. More drinks. The school budget. More drinks. Unpleasantness. More drinks. Then off to our rooms.

But there was more. What happened then? She got angry and upset again. She left her room and went to...Oh God...Charlie's room. She had wanted to have it out with Charlie for being an insensitive bastard last night. She had got really upset with him...she had cried...Charlie had comforted her...and then...*Oh God, Oh God, Oh God. What did I do? What did we do? Oh God.*

CHAPTER 10

At 8.50 am Peter surveyed the Palace Hotel private breakfast room. It was just as shabby as it looked last night but this morning it had been turned into a room for the five of them to have breakfast in peace, hopefully! For a modest-priced pub/restaurant/hotel they had made an effort to provide a varied buffet breakfast. On the sideboard next to the dining table was a selection of cereals in plastic boxes, white and brown sliced bread and a toaster, jams and marmalade, a bowl of fruit and five Danish pastries. There was also a small menu on the table offering a full English cooked breakfast or vegetarian equivalent.

Peter made himself a cup of tea from one of the flasks of hot water. There were sachets of a variety of teas and coffees and brown and white sugar. Peter was impressed with the hotel's catering generally and would have graded them as *Outstanding* if it had not been for the milk. He hated those miniscule plastic cartons with the impenetrable sealed lids which always managed to take their revenge on Peter as he tried to prise them open.

The sofa and some armchairs still remained at one end of the room. Peter eased himself down onto the settee, drank his tea and waited for signs of life from the rest of his team.

At 9.00 am Neil arrived.

"Good morning Neil," said Peter.

"Oh! Good morning. You startled me. I thought I'd be the first one down this morning. I was going to grab something quick to eat and then shoot off, if that's OK? I've got a few things to do today," said Neil hoping Peter wouldn't ask him what the things were that he had to do.

"That's fine Neil. I expect we'll all want to get away fairly soon this morning. We all have things to do, normal things that don't involve Whatmore. Did you sleep well last night? It's sometimes difficult trying to sleep in an unusual bed."

"Yeah, it is," said Neil easing himself into an armchair. "I must admit I woke up several times in the night. It's strange, after the week we had with Ofsted I was so tired I thought I would sleep all night but things just kept spinning around in my head."

"I know the feeling. I kept thinking about the possible consequences if we'd failed Ofsted. I had to remind myself a couple of times when I woke up in the night that we were judged a *Good* school. It's funny how your mind plays tricks on you. We should have been really happy last night and yet we all seemed anxious and stressed out."

"I think we were all just tired. Last night would have been fine had it not been for the discussion about saving money on staff. I suppose some of us, including me, over-reacted."

"It wasn't your fault. I shouldn't have brought up the issue last night. I should have waited for a better time to discuss the matter with the team. It wasn't fair dumping the school's financial problems on you when we were supposed to be celebrating and enjoying ourselves."

"Oh well, it's done now. I'm sure we'll re-visit the discussion next week in our SLT meeting. Hopefully we'll be less tired by then and possibly more sober!" Neil tried to smile but the attempt ceased abruptly as Charlie entered the room.

"Don't get up!" said Charlie cheerfully as he bounced into the room heading for the fruit juice. "Just been for a walk around the grounds. Nice morning. Might go for a run when I get home."

"God, you're bright and beautiful this morning Charlie," said Peter, "particularly after the tanker full of booze you drank last night!"

"I thought I was quite conservative last night – unlike some I could mention."

"I was just telling Neil that things got a bit strained last night. I think we were all feeling the effects of the inspection," Peter said hoping for some sort of absolution from Charlie.

"Perhaps you're right. Things were said that perhaps shouldn't have been. I think we need to forget about it all now and start again on Monday." Charlie was standing between Peter and Neil but looking at neither of them.

Neil looked up at Charlie and addressed him for the first time since he came into the room. "The trouble is it's not that easy to forget. There's still quite a lot to sort out, isn't there, Charlie?"

"I know, I know." Charlie raised his hand slightly, which could have been interpreted as a cross between surrender and apology.

"Anyway," Peter interjected, sensing an uncomfortable atmosphere returning and waffling back into leadership speak, "we are a team...one leadership body...and we're all responsible for each other...and we have to learn lessons..."

"Good morning," said Sobia walking quietly in. "Sorry I'm a bit late but I was on the phone to my husband. Then the boys wanted a word with me. You haven't started breakfast yet?"

"No, we were just having a drink first," said Peter thankful for the distraction. "Did you sleep well?"

"Quite well, thank you. Is there some tea?"

"The thermos flasks are over there," said Neil pointing across the room.

"Do you think we should wait for Julie or start breakfast?" asked Peter. "I know Neil has to get off fairly quickly."

"Yes, I do too," said Sobia. "Shall I go and knock on Julia's door, see if she wants breakfast?"

"I'd leave her, if I were you," said Charlie as he walked away from the group heading for the breakfast bar.

"OK then, let's eat," said Peter. "Does anyone want a cooked breakfast? They will do us a meat or veggie full English."

There was a unanimous response. Nobody could face a hot greasy breakfast and each of their tired heads settled on a token breakfast of cereal or toast and so did their stomachs.

The four of them sat down at the table and deliberately tried to keep the conversation as light as the food in their dishes and on their plates. They chatted about plans for the rest of the weekend. Sobia was taking her boys out somewhere to give her husband some time on his own, Charlie was going for a run followed by a round of golf with some friends, Peter was shopping with his wife and then to compensate Rachel was going with him to see the latest Star Trek movie and Neil...well, he was running unspecified errands in the morning and then meeting up with friends later on in the day. The gathering would be virtual but the rest of the team did not need to know this.

Just then the door opened and Julie walked in.

"Hi folks," Julie said, "Sorry, I overslept."

There was a chorus of "Morning" aimed at her. The other four were all subtly craning their necks to look at her without trying to stare. Julie Osborne, an attractive smart young woman, looked anything but that this morning. Her hair was wet from her shower, her face was pale and lacked colour and make-up. She looked as if she had aged overnight.

"Sorry I'm late for breakfast but I didn't really feel like eating. I'm glad you started without me."

"Are you OK?" asked Sobia, a concerned look on her face.

"Yeah, I'm fine. Just didn't get much sleep last night. It's my fault. I drank too much last night...I'm sure you all noticed..."

"It was a celebration. That was the whole point of staying here overnight so that we could have a drink or two..." said Peter trying to sound upbeat. "Would you like anything to eat... some cereal or toast?"

"No thanks Peter. Food and hangovers don't really go together. When I get home, I'll go to bed and sleep it off for a few hours. For now, I'll just stick to coffee."

"You weren't the only one not to get a good night's sleep last night," said Peter. "Most of us found it hard to de-stress after the week we had. Worrying about the future...tossing and turning..."

"Yes... we all found it hard," said Charlie peering into his cereal bowl with an inscrutable smile.

"I didn't either Julie, if it's any consolation," said Neil. "What with the worries of Ofsted and then the news about the school's finances last night. It was an unsettling week all round. Life doesn't feel very positive going forward, does it?"

"Yeah," replied Julie staring into her black coffee cup. "The clock is slowly moving forward and yet we all seem to be going backwards. Everything's getting worse."

A silence fell over the group for a second or two which gave them all time to reflect and take stock. It felt an eternity before Peter Burlington broke the spell. "C'mon Julie, you're just hung over. Things aren't that bad. We can get through this if we take the long view." He had not a clue what Julie had been referring to.

"Talking of time, is this your watch Julie?" asked Charlie innocently. "I think you must have dropped it somewhere."

Julie reached across the table and took it from Charlie without eye contact or acknowledgement.

There was another long silence.

After a second eternity Julie got to her feet. "I don't know about you Sobia...but I wish I wasn't a woman some times. I'd like to be a man."

"I know what you mean," said Sobia pensively.

"I think I need to go, if that's OK with everyone?"

"Sure. That's fine," said Peter. "I think everyone is making tracks." He stood up and made the briefest of closing remarks to round off the so-called celebration. "Thank you everybody for staying over. Remember, Whatmore is a *Good* school, we're a good team and good times will keep rolling if we work together..."

Charlie playfully started singing 'Let's Work Together' by *Canned Heat*. The other team members either looked at him in bewilderment or groaned.

That was the cue for every boy, girl, woman and man to leave the scene and try to safely navigate a route through their own separate worlds.

ACKNOWLEDGEMENTS

Many thanks go to the many people for helping me directly or indirectly with this novel.

I will start by thanking the playwright John Boynton Priestley. It was his play, "An Inspector Calls" that gave me the idea of the plot structure for my first story about an apparent Ofsted inspection. For this companion novel I have used another one of Priestley's 'time' plays called "Time and the Conways" and adapted the time-shift plot to explore my main characters' pasts, presents and futures. Consequently, "Time and the Consequences" calls into question whether my first novel ever existed in the first place! I can assure you, though, that it does exist and can still be bought as a hard copy or as an electronic version!

I would also like to thank Peter, Charlie, Julie, Sobia and Neil for letting me interfere with their lives. Working in a secondary school is hard enough without me creating havoc for them.

Also, thanks to all of the bands who have performed tirelessly for me while I have been toiling away at my laptop – particularly Caravan, Procol Harum and Steamhammer.

A special thank you goes to my lovely wife, Ann. She has encouraged and supported me through the good days and the days that require improving.

Thank you to APS Publications, particularly Andrew Sparke for his support and guidance.

Thank you for reading "Time and the Consequences."

Until the next time!

IAN MEACHEAM

Ian Meacheam has spent most of his working life in education. Consequently, he is well versed in the trials and tribulations of school leadership and Ofsted inspections. He lives in Lichfield with his wife. Ian also writes short stories and poetry.

FICTION FROM APS BOOKS
(www.andrewsparke.com)

AJ Woolfenden: *Mystique: A Bitten Past*
Davey J Ashfield: *Footsteps On The Teign*
Davey J Ashfield *Contracting With The Devil*
Davey J Ashfield: *A Turkey And One More Easter Egg*
Fenella Bass: *Hornbeams*
HR Beasley: *Nothing Left To Hide*
Lee Benson: *So You Want To Own An Art Gallery*
Lee Benson: *Where's Your Art gallery Now?*
Lee Benson: *Now You're The Artist...Deal With It*
Lee Benson: *No Naked Walls*
TF Byrne *Damage Limitation*
Nargis Darby: *A Different Shade Of Love*
J.W.Darcy: *Ladybird Ladybird*
Chris Grayling: *A Week Is...A Long Time*
Jean Harvey: *Pandemic*
Michel Henri: *Mister Penny Whistle*
Michel Henri: *The Death Of The Duchess Of Grasmere*
Michel Henri: *Abducted By Faerie*
Amber J Hughes: *An Injection Of The Unexpected*
Hugh Lupus *An Extra Knot*
Ian Meacheam: *An Inspector Called*
Ian Meacheam: *Time And The Consequences*
Tony Rowland: *Traitor Lodger German Spy*
Andrew Sparke: *Abuse Cocaine & Soft Furnishings*
Andrew Sparke: *Copper Trance & Motorways*
Phil Thompson: *Momentary Lapses In Concentration*
Paul C. Walsh: *A Place Between The Mountains*
Paul C. Walsh: *Hallowed Turf*
Michael White: *Life Unfinished*